More Than Crave You

MORE THAN WORDS SERIES BY

SHAYLA BLACK

MORE THAN CRAVE YOU
More Than Words, Book 4
Written by Shayla Black

This book is an original publication by Shayla Black.

Print Edition

Cover Design by: Rachel Connolly
Photographer: Sara Eirew Photographer
Edited by: Amy Knupp of Blue Otter

ISBN: 978-1-936596-50-8

PRAISE FOR *MORE THAN WANT YOU*

"Highly recommend! Shayla Black delivers once again with this passionate and sexy novel… A beautiful love story with a twist that you'll never see coming!"

—Meredith Wild, #1 New York Times Bestselling Author

"Amazing! Everything I didn't even know I needed or wanted in a romance novel. Hot. Spicy. Addicting."

—Rachel Van Dyken, #1 New York Times Bestselling Author

"Sexy, passionate and oh-so-clever! An intriguing love story!"

—Lauren Blakely, #1 New York Times Bestselling Author

"You'll hate him and then you'll love him! A sexy read with a surprising twist."

—Carly Phillips, New York Times Bestselling Author

"I'll play house with the hot real estate mogul Maxon Reed any time! Shayla Black's fans are gonna love this new series!"

—Lorelei James, New York Times Bestselling author of the Need You series

PRAISE FOR *MORE THAN NEED YOU*

5 Stars! “I adore Shayla Black! She masterfully delivers story after story full of passion, love, heartbreak, and redemption.”

—Chasing Away Reality

5 Stars! “I love this book!!! It has all the elements that takes you on an emotional rollercoaster.”

—Romance Between The Sheets

“So real and so raw! Be prepared to fall in love, have your heart broken, and then carefully mended back together by a master.”

—Shayna Renee’s Spicy Reads

5 Stars! “Ms. Shayla Black has once again reached inside my chest and shaken my heart with this emotional story…”

—Amuse Me Books

PRAISE FOR *MORE THAN LOVE YOU*

5 Stars! "The perfect blend of romance, lust, love and standing in your own way. I love the story."

—Alpha Book Club

5 Stars! "I loved this story and Harlow and Noah were the perfect couple. They were funny, had the faults and fears and in the end, their story was great."

—Wicked Reads

5 Stars! "One of the best books I've read in months! I love this book!"

—Magic Beyond The Covers Book Blog

5 Stars! "HOT and Sexy!"

—Tasty Wordgasms

ABOUT *MORE THAN CRAVE YOU*

I'm Evan Cook—billionaire tech entrepreneur and widower. Professionally, I've got it all. But since my wife died, my personal life has fallen apart. Remarrying seems like the obvious answer, so I place an ad. I'm not asking for much. The ideal woman only needs to be smart, organized, pretty, and helpful—both in and out of bed—without expecting romance. I never thought to look right in front of me...but it turns out that Nia Wright, my sexy, sassy assistant, just might be the perfect candidate.

After an unexpectedly hot night together, I'm ready to stop interviewing strangers and simply marry her. On paper, she ticks every box on my list. Best of all, she's far too sensible to fall for me. I didn't see the flaw in my logic until it was too late. I never thought I'd lose my heart for the first time. And I definitely never imagined Nia could consume me. But she's harboring a secret that could tear us apart. Can I prove I more than crave her before it's too late?

There are infinite ways to tell someone you love them. Some of the most powerful don't require words at all. This was the truth rolling through my head when I first conceived of this series, writing about a love so complete that mere letters strung together to make sentences weren't an adequate communicator of those feelings. Instead, for this series, music was my go-to choice.

I *love* music. I'm always immersed in it and spend hours a day with my ear buds plugged in. I write to music. I think to music. I even sleep to music. I was thrilled to incorporate songs into the story I felt were meaningful to the journey. I think of it this way: a movie has a sound-track. Why shouldn't a book?

So I created one.

Some of the songs I've selected will be familiar. Some are old. Some are newer. Some popular. Some obscure. They all just fit (in my opinion) and came straight from the heart. I listened to many of these songs as I wrote the book.

For maximum understanding (and feels), I recommend becoming familiar with these songs and either playing them or rolling them around in your head as you read. Due to copyright laws, I can't use exact lyrics, but I tried to give you the gist of those most meaningful to Nia and Evan's story. I've also made it simple for you to give these songs a listen by creating a Spotify playlist.

Hugs and happy reading!

FIRST DATE – Blink 182

FALLINGFORYOU – The 1975

YOU AND ME – Lifehouse

KISS ME – Sixpence None the Richer

GOD ONLY KNOWS – Beach Boys

THANK YOU – Dido

TRULY – Lionel Richie

BOO'D UP – Ella Mai

A COUPLE OF FOREVERS – Chrisette Michele

GOODBYE – Natalie Imbruglia

BREATHE AGAIN – Sara Bareilles

FALL BACK IN – Plumb

IT'S NOT OVER – Daughtry

WHATEVER IT TAKES – Lifehouse

IF – Bread

Love has no color.

CHAPTER ONE

Evan

Seattle, Washington
Thursday, November 2

> *Successful young entrepreneur seeks wife, business hostess, and sexual partner. Ideal candidate is between twenty-two and thirty, polished, intelligent, organized, educated, and attractive. No children or romance. Sense of humor optional. Must relocate to Hawaii.*

As I read the words I printed moments ago, I make my way to my assistant's desk. "What do you think?"

When I hand Nia Wright the page, she scans it, then scowls at me with incredulous dark eyes. "A personal ad? *This* is how you're going to replace Becca?"

I pluck the paper from her grasp, jaw clenched. "No one can replace her."

My wife and unborn child were killed in a car accident just over six months ago. Since I turned sixteen, Becca was my constant. Without her, the penthouse we shared feels too quiet. I have no one to talk to. My sex drive is raging. I'm empty.

I'm lost.

"So why would you try with a stranger?" Nia shakes her head.

She asks a fair question, and I'm forced to reexamine my original conclusion. But no. The answer still seems obvious.

"Training one woman to fulfill my corporate and personal needs, then compensating her with money and job security seems far more logical than paying a handful of contractors who aren't invested in our business relationship."

I could do that, of course. At almost twenty-seven, I helm a growing company that's worth over a billion dollars, so money isn't the problem. But hiring five people to do what one can seems inefficient and wasteful. Illogical. Imbecilic. And while I don't have a moral problem paying a professional and see little difference between engaging a chef or a prostitute for their services, Becca would have seen it *very* differently. Yes, she would want me to move on. Until now, I haven't. But I would never intentionally disgrace or dishonor my wife.

"Do you think having a stranger beside you will really improve your quality of life?" Nia asks pointedly.

It's a calculated risk, but one I'm prepared to take. "I don't think it can be worse."

She scoffs at me like I'm an idiot. From any other employee I wouldn't abide the insubordination. Nia is different. She's repeatedly proven she's both loyal and levelheaded—two qualities I require. I value her opinion; it's the reason she's my right hand in all things related to Stratus Solutions, the tech infrastructure powerhouse I started six years ago with nothing but twenty-five hundred dollars, a little hardware, my coding skills, and serious grit.

"Then you haven't thought this through. And your ad is a lie."

It's my turn to scowl. "What? Every word is true."

With a sigh, she stands and snatches the page from my hand once more. "What this *should* say is: Brilliant workaholic seeks June Cleaver in the living room and Lolita in the bedroom. Ideal candidate is a supermodel who's mute until I require her to serve guests or service me. No risk of emotional entanglements. Must be at my beck and call."

Okay, maybe there's a smidgeon of truth to her version of the ad. "Somehow, I suspect that would bring in far fewer responses."

"You think?" She rolls her eyes. "The whole idea is inane. The way this reads, I don't know whether to post it on eHarmony or LinkedIn."

"If I want the right woman for the job, I have to outline all the duties I expect her to perform so I can find the most qualified candidate."

Nia huffs at me. "You're talking about marriage, not a middle manager. Why not take someone you know on a date? See if you like them. Spend a few months together, figure out if you're suited for a deeper relationship. Use the time to get over Becca. Why are you shaking your head at me?"

"I intend to be married before Christmas. Everything in my non-work life is a disaster, and I'm too busy preparing for the move to Maui and fending off this hostile buyout to clean it up." Best leave tidying my mess at home to a professional. "So I want you to place this ad everywhere you can think of today, screen all the replies, then give me a slate of the most qualified applicants by next Friday."

She braces her hands on her hips, which are covered by a snug charcoal skirt. "You want me to help you *pick* this wife?"

I'm confused by her question—and her obvious displeasure. "It makes sense. You know me well, and you're an excellent judge of character."

"Have you ever been on a dating site?"

"Of course not." Until Becca's death, I was happily married.

"Do you have any idea how many crazies and gold-diggers an ad like this is going to attract?"

"I'm socially awkward, not naive. Of course I do. That's why I'm lucky to have a savvy woman like you."

Nia sits stiffly. "Fine. I'll get it done. But really, have you at least thought about trying to date someone in your social circle? Someone you know isn't crazy?"

"Who would that be? You're the only single female I know who meets my list of qualifications. And you're dating"—I snap my fingers, trying to remember the name of her latest boyfriend—"Brett?"

"Brick," she corrects.

As in dumber than? I haven't met him; she didn't bring him to the company picnic this summer. But he sounds like a douchebag.

"Him. Sorry. I can never remember who you're seeing." It changes so quickly.

"I broke up with him in June."

That explains why she didn't mind working more hours over the summer. "I'm surprised. You said he was smart, ambitious, and well-employed."

"He is. But he was a lot of talk and not much action."

I frown. "He didn't follow through on his promises?"

"Do I have to spell it out?" She sighs. "Brick sucked in bed."

"Oh." I clear my throat, trying to imagine Nia naked with this guy. I can't. She's pretty, I guess. Exotic. Her skin is a pleasing cocoa shade. She's got the kind of curves often photographed for the purpose of rousing a man's libido. I've simply never thought about my assistant like *that*. It's unprofessional. I won't start now. "Next time, remind me not to ask about things that are none of my business."

Workplace harassment is such a hot-button topic. I'd rather not be sued for discussing inappropriate things in the office. But I also value Nia as an assistant and a human being, too. I don't want her to think I'm not listening if she has something to say.

"No." She waves my words away. "I got too personal. Sorry. I haven't had anyone to talk to and…" She sighs. "I wish I understood men. Since I never had one to figure out growing up, I feel like I'm forever confused."

Nia doesn't like to talk about her father. He wasn't a part of her childhood. He impregnated her mother, who worked for him, then bought the woman off when she broke the news of his impending fatherhood. Her mother raised Nia alone, not marrying or even dating seriously before tragically succumbing to a case of the flu two years ago.

"I doubt I'll be much help." I'm aware that I function differently than most men. They thrive on competitive sports, beer chugging, and dirty jokes. I much prefer a good mental challenge, fine scotch, and video games. "You don't date my type. I was called a brainiac and a computer nerd growing up. But I drew the line at Dungeons and Dragons."

My quip somehow makes her laugh. "Good to know you have boundaries. It's just...some guys really seem to forget there's another person in the bed. Hell, in the relationship. I've done some soul searching since I ditched Brick, and I've decided I'm not dating guys I barely know anymore. We have to be friends first." Surprisingly, she wraps her fingers around my shoulder. "Which is something you should consider, rather than placing an ad. Don't marry just anyone. You'll be miserable. Why don't you let me help with your disorganization? It will give you some time to find a more permanent solution. You know I love whipping a good mess into shape."

"That's generous, but I don't expect you to cook or clean for me after you've worked all day, too. Grocery shopping and running errands aren't in your job description, either."

Plus, there's the sex issue. I glance at Nia again. She's actually more than pretty, now that I'm actually looking. She's beautiful. Striking. Taking her to bed wouldn't be a hardship.

And I really need to get off this train of thought.

"It's not a big deal. I need to cook for myself anyhow. It's actually easier to toss dinner together for two. I can show you how to grocery shop online. Cleaning up...I'll tackle what I can, teach you how to manage some yourself, and help you hire out the rest. We'll figure out the other errands. The dry cleaning should be simple since we use the same one, right?" When I nod, she goes on. "See? We got this."

"I appreciate you trying to—"

"Save you from getting into a rebound relationship with someone who will probably make you miserable." She squeezes my shoulder one more time before letting go. "That's what I'm doing because you deserve more. Don't you want to spend the rest of your life with someone who will actually care about you?"

Maybe that will matter eventually. Right now, I can only see my current slew of problems and the fact I'm not dealing well with them. Of course, she's phrased the question so I'll sound like an idiot if I say no. And maybe I am. Becca often had to explain her brand of logic to me since my emotional IQ is apparently something close to my shoe size. But

Nia and I have similar problems, though in reverse. She doesn't understand men because she grew up without a father, and I barely remember my own mother, who died when I was five. None of my foster families filled in the gaps. So females confuse me. I'm not saying I've never made a decision based on feelings…but I've done it fewer than five times in my life. Daily? I couldn't handle that.

"I don't expect you to take care of me outside the office, Nia."

"If it will keep you from making the biggest mistake of your life, I will." Then she sends me a coaxing smile. "Let me cook tonight. I'll make some of my great-aunt's famous New Orleans gumbo…"

Nia brought the spicy, soupy heaven to an office potluck once, and my taste buds instantly fell in love. Besides, I haven't had a home-cooked meal in months. "Your bargaining tactics are cutthroat."

She shrugs as if she can't help herself. "I learned from the best."

That's true. Nia has paid attention through every step of the negotiations my college buddy and current CFO, Sebastian Shaw, and I have taken with cash-rich Colossus Investment Corporation. I've declined their three offers. The first two simply failed to offer me market value for my cutting-edge data storage technology. The most recent buyout approached fair…but still wasn't lucrative enough.

With a sigh, I give in to my assistant. I've never been good at saying no to Nia, especially when she presses on my weak spots. My stomach is definitely one. "All right. I appreciate the help and the meal."

"While the gumbo is simmering, we'll tackle some of the projects around your place and hopefully start getting your life back in order."

"Thanks. I'm lucky to have you in my corner. Who knew that hiring a girl with moxie straight out of college would be one of the best things I ever did?"

Nia's smile seems to brighten everything around her. "Who knew that taking a chance on a newish but growing company with a ridiculously intelligent founder would end up so great?"

For the first time in what feels like forever, I relax. "I'm assuming gumbo takes a while to cook. So what time should I leave here?"

"If I get all the ingredients prepped and on your stove by five-thirty, we'll be eating about eight. That all right?"

Actually, it will be perfect. I can barely remember the last time I didn't spend an evening alone. "Sure."

"See you at your place then."

"Thanks."

If anything, her smile widens. "It's my pleasure."

WHEN I ARRIVE at home, it's almost six. Nia is waiting in front of my door with bags of food and a big cooking pot at her feet. She's dressed in a gray sweatshirt that clings to her shape, along with a matching pair of leggings that hug her from thigh to ankle. I stop. I've rarely seen her in casual clothes, and never in anything this formfitting. The effect is nothing like her usual suit with skirts and silky blouses. She looks relaxed. Female. Lush. I gulp. No wonder she's never lacking for dates.

I shove the thought aside.

"Sorry I'm late." I rush from the elevator, opening my door with one hand and scooping up bags of groceries with the other. "I'll get those."

I feel more than vaguely guilty that she carried everything up by herself. Becca always did the same, and I hated that I was never around to help. But Nia is volunteering to organize my life. I can't repay her by being a slacker or seeming like an ungrateful asshole.

"No problem," she insists as she follows me inside, then gasps.

I'm not surprised. The place looks like a hurricane hit it. She's only ever been here to drop off work when I was sick. Becca insisted on personally keeping this place spotless back then; she couldn't tolerate chaos of any kind and wanted control of her surroundings. After my OCD wife was gone, I didn't have any clue or inclination how to keep the house the way she had.

I lead Nia to the kitchen. She sets the pot on the stove, then turns in a circle, hands on her hips. "You weren't kidding. This is a wreck."

I wince, aware that just about every dish I own is piled in the sink. The overflow clutters the counters. I probably shouldn't spring my bedroom and bathroom on her, too. "Unfortunately, no."

"Okay…" She sets her purse aside, gets the gumbo heating, then pushes up her sleeves. "Do you know how to start the dishwasher?"

"I'm sure I could figure it out."

"But you haven't tried?"

I shake my head. "No."

Until a couple of weeks ago, I spent all my time at the office. It kept me from thinking about how empty my house was. Since the terrible April day Becca perished, I've spent as little time here as possible to avoid the reality that I'm alone. I plump up the pillows in bed beside me to mimic the feel of her taking up space in our king-size bed. I even downloaded an app to simulate the sounds of her breathing beside me. Lately, it's working less and less. Most nights, I stare at the dark ceiling and try to come up with a logical answer to the emptiness around me. The wife idea still seems like the best solution.

"I'll…um, look into that while you tell me where you placed my ad."

Nia hesitates, then reaches for the faucet and flips it on. "I haven't had a chance yet. Most dating sites want you to fill out a profile, not give them a couple of sentences about your prospective mate."

"Profile?" That sounds tedious and time-consuming.

"Yes. After all, you're not the only person selecting someone from the database; a woman has to choose you in return, based on your answers to the questions. Prospective dates looking at your information will want to know what your interests are, what you like to do with your downtime, what your religious and spiritual philosophies are, how your best friends would describe you and—"

"I'm looking to hire a wife, not begin an actual romantic relationship. A dating profile would be a complete waste of my time."

She shakes her head as she begins washing out the dishes in the sink. "Well, not doing it cuts down on your possibilities. Would you prefer an overseas mail-order bride?"

"I don't have the patience to deal with government bureaucracy and paperwork. I want someone already in the country legally."

She sighs. "I was kidding, and the fact you thought I was serious is scary. I'll do what I can, but don't say I didn't warn you. Put the glasses on the top rack of the dishwasher."

I do as she instructs with a frown. "I can't possibly be the only wealthy man with this problem."

"Evan, seriously? Most already have wives and are looking for a lay on the side."

She has a point. "Maybe I should call Harlow, Keeley, and Britta."

"You know I applaud you for getting to know your newfound family, but you met your sister and your brothers' wives six months ago. Do they know you well enough to help you find a woman who can make you happy?"

I tracked my long-lost siblings down during a relocation scouting trip to Hawaii. Despite the fact my siblings and I share a biological father, they're still somewhat like strangers, but… "They already live in Maui and probably have single friends."

"They don't know who you are, what you want, or what you've been through." She shuts off the water to face me. My face must tell her I don't care about any of that because she sighs. "Besides, if you wait until you move to Maui to meet someone, you won't be married by Christmas."

"I'm going for Thanksgiving in a few weeks. I'll ask them to introduce me then."

"You're really serious about finding someone right now?"

"I'm serious about filling the position of wife as soon as possible."

Exasperation fills her face. "Then let me handle it. I'll figure something out quickly."

I shake my head. "If you'll simply screen the candidates, I'll take it from there."

"I'm worried what—or who—you'll come up with if I leave you to your own devices."

Nia might have a point. My interpersonal skills suck. I was lucky Becca understood me and didn't have romantic expectations.

"All right. I'll give you until Thanksgiving to find me someone. But I still want that ad placed as backup."

"Fine." She doesn't sound fine with it at all, but focuses instead on showing me how to scrape off the crusted food from my dirty dishes, then place them in the dishwasher. "How is it you never figured out how to clean your own kitchen? Didn't you ever live alone?"

I laugh. "For eight disastrous months before I got married. After that, Becca did everything."

"None of your foster families made you load a dishwasher?" She sounds shocked.

"Nope. I did other chores, but I blocked out a lot of my life before I went to live with Diana. As long as I kept her old cottage in working order, she took care of what little cleaning got done."

The day I turned eighteen, I packed my bags and left my foster mother's house. Diana was great, the closest thing to a mom I have left, but once the state stopped paying her to look after me, she didn't need a financial burden under her roof. There aren't many jobs in rural Washington State, especially for a starving artist who's never held a job longer than six months. Besides, she swears that she and the wind are conjoined twins, so she goes wherever her sister takes her. Since she gave me a much-needed, if off-beat, home for six years, I now give her financial security so she can breeze across the world.

"Growing up, Mom and I took turns with the chores. Her motto was that doing everything for me wouldn't teach me how to fend for myself. That's why I can both cook and do some home repair. Now, I'm going to help you." She holds up a casserole dish. "What did you make in here?"

"Nothing. One of my neighbors brought me lasagna shortly after Becca's funeral." I probably should have washed and returned it, but I didn't want to spend any more time in Becca's kitchen than I had to. Her absence simply reminds me too much of the fact I'm alone.

"You know, if doing dishes were more like rocket science, you'd probably understand it better."

"No doubt you're right," I admit wryly.

"Put some dish soap and hot water in this, then set it on the counter to soak." Nia shoves the dish in my hand.

A thick layer of black and green crusts the bottom. "It looks like something that belongs in a Petri dish."

"It totally does." She rolls her eyes, but there's a smile hovering at the corners of her lips.

I smile back, then finally remember that I have a few manners. "Wine?"

Nia turns to me with raised brows. "You have some?"

"Yeah." I don't mention that most are bottles people have given to me over the years—birthdays, corporate events, congratulations on a great year/new offices/coming baby sort of thing. I simply open the pantry door. "I've got a collection. Take a look."

She strolls toward the mostly empty shelves. "Keep working on that pile of dishes. We should probably have some zippy white with chicken and seafood for dinner, but I love me a good red. Merlot it is. That okay?"

"I guess. I've never tried it." Becca didn't drink, and I only imbibe when I'm hanging out with Sebastian.

"I'm beginning to think my mission in life is to expand your horizons."

I only know random details about Nia's past. She grew up in Georgia, then decided she wanted a totally different experience while she pursued higher education, so she applied to institutions in the northeast and northwest, finally deciding to attend the University of Washington. She graduated with honors in four years with a degree in communication and a minor in business administration while holding down crappy minimum-wage jobs. She filled the summers of her college years with adventures—backpacking through Europe and building clean-water facilities for rural South American villages. For graduation, she saved up for an epic trip, journeying to Africa by herself to see the other side of the world. I give her tons of credit, especially since I don't step out of my shell much.

"If anyone could, it's you."

She looks proud of herself as she wags a finger at me. "Don't you forget it. Corkscrew?"

I shrug.

"I'll look around. You keep washing."

I hear her rummaging through drawers, muttering softly to herself as I continue to work at the mountain of glass and china that's been stacking up for months. At least the stove is relatively clean since I've hardly used it.

"Ah-ha!" After some clinking and rattling, she holds up the implement, triumphant. "Found it." Moments later, she has the bottle open and she's poured some into two clean glasses. "What should we toast to?"

"Me getting my act together?"

"Other than this domestic mess, no one has their act more together than you. How about…new possibilities?"

Like a clean house and a new wife? "To new possibilities, then."

We clink glasses and sip. It's not awful, actually. I'm surprised.

For the next two hours, we talk about work and fix the abysmal state of my living room while I try to ignore the spices wafting through the place and making my stomach rumble. Becca preferred bland food, but I like something with kick. What Nia is simmering smells divine.

By the time it's ready, she's reorganized half my cabinets, directed me on how to scrub my refrigerator from top to bottom, and sorted months' worth of magazines and mail off the kitchen table and into either the trash or my home office.

My penthouse is beginning to feel something approaching normal again. But it's not home anymore.

I swallow a bite of gumbo and peer across the table at Nia. I realize that I know her…but I don't. She's told me an assorted collection of her facts and memories, but I don't know the kinds of things that belong in her dating profile. I don't know what makes her tick.

"Uh-oh," she mutters and washes down a bite with her wine. "You're staring at me like I'm a problem you have to solve. That scares me."

I laugh. "I'm not going to add you to my project list when I get back in the office tomorrow."

"Thank god."

Again, I stare at her. I'm used to seeing Nia five days a week. But have I ever really looked at her?

"You know, I was thinking earlier…" she begins. "It's going to be weird come January, when you've relocated to Maui. You won't be in the office beside my desk anymore. If I have a question, you'll be far more than a few steps away."

I didn't think about it like that. Working remotely has never been a problem for us; we've done it when I've traveled. But suddenly I'm wondering whether having Nia twenty-six hundred miles away makes sense. I rely on her for so much. "You have a point."

"Maybe…you don't have to move that far away."

I've considered this thoroughly. It might be one of the five emotional decisions I've made in life. "I can't stay in Seattle."

Too much history. Too many memories. No real connections…except maybe to Nia. Suddenly, I'm loath to leave her behind.

Her face softens. "Maybe if you sold this place and found another—"

"The only family I have left lives in Maui."

"I know, but do you have to move near them? They're all recently married and getting ready to have babies. Will being around a bunch of expectant newlyweds really make you feel less alone?" When I frown, she holds up her hands. "Sorry. I said too much. Of course, they're your family, and it's your call."

"I understand the move seems sudden to you. But my mind is set."

She nods, not exactly thrilled but accepting. "What I should say is, if you decide you'd work better with me in Hawaii, then when you move, I'll go, too. I know you said I don't have to relocate, but…"

I didn't ask because she has a life here. Because she was always involved with someone. Because it didn't seem necessary. And maybe because Becca always insisted I'd benefit from a more experienced assistant. Whatever the reason, I'm now rethinking my decision to leave

Nia behind.

"Just putting it out there," she says, staring into her wineglass. "I mean, since you're taking Sebastian—"

"I couldn't have stopped him from coming if I tried. He hates the gray and the rain here." And I suspect I'll miss them. They suit me, especially these last six months.

"Yeah, he's been vocal about that."

"Thanks for volunteering to come along. I'll give that some serious thought."

"Whatever works for you." She shrugs. "I don't have any family or specific reason to stay, so…why not?"

We finish dinner, sharing the rest of the bottle and some comfortable business conversation. By the time we push away from the table, it's shortly after nine. The moon hangs like a big silver orb over my insane view of the Space Needle and Elliott Bay. I'll miss this scenery, but I'm confident that Maxon and Griff, my two half brothers who are successful Realtors in Maui, will find me something equally stunning.

Nia begins to clear the table, and I follow suit, helping her stack everything in the sink. She puts the lid on the pot of gumbo and shoves it in the refrigerator. "There's enough leftovers for you to eat another meal or two. I'm going to let you do the dishes so you can practice your new skills."

I know it's good for me, but… "Am I supposed to appreciate that?"

She laughs, and I'm struck by the glow of the moonlight on her dark, gleaming skin. By the flash of white teeth against her rosy lips, by the fall of her fat, loose curls cascading over her shoulders and toward the plump breasts I never really realized she had before this moment.

Shit. I have to stop thinking about those. About her. I'm her boss; our interaction can't be personal.

"I know you won't, but think of this as tough love," she joked. "Now…do I even want to know the last time you changed your sheets?"

Her question makes me freeze. I'm sure I look somewhere between lost and ashamed. The truth is, Becca changed them two days before she died, and I've never had the gumption to take them off. I thought about it, but every time I tried, I felt like I was ripping another reminder of her out of my life. Even months after her death, Becca can still inspire guilt in my technically geared heart.

"Don't ask," I admit finally.

"Do you know how?"

Vaguely. "Yes."

Nia cocks her head as if she's reading me. After three years as my "work wife," I have a terrible feeling she actually can. "Do you want me to do it?"

I swallow, then nod. Becca is gone and she isn't coming back. Keeping her sheets on the bed won't change that. "Please. I'll find a clean set."

"All right." She follows me down the hall. "I'll stick the dirty ones in the washer before I go."

"Trash them." I don't want to see them again. And I won't be taking them to Hawaii.

Everything there will be new, never touched by Becca.

"If you're sure... What about the rest of your laundry?"

I'm surprisingly embarrassed to admit that I've been ordering new pairs of underwear and socks every week. Most everything else goes to the dry cleaners. "If you'll show me how to work the washer and dryer, I'll do it."

"I'll get you started," she assures softly as we reach the bedroom I once shared with my wife and flip on the light. "Whoa."

Yeah, spread across the room is a jungle of shoes, neckties, socks, and T-shirts. "It's a disaster. I know."

This used to be my haven, my favorite spot to read one last report before bed or watch TV on the weekends. Now, I hate to come in here. Every time I do, Becca haunts me. Tonight, the sensation is strong. I feel guilty for being so eager to leave this place behind.

"Well, the good news is, it's fixable."

"Thank you. Really," I murmur, feeling an odd urge to...I don't know. Hug her? No, something more, but physical contact is not an appropriate way to express my appreciation to my assistant. Besides, what's rolling through my head now is muddier. My urge to be closer to her isn't strictly professional, and I don't understand. "I'll leave you to it and do the dishes."

Nia nods as I go. After I rinse off tonight's bowls, I tuck away the last of the pans we washed by hand earlier. Then I empty the dishwasher, only to fill it up again. I'm not really sure where any of the clean stuff belongs, so I shove everything somewhere and hope I can find it again.

In that thirty minutes, she's organized my room, remade my bed, and started my laundry. As I begin down the hall, I can hear her muttering to herself. It's nice to have someone else in the house. She's been good company. I'll hate to see her leave. But soon she'll have to head home. She's already gone above and beyond. I can't insist on her company until exhaustion finally takes me somewhere around two a.m. And as questionable as my thoughts about her tonight have been, I don't know what would happen. It's better if I let her go.

Even as I tell myself that, I walk into the bedroom for more of her company. And I stop short when I get an eyeful of Nia.

She's on her elbows and knees, obviously searching for something. All I can see is her bent over. Her soft, round ass fills my vision. In that instant, I want to sink my hands—my teeth—into that.

Holy shit.

I stop breathing. I stop blinking. A lightning bolt of lust jolts me. I can hear my jagged heartbeat suddenly thudding in my ears.

It's been nearly two hundred days since I've had sex. I see beautiful women all the time. Seattle is full of them. Hell, Stratus Solutions is, too. Since Becca's death, some of her lithe, lanky yoga friends have even hinted they'd be interested in comforting me with more than a homemade casserole and a hug. I haven't truly been tempted.

Until now.

With a huff, Nia tosses her hair back and sits on her heels. Her thin gray sweatshirt rides up, the band at the bottom circling her tiny waist, accentuating her curves. Her hair, which she usually has pinned up in some complicated twist at the office, falls in ebony waves halfway down her back.

Suddenly, she whirls around. I should look away…but I can't. She's flushed. Her eyes are bright. And a goddamn strip of her smooth, bare abdomen shows below the hem of her shirt, flirting with my overloaded senses. I gulp and hope she can't see how hard my cock is. For her.

I need to think of something to say—fast.

Nia rescues me. "Do you know how many socks are under your bed?"

I press my lips together and try to pry my thoughts off her body. When I attempt to focus on her question, the shock of my sudden attraction has my brain boomeranging away from the clutter and back to all the things I can suddenly picture doing with her. To her.

Somehow, I manage to shake my head. "No idea."

That's my honest answer. I have no idea what's going on. Why this is happening. What I'm going to do next.

She scoffs. "You must have tossed them under here at some point. I've managed to find what I can. Once the washing is done, you'll probably fall a few pairs short. Oh, and did you know there's some painting canvases under the bed?"

"Yes." I try not to flush.

"Were they Becca's?"

They're mine. Diana taught me to paint as a teenager. I used to find it soothing. When I couldn't sleep or when I couldn't solve a business problem, something about turning off the analytical half of my brain and focusing purely on the creative when no one was watching and there were no rules to follow would free up my subconscious enough to untangle my dilemma.

All that ended when Becca perished. A few brush strokes across the canvas weren't going to change the fact that she was gone. My will to dig for what little creativity I possess dried up. I shoved everything under the bed and left it there for good.

I don't lie to Nia. Instead, I simply shrug. "I'll move them later and see if I find any socks underneath."

"Okay." She stands, a handful of mismatched socks in her grip. "I'll toss these in the hamper. They can go in the next load."

We make our way to the laundry room, her talking about water temperature and me trying not to fixate on the sway of her pretty ass.

A few minutes of torturous laundry talk later, she meanders back to the living room. I can't take my eyes off her as I follow. When she stops, I do, too. And I realize I'm standing closer than I should. My breathing becomes harsh as I watch her turn in a slow circle and take in her handiwork.

"This looks better." She nods, seemingly pleased.

"A lot. Thank you for everything."

"Happy to help. Can I do anything else for you tonight?"

She can't possibly mean that the way it sounds. I only hear suggestion because I suddenly have sex on the brain. Still, how do I answer?

"I, um…" *Want to fuck you so bad.*

Dear god, did I just think that?

"You what?" She looks somewhere between concerned and confused.

If I pushed her against the wall, laid my lips over her soft, pillowy ones, and kissed her hard until her frown melted away, what would she do?

The question makes me sweat.

"Nia, I—"

Before I can figure out what I'm going to say, the doorbell rings. I let out a long breath. *Damn it.* Since it's nearly ten o'clock, that can only be Sebastian. I don't know whether I'm cursing the fact he's interrupting whatever might be developing between Nia and me or thanking god he's come to save me from making a catastrophic mistake.

"Open up, loner." Sebastian knocks on the solid wood between us. "I have a problem to discuss and a bottle with your name on it."

Nia grabs her purse from the nearby chair. "Sounds like he does this a lot."

"All the time." I know he's trying to make sure I don't spend too much time alone. Usually, he's a welcome distraction. Tonight, I wish he'd stayed home and watched the damn football game.

"Well, I'll go and leave you to your guy time. If you think of anything else you need help with, let me know. I'm not busy tomorrow night."

She doesn't have a date on a Friday night? I'm both shocked and thrilled—and have no right to feel either. "I think I've got it now that you've helped me back on my feet."

I have to say that because if I invite her over again, I'm worried I'll tell her that I need help with my cock and she can best assist me by stripping and spreading her legs.

Yeah, that's way past unprofessional, veering into lawsuit territory.

"Okay, then. See you in the morning."

"Jesus," Sebastian shouts. "Are you taking so long to come to the door because you're shitting or masturbating?"

A laugh slips from Nia's lips before she covers it with her hand. "I thought he was only impatient in the office."

I shake my head and focus on replying now that Bas has totally killed the moment. "He's far worse away from it."

She winces. "Have fun with that. I'll spend the rest of the evening doing something more fun than appeasing Bas. Tearing out my toenails comes to mind."

"He's not that bad."

Nia raises a skeptical brow. "Uh-huh."

"Oh, my god. Stop whacking your weenie and open the damn door." Sebastian pounds on the wood.

"Shut up," I call back, a smile lurking at the corners of my lips. "I'll open it when I'm ready to."

"Why don't I save you the trouble?" She grasps the knob and turns, then yanks the door open. "Hi, Bas. Glad to see you're behaving like your usual charming self."

"Nia..." One of my best friends for the last decade says her name like she's a welcome surprise. "I didn't know you were here, especially so late."

"I'm helping him."

"Yeah? I can think of a few ways you could do that," Bas drawls suggestively.

Despite the fact he's not thinking anything different than I did a minute ago, he said it out loud. I find his suggestion disrespectful, out of line. Most likely, so does Nia. I won't tolerate it.

"Get your mind out of the gutter," I snap and shove him against the wall, teeth bared. "And shut. Up."

Bas blinks and raises his hands in surrender. "Hey, I was teasing. I didn't mean anything..."

My scathing glare thankfully motivates him to close his mouth.

I turn my attention back to Nia, who's edged out the door. I can't help myself. Before I think better of it, I reach out and cup her shoulder. Electric heat sizzles across my skin. My knees nearly buckle.

Shit.

"You all right? I can walk you to your car."

Nothing should happen to her in the parking garage. It's secure and open only to residents of my upscale building, but I don't like her walking in the dark alone. I don't want our evening to end like this.

I also don't want to be apart from her.

"I'm fine. Good night."

"Night, sweetheart," Sebastian calls with a wave before he shuts the door behind her. The moment we're alone, he leans against it with a raised brow. "So, how long have you been fucking Nia and how did I not know?"

CHAPTER TWO

Saturday, November 4

"TELL ME AGAIN why we're here. Wherever here is," I say to Sebastian as I exit his sedan.

"There's something I think you need to see."

Since this place is a theater of some sort, I doubt it has anything to do with work. The giant sign out front in old-fashioned lettering simply reads BBB REVUE. I have zero idea what that means, but as Sebastian strolls inside and speaks in low tones with a hostess sporting a corset, fishnets, and not much else, I look around. The place is almost theatrical, like something out of a Victorian house of ill repute. Dim lighting and red velvet, lots of dark wood, flourishes, and detail. Booths line the walls. There's a balcony above with cozy round tables hugging the railing, providing a view of the floor and stage below.

"What is this place?" I murmur to Bas as the hostess leads us to a table almost front and center yet still somehow steeped in shadow.

"Just…wait." As we sit, he flashes me a smile. "You'll find this interesting."

Bas's idea of interesting worries me.

We've barely managed to sit when a waitress, also wearing next to nothing, sidles up to our table. "Hey, boys. What are y'all drinking tonight?"

"Scotch," Bas answers.

"Make it two," I add.

"Great." The blonde with this southern accent gives us a saucy smile. "I'm supposed to tell you that the appetizer of the night is calamari, but that stuff smells so awful I swear it's gonna re-grow legs and walk itself away. Want some?"

With that glowing recommendation? "I think we'll pass."

She leans in, giving me a perfect view of her spilling cleavage. "Smart man."

Sebastian clears his throat. "I'm the guy who insisted we come here tonight."

The waitress laughs, then ruffles a hand through his thick, golden waves. "Well, that makes you even smarter. Whatcha doing later?"

Since she punctuates her question with a wink, she's not serious. At least I don't think so.

What kind of place dresses their waitresses like turn-of-the-century hookers and allows such outrageous flirting? This isn't a strip club. There are no poles, no loud music, no one named Destiny shaking her hips and losing her top to the strains of an overplayed 80s metal classic. But I don't know what to think.

"Well, now." Bas grins. "That depends on you, darlin'."

He's good at turning on the charm. He manipulates women the same way he manipulates numbers—smoothly, efficiently, and perfectly. Truth be told, I've always been a bit in awe of his pickup skills. Not because I want them, but they're infallible. I've never had that knack with women. I've never needed it. I first kissed Rebecca Martin when I was sixteen. We were inseparable after that. Married two years later. I've never thought much about what I'd do with another woman.

Which is why my sudden urge for Nia is blindsiding.

I was hopeful when I sauntered into the office yesterday that the odd feelings would be behind me, that I wouldn't look at her and immediately think about peeling away her clothes and bending her over my desk. Unfortunately, I was overly optimistic. She swayed in yesterday morning, wearing something she's worn a dozen times: a crisp white blouse, a black skirt with a slit halfway up the back of her thighs, and stilettos with straps that wrap around her ankles. Suddenly, those shoes are screaming "fuck me!" In that moment, I really, really wanted to oblige…like I wanted to on Thursday night. And last night. Tonight isn't looking much better.

Not long after Becca's death, my desire for sex resurfaced. I didn't want another woman, per se. Just relief. My hand has been getting a hell of a workout, but I've never had a body or a face to put with my imaginary bed partner. Now, I can't get Nia out of my head.

This is a problem I didn't foresee.

Bas and the waitress laughing bring me out of my reverie. She looks ready to fall for his flashy good looks and smooth charm. But the blonde flits away moments later, and my buddy watches her go with a sigh.

"You brought me here to be your wingman? You don't need backup to get laid, and I have a mountain of work I could be doing." I move to stand.

"Don't leave. I brought you here because a) you can't work all the time, b) you have to stop avoiding the fact that you need to move on from Becca, and c) like I said, there's something you've got to see."

"Something here? What?"

He shrugs, but his face is full of mischief.

"Oh, I get it now." I shake my head. "You think *I* need to get laid."

"I know you do. But not by just anyone. That's not your style." He leans back and peers at me. "First, are you sure there's nothing going on between you and Nia?"

In my head doesn't count. "We beat this dead horse the other night. She took pity on me because I hadn't had a home-cooked meal in months and my apartment was a disaster. Stop reading more into it."

"Ever think about why she'd bother? Why she'd care?"

Actually, I have. "Because she's a nice person who likes to help others. She's done some babysitting for Marcy when her husband was out of town and her older son had a soccer game. She also helped Don and his wife when they moved into a new place over Fourth of July weekend. I'm not looking for ulterior motives."

Mostly because if I thought she was hot for me in return, I'd be way more tempted to throw caution to the wind, risk a lawsuit, and carry her off to my bed.

Then you'd have no assistant, dipshit, and where would you be?

"You should. I think she's got a thing for you."

I scoff. "I think you're insane. I also think you should drop it."

If he doesn't, I'll fixate on the possibilities. Nia is not only the first female who's stirred my interest since Becca, but she's the only one who's ever made me feel like my blood is boiling. I don't understand it; I've barely touched her.

"All right. Let's sit back, enjoy the show, and see what tonight brings."

Whatever he has planned will at least be more entertaining than his October profit and loss statements. Maybe this show, whatever it is, will help me keep my mind off the newest offer Colossus Investment Corporation submitted just before five o'clock on Friday...and the fact that today my son or daughter was supposed to have been born.

In March when the obstetrician gave Becca and me the baby's due date, November fourth hadn't sounded that far away. Before we even left the office, she was furiously making plans to hire a decorator for the nursery and interview potential nannies. We even discussed private schools.

I had no idea then how different my life would be now.

"Sure," I say finally. It's probably better—and healthier—than sitting in my penthouse alone, stewing about my worries and lamenting all I've lost.

The waitress returns with another sassy grin, a few drinks, and a veggie tray on the house. Over the next ten minutes, I see more women dressed suggestively bustle in and out of the curtain draped across the stage, some showing thigh or ass to appreciative audience members. Others outright wriggle, flirt, and tease.

"God, I love kittens," mutters the forty-something guy behind me.

I lean in and peer at Bas. "Kittens?"

He smiles. "They help the show run smoothly."

"What kind of show?"

Before Bas can answer, the room goes dim. A spotlight hits the stage. Then a man in a red velvet tux centers himself in the beam of light, mic in hand. "Welcome! Who's ready for a swinging Saturday night?"

The crowd cheers raucously. Even Bas, who is never a joiner, claps and whistles.

"Who are our experienced guests? Let me hear you."

My buddy surprises me by applauding even louder.

"You've been here before?"

"Yeah. Last weekend with one of my basketball buddies. One visit, and I knew I had to come back. We'll see if you feel the same."

On that cryptic note, he leans back in his chair and focuses on the stage, leaving me no choice but to do the same. I nervously bite into a stalk of celery and wonder why the hell I'm keyed up.

"A lot of returning friends here tonight," the emcee praises. "Always good to see you. And who are our virgins? Raise your hand. Don't be shy."

When I sit quietly, Bas kicks me under the table. Grudgingly, I lift my arm above my head. The spotlight zips around the room and zeroes in on me before highlighting a few others, then returning to our host.

"Excellent. Let's get your cherry popped. Who's ready for a great show?"

If anything, the decibel level goes up again. People, especially men, are excited. My disquiet returns in earnest.

"Then get ready for the Bawdy Boudoir Burlesque Revue!"

Music fills the air—trombones and saxophones mostly—giving the old music a lively, sexy vibe. Then the curtains part, and an artificial redhead hustles onto the stage in a stark black pea coat, a top hat, and heels. Behind her, a dozen women all dressed in French maid costumes cluster around her. The live horn section goes silent before prerecorded music fills the speakers around the club. It's whimsical and cheeky and suggestive as hell, especially when the redhead peels off her coat and tosses it aside, revealing a glitter-studded bra and thong, then proceeds to undress even more until she's covered only by a pair of feather dusters and a couple of pasties.

"Burlesque?" I raise a brow across the table at Sebastian. "This is what you think I need to see?"

He nods, barely taking his eyes off the stage.

"Bas, I don't need to gawk at half-naked women."

"Keep watching. It'll get better."

In what way?

As soon as the nearly naked redhead flounces off stage, her pale ass swishing to the closing beats of the music, another horde of women race front and center, dressed in what I can only describe as Flamenco garb—ruffled skirts, low-cut necklines, and bright red lipstick. A Latina beauty shimmies her way on stage, dressed in a skimpier, drop-dead red costume. A shirtless beefcake follows in her wake. They dance together…if you can call it that. It looks like vertical, rhythmic sex to me.

I don't want this woman, but I sure would like some action. Unfortunately, right now I can't picture doing it with anyone except Nia.

After a striptease down to a G-string and some swinging tassels, the brunette and her partner tango out of sight, littering the floor with glitter and sequins.

The waitress slides by in silence and brings both Bas and me another drink as the Latin dancers are replaced by a busty blonde barmaid in a parody of traditional German garb. A corset thrusts her boobs up, and her skirt looks indecently short. Her white knee socks are a schoolgirl throwback and utterly at odds with her shiny black heels. She carries two big steins as she skips to a cluster of men in the corner whose tongues practically hang from their mouths. Instead of setting the big mugs down, she turns and bends, wriggling her backside and revealing a tiny thong. One bare cheek is painted with the word SPANK. The other reads ME. The middle-aged man closest to her happily complies.

A few minutes later, the barmaid is replaced by an Asian woman wearing a dress in transparent green vinyl. She stirs a giant pot like a mad scientist with a seemingly evil smile, then leads one of the male dancers clad in a business suit into her lair, tossing off her dress and tempting him with come-hither glances until he dives into her concoction and emerges wet and horny and nearly naked. Another sex-standing-up number ensues.

I still don't know why Bas insisted I come. All the sexual reminders are only revving me up.

As the latest duo leaves the stage, I reach for a couple of bills in my wallet. "Thanks for an interesting evening, but I think I'm going to call an Uber and head home. It's getting late, and I'm tired."

"Tired?" he parrots. "It's barely eleven o'clock on a Saturday night."

I shrug. "I haven't slept much."

Try not at all. Instead of seeing Becca all around the apartment, I'm now imagining Nia. In my kitchen. In my bedroom. In my bed.

Why the hell can't I think of anything except her?

"Give me until midnight. It will make sense by then."

I'm not wavering. "I'm done."

Suddenly, he shoots me a challenging grin. "That supplier you hate dealing with so much—what's his name?"

"Bill Rhodes."

"Right. When he comes into town for his next quarterly schmooze, I'll volunteer as tribute and go golfing with him for you. I'll even do the dinner bit."

I sit. Now I'm tempted. I don't like Bill Rhodes. I like golfing even less. Spending twelve hours with the man is pure torture. "You're mean."

"I'm helpful," he corrects.

"If you were helpful, you would have volunteered to deal with Bill without coercing me to stay."

"I'm doing this for you. You'll thank me later."

Before I can ask how that's possible, another act trots on stage, this one a heavy thirty-something comedian. He's a dead ringer for Jackie Gleason back in the day. Speaks like the actor, too. I only know that because when I was growing up, Diana loved to watch reruns of *The Honeymooners*. He's funny. I relax, finding him easy to enjoy.

A half hour later, the emcee who had appeared earlier in his red velvet tux now flits onstage in a green corset, full makeup, and crazy heels. Gotta say, it looks damn awkward with his handlebar mustache.

Sebastian laughs, then gives him a considering stare. "I'm kind of impressed."

"Don't think you'd look that good in a corset?"

"I'd look better," Bas scoffs. "But I sure as fuck couldn't walk on those heels."

The man has a point. Neither could I.

"Now, for our grand finale this evening… The moment you've all been waiting for. Let's give a big BBB welcome to the one, the only, the most beautiful goddess of burlesque, Precious Noire!"

The man backs off stage, and the curtains part. An African-American woman wearing a white sequin dress that hugs her body and covers her from head-to-toe waltzes into the spotlight, hair secured demurely at her crown. A mask covers most of her face, except for a pair of red-painted lips that do crazy things to my libido.

As the music turns bawdy, she slinks forward, the slit in her costume revealing her thigh and teasing me with a glimpse of her hip. With one hand, she flicks open a huge white feather fan and covers the tempting valley of her cleavage before she shoots a coy glance over her shoulder. I look to see a man following her wearing a pair of tights…and nothing else. He's hard as hell and makes no move to hide it.

The ridiculously shredded and ripped male dancer approaches her from behind and wraps his pale hands around her dark shoulders, caressing his way down her arms. She gives a shiver and a wriggle. Then he finds the slit in her skirt and flares it wide, revealing her sleek thighs and a small red glitter-studded brief beneath.

Holy shit, she's sex on stilettos. I feel myself start to sweat.

When she lifts her knee in front of her then slowly opens it to her side, the man behind her takes her thigh in hand and lowers his mouth to her exposed neck. She tosses her head back, lips parted. My cock responds immediately.

This woman is sensual in a way I've never seen, not in person. Sure, movies and whatever. But somehow being in the same room with her makes it real. Her sexuality is tangible; I feel it.

In that moment, I would gladly have walked on stage and offered that man a million dollars to give her to me.

Instead, I shift in my chair and find myself barely breathing as I wait for what comes next. They don't keep me hanging for long.

The guy spins her to face him, anchors her thigh above his hip, then bends her back over his supporting arm. She arches, face upside down for the audience, as she throws her arms wide in total trust.

As I watch him touch her, I'm jealous. Which makes no sense.

But that gnawing envy only grows when he uses his free hand to unfasten the front of her dress. Slowly, slowly, he exposes a glittering red-and-white bra with dangling loops and feathers, all designed to snare a man's attention. I can't stop looking at her as he caresses her dress off one shoulder and nibbles at her flawless, gleaming skin.

When he raises her to face him again, she backs away as if she's taunting him, but he grabs her dress by the other shoulder and gives it a tug. The garment falls away from her body, giving me a spectacular view of her ass, her plump, pert cheeks almost totally exposed. Her waist looks incredibly small above her lush hips. And when he thrusts his hands in her hair and unpins it, the mass of dark curls tumbles halfway down her back...drawing my eyes to a shape that suddenly looks familiar.

I zip a shocked stare over at Bas. "Is that Nia?"

"You figured it out quick. I'm impressed. It took me until Thursday night to be sure that's her."

Thursday night? When he saw her at my house? "Why then? What made it click for you?"

"Her ass. When I saw it in those gray pants..." He shrugs. "It's unmistakable."

He's right. I want to be furious at his observation, but how can I fault him for identifying the copious beauty of her taut, juicy backside when it's so obvious?

"Stop looking at her," I bark, even as I realize my demand is ridiculous.

The whole room is transfixed by Nia.

"Are you going to beat me up?" He glances around him. "Are you going to beat every other man up?"

I grit my teeth and try to hold in an explosive fury I can't explain. It isn't logical. First, she's choosing to be here, exposing her body to whoever walks through the door. I don't understand why, and I'll demand to. Except…I have no right. She's not my wife or my girlfriend. She doesn't owe me any explanation about what she does when she's not working for me.

I hate that.

Fists clenched, I stew and watch the son of a bitch dancing with her toss her dress across the stage and trail his palm down her body from her neck, over her cleavage and abdomen…then lower. I don't want to know what part of her he's touching now. I simply want to throttle him.

"You going to tell me again there's nothing between you two?" Bas baits me.

"I've never touched her."

"But you want to."

I ignore the knowing smirk on his face. "Drop it."

"You wanted to leave earlier." He pushes away from the table. "If you're still ready to get out, I'll go, too."

"Stay where you are."

Bas has made his point, and I can't fail to understand. Somehow, Nia has become more to me than an assistant.

What the fuck am I going to do about it?

As the slide of a trombone turns more suggestive and a sax further heats the mood, Nia faces the audience and lures the man on stage with a flirtatious roll of her body, even as her palms trace her curves from breast to thigh. She thrusts forward and arches back to the beat of the music in a smooth rocking of her hips, simulating sex. Ecstasy seemingly transforms her.

I want to put that expression on her face for real. I'm compelled to. I don't think I'll be complete until I know at least once what she looks like, sounds like, feels like as she's coming for me.

This is stupid for so many reasons. Completely illogical. And I right now, I can't bring myself to care.

Her partner sidles up behind her, takes her hips in his grasp, and rolls his body with hers. Jesus, they're simulating sex so realistically. If they were naked, I'd believe he was actually palming her ass and sliding deep inside her.

I'm about to burst. I grab the arms of my chair and try to keep my shit together. I remind myself this is an act. None of it is real. But their bodies are so in synch, so fluid together that I can't help the nasty suspicion Nia and this guy have fucked before.

The thought burns. I seethe. She isn't mine. But I goddamn want to be the one inside her now.

Then the man reaches around her, knuckles brushing her collarbones before he spins her to face him again. He seems to cup her breasts in his big hands. Seconds later, he pulls her bra away and tosses it aside. Then he reaches farther south and removes a layer of embellishment from her briefs, shrinking her thong and exposing even more of that luscious ass.

With her back to the audience, Nia flares out both of her big white fans to cover the front of her body and turns to the small crowd once more. She seemingly looks right through me as she smiles, purses her lips, and teases everyone with what we can't see.

I'm torn. On the one hand, I feel as if I'm going to explode if I don't feast my eyes on what's behind those feathery shields right now. On the other hand, if she flashes me, she flashes every other man with a stiff dick in the room. The thought makes me homicidal.

But Nia doesn't know or care what I want, she merely goes on with her act, sliding her hips from side to side in a slow, sensual rhythm while her partner gyrates behind her, his lips all over her bare shoulders, as he takes hold of her wrist and slowly pulls the fan away from her breasts. They are ripe and real, symmetrical and smooth—and covered only by a pair of red pasties with matching dangling tassels.

She shimmies, gives the crowd a seductive brush across the swells with her fingertips, and closes her eyes in pure pleasure as her partner wrests the fan from her grip, then reaches for its twin in her other hand, which still sways over the mystery between her legs. The music ramps up. He seemingly thrusts into her from behind again, then yanks the frond of feathers away from her body and chucks it to the other side of the stage.

I gasp. Hold my breath. Stare. The tiny thong she's wearing leaves her close to exposed. It's antagonizing me. It's arousing me. Shit, the elaborate mask on her face covers more than her pasties and her thong put together.

Something shifts inside me. I already know I'm never going to be the same. And Nia keeps dancing, taunting me as if she has no idea she's utterly ruining me.

Holy fuck, how did I have absolutely no inkling for the last three years how sexy she is? I already understand I can't unknow that now. And I'm beginning to suspect that tonight, I'm going to cross a line I may regret.

But I can't stop myself, not when Nia's every move seemingly goads me toward her.

As the music comes to a bumping, grinding halt, she turns one last time, hips rolling as she spins slowly, treating me to a final glimpse of her world-class ass before she strikes a pose. The music stops. The theater falls dark.

The entire place erupts in applause.

That's my cue. I stand.

"You going to find her?" I hear Bas over the thunder of her ovation.

"You're fucking right I am."

As the house lights come up, he slides his keys across the table with a smile. "Take these. I'll catch an Uber home."

I scoop them up, then hesitate. "Am I making a mistake?"

"How can you be? Whatever happens next is far better than you sitting at home, drowning in guilt over a woman who's long gone. And I've never seen you want something as much as you seem to crave Nia right now."

It's ugly, but he's right.

Fuck it. I'm about to make emotional decision number six. And I don't care.

JAW CLENCHED, I slip through a door marked EMPLOYEES ONLY and hang in the shadows, acting as if I belong. No one calls me out or questions why I'm here. The scene is crowded and chaotic. Dancers surround me, half-dressed in their costumes or emerging from little rooms on either side of the narrow hall in street clothes.

Beside me, the German barmaid looks surprisingly girl-next-door now that she's in a pair of jeans and a pink T-shirt with a kitten ironed on the front.

I turn to her. "Where's Nia?"

The blonde looks surprised that I know Precious Noire's real name. And she probably she sees my agitation. "Last door on the right."

I don't have the composure to speak words of thanks. Instead, I nod and charge down the hall toward what might be the stupidest mistake of my life.

I move through the sea of bodies, shrugging past the Latina dancer, a few of the French maids, then bump into my assistant's handsy dance partner. I stare him down. He looks at me blankly. One thing I realize instantly? My gaydar is absolutely silent. He's every bit as straight as I am.

As he hovers protectively around Nia's dressing room, I snarl and shoulder my way past him.

He grabs my arm. "Where do you think you're going?"

"To see Nia. Let go."

His eyes narrow. "Is she expecting you?"

No. In fact, I'm about to shock the hell out of her. I don't know if I'll be unwelcome, but I'm going to test Bas's theory that she wants me. If he's right…this could get messy really fast.

I shake him off, barrel inside the room, and shut the door. Behind me, I immediately hear the asshole jimmying the knob. I throw my weight against the portal to keep him out and lock it behind me.

Nia whirls to the sound of my intrusion, dressed in an inch of stage makeup, a silky white robe—and nothing else.

The moment she recognizes me, her mouth drops open. Shock spreads across her face. "E-Evan?"

"Nia." I can't find more words. I can't do anything except stare and put one foot in front of the other. I certainly can't defuse the anger and possessiveness I know I have no right to feel.

"What are you doing here?"

"That's my question for you," I growl. "Why the fuck are you taking your clothes off for strangers?"

She rears back and blinks at me. I don't think she's ever heard me curse. I keep the office professional, totally aboveboard. But I can't manage decorum now when she's breathing hard and her nipples are poking her thin robe.

She raises her chin and glares at me. Everything about her demeanor is like waving a red cape in front of a bull.

"It's burlesque, not stripping," she snaps. "I don't do this for money. I do it because I enjoy dancing."

"Yeah? You enjoy that asshole's hands all over you, too?" Even though the logical side of my brain tells me I'm way out of line, I point at the door behind me and stalk closer to her. "You enjoy sex standing up with him?"

Her nostrils flare. Her mouth presses into a firm line. "Last time I checked, *boss*, I don't have to justify my personal life to you."

The fact she's right only pisses me off more. "You do when your behavior reflects badly on Stratus Solutions."

She shoots me a quelling glare. "You'll have to do better than that. No one in the audience knows who I am. I never take off my mask and I never use my real name. Nothing I do on stage can taint your reputation." Arms crossed over her chest, she saunters closer. "Why don't you be honest and tell me what's really bothering you? I know you're not this mad simply because I was dressed a little risqué and gyrated on stage with Kyle?"

I debate the wisdom of blurting the truth. The rational part of my brain tells me to shut up, leave, and act on Monday like nothing happened tonight. Every other part of me knows that ship has sailed. My cock is especially eager to lay my cards on the table, grab Nia in my arms...and not worry about what happens next.

"You're right. I'm mad because I think you've fucked him."

She jerks as if I've slapped her. "Not that it's any of your business, but we haven't been together in almost two years. Thanks for letting me know you think I'm a whore."

Hearing I was right royally pisses me off. Having her put words in my mouth kills what's left of my patience, stripping away anything resembling professional civility.

I try not to squeeze her arms as I drag her close. "I *never* said that. Or thought it. I'm telling you that I can't stand knowing he's touched you. I don't like the fact you still have anything to do with him. I don't even understand why I'm here yelling and angry. I'm just..."

How the hell do I put the storm raging inside me into words? No clue, but I need to get it all out somehow or I'm going to explode.

"Jealous?" Soft surprise crosses her face.

Something about her confusion rips the confession from me. "Yes."

"Because you...want me?"

I grit my teeth and try again to think through the wisdom of spilling all this to her. But I can't keep it in. The softness of warm silk and hot woman under my palms almost undoes me. "Yes. I know I shouldn't. I've spent forty-eight hours telling myself what I'm feeling is ridiculous and I can't allow this—whatever it is—into our perfectly comfortable, efficient working relationship. But I can't turn it off. I can't fight it. I can't pretend it doesn't exist."

"Is that what you'd rather do? Bury your head in the sand and not feel it?" She looks hurt.

Her expression makes me feel like an asshole. Nia always asks insightful questions. Why should now be different?

I shake my head. "For the first time in months—maybe years—I feel alive."

Nia stares at me in silence, her gaze fused to mine. I swear I see a hundred thoughts whip through her head. For once, I can't read a single one.

"Say something." If she doesn't soon, I don't know what I'll do. I don't even know if I can be responsible for what happens next.

"Have you been drinking?"

"Not enough to drown out how much I want you."

"In spite of your opinion about my sexual past? And what about our working relationship?"

She's not wrong, but they're barbed questions. I have to maneuver around them carefully. "Nothing matters to me except touching you right now."

Before Nia can chew on my answer and remember all the reasons she should say no, I pull her against me. She gasps. The instant her soft body makes contact with my hard, aching cock, I groan and hold her tighter, cupping her face and lowering my mouth to her parted lips.

CHAPTER THREE

BENEATH MY HANDS, Nia freezes.

I stop, realizing I didn't ask the most important question of all. "Do you want me, too?"

My ragged breaths punctuate the air as she scans my face, seemingly searching for something. I don't know what.

Suddenly, she lunges for me, tosses her arms around me, then plants her mouth across mine.

The moment our lips meet is a shock of unbridled thrill. Desire floods my system, saturating my senses and shutting down my brain. I groan as I push my way past her soft lips and thrust my tongue against hers. Her moan of acceptance and her fingers clutching at my shirt are all the confirmation I need.

Without hesitation, I wrap my arms around her and fill my palms with her succulent ass, then lift her against me. I spare a brief moment of thanks for my logic that a daily gym habit makes for a healthier human. Holding her against my throbbing shaft so I can grind her against me is easy. And so sweet it sends a shudder of arousal through my entire body.

Nia opens wider to me with a throaty groan and rolls her hips in sync with mine. The friction staggers me. My knees nearly buckle. The heat between us…it's going to consume me. But if I don't get inside her in the next thirty seconds, I'll spontaneously combust.

I tear my mouth from Nia's. We breathe hard together as I scan the room. "Bed?"

"Futon." She points to an area behind a dressing screen at the back.

I nod and take her mouth again, along with five ground-eating steps to the comfortably rumpled gray surface.

As I lay her down, I grab the sash securing her robe in my fist. "Do you want me to stop?"

"No."

"Do you want me inside you?"

She gives me a jerky nod. "Now."

God, is this actually happening? Three days ago, Nia was the ideal assistant. Right now, she's my ultimate fantasy.

Breath sawing, I rip her robe open. She's completely bare. I appreciate the generous curves and shadowed valleys of her body while I tackle my zipper. The instant my cock springs free, I take myself in hand and align my aching crest against her silky, slick opening. "Last chance. Or I'm going to fuck you."

Nia wraps her thighs around me and presses kisses up my neck. "Hurry."

Normally, I'd debate the wisdom of this decision long and hard. I'd make a pro-and-con list, study my options from every angle, then choose the most logical conclusion for the desired outcome. Tonight, the primal part of me has stripped my brain down to its base functions. I don't care anymore if this isn't smart, if I'm being irrational, or if I'll regret the hell out of this.

I need Nia Wright now.

I grip her hips in my fevered hands, seize her lips, then thrust into her like I'll die if I don't feel her around me. Because I will.

And as I submerge myself inside her, Nia takes every inch. I let out a long, tortured groan, straining to surge as deep as I can. My eyes nearly roll back in my head as pleasure bombards me. How the fuck did I not realize until this moment how perfect she would feel, all soft and welcoming around me?

Then I'm not thinking anything because Nia arches and cries out, breaking our kiss to gasp and toss her head back. Her nails dig into my shoulders as her pussy clamps down.

"You're tight," I growl.

"You're filling and stretching me. It burns. Oh, damn. Yes..."

Under me, she gyrates and sways, her hips rocking back, sliding the tight paradise of her pussy up my sizzling length until only the head of my cock is bathed in her heat.

I clench my jaw, bare my teeth. Anything less than buried balls deep is unacceptable.

"Don't," I warn, shoving my hands under her, digging my fingers in her ass, and spreading her wider for me.

"What?" The way she pants the word screws with my brain and plays tricks on my overloaded libido.

"Don't try to get away from me. It's too late for that."

Then I pull her closer with all my strength and I drive inside her, thrusting deeper than before. I barge into a spot far inside her depths, and she keens again. Her nails dig harder.

"That's so good," she pants in my ear. "Hell, yes."

Her words encourage me, but her body shifts away from me once more, until she's almost dislodged me from her tight clasp. In some corner of my brain, I realize she's prodding me to move with her, to thrust in and out and generate friction between us until we reach a cataclysmic end. But the primal urges of my body are telling me to plunge as deep as possible, hold tight, and stay there until the end of time.

I take her mouth again, biting her bottom lip as I squeeze her derrière and push my way back inside her. The nip leads to a press of lips. Her taste lures me deeper, so I force my way into her mouth. Not that she fights me. No, she welcomes me with more animal sounds and a seductive swirl of her tongue.

I think we've come to a mutually satisfying position when she starts wriggling in my grasp again, trying to put distance between us.

"Goddamn it," I hiss.

"Move with me, Evan. Slide in and out. I want to feel every amazing inch of you against me."

When she puts it like that, I want that. I want it right now. And don't I want to see her come? Yes. I have to see her face, feel her grip, hear her cries—and know I made her unravel for me.

At the thought, something savage inside me comes off its chain. My heart lurches into high gear. My body revs, every muscle tense. My stare penetrates her unblinking gaze, just as my cock does to her sex. She looks breathless, full of anticipation, and so damn aroused it's making me dizzy and crazy and unhinged.

"Fuck, yes."

I barely see delight fill her face before I rear back and begin to pound into her. Deep, long, rapid-fire strokes that are an all-out assault on whatever barriers she has between the sensations we're sharing and the orgasm I intend to wring from her body.

As I plow into her over and over, sweat beads my brow. My fingers go numb. My head is completely silent except for the roaring heartbeat thrashing between my ears. Pleasure deluges me.

Nia begins to tense. Her encouraging moans pick up speed and octave until she's delivering them against my skin as she's sucking at my neck and crossing her ankles behind me as if she never intends to let go.

My lungs work like a bellows as I inhale ragged breaths and exhale with rough grunts. Pressure builds. My senses expand until all I can comprehend is Nia. Her skin is like velvet under my fingertips. Her lips against mine are unexpectedly sweet. Her scent around me is intoxicating as hell.

She's everything I've been seeking for longer than I care to admit.

Under me, she scratches and strains, crying out and writhing. I'm seconds from bursting in a devastating explosion of ecstasy beyond anything I've ever felt. I want it. I need it. I crave it—and her—so badly I don't think I can take another breath without giving into the towering pleasure about to crumble me under it.

But the way Nia is moving, desperate and wailing, she's climbing...but not yet on the edge.

There's no fucking way I'm going over without her.

I don't even know who I am or where this insistence is coming from. I feel compelled to thrust my hand in her hair and tug until our eyes meet as I rise upright and change the angle of my thrust. Then I set my hand on her hip—and my thumb over her clit.

I rub the sensitive nub. "You're going to come for me, aren't you?"

Her eyes half close with a sob of yearning and a bending of her spine. "Yes."

"What? Say it louder," I demand so I can hear her moan for me again.

"Yes!"

Her pleading arouses me like nothing else. I have to have more of it. I'm greedy for more of her passion, her supplication.

"Tell me again. Say it now."

"I'm going to come for you…"

And she is. Her bud swells and hardens under my thumb. In this position, I see the rush of blood making the undertone of her rich, umber skin even darker. Her throat works. Her lips part. Her nipples bead to perfect points as her chest rises and falls. A glance down the long line of her torso keys me up more, especially when my stare settles on her swollen pussy, so pretty and plump and perfectly bare.

"Do it," I bark in desperation. "Fucking now!"

She reaches out futilely to grab the futon and arches, her spine twisting. I shove in again, feel her squeeze me so tight it's hard to push deeper. But I grit my teeth and persevere. I'm going to watch her come apart for me, then I'm going to follow her into the abyss of pleasure and climax like I never have. I already know it, feel it.

"Yes." She nods frantically as she grabs on to my arms and grips hard. "Yes! That's it. It's so good… I'm there. Evan!"

She screams. Under my touch, her clit turns to stone. Her body bucks as her pussy rhythmically clamps and squeezes me. Ecstasy sharpens her face, and I already know I'll never forget the way it transforms her mouth to an *O* and her body to soft putty in my hands.

My stare is still fused to her, watching the most beautifully mind-blowing sight I've ever seen when rapture overtakes me. I want to watch her through every moment of her peak, but my own crushes me. I'm forced to close my eyes as I erupt and ride the relentless, stunning agony ripping away my breath and ruining my sanity.

This night and this moment—hell, this woman—have destroyed me.

As I struggle to catch my breath, she huffs and gasps. I open my eyes and find her staring. The jolt of our connection whacks me. Then a thousand thoughts hit me at once. Not only did I have sex with my secretary, but for the first time ever, I had intercourse with someone other than my wife.

"Oh, god," I spit out, my face tightening. "What just happened?"

She cups my cheek in her soft palm. "Don't do this, Evan. Don't ruin the moment."

It shouldn't have happened in the first place. My logical brain knows that. Guilt screams at me. Becca never liked Nia; she would have disapproved. Plus, we work together. What happened tonight will make everything damn awkward from now on.

Despite all that, I can't bring myself to wish it hadn't happened.

"Did I hurt you?"

Nia frowns. "Do you think I'm made of glass? Would I have been screaming for more if you had?" She caresses her way up my arms and wraps hers around my neck, bringing me closer. "It was amazing."

"It was." I can't lie about that.

"Then please don't regret it."

I can't promise her I won't. Instead, I hover above her, stare into her earnest face. We're so close. If I lean in, I could kiss her…like I'm dying to now. I don't, though. "What happens next?"

She shrugs. "Whatever we want."

Nia should think twice before saying that. Even now I'm realizing that I should get off of her, put my clothes on, and try to forget this monumental breach in our professional relationship. The other part of me is pretty sure I can't shove that genie back in its bottle. And if I know her door is always open… Well, guilt aside, I'm always going to want her.

Because sex with Nia turned me inside out, and no amount of logic is going to change that fact.

"Can we really work together after this?" My hand tightens on her hip. My cock is still hard inside her. "Truly?"

She continues to caress me as if we don't have a care in the world. "Why not? We're both adults. We're responsible. We can separate private from professional."

Logically, that sounds correct. Realistically? I don't know. I've never tried to focus on work while the person I crave on a base, naked level is knee-deep in all my professional affairs.

For now, I nod. I'll go with her assumption unless and until it proves untrue. "I hope you're right."

"I am. We'll just...work it out. We have to." Her face softens, and she rises to brush a kiss on my lips. "But this can't be the only time we're together."

Despite all my reservations, I don't hesitate. "You're right. It can't."

Though it should be, and I damn well know it.

Nia lets out a breath as if my agreement is a relief. Doesn't she realize tonight completely shook my world?

Maybe not. Maybe she has amazing, spontaneous sex with other guys all the time.

I hate that fucking voice in my head. I hate even more that it might be right.

"Do you want to come to my place for the night?" she whispers hopefully.

Absolutely. That's my first thought. Then I stop myself. "I have a mountain of work so I can be ready for Monday."

But sifting through the latest buyout offer isn't the only reason I decline. I need time to digest what just happened. Nothing about tonight fits my concept of sex. Nia gave me so much more than I expected—or was prepared for. I also need space to reconcile the fact that, in the blink of an eye, Becca is no longer the only woman I've ever shared passion with. And that it's not my late wife I'm pining for now.

For a reason I can't comprehend, that fact hits me hard. I withdraw from Nia's soft body with a grimace. Immediately, I feel colder. Alone.

Beneath me, she gasps. "Towel on the vanity. Shit."

When she points a few feet away, I jump up and grab it, then hand it to her. "A mess? I'm sorry. It's been…since Becca."

"I figured." She begins to clean herself up.

I take the towel back from her grasp and handle the task. After all, I made the mess. And it gives me another reason to stay close, touch her.

"Evan, I-I need to tell you something," she says suddenly. I'm surprised her voice is shaking. "I just realized we didn't use protection, and I'm, um…not on birth control."

"What?"

Somewhere in the back of my head, I hear myself snapping the question. But of all the things I imagined Nia would say next, that bomb never occurred to me at all. It should have. Neither of us were mindful enough to think about a condom. But if she has the kind of active sex life I'm imagining she does, how has she not been pregnant twenty times over?

"I can't," she explains. "The pill gives me migraines. IUD gave me awful mood swings. I usually insist on condoms, but everything with us happened so fast."

That's an understatement. I touched Nia and utterly lost my head. I stopped thinking about anything except how fucking good she made me feel. And Becca was on the pill for years before she decided she wanted a baby. Neither one of us ever had another sexual partner, so I've never used a condom in my life. I didn't pause long enough to realize how different everything would be with another woman.

Of course, when I think about it, that fact is so obvious I feel like a fool. But I try to keep calm and collected and hide my death grip on the towel as I wipe myself dry. After losing Becca and our baby in an instant, I can't think about the possibility of another pregnancy.

I haven't recovered from losing the last one.

Finally, I tuck my cock back in my pants and rearrange my shirt. Nia doesn't move, just lies sprawled across the futon, breasts moving softly with each breath, still naked as she studies my expression.

"I should have said something sooner."

Her face is so full of apology I can't possibly think she allowed me to have sex with her unprotected on purpose. But it's not okay. "I'm equally to blame. I should have asked."

"I'm early in my cycle. It should be okay."

But there's no guarantee. That's utterly fucking terrifying.

I swallow back my tension. "If you're ready to go, I'll walk you to your car."

"Are you sure I can't persuade you to come home with me? French toast in the morning..."

Her offer is tempting, and she tries to give me a flirty smile. But I see the uncertainty on her face. I'm probably a complete bastard for leaving her now, but my head is bubbling like a volcano. I've always been even-tempered, not prone to being swayed by any particular mood. The disquiet unsettling me now makes me wonder if somehow Nia has changed me.

"I can't." I also stifle a promise to take her up on the offer another time. I don't know if or how Nia and I will make us work.

If you can't deal and you break it off with her, then she becomes angry, disillusioned, and bitter, what then?

Nothing good.

"All right." Now her voice sounds clipped, a little hurt, as she wraps her robe around her body and covers herself from nearly head to toe again.

"Nia, what happened tonight can't change anything at work. No one can know."

She looks away and crosses her arms over her chest. "Sure."

I've hurt her. Son of a bitch. Whatever this is between us is barely ten minutes old, and I've already screwed up. Maybe I'm not wired for meaningful human interaction. Maybe the only woman who could ever understand me is cold and buried and gone forever.

"I'm sorry, but keeping what happened a secret makes sense—for both of us," I murmur, then realize if I keep talking, I'll only say more things that only upset her. "We'll talk more on Monday, all right? I'll see you then."

"See you."

As soon as Nia nods, I tell myself to turn around and leave. I shouldn't linger or give her false hope that I might stay the night after all or give her any reason to think I'm romantically inclined. But I can't make myself leave when she's distressed, especially when everything that's wrong is my fault.

Before I can tell myself not to, I take her by the shoulders, tug her to her feet, and pull her against me. Just like before, the minute I touch her, I don't care whether being with her is right or wrong. I simply need. The yearning on her face says it's the same for her.

She meets me halfway as I dip my head and kiss her slowly, tenderly, so unlike the way I assailed her mouth when I entered the room. It feels different to take my time, to savor her scent and flavor, to be kissing her not in passion but affection. But it doesn't take long before my head swims, my heart thuds, and my cock goes stone hard.

Fuck, she's potent, and I have a feeling that if I'm not careful, she could become a distraction. A weakness. An addiction.

Somehow, I manage to dredge up the will to stop enjoying her mouth, press a kiss to her forehead, and step back. "Bye."

CHAPTER FOUR

Monday, November 6

"MORNING. I BROUGHT donuts." Sebastian tosses a box of a dozen on the conference table in my office and parks himself in a chair. "Dig in, and let's roll through these numbers."

It's just after seven a.m. I came in early. I often do because there's always plenty of work. But today was a no-brainer. Why stay home when sleep is elusive and productivity is nonexistent?

The reason for my restlessness will be here in less than an hour. Nia and I haven't spoken since Saturday night. I'm torn. On the one hand, I must maintain status quo at the office. There's too much happening with Stratus for us to lose focus. On the other hand, I spent yesterday missing her in a way I don't understand. My thoughts are jumbled. I have urges where she's concerned.

I don't like this. I'm never conflicted. Why is everything different?

With Becca, I never felt this sort of internal chaos. She liked me; I liked her. We bonded because we had both suffered through terrible home lives and crappy foster families. Diana saved me at twelve, but I plucked Becca out of her living hell as soon as I legally could. She was grateful and took care of everything not related to my burgeoning business. I enjoyed her company. Sex was nice. Life was good.

Nothing about being inside Nia could be termed nice. What we did wasn't merely pleasant. It was raw, compelling, unforgettable…

And confusing as hell.

Yesterday, I resisted comparisons, but Becca is the only other sexual partner I've had. Isn't it natural to wonder why being with one woman is vastly different than performing roughly the same act with another? The only conclusion I can draw is that Becca had been providing me regular relief with her hand before we spoke our vows. Nia ended a terrible months-long celibacy, broken only by masturbation that had become both regular and dull. I was simply pent up. Surely if I had sex with her today, I wouldn't feel that same blood-churning, heart-pounding, gotta-have-it-now urgency.

"Evan?"

I whirl around and face my CFO, trying to look as if I've been completely attentive. "Yeah. The numbers. Let's do it."

"I already was. You didn't hear a word I said." He sighs. "It's none of my business, but what happened between you and Nia after I left on Saturday night?"

"You're right; it's none of your business."

Bas is my oldest friend. I couldn't lie to him if I tried. First, he reads me too well. Second, I won't deceive him. But I have no problem telling him to butt out.

"Oh, my god. You fucked her."

I remain absolutely mute for a long moment, gritting my teeth. I can't tell whether he's more shocked that I finally took his advice about moving on from Becca or that I did it with my assistant.

"Friday's offer was an increase of fifteen million cash and another thirty in Colossus stock options when their IPO goes public next summer." I change the subject. "It's more lucrative than their former offer and closer to market value."

"Not going to talk to me, huh?"

"About Nia? No. About this offer, sure. All day long. My big complaint is that we can't possibly know the price of their stock once the IPO goes public. So the valuation of the offer could suffer significantly following the initial offering."

"You don't believe that. Douglas Lund has almost tripled the size of their organization since he took over five years ago. The man is financially brilliant, and there's no way he would suddenly steer that ship in the wrong direction. My guess is the value of that stock will go up at least another twenty-five percent in the first six months."

Bas is probably right but… "If it doesn't?"

"You're still walking away with almost five hundred million in cash and other stocks that bring the value of the deal up to a billion dollars. All you have to do is sign a few papers and stay on as COO for two years. Then you'll be thirty and filthy rich, and you can spend the rest of your life doing whatever the fuck you want. Take it."

Everything he says is valid. I've had similar thoughts. All totaled, it's the sort of money that means not only would I never have to work another day in my life, but neither will my kids, my grandkids, or their children. I would, of course. I've never been an idle man, and I don't like people who lack goals or fail to embrace challenges. So I'll definitely find another business to build and succeed at—and I'll have the luxury of taking my time. Most people only dream of this financial independence. I certainly never fathomed having this much money as a poor kid in foster care. And I'd not only achieve my dream of making a billion by age forty, I'd beat it by a decade.

"Unfortunately, the deal, as is, still isn't right."

He gives me an exasperated sigh. "What's your hesitation? Is it because you built Stratus from the ground up? Hell, I joined you barely three months after you started, so I'm as attached to it as you are. If I were a selfish bastard, I'd talk you out of accepting the deal because I'll probably be downsized once the Colossus people take over. But I'm okay with that because this is best for you. I know you're sentimentally attached—"

"I'm not a sentimental man."

"Not about much. I understand why this might seem different, but saying yes is the right move. You're never going to get another offer like this, buddy."

"I disagree."

"You think your technology will remain wave-of-the-future long enough that another behemoth firm will decide you have the best data storage solution for individuals and corporations alike and be willing to pay you an obscene amount of money for your infrastructure and proprietary technology?"

"I don't think there will be another buyer; you're right about that. I'm saying if I take this particular offer, I'll be leaving money on the table."

"Oh, I get it. You want to make Lund bleed because you loathe him. Be careful with that…"

Admittedly, he's an egotistical, middle-aged prick who treated me like a snot-nosed kid when we first met. Since then, he's continued the trend, all but patting me on the head and rubbing me the wrong way. I don't mind sticking it to him, but I wouldn't do it if I thought I'd be screwing myself in the process.

"I've done business with people I disliked in the past. I'm not here to make friends; I'm here to negotiate the best deal possible. But as you just pointed out, if I sell, you might be laid off. Any of Stratus's existing employees are at risk." I employ nearly seven hundred people now. "They deserve whatever protection I can negotiate to compensate them for their years of loyalty and hard work."

Bas gapes at me. "Wanting more money out of the deal, I understand. You may be right that Lund can cough up more. But you can't possibly be willing to blow a billion dollars to coddle your existing workers. C'mon."

"I'm not," I assure. "But if I can ensure their futures for a bit longer—and yeah, stick it to Lund—I will."

"Just don't worry too hard. Everyone who works for you is smart. They understand the corporate game. If they're unhappy or they see the writing on the wall after the sale, they'll start looking for other jobs. Negotiate whatever terms you can, say *adios*, then laugh all the way to the bank."

"Don't be an ass, Shaw." Nia strolls in, wearing a figure-hugging dress in a teal shade that makes my breath catch, beige heels, and a smile.

Holy shit. After one glance, I'm beyond eager to peel every stitch off her, toss her onto the table, and shove my way between her legs.

So much for my theory about being sated and disinterested.

She looks different this morning than she did on Saturday night—without the inch of black eyeliner, false lashes, stark red lips, and all the glitter. Today, her makeup is subtle. Browns accentuate her eyes. Her cheeks have a hint of a flush. The lights in the room catch the soft glow of her lustrous skin. Her lips are a sheer berry shade that makes me desperate to kiss them.

How did I look at her for three fucking years and see an assistant, not a woman? A lover? No idea. I only know I can't do it anymore.

Bas flashes Nia a huge smile. "Wright, you know that's part of my charm."

They've been on a last-name basis in the office forever. They're usually friendly. Today, I don't like the speculative way Bas eyes her.

"Ha! What charm?" She raises a brow at him. "Think about this from the employees' point of view. Take Perkins, who's been counting the days until his retirement in three years. He's going to rely on that pension. What happens if Evan sells out and Colossus changes the benefits structure? Will he still be able to spend his golden years in the Outer Banks fishing or will he eventually have to go back to work? And what happens to the employees on tuition assistance? The ones who rely on our health plan? Hell, what happens to the workers they lay off? Will all of them find new jobs they like half as well? Will any of them?"

And what about Nia herself? I'm her first employer out of college. She's scarcely worked for anyone but me. What if she ends up assisting someone who doesn't treat her with respect? Or what if she finds herself working for another executive who's attracted to her, he touches her, and they…

Fuck.

Unacceptable. If I sell, I'm taking her with me. Well, provided she'll follow. Right now, I don't know. She hasn't acknowledged me since she entered the room. Is she going to act like I wasn't inside her, as deep as a man can get, less than thirty-six hours ago?

"Good morning, Nia."

"Morning," she says absently as she sets her purse and coffee cup on the table, then slides into the chair between Bas and me.

That's it? Is she going to look at me at all? "Do you have specific suggestions?"

"To protect the employees? Make Colossus honor your benefits for three years. Tell them they can't lay off anyone for eighteen months. Force them to provide education assistance and placement services for any Stratus employees they release. You know the drill."

"It's a stop-gap measure. Nothing will protect them indefinitely after I'm gone." I don't know why I'm playing devil's advocate with her when I agree those are concessions worth obtaining. Am I that desperate to make her talk to me?

"Nothing ever will," she argues. "But if you're actually serious about selling…"

"You think I shouldn't?"

"Saying no would be stupid," Bas cuts in. "He's young and connected enough to build another business. Or he could just kick back. Take up philanthropy. Buy his own tropical island. Whatever he wants."

It's hard to argue with his logic. If I were in his shoes advising me about this buyout, I'd probably tell me to negotiate those last few terms and dollars I want, then take the deal.

"No one will care about this business the way Evan will. And I think he'll regret selling." She shrugs as if it's obvious. "His heart is with Stratus."

I scowl. "Hearts don't belong in business."

She purses her lips together, disappointment tightening her face as she looks over at Bas. "Pass the donuts, Shaw."

Dutifully, Bas does, along with a stack of paper napkins. She opens the box and pulls out a Boston cream, then lifts it to her mouth. When her lips envelop the chocolate-covered, cream-filled concoction, she bites down with a long, low moan. I get hard instantly. Suddenly, I can't help remembering her groans and whimpers when she dug her nails into my back while I stroked inside her.

This train of thought isn't helping our discussion. Or my mood. Something angry overtakes me with every passing moment she acts like nothing at all happened between us.

"I'll take one," I say to her—not because I actually want a donut, but simply because I need her to look at me.

She hesitates, then gives the box a shove, sliding it across the table. Finally, she lifts her lashes and glances my way. Our eyes meet.

Instant zing.

"It's nice that you want to ask for protections for the employees, but I should advise you that it's a risk," Bas points out. "Lund is a hard-ass. Going in with demands might piss him off."

"I don't think so. He's already proven he wants Stratus. If he's come back to the table repeatedly and he's given me an offer this close to market value, then something simple like assurances for the workers won't chase him away, especially since he needs the know-how of the staff. He's smart enough to realize that. That's why he's asking me to stay on as COO for two years."

"I hope you're right," Bas mutters, focusing on the box of donuts. "You going to eat one and pass the rest along or hoard them all?"

With a scowl, I pluck one from the selection and drop it on a napkin, then shove the rest across the table. "I'm right."

He grabs one out of the box. "Well, on the plus side, us countering could be construed as interest we've never shown before. Do you want me to prepare something for you to present back to Colossus?"

"Put something together. I want to look at it when you're done, but I'm going to have you present instead."

"That won't make Lund happy. You know he wants to pal up with you."

I snort. "Whatever. I want the best deal for me and for Stratus. Looking too eager won't get me there."

"Fair enough. Wright, why don't you come with me and share your ideas? We'll whip this into something we can send over."

"Sure." Nia slips the last bite of the donut into her mouth, and when it oozes cream onto her fingers, she catches it with her tongue. "Be right there."

I watch the sensual pursing of her lips and the slide of her slick tongue as she sucks her finger clean. Instantly, I go from hard to aching so badly I nearly lose my composure. Worse, I can't tell if she's trying to torment me or if she reconsidered our hookup during her lazy Sunday and decided it wasn't that great after all.

When Bas disappears out the door, Nia stands, then grabs her coffee and purse. "It shouldn't take me too long to gather my thoughts and format everything. You'll definitely have a draft to approve by the end of the day. I also gave your personal ad some thought. I think I know what to do. You'll have a list of candidates by Friday."

As she takes the doorknob in hand, I stand. "Wait."

Nia turns and blinks, staring expectantly. "What's wrong? Did I forget something?"

She's really going to act as if we didn't share excruciating pleasure? "I don't know. Did you? Did you actually forget we had sex?"

WITH A SIGH, Nia cracks the door open and peeks into the hall. No sign of Sebastian or anyone else. When she shuts the door, she takes in a bracing breath as she turns to me. "What do you want, Evan?"

"For you to talk to me. For you to acknowledge that something more than nothing happened between us."

Her expression tightens. "After you zipped your pants on Saturday night, you told me nothing could change between us at the office. I'm honoring your wishes."

To her credit, she is behaving as if it's any other day. She's not giving me longing, lingering stares. She's not coming on to me now that we're alone. She's not acting as if she has any idea what it feels like when I sink inside her and ride her to climax.

I asked for this. But now that she's complied, I hate it. "I didn't say that to hurt you."

She shrugs like it's no big deal, but I see pain ripple across her face before she blanks her stare again. "You needed relief. And you see me all the time, so you know I'm safe. I'm not the crazy girlfriend type who will do anything and everything to snare a man. And when you saw me dancing nearly naked at the club, I probably seemed easy. It makes sense that you'd pick me to let out some of your pent-up sexual frustration. It's fine. I hope you feel better now."

Balancing her coffee carefully, she twists the knob.

Without thinking twice, I brace my palm against the door, ensuring she can't open it. Then I lock it and lay my other hand against the hard surface, caging her between my arms, thanking God this conference room doesn't have any windows. I'm not touching her anywhere—yet. But I want to so badly it's all I can think about.

"I didn't storm into your dressing room because I thought you'd be easy to nail. I don't know what I was thinking, but it certainly wasn't that you'd spread your legs simply because I asked you to. And it wasn't with the hope you'd take the edge off my sex drive. And it damn well wasn't because you're 'safe' or 'convenient.'" I rake a hand through my hair. "I did it because I couldn't stop myself."

"Well, itch scratched, right?" The only hint I have that my nearness is getting to her is the little pulse pounding at the base of her neck. Otherwise, she looks maddeningly cool. "You're moving on. I got it. We'll forget it happened and go back to normal."

Has she lost her damn mind? "You think I'm going to forget what we did? That I even could?"

As soon as the words are out, I wish I could take them back. Maybe she's capable of hookups and one-night stands. Maybe she didn't find the sex we shared particularly memorable or special. Maybe she doesn't want me anymore.

"What are you saying, then? I don't know what you want."

For her to forget about maintaining office decorum between us and to kiss me until I drown in her taste. "I want you. I want what we had on Saturday night again. I know we have to maintain a professional environment here. If anyone suspects we might be carrying on a torrid office fling, it could undermine us both."

She tilts her head and nods. "You're right. So let me out. I'll find Bas and get to work."

I don't budge. "I didn't say anything about keeping things status quo away from the office."

"So what do you think this looks like"—she gestures between us—"when we're not boss and assistant?"

Great question. "I don't know. I haven't thought about it beyond the fact I know I want more of you."

"Hmm. But you want to get married next month to someone you don't yet know. How will that work?"

Another great question. "I don't know that, either. We'll take it one day at a time, I guess."

"I see." She pastes on a bright smile. "Well, in the meantime, if you don't want anyone to know we're fucking on the side, unlock the door and let me leave."

I know she's right and yet… "Two minutes more. What are you doing tomorrow night?"

"I have a hair appointment."

"Wednesday?"

"Dress fitting. I'm a bridesmaid in a friend's wedding."

"And I'll be out of town Thursday and Friday." I sigh. Of all the challenges we face, I can add our busy schedules to the list. "Saturday night?"

"I'm dancing."

Her words ping around in my head. I freeze. "You mean you're taking your clothes off for strangers again?"

"If you want to boil down the art of burlesque to its most tawdry element, I guess so."

I'm being unfair. Possessive. An ass. I exhale, trying to see this from her perspective. But all I can picture are men with hard dicks staring at her and imagining themselves touching her the way I did, particularly that ex she dances with.

"What if I don't want you to?"

"I'm not going to give up something I love or who I am for any man, especially not one I hooked up with once. Besides, I signed a contract. I perform for the next two Saturdays. We're negotiating more performances in early December and all of January."

So basically, she doesn't care if I don't like it. And why should she? Unless I put a ring on her finger, I have no right to tell her what to do.

Now there's an interesting idea…

"You're welcome to come back to the club and watch if you want. But if you do, no more sex in my dressing room. I took a ration of crap from Kyle after you left."

"Your ex-lover?" She gives a damn what he thinks?

Nia sighs as if she's digging deep for patience. "He's now just my partner and my friend, one who happens to think screwing my boss is a terrible idea. And if we're going to fight about this, maybe he's right."

"We're not fighting," I bite out—then catch myself.

Well, Nia isn't fighting. I am. Damn it, how many other ways can I not act like myself? Why am I so tied up in knots?

"Good. I'm getting to work now. Can you step aside and let me go?"

I need to. If I don't, Nia can legitimately claim I'm harassing her. And that's the last thing I want, especially since I need her to talk to me.

"Can I see you on Sunday, then?"

She hesitates, then looks like she's gearing up to tell me something I don't want to hear. "Kyle and I have practice. But even if we didn't, I'm not sure you and I should see each other away from the office until you decide what you want this to be. Are we having casual sex or starting some sort of a relationship? Until you can answer that question, I'm not sure there's any reason for us to get together." She gives me a nudge, and I move out of her way because I should. And because her question bowls me over.

What *am* I doing with her?

"All right. We'll talk next week."

I half expect her to shrug me off. Until now, she's acted like my decision doesn't matter one way or the other to her. Instead, her face softens. "I hope so."

When she turns the knob and twists out of the conference room, I don't try to stop her.

I have a week to make up my mind. I already hate the thought of letting her out of my sight, though not as much as I hate the thought of her with Kyle. But I know where my thoughts are heading…

CHAPTER FIVE

Monday, November 13

IT'S BEEN AN excruciating week since Nia and I have had anything that resembles a personal interaction. Every second sucked, but I've made up my mind. I know exactly what I'm going to say the minute I can get her alone.

I just wish I knew what she was thinking. No, feeling. Nia is sensible, but ultimately she leads with her heart.

Before I left town, I tried to see her again. She was always in a meeting or training some of the newer administrative assistants or on the phone. I tried to call her when I arrived in LA. We never connected. On Saturday night, I debated the wisdom of returning to the BBB Revue. But I was in no mood to watch Kyle put his hands on her and dry hump her like he's never had a better thrill. I doubted I could have been responsible for my behavior.

So I waited, buried myself in work, digging into Lund's reply to my counter, which provides hardly any additional money. It does give me a lot of assurances for my employees…just not enough. So it didn't take me long to realize my answer is still a no. And that left me too much time to fixate on Nia.

What will she say when I tell her what I've decided?

I glance at the clock in my office. Five minutes until eight. She's usually here by now. I'm anxious to talk to her. Eager for any chance to touch her. She's consuming my brain.

"Morning." She waves as she breezes past my office door on her way to her desk. Today she's chosen to torment me with a camel-colored dress and black heels that show off her rich skin and feminine curves.

I want her. Now. I envision her in my office, spread across my desk, her sexy shoes on the arms of my executive chair as I make a meal of her body. She's both vocal and a screamer, but for the chance to have her on my tongue—and on my cock—I'd find a way to make it work in the office.

For now, I swallow back need and nerves, and hope she doesn't notice I'm hard for her. After waiting days for this moment, I'm nervous. I wipe my hands on my slacks. "Morning. Come in. Let's talk."

"No time," she says as she deposits her purse and coffee on her desk, giving me a prime view of her unforgettable ass. Then she whirls to me with an apologetic expression. "Your first appointment is in two minutes."

"Appointment?" When I looked an hour ago, my calendar was blessedly empty today.

She sighs in frustration. "Did the calendar not sync again? Sorry. You should have eight new invites for today, one at the top of every hour, minus an hour for lunch."

"Who am I seeing?"

"Your candidates."

"For what?"

Confusion knits her brows. "The candidates you asked me to find for your wife. Hang on..." She dashes back to her desk and opens a drawer, then pulls out a file folder and puts it in my outstretched hand. "I printed off the profiles and corresponding documentation for the women I ultimately chose for you to interview. These are the best of the best. The others..." She winces. "Let's just say I laughed a lot compiling this list late Friday afternoon. If you'll open the folder, the profiles are arranged in the order in which you'll meet the candidates, just like the last few jobs you filled. It should all be straightforward. But let me know if you have any questions."

Before I can ask if she's serious, the phone at her desk rings. She answers promptly. "Nia Wright speaking." A pause. "Excellent. Yes, please send her up." Another pause. "Her visitor badge only needs to be active for an hour. In fact, all of the visitors I receive today will need the same access." Another head bob. "Thanks."

"Nia, when we talked about this, I asked for a candidate slate. I wanted to look at the list and choose. I didn't ask you to set up a face-to-face with anyone. I never intended to interview potential wives in the office. I don't know what Joy at the reception desk thinks is going on—"

"I told all the candidates to indicate they're party planners we're considering for upcoming corporate events. Only you and I know the truth."

"Thank you for the discretion, but I would have liked the chance to talk to you before interviewing these women. You asked me to think about what I want next between us, and I have. We need to discuss—"

"And we will." She nods. "I'm sorry if you're not happy. I tried to take the initiative and start the process rolling since you said you were in a hurry to be married."

"Call everyone and cancel."

"I can't. I arranged to have five of the candidates flown in just to meet you. I have their email addresses, of course. But I just realized I don't have any of their phone numbers." She tsks at herself as if she's annoyed by her lapse. "I was so scattered on Friday. Sorry. I'll be sure to ask for their full contact information when they arrive."

"I don't want to talk to any of them, Nia."

She gives me an apologetic grimace. "I understand, but as long as they're coming, it seems smart to get to know these cream-of-the-crop candidates and see if one could be the next Mrs. Evan James Cook. How can you know who's out there if you don't look, right?"

Before I can correct her, I hear a knock. Nia hustles across the room and opens the door.

"Hi," I hear her say. "Welcome. Can I take your coat?"

"Here. So where's the rich guy who needs a wife? This better not be a scam…"

"Not at all." Nia rushes to hang the woman's coat on the tree, then gestures to my office. "Right this way."

I stand. I haven't even seen this woman and I already don't like her. I don't care what she looks like, how interesting she might seem, or how good she is in bed. She was rude to Nia. That's a deal breaker for me.

From around the corner, a stranger enters my office. A honey blonde with her tresses in a messy bun. She has black-rimmed blue eyes, an artificial orange tinge from chemical tanning, and an unlikely pout that's probably the result of lip injections. She's wearing a red two-piece suit…of sorts. The top is something off-the-shoulder with a ruffle that flirts with her too-large enhancements that I can't help but wonder if they're meant to compensate for what she lacks upstairs. The blouse ends at the top of her rib cage. After a strip of bare midriff, the high-waisted pants cling to her like a second skin, ending at the ankle. Her shoes are so sky-high I have no idea how she's walking.

When she catches sight of me, she pauses and eyes me with approval. "I'm Brittanii with two *I*s. And two eyes." She points at the pair on her face and laughs at her own joke.

"I'm Evan." And I'm not at all amused. "Sit down and tell me about yourself."

Nia peeks her head in. "Coffee, anyone?"

"Caffeine is, like, bad for you. Do you have any organic green tea, preferably steeped in filtered water? I don't trust tap. Who knows what they put in there?" Brittanii shudders, then turns to me. "You know what I mean?"

I'm aware that in a dating situation it's probably polite to agree with her statement, about which I'm basically ambivalent. But I don't have a fuck to give in order to acknowledge her. "I don't need a refill, Nia."

"Excellent. I'll see you when you're finished."

If I didn't think my assistant incapable of subterfuge and enjoying this farce at my expense, I would be deeply suspicious. But as she closes the door, leaving me alone with Brittanii, I'm unable to ask Nia any of the pointed questions whirling through my head.

"So you're looking for a wife?" my first candidate says. "What kind of arrangement are you after? I can look pretty. I can hire caterers. I mean, your ad said you were looking for those things. And sex. I'm good with that since you're not a troll. The ad didn't say if you were looking for something long-term."

Is she for real? "How long do you think a husband and wife should be married?"

I'm not really interested in the answer, but if I'm stuck with her for the next hour, I might as well let her horrify me.

"I don't know. I guess until they both feel like moving on."

I frown. "How long was your longest relationship?"

She pauses, obviously reflecting. "About eight months."

"Who usually breaks up with whom?"

"I get bored, you know? Of course, I usually date hot guys who are often poor, so we have nothing interesting to do. I mean, even sex gets stale after a while, right? What about you?"

"I was married for nearly eight years. We dated for two years prior to that."

"Wow, that's a long time. But then you got bored? It happens."

"Actually, I'm single because my wife and unborn child died in a car accident."

"Oh." She has the good grace to look contrite. "Well, you don't seem like you'd be boring since you're rich and hot. Even if you're a snooze in bed, if there's, like, shopping, I'll be the best wife ever."

I'm done. Truthfully, I was already disinterested before she opened her mouth, but now I'm completely annoyed. I don't deal with laziness, sponging, or idiocy well in general. And this woman seems to represent all of the above.

"Did you go to college?"

"Long enough to join a sorority, meet frat guys, and go to parties. Who, but nerds and losers, takes that academic stuff seriously?"

"Me. I graduated summa cum laude in three years with a double major in business management and economics."

She wrinkles her nose. "Summa what?"

"Top one percent of my class."

"Oh. So, you're, like, smart?"

"I like to think so. And I value intelligence. Tell me why you think I should choose you."

She pauses and smirks as if the answer is obvious. "Have you looked at me?"

I have. Not only is she vapid, she's conceited. "I prefer substance to aesthetics."

"To, ah...what?"

"After sex, looks will only engage me for so long. I need someone smart, witty, and interesting. Are you well read?"

Brittanii hesitates. "*Cosmo* and *Vogue*. I don't read, like, books. It takes too long, and they're usually yawn-worthy."

I'm completely unsurprised. "Have you traveled?"

"I'd like to. I thought seeing the world was part of the package."

"What are your hobbies?"

"Um, well...there's tanning. And shopping. I'm a good dancer. I get down at clubs almost every weekend. You like going out?"

"Actually, I work somewhere around seventy hours a week. I tend to prefer quiet weekends at home."

"Ugh, that sounds like something my dad would say. We'd have to do something less boring or this won't work."

"It won't work, regardless, Brittanii. Thank you for your time. Let me show you to the door."

Wide-eyed, she huffs and rises to her feet. "You're serious? You're turning *me* down?"

"I am."

"Ugh. And I gave up a nail appointment for this."

"Good luck finding a man who finds you perfect and charming just as you are." If he does, he won't be any smarter or more ambitious than she is, and they will probably suit each other perfectly...as long as he comes equipped with an endless trust fund.

"Well, good luck finding someone better-looking than me. And when you can't, don't call."

With that lovely parting shot, she flounces to my office door, yanks it open, and storms out. She snatches up her coat with such force the rack topples over. She never looks twice at it, much less bothers to pick it up. Then she slams the ante door.

Nia stands behind her desk, blinking in shock. Then she checks her watch. "Eighteen minutes?"

"We didn't suit."

"Sorry. At least she was every bit as pretty as her picture suggested."

I shrug. "That hardly matters. She's not my type. But we have almost thirty-five minutes before my next appointment arrives. I think you and I need to have a serious conversation."

"I can't." She grimaces. "There's an emergency with the copier, and you know I'm the only one who can finesse that silly machine. If I don't go now, the new assistants on the third floor might melt down. Back in thirty!"

Before I can stop her, she's gone. I curse.

The rest of the day doesn't improve.

Candidate number two is a beautiful Latina girl. Nia returns to my office with her in tow and introduces her as Camila. After we shake hands, my assistant leaves us alone with the quiet snick of the door. The woman sits in the chair opposite my big desk, crosses her slender legs, and looks everywhere but at me.

"Hello." I prompt. "How are you?"

She pastes on a smile. Despite the expression being completely false, it transforms her face from pretty to stunning. I might believe she was happy if her eyes didn't say something else entirely.

"Fine."

It's a polite lie. I don't pry. I used the same BS line after Becca's death when I didn't want to answer questions or be reminded about my loss.

"How are you?" she adds, seeming to remember that she's here for a job interview of sorts and she should engage me.

"I'm all right, Camila. Thanks for asking." I don't have any interest in marrying this woman, but she seems as if she's sad and clinging to her composure by a thread. "Tell me why you answered my ad."

"I'd like to get married, and I'm not interested in romance. We have that in common."

A week ago, that was true. Then, she would have seemed perfect.

Not anymore.

"Why are you against emotional entanglements?"

"Why are you?" she counters.

"I'm a widower. I need companionship and assistance. I'm not ready for more." I lean forward. "I was blunt in the ad because I didn't want any misunderstanding."

"Thank you for explaining. I'm sorry for your loss. I'll be equally honest. I was supposed to marry my high school sweetheart next month. Three days ago, I found him in bed with my sister." She laughs bitterly. "If I hadn't mistaken the time of my wedding dress fitting, I would never have caught them."

Ouch. No wonder she's taking the nuclear option. "So, you're looking for a husband and revenge all at once?"

"Do you blame me?"

"No." But this has disaster written all over it.

"He keeps calling and coming by, telling me how sorry he is, that he still loves me and wants to marry me. If I make that impossible, he'll go away."

Maybe. I don't know this guy, but I do know this situation is too much drama for me. I don't have the time or inclination to deal with it. Besides, Camila would eventually regret jumping into matrimony with a stranger before she's resolved her relationship with her fiancé, and we'd wind up divorced.

"I think that's something the two of you need to work out before you bring a third party into the situation."

"So you're rejecting me, too?"

She looks both stunned and near tears. I doubt she cares about me, but she seems too fragile to handle more emotional upheaval now.

Across the desk, I take her hand. It's uncomfortable. I'm not much for extraneous touching, but she needs human contact. I'm the only other person in the room.

I don't know why I'm not a "hugger." I have vague recollections of my mom holding me as a kid. But after she died, my various foster parents over the next seven years didn't show much affection. That suited me. Even Diana, as kind and jovial as she is, isn't terribly touchy-feely.

Growing up, I wondered if Barclay Reed, my biological father, would have loved me. After meeting my half siblings, I gather the answer is no. Maxon especially has nothing but contempt for the man. If he's truly guilty of bilking clients out of their money for decades, then I'm glad he wasn't a part of my childhood. I hope he'll get what he deserves in his upcoming trial. I'm all for making a buck, but not by stealing it.

"I'm not rejecting you," I say softly. "I'm preventing you from making a mistake. If I married you, I would be doing you a disservice."

I don't know her personally, but I know her type. She's the sort of woman who wants to marry for love, not as a fuck-you to her ex. It would never work.

She's gone less than five minutes later. This interview was even shorter than the first, and when I escort her out of my office, Nia's desk is empty. I curse. We need to talk, damn it. I have to tell her what I'm thinking, but I'm beginning to suspect she's dodging me.

Stratus Solutions' offices aren't massive, so I go in search of her, only to discover she's already fixed the copier and moved on. I text her. No answer.

Grumbling, I make my way back to my office. There she is—with another candidate, a pretty redhead with a chip on her shoulder. That meeting lasts less than ten minutes—I'm getting faster at dismissing women I don't want—but Nia is gone again. A glance at my calendar tells me that I'm finally free for lunch after the next potential wife. She turns out to be a blue-eyed brunette waif who looks too much like Becca. Strike one. She's ten minutes late, then somehow blamed me for her tardiness. Strike two. She spent most of our seven minutes together Snapchatting with someone and barely giving me an "uh-huh," even when I didn't ask a yes-or-no question.

As soon as I dismiss her, I catch sight of Nia down the hall, slipping into a conference room, and march toward her. When I approach from behind and grab her shoulders, she gasps and whirls to me with a frown.

"I didn't expect you here, especially so soon. You didn't like Felice, either?"

"No. I escorted her out and came to find you. We need to talk, and it can't wait."

She gives me an apologetic shrug. "Sorry. I need to run some errands for lunch."

"You're avoiding me." In fact, given that she's set up a makeshift work station in here, it's clear she's camped in this room for that purpose.

"I'm giving you privacy." She drops her voice. "You're interviewing for a wife. I'm sure you don't want me to overhear your conversations."

Is that really why she's been keeping her distance? I don't know and I'm tired of guessing.

"I don't care if you hear my conversations. You and I bypassed strictly professional when we hooked up. You asked me if we were having casual sex or starting a relationship. You said you didn't see any reason for us to spend time together until I could answer that question. Now I can." I shut the door. "We're going to talk."

SINCE NIA HAS always been independent and forthright about expressing her opinions, I'm not shocked when she crosses her arms over her chest and raises that dark brow at me like I've pissed her off.

With a sigh, I realize I have to stop demanding. First, she's not merely an employee. Second, that tactic will never work with her.

"Please. Sit," I add as I grab the closest chair and plop in it.

She hesitates, then lowers herself into the big leather chair beside me.

"All right. Let's talk."

"After a great deal of consideration, I've realized the status quo isn't working. I can't work with you and be purely professional anymore. To manage that, I can transfer you to Bas or another of the executives—"

"That's how you're going to deal with what happened between us?" Nia leaps out of her chair, betrayal streaking across her face. "Listen, you barged into *my* dressing room and acted butt-sore because I was dancing in public—which you had no right to do. Burlesque is something I've been doing for almost five years. I love it. I *so* look forward to Saturday night. But suddenly you were in my face, practically foaming at the mouth about what, my lack of modesty? My partnering with someone I screwed a couple years ago? But I got caught up in the moment, believing you'd only be jealous if you felt something for me. Afterward, I remembered you're not emotional and probably hadn't had sex in months." She sniffs. "I've given you three years and now my body, Evan. I could be pregnant. And your response is to get rid of me? Fuck that. I quit."

When she glares my way and barrels toward the door, I jump from my chair. I've got one shot to grab her before she escapes. Thankfully, I snag her by the wrist. Tightening my fingers, I draw her in until our chests brush. This is the closest I've been to her in over a week. All at once, I'm soothed and stirred. I don't know what to think or how to stop the loss of control. The only thing I know is the truth.

"I won't accept your resignation. You're right that I'm not normally emotional. But this…is different. Being with you makes me different. I can't not want you. Suddenly, when you're around, my concentration is shot. I don't have the control I should. And if I don't change something, it's only a matter of time before people guess what happened between us."

She cocks a fist on one hip. "Maybe that wouldn't be so awful. Dunstead is dating Melissa, that customer service manager. They're not hiding anything. And they're making it work. Why would we be any different?"

"Because she works with him, not for him. Their contact on the job is limited to an occasional meeting. You're barely six feet from me most every day. How long do you think it would take before I started peeling off your clothes in the office? And what happens if our relationship goes south? It will be awkward. And the possibilities for sexual harassment lawsuits are almost endless."

"So, because you can't handle yourself or you're worried I'm petty enough to hire some shyster to rip you a new asshole, you're going to demote me?"

"No. You're misunderstanding. If it comes to that, you won't lose salary or benefits." Somehow, I'm saying this all wrong. We're getting into an argument I never anticipated and I'm unprepared for. How do I turn things around? Becca never argued with me, so this entire interaction is foreign.

"But people will talk," she counters. "They'll speculate about why you suddenly kicked me to the curb professionally. They'll either think I couldn't handle my job anymore or they'll realize I was fucking the boss. Either way, my credibility will be shot."

Nia has valid points.

"All right, then. Once I move to Maui, you stay here in Seattle and continue to report to me." Then I won't be tempted every moment I'm in the office with her.

"Our opportunities to see each other will be limited." Her tone is neutral, but it paints a picture I don't like.

"Forget I said that," I bark even as I mentally acknowledge my suggestion would solve a lot of problems. But for a reason I'm unable to pinpoint, I can't have Nia that far from me. "Last week, you offered to move to Hawaii, and I said I would consider it. I'm far more efficient and productive when I have you with me. So I think you need to come, maybe work for Bas."

"But if I'm working for him, then I won't be organizing you."

Is she just determined to be argumentative today? "Or we could forget this entire debate about where you'll be living and who you'll be working for. And you could simply marry me."

Nia freezes. "What?"

"I don't want these 'candidates' you've lined up, none of whom suit me, by the way."

"You've only talked to four."

"That was four too many."

"I genuinely gave you the best possibilities among the women who replied."

"I'm not questioning that. You told me this ad would bring in the crazies, and you were right." Again, we're getting off topic. I need to stop being discombobulated by my nerves and her nearness and get back to what I planned to say. "The truth is, I came in to the office today, prepared to tell you to withdraw the ad because I want to marry you."

She bites her lip and frowns. "Why?"

I'm prepared for this question. "We make sense. Our working rapport is phenomenal. We communicate well. Our relationship won't cause much splash around the office if we're married. Plus, the sex is...beyond."

"But there has to be more between us than that for the marriage to succeed."

I frown. I'm not sure what she's getting at. "Statistically, most marriages that end in divorce fail because of issues arising from money or sex. Neither will be a problem for us. I understand we'll have some adjustments to make—"

"Yes. Because working together isn't like living together. If your ability to clean up after yourself is any indication, you and I would have some major clashes. I like a tidy space, and if I only make half the mess I'm not fixing it all by myself."

"I can endeavor to pick up more." Getting in the habit would probably be good for me. Hygienically speaking, it's not good to live in filth. I should have considered that obvious fact sooner. "If you show me what to do, I'll help."

"Great—"

"So, when do you want to get married. This weekend?"

"What? Hang on." Her expression says I must be crazy. "Cleanliness isn't the only issue. There has to be mutual respect."

"I respect you. Very much." I frown. "I never meant to give you any reason to think otherwise."

"You haven't, but I needed to say it. And like I mentioned before, I'm making it a policy to only get involved with guys I'm friends with first. From now on, I want to really get to know someone before I dive in."

"You and I know each another well."

"But not personally. I don't know your favorite potato chip."

"I don't eat them, actually. You know they're not good for you, right? The fat content is high, and the calories are empty—"

"Evan, of course I know they aren't good for me. I'm making a point that there are lots of things we don't know about each other. And for the record, we can't be friends if you don't eat potato chips. Or donuts. You took one of Bas's the other day, then failed to eat it."

"I prefer a clean diet, but I will incorporate more of your favorite things if it will make you happy. See, I know marriage is about compromise. I'm willing to do that."

"That's helpful…but not enough to base a marriage on. We've never even been on a date."

"I never dated Becca, and it worked out fine."

Well, we never dated in the traditional sense. We held hands in high school because it made her feel happy and safe. We sneaked in some petting because I wanted to know what girls and sex felt like. But her foster father didn't approve of her having a boyfriend and tried to keep her too distracted at home to be with me often.

Nia purses her full lips into a grim line. "I'm glad that's how it worked for you two, but *I* won't get married until I'm sure it's right. If you're still marrying for the reasons you stated in your bride-wanted ad, we're going to fail. I'm more than a hostess, a maid, and a lay."

"Of course you are. That's the other reason I think you and I will suit well. We'll be far more comfortable with each other than I would be with a stranger. We can keep our working relationship intact. And we can explore all the other ways we're good together." Because, guilt and confusion aside, being inside Nia is something I'm eager to do again—the sooner the better. "If you'd feel more comfortable dating first, we can try that. We'll have to navigate the office, keep our personal relationship quiet. We'll date as much as you like until the move to Maui. Before we leave for good, I'll ask you to marry me again."

I hope her answer will be different then. I don't know what I'll do if she says no. That's something I never worried about with Becca.

"I'm not convinced I can be sure I want to marry you—or anyone—in six weeks."

"That's all the time we have. I'm not planning to move alone." I let that sink in. "If I haven't convinced you by January second, then...you stay here in Seattle and I'll find you another appropriate supervisor." And I'll figure out how not to lose my mind. "We'll float the story that you didn't want to move, and I decided I needed someone local. Done."

There's no way not to hear the frustration in her sigh. "I don't like ultimatums."

"I'm not intending to back you into a corner. I'm simply stating my position; I only intend to be single until I move to Maui. I've agreed that we'll date, despite the fact I think it may be somewhere between unnecessary and a waste of time. I know what and who I want, Nia. That's you. But I'm slowing down, compromising, and dating to make you happy."

"What about Saturday nights?"

She means when she's performing half-naked with that totally straight asshole who I have no doubt wants to take her to bed again. I very much want to insist that Kyle can't touch her, even in a dance. But Nia has already made herself clear that she's unwilling to stop something she genuinely enjoys. In truth, I don't like the idea of taking away an activity she loves. I'm also not thrilled with the idea of her bumping and grinding with her ex. But I stifle my objections. Once we move to Maui, it will be a moot point. There will be no Kyle and no burlesque, just settling into our new house and our new lives, along with lots of newlywedded sex.

"I won't interfere. I may insist on being present, however."

That takes some of the starch out of her attitude. "If you're okay with it, I want you there."

Since that's settled, even though I'll have to find some way to keep my sanity, I nod. "Should we go out on our first date tonight?"

"I can't. Every other Monday, I teach a burlesquercize class at the club. It's another way for them to increase revenue, and I get a workout in as well. I'm not done until eight, and after that, I'm wiped out."

Clenching my jaw, I strive for patience. I know she has a life apart from me. I simply don't like anything that prevents me from spending time with her since I suspect she needs every spare moment to decide if she wants to be my wife. On the other hand, she was softer and sweeter after her orgasm. Maybe I just need to get her back into bed.

Behind my zipper, my cock gives that idea a standing ovation.

"When are you free?"

"Tomorrow night should be good."

"Excellent."

She hesitates. "What do you want to do?"

In truth, I don't know. I've never planned a date. When I was married to Becca, if she wanted to go someplace, she would simply make her wishes known, and I'd either work it into my schedule or encourage to her to go with one of her yoga friends.

"Is there anything in particular you're interested in?"

Nia shakes her head. "Plan something you'd enjoy, so I can see what you're into. On the next date, I'll do the same. If we take turns, we'll both get a good idea of what the other likes. It will help us figure out if we're actually suited."

I'm already convinced since I've never felt anything quite like this. But if that arrangement will make Nia more comfortable… "Fine."

"Good." She checks her watch. "I should probably head for the reception desk. Your next appointment should be here in less than ten minutes."

"I'm done interviewing wives, Nia. I don't care how you cancel the last four. Make it happen."

Thankfully, she doesn't argue. "I'll get it done."

"I know you were taking initiative, but I can't handle any more."

She represses a grin. "Sorry."

I shrug. We stand close. I want to touch her, but I simply stare and tell myself to back down. I really should keep things clandestine around the office...but I'd rather spread her across the conference table and feast on her.

"I'll go tell Peyton, your next appointment, that you're no longer available," she says, ending the sexually charged moment.

"Please."

"She'll be sad that you won't be funding her new cosmetics start-up."

"I don't care." I slant Nia a speculative stare. "Since we're officially dating, does that make me your boyfriend now?"

"I've never dated my boss before. But...I guess so."

"I like it." I lean in, feeling the heat of her cheek almost against mine. Then I whisper in her ear, "But I'd rather call you my wife."

She shivers. "Evan...we had great sex one time. That doesn't mean it's going to always be explosive. Or even good. And it definitely doesn't mean we'll suit long-term."

"I think it was a damn telling indicator of our compatibility." I barely resist nuzzling her neck. "You should get out of here before I stop caring about our professional reputations and find out for sure."

Nia drags in a shaky breath. "I'm going. We'll talk more about this tomorrow."

"We will." And if I have my way, when we're on this date, we'll do a lot more than talk.

CHAPTER SIX

Tuesday, November 14

WHEN I PULL up in front of Nia's place, I put my BMW in park and stare. I've never been here, and I don't know what I expected, but it wasn't anything like this.

I live in a sleek glass high-rise that's industrial, efficient, and green. Everything is solar and built with responsible convenience in mind. Nia's home isn't typical urban living and isn't focused on proximity to java while reducing her carbon footprint. Her cottage is full of character and oozes charm.

When I step out of my sedan, I follow a brick walkway that leads to a simple black gate. Beyond, freshly painted gray siding frames a white door rich in detail. Two dark wrought iron sconces flank it and illuminate the little mosaic porch. Tall topiaries stand on either side like sentries, rimmed by evergreens and an occasional splash of tiny white flowers. I'm surprised by how lush and summery her yard looks, despite the fact Thanksgiving is less than two weeks away.

Nothing about this place looks practical. It's probably a hundred years old—especially the windows. It likely doesn't even have air conditioning. She parks on the street. Her neighbors are almost on top of her. And I wonder if there's an ounce of insulation in this structure.

On the other hand, it's just like her—different, unexpected, wonderful.

The thought makes me smile as I knock, mixed bouquet of flowers in hand.

When Nia swings the door open, I can't help but stare. She's dressed in a white sweater that flashes a hint of cleavage, figure-hugging jeans, and black lace-up boots that climb halfway up her sleek thighs.

"Hi." Since I'm having trouble finding my breath, it's the most intelligent greeting I can manage.

She grins. "Hi, yourself. Are the flowers for me?"

"Yes." I manage to stop salivating long enough to hold out the bouquet to her.

"That's sweet." She holds them under her nose and sniffs. "But I know you, Evan. This wasn't your idea. Did a website tell you to bring flowers on a first date?"

I laugh; she knows me too well. "No. I called Harlow, Keeley, and Britta for advice. My sister suggested I keep you horizontal and naked until you agree to whatever I want. According to her, Noah used sex to persuade her to marry him. Keeley was more subtle. She gave me a collection of appropriate songs to play in the car for mood music."

"Are you planning to?" she asks over her shoulder as she retreats to her kitchen to stick the flowers in water.

The view of her backside is every bit as lust-inducing as the view from the front. I don't remember ever being fixated on a female's ass, but I swear Nia's might be the single sexiest part of a woman I've ever noticed.

"Or not?" she asks into my silence as she sets the vase of blooms on her kitchen table.

I clear my throat and find my brain. "You know I thoroughly prepare for meetings, so I figured it couldn't hurt."

She smiles. "I do know. Which means Britta suggested the flowers?"

I nod. "She didn't say what kind. I guessed. Do you like them?"

Asking makes me sound uncertain. I am, but I hate the reminder that, other than Rebecca, I have zero experience dating…while Nia has so much.

"I love them," she assures, her dark eyes lingering and warm. "Let me grab my purse, and we can go."

She disappears for a moment, then returns, bag looped on her shoulder. After she shuts off a couple of lights, she shoves the key in the lock and flips a gaze to me over her shoulder. "So what are we doing tonight?"

"Dinner first." I escort her to the car, hoping like hell she likes what I have planned. "I assume you're hungry."

"Starved. While you and Bas and that group of contractors went to lunch, I stayed behind to type up the meeting notes."

I frown. "You never ate?"

"No time. I had an orange when I got home."

"Why didn't you tell me?" I question as I open the passenger door for her.

"What were you going to do? You had to deal with four grown men willing to get on their knees and beg for your business."

I jog around and slide in beside her. "You're not wrong. They didn't even stifle their groans when I said Stratus wouldn't be making a decision until the first of the year."

Nia smirks. "I'm surprised no one offered you a blow job to hurry your decision."

"They looked desperate, and I'm pretty sure it crossed their minds. But, um…" I shake my head. "Not my type."

"You mean you're not attracted to beards, plaid shirts, and a more-than-passing knowledge of Java programming?"

"Not even a little."

Her laughter fills the car, and I realize that, if I've heard the sound before, I don't remember it. I haven't amused her much over the years. Worked her a lot? Yes. Frustrated her a lot? Probably so.

But tonight we're not at work. And the fact we're on a date seems surreal. Though she's been my assistant for years, that circuit-frying encounter in her dressing room scrambled my brain so much that my thoughts about her no longer compute the way they used to.

This morning, she greeted the arriving contractors with a smile. Instead of absently thanking her while preparing to get down to business, I had to ruthlessly restrain my fantasy of stripping off her dress. As she showed them to the conference room and brought us all coffee, I forced myself to act as if I have no idea how it feels to have every inch of my cock buried inside her. And when one of my visitors eyed Nia like a prime slab of beef, I had to bite back a possessive growl.

Fast forward ten hours. Now, she's not merely my assistant, but also my girlfriend. I can shed the professional straightjacket and treat her like a woman. Except…I'm unsure how to proceed.

As we pull away from the curb, I focus on the plan I've been concocting since Sunday and connect my phone to my sound system. Rush hour is tapering off. Keeley's recommended tunes calm me and fill the silence.

The first I've never heard. Blink 182 is a band I'm familiar with, but not this song, which is appropriately titled "First Date." It's got a punk rock vibe and it's kind of catchy and fun.

Nia bounces in her seat, seeming to like it, too. "Keeley nailed this one. From everything you've said, she sounds cool."

"She is, though she's somewhat hippie and quirky. Maxon is usually very serious, so they're interesting together. From what I gather, he was a complete bastard before they met. Now, they seem really happy."

Before she can comment, the next song begins. It's another unfamiliar tune, not that I'm surprised. I usually prefer silence, and I've never cared what everyone else is listening to. According to Keeley's cheat sheet, this one is "fallingforyou" by The 1975. It's a mellow song with an unexpected beat and a slightly sexy vibe. It's one I'd listen to again, especially when Nia turns to me with a glance that makes me wish we'd stayed at her place.

When the male vocalist sings that he touches her leg, I do the same. On contact, my body jolts. My heart lurches. I squeeze her thigh when he croons that he doesn't want to be just her friend. I relate to that.

Then he admits he's falling for her. Is that what's happening to me?

I let out a steadying breath. It can't be. It's too soon, and I won't fall in love again. I'll commit to a relationship of mutual trust and respect, especially since the benefits with Nia are incredible. But that's it.

"I like it," she says at the end. "Who is the band?"

I hand Nia the page Keeley emailed. "Here's a full list."

She scans it. "Eclectic. I don't know half these songs."

"At least I'm not alone in that." I shoot her a wry grin as another tune starts. "But I've heard this one."

"'You and Me' by Lifehouse? Yeah."

It's an earnest song about a guy who's realizing he feels more for a woman than he once thought. He sounds confused but mesmerized by her.

Join the club, pal.

The simple melodic strains of the guitar end the song as we arrive at our destination. I park the car near the front door and hop out to retrieve Nia. She steps from my gray sedan, then looks around. "The Living Computer Museum? This is where you're bringing me?"

"You said to pick something I enjoy. I actually come here a lot." Especially since Becca's death. She always hated this place, but I appreciate the peace and the orderly surroundings.

Nia gives me a slow nod as she takes everything in. "All righty."

I smile as I lead her forward. "It's a lot more interesting than it sounds. I promise. Give it a chance."

She glances at the sign beside the door, then stops mid-step. "They're closed."

"To the public, yes. Not for me."

When I knock twice on the glass, a ginger with a bushy beard wearing a black button-down shirt stitched with the museum's logo lets us in, then locks the door behind us. "Welcome, Mr. Cook."

"Thanks, Aiden." I read his nametag. "Where do we start?"

"Everything you requested has been arranged. Come this way…"

I gesture Nia in front of me to be a gentleman…and because I can't resist the view of her ass. Soon, we reach a door tucked into a back corner of the museum, and the guide ushers us upstairs, into a private room with lights dimmed. Candles flicker on a table set with crisp linens for two against the window overlooking the museum relics of machines from bygone eras.

Nia takes in the room. "This is amazing. Wow..."

After I pull out her chair, she slides in. As I do the same, a waiter brings us wine—I remember she likes reds—along with our salads.

Across from her, I can't stop staring. How did I see her for three years without seeing how beautiful she was? "You're surprised?"

"Shocked. You did all this just for our date?"

"I did it for you."

"Without help?"

"Well, not exactly," I admit wryly. "When I called here to ask about a private, after-hours tour, they connected me with the catering manager, who was full of suggestions. So we'll have dinner, then the guide will show us around. I'm hoping you'll see why this place fascinates me."

Machines make sense. No emotions. No gray areas. No unpredictability. Just binary code. Just black and white. When I'm here, I forget my problems and lose myself in the technology that has transformed the world.

"I'd like that. Thanks for going to so much trouble to make this special." She rims her wineglass with one finger, then looks my way. "It's interesting, dating you suddenly."

"I was thinking the same thing earlier."

"There are things I know about you and lots I don't. I think we should treat this like any first date. Talk and learn about each other. I'll ask you some questions. You feel free to ask some, too. You know?"

Not really, but I'll play along. "All right."

Nia finishes her bite of lettuce. "So, how did you meet Becca?"

I wasn't sure what I expected her to ask first, but that wasn't it. "In high school. We found out we were both foster kids. I was in a good home by then, but her situation was terrible. We started talking because I was a little older and she wanted advice about how to handle her foster parents. I quickly realized she needed way more than someone to offer an ear every now and then. I was sixteen, so there wasn't much I could do to intervene, but I stayed on her guardians' radar. Things were always tenuous. She was afraid."

"They were abusive?"

"He was. When stuff happened, the wife was suddenly blind, deaf, and mute. I did the best I could to look out for her, but Child Protective Services never seemed to have a spare caseworker to investigate Becca's claims. We got married the day she turned eighteen. She went straight from being their ward to being my wife. From then on, I took care of her, and she took care of me." I wolf down a bite of salad and regard Nia across the table. "What about your first boyfriend?"

"Serious one? Not my middle school crush, right?" At my nod, she swallows another bite. "I was a cheerleader, and Jayden played running back. His senior year, he put up more points than any other high school football player in the state. We dated for almost two years and broke up just before graduation because we were both going to college hundreds of miles apart. And because I found out the football wasn't the only thing he was scoring with."

"He cheated?" I dive into my salad, unable to imagine why anyone would so intentionally and flagrantly break his bond with Nia. Besides being beautiful, she's interesting, genuine, and smart. To risk losing her for fleeting pleasure seems illogical.

"Apparently a lot. I think I knew on some level. I wasn't in love with him or anything, so I probably didn't care as much as I should have. Anyway, when I realized we were going in different directions and that being without him was actually a relief, I broke it off."

"I'm glad. I don't understand people unable to keep their commitments. You deserved better."

"Thanks." She cocks her head. "After him, I dated off and on in college—all kinds of guys—black, white, ambitious, lazy, snarky, sweet, smart, and some less bright...who had other attributes to make up for their lack of brains." She laughs at herself. "But I started going out less frequently when I hired on at Stratus. I was too busy to put up with guys who were either self-absorbed, wanted to party, seem married to their careers, or only looking for a hookup. The dating pool out there is terrible."

"Based on the women I met yesterday, I'm glad I'm here with you, rather than swimming in it." Before I can say more, a waiter wheels out a cart with two domed dishes and a basket of steaming bread, then takes our salad plates away. "I didn't expect you to find candidates for me while I was in LA. I certainly wasn't expecting to interview anyone yesterday."

"I figured that if you want to be married before you move, we couldn't afford to waste time."

It's not an illogical conclusion. "You didn't know I'd changed my mind."

We pause as the waiter sets our dishes in front of us and lifts the lid to reveal filet mignon, asparagus, and a steaming baked potato. The heavenly smells waft as the waiter walks away. I'm surprised when Nia doesn't dig in.

"Your food look okay?"

"Yeah, I'm just...not sure why you decided you want to marry *me*. You listed your logical reasons, but what about feelings, Evan? Are you going to care about me? Will you be okay with whatever feelings I might have for you? I know you don't want 'entanglements,' but how do you expect to live with someone for the rest of your life and not be connected more than mentally and sexually?"

Once again, Nia asks great questions. I consider as I fork in a bite of steak. "I didn't say I wouldn't care. I won't love again, but I promise I'll always do my best to make you happy."

She's quiet for a long moment. "So you loved Becca?"

"Of course I did."

After all, if I hadn't, I could never have been married to her happily. But...Becca didn't inspire the kind of passion in me that Nia does. I didn't ever think I would lose my mind if I had to go another day without being inside Becca. She didn't linger in my thoughts—until she was gone.

"Did you ever tell her you loved her?"

"Sure." I don't remember a specific instance, but I must have. "Not often, but neither of us required verbal reassurance. Maybe we weren't a typical couple, but we were secure in our marriage and knew we were together until death parted us."

I just never expected that would be so soon. Or that she'd take our child with her.

Nia presses her lips together as if she doesn't like something about my answer. "What about your foster parents? Tell me what they were like."

Where is she going with this? "I had a lot of them over the years, some pretty rough. But I always had computers and the Internet to help me escape. I got by. Then Diana came along when I was twelve, and I finally had a good place to finish out my time in foster care."

"Did she ever tell you she loved you?"

Why does Nia seem so hung up on love?

"Not in so many words. Diana is a free spirit. She raised me for money, and I never let myself forget that. But she taught me a lot about respecting the Earth, about healthy eating, and about art. She taught me how to laugh. She never had to speak words for me to know I mattered."

Nia nods as she swallows a bite. "Do you remember much about your mom, since she died when you were so little?"

"Not really. I have a vague recollection of her ruffling my hair as I sat on her lap beside the Christmas tree. That was a few months before she passed. The only other thing I remember is the way she always put her arms around me, kissed my cheeks, and called me her little man. I wonder sometimes how different my life would have turned out if she'd lived."

"Maybe not as much as you think. You're brilliant, ambitious, and hardworking. Nothing was going to change the fact you were destined for success." She nibbles her lip as if she's debating the wisdom of whatever is rolling through her head. "Tell me about finally meeting your biological father. You didn't say much after you returned from Harlow's wedding in June."

"Not much to say." Barclay Reed was there with his wife, Linda. Looking into the face of the man who contributed half of my DNA and realizing he's not only a stranger but an asshole rocked me. "We talked for three minutes. He seemed far more interested in selling me on 'investment opportunities' than learning about his grown son as a human being."

By the time I walked away from him, I felt nothing but contempt.

"Did he even try to explain why he never took you in?"

"No. He didn't have to. Harlow and I were born three days apart. I'm sure the last thing he wanted was for his wife to know he'd knocked up his secretary at roughly the same time he'd impregnated her. And I doubt she wanted to raise his bastard."

Nia grimaces. "But you were a kid when your mom died, and he cut you loose to save his own ass."

He did. "Well, I think Karma got the last word since, according to Maxon and Griff, he might well be going to prison."

She knows this part of the story, so she's not surprised, just snide. "It sounds like you didn't miss much by not growing up with him."

"According to my half siblings, I should consider myself lucky. I don't know about that. But at least they seem fantastic, so something good came from the whole mess." I sip my wine. "That's enough about me. What about you and your father? You've never said much about him."

"I don't know much. While I was growing up, he met his financial responsibilities. He even put me through college. But we've never met." None of that is news to me, but when she pauses, I have a feeling she's about to tell me something big. "I don't even know his name."

My jaw drops. "Seriously?"

"Yeah. When I was a kid, my mom always said she'd tell me when I was old enough to understand. But when I got older, she admitted she couldn't answer my questions because the two of them had reached a settlement, which included her signing an NDA."

"And this nondisclosure indicated she couldn't tell his own daughter his identity?"

"Apparently so."

"Why the hell would he not want you to ever know about him?"

"So I couldn't come after him and his money as an adult, I guess. Oh, don't look so shocked. He was married, rich, white, and well respected. And he knocked up his young black maid. My mom admitted she fell for his charm and smooth tongue, even though she knew better. Predictably, when she told him she was pregnant, he broke it off. It didn't matter that she loved him. He never talked to her again, except through lawyers."

I'm furious on behalf of Nia and her mother. "His behavior was irresponsible and unforgivable."

"Cowardly and short-sighted, too." She shrugs. "When I was a kid, I used to play with other children and be envious of their really involved daddies. My mom always claimed his absence in my life was a blessing in disguise. Maybe it was, but it never felt that way. I've always wanted that typical TV-perfect family, you know? Hell, any family at all. I still do."

"I guess we both wanted family growing up because neither of us had an ideal childhood."

"Probably. So…if we both want family, does that mean you still want kids? After everything that's happened, do you see yourself having children with your second wife? Maybe with me?"

It's a question I should be prepared for. I've been asked if I still want children, and I thought I knew the answer. I want family…but I don't feel anywhere near ready to risk conceiving a tiny human with my DNA, only to possibly lose him or her again. Becca's absence in my life has been difficult. But as November came and I was confronted with the due date of the infant I'd never get to hold, I've been wracked by pain and guilt. Why did I survive while my wife and child died?

"Not this soon after losing Becca and the baby. Maybe in a few years." But even the thought of it terrifies me. "Maybe never."

Nia softens. "You've been through a lot, Evan. I know. I've watched you struggle, and I hurt for you."

"Thank you for picking up a lot of slack in the office when I couldn't."

"It was my job and my pleasure. But if you seriously want to marry me, I have to be honest. I'm eventually going to want kids, at least two. If you're not sure you'll ever be ready for that, this won't work. I also want a man who can tell me he loves me and mean it. Not today. Not even next week. But someday. I'm not sure that's you. Your childhood was rough, and no one gave you the affection you deserved. Becca didn't need to hear how you felt, but I do. If that's a problem, I should call your other four candidates back tomorrow and let you interview them."

Everything inside me seizes up. Having another wife pregnant and vulnerable terrifies me. I'm equally afraid of telling another woman I love her.

But Nia walking away scares me most of all.

It's a feeling, so I know it isn't logical. But that doesn't make what's churning in my gut any less real.

"Don't. I want you with me and I want you to be happy. We'll negotiate, work something out. But I need more time to come to terms with everything."

She nods. "You'll have the next six weeks while we're dating to figure it out."

I've had six and a half months so far and I've untangled nothing. Does she think the next six weeks will somehow magically make everything clear?

Then again, I've only given her six weeks to figure out if she wants to spend the rest of her life with me.

Nia reaches for bread and breaks into my thoughts. "I guess it's weird to be talking about the possibility of love and babies on our first date. On the other hand, you've already asked me to marry you and we've had sex. We're doing everything ass-backwards."

I have to laugh. "That we are."

The rest of the meal passes in companionable conversation—and a lot of Nia moaning about the chef's amazing ability to elevate cheesecake to orgasm on a fork. I'm not usually a fan of desserts and sweets, but I agree with her assessment.

When we're done, I help her from her seat and we head downstairs. As we open the door and find ourselves on the museum floor, Nia takes it all in. It's odd to see the place devoid of people. The main space almost looks like an office building from an old TV show. Gray metal grids hold up flecked ceiling tiles. Track lighting illuminates the putty-colored walls, along with various exhibits and the walkways between them.

"You two ready?" Aiden asks as he approaches.

I defer to Nia, and she nods. "Yeah. Let's do it."

He walks us through photos of some of the earliest computers.

"Colossus was the first electric programmable computer. It went into service in December 1943," Aiden says, then looks at Nia. "Any guesses what it was used for?"

"Given what was going on then, did it have something to do with the war effort?"

"Exactly." I smile at her. Even if computers aren't her thing, I like that's she curious enough to listen and play along. "It was created to help British code breakers read encrypted messages they intercepted from the Germans."

"Wow. I had no idea. And what about this?" She points to the next exhibit, a photograph of one of my personal favorites.

"ENIAC."

"Any what?"

Aiden laughs. "It was one of the earliest digital computers. It took up eighteen hundred square feet. Which is bigger than my whole apartment."

"The picture is mind-blowing. Multiple people standing there, being dwarfed by all the walls, wires, connectors of this machine." She looks amazed.

I can't help but smile. "They were. ENIAC used eighteen thousand vacuum tubes and weighed almost fifty tons. It was very state-of-the-art for 1946."

"I had no idea computers started so early."

"Absolutely. And look how far they've come." I pull my phone from my pocket. "Even simple things you do with this little device would have taken up a whole room seventy-five years ago."

"For sure," Aiden agrees. "Next, we have the first stored-program computer, another British creation called EDSAC. In 1949, it performed the first graphical computer game. Despite the fact it, too, took up a whole room, it was nicknamed Baby."

That makes Nia laugh.

Over the next couple of hours, Aiden walks her though the first computer with RAM from the 1950s, the first desktop computer from the 1960s, along with teletype units, dumb terminals, and giant Unix machines, which could be used by more than one person at a time. As we continue moving through the advancements in the decades that followed, she gets a huge giggle out of the first laptop computer, the IBM5100.

"This would crush me," she protests. "It's huge!"

"By today's standards, it's ridiculous. But this was 1975," I argue. "So fifty-five pounds with a five-inch display was the latest. And by 1981, a laptop's weight had been cut to less than half, so progress was happening pretty fast. Sometimes, I think it would have been cool to be alive during the groundbreaking phases of computer development. And yet the limitations in technology would have been so frustrating."

"You wouldn't have known any better."

"I would have seen the possibilities."

Nia nods. "You always have to look at those…"

I'm hoping she means more than the computers. That maybe she means us, too.

When we work our way through the rest of the museum and I thank Aiden for his excellent tour, I can't resist putting my hand on the small of Nia's back as I lead her to my car. "You didn't hate that place?"

"No. I actually enjoyed it. I had no idea computers were so old and varied and had gone through so many types and versions. I tried to take it all in, but I'm on information overload. I'm sure I missed some details."

"I visit once a quarter or so and I almost always find some nugget of information I previously overlooked." I help her into the car.

As we head out of the parking lot, I look her way. I know it's late. I know we both have to work tomorrow.

But I don't want to let her go.

The streets are deserted, so we reach her house in the short time it takes for Keeley's next song to fill the space. Sixpence None the Richer pleads in lilting, feminine tones to "Kiss Me." I only know this song because Diana loved it and played it whenever she was feeling optimistic about some new girlfriend or another she hoped might fall in love with her. The lyrics are chanting through my brain as Nia sings along just under her breath.

Yes, I want to kiss her beneath the milky twilight. Hell, I'm aching to kiss her anywhere. I'd love to kiss her now.

The night we had sex is emblazoned in my memory…but it's a blur. Everything happened so fast it was almost an out-of-body experience. My inexplicable anger at seeing her naked for a room full of strangers with Kyle's hands all over her, followed by the raging lust that overtook everything, especially my inhibitions and common sense. When it was over, I was breathing hard, stunned, reeling with guilt, yet flush with a bone-deep satisfaction I'd never felt. But the details—the way she smelled, tasted, kissed—aren't clear. And I need them to be.

When I take Nia's hand and stare at her through most of a stoplight, she glances my way, assessing me from beneath her long, dark lashes. The sheer rosy tint of her lip gloss snags my gaze as her lips curl up in a knowing smile. She remembers that night, too. My heart thuds. Beneath my zipper, my cock does handstands. God, the chemistry between us keeps brewing, bubbling under my skin, boiling me with anticipation. This need is something new, unsettling, and addicting.

I exit my Bimmer and help her out. I keep her hand clasped in mine and hope my palm isn't sweating as I lead her to her door.

Under the bubbled glass of her porch light, I give in to my need to touch her, curling my hands around her shoulders. "I want you."

She meets my stare. "I want you, too."

"Thank god." If I had to leave tonight without feeling her under me, I don't know if my sanity would survive.

I tug her close and lean in. Her grip on my arms tightens as she closes her eyes and offers up her mouth. I don't hesitate.

As I crush her lips under mine, I glide into heaven. She's warm and velvety and lush, like I remember. But so different. The night I barged into her dressing room and into her body, she looked like a siren luring me with her red lips and a barely there robe. She felt like a woman, like temptation and sin. Tonight, Nia is more natural, almost vulnerable. I want to surround her, comfort her. Pleasure her. But it's more. I want to make her forget every man who came before me.

I don't even know if that's possible, but I damn sure want to try.

Yet when I deepen the kiss to soften her, she does something to me instead. She arouses me, of course. But she also…comforts me. I don't know why, but one kiss from her, and my anxiety seems to melt away.

I feel nothing but her. I lose my head to her. I drown in her.

When I grip her tighter, Nia moans, wraps her arms around my neck, and sways closer, pressing her body to mine. I part her lips. Her tongue dances against mine. She flicks, then retreats in a teasing sweep. Desire slides through my veins like a narcotic. I'm reeling. Blood rushes. Thoughts about anything besides getting her naked, panting, and under me stop.

I don't understand what Nia does to me. It makes no sense, but I don't care. I can't stop myself from nudging her against the side of her porch, notching my cock against her softness, and groaning long and low into her mouth.

When I rock between her legs, Nia tears her lips from mine with a gasp, clawing into my shoulders and tossing her head back. Moonlight and arousal make her glow as she stares at me, blinking and breathing and seemingly stunned.

"If we keep this up out here, your neighbors are going to get an eye-ful," I joke. "I don't think you want that."

Slowly, she nods. "You're right."

Thank god she agrees. All she has to do is open the door and let me in so I can put us both out of our misery.

Instead, she plants her palm in my chest and gives me a gentle push. "I think we should say good night."

I freeze. Am I understanding her correctly? "End the date now?"

"Yes." She withdraws her keys from her purse. "I had a really good time with you. I appreciated the museum and the conversation. Both told me a lot about you that I needed to know."

That's great but… "You said you wanted me?"

"I do, but I don't think we should have sex tonight. After all, it's our first date."

"But we've already had sex." I know she hasn't forgotten.

"Yes, but now we're dating. Since we're also talking about marriage, what's happening between us isn't a hookup." I must look as confused as I feel, because she pauses, seeming to gather her words. "After what happened in the dressing room, you said you needed time to think, so I gave you space."

She did, and I appreciated it. "And now you need some?"

"I have to ask myself if I can marry someone who may never give me children and may never love me."

Instantly, I want to protest…but what can I rail against? She's not saying anything that isn't true. And doesn't she deserve everything she wants in life? Especially to be loved?

"Evan…" she goes on. "Don't be disappointed. The sex would probably be really good, and god knows I would love your touch…but it would muddy everything."

She's probably right. Rationally, I know that, yet I find myself grappling. My libido wants to change her mind. The rest of me realizes I have to back down. If I don't, Nia may think I'm more interested in sex than in her.

Dragging in a ragged breath, I step back. "I understand. Everything is happening fast, and I'm asking a lot of you. Of course you have to think about it. Just consider that, no matter what, we could be our own family, and I will always endeavor to make you feel like the most important, beautiful woman in the world, especially in bed."

She tears up. "I think you mean that. Now I have to ask myself if that's enough."

Wednesday, November 15

I'M STILL TROUBLED by my conversation with Nia last night when I walk into Stratus's lobby to see her arguing with Douglas Lund and some other puffed-up suit. I presume it's one of his staffers, whom I've never met. They don't have an appointment, so why the hell are they here?

Then Nia distracts me. She's wearing a red dress that gathers at her small waist, flares over the tempting curve of her hips, and ends at mid-thigh. Her stilettos and professionally dismissive smile round out the look.

"Mr. Cook's calendar is very full. You'll need an appointment to see him. He's on vacation for two weeks beginning next Monday. So his next available opening is"—she glances at her phone—"December fifth at two thirty. Would you like me to put you down then?"

"Look, Ms…" The silver-haired Wall Street bigwig glares impatiently.

"Ms. Wright. I'm Mr. Cook's executive assistant. He doesn't have time to see you today."

"He hasn't made time to see me since he flew out to New York months ago. I've sent my people here to reason with him, and he never has time for them, either. I call, and he dodges."

Nia crosses her arms over her chest. "He's a busy man with many priorities. Would you like his next available appointment?"

"I need to see him today. I have something he'll want to see, I guarantee it. I suggest you find him. If he misses this opportunity, he won't be happy. And I'd hate to see you out of a job."

Is that asshole threatening her?

"I'd hate to lose my job, too, Mr. Lund, which is why I won't be disturbing him for your unscheduled appearance. You'll have to make an appointment. If December fifth doesn't work—"

"It doesn't," Lund growls and begins to lean into her personal space.

"Do we have a problem here?" I speak up from the door on the far side of the room.

She raises her chin. "Everything is fine. I'm just explaining to Mr. Lund that you're unable to see him today."

"I have a final, very lucrative offer for you, Cook. I came to present it in person and pitch to you all the reasons you should take Colossus Investment Corporation seriously."

His pompous shit annoys me. But it's business and it's money. I didn't get where I am by being pigheaded, closed-minded, and illogical. If he's come all this way and is barging into my lobby insistently, I bet he's finally going to give me an offer I can take.

I glance at Nia. She's come to the same conclusion. But I see that stubborn set of her chin. She doesn't care about the offer; she doesn't want me to sell.

As much as I hate putting any more breeze in this windbag's sails, I nod at Lund. "You have ten minutes. Follow me. Nia, can you call my eight a.m. and tell him I'm running late?"

She presses her lips together in displeasure but nods. "I'll take care of it."

As I march toward my office, I presume Lund and his lackey are following.

An unfamiliar voice stops me. "Nia, is it?"

When I turn, Lund's sidekick eyes her openly and speculatively.

She draws up and lifts her chin. "Yes. Can I help you with something?"

"I…I, um, was wondering if you could point me to the restroom."

This dude is in his mid-thirties, tall, and seemingly suave with his blond hair and movie-star blue eyes. And he can't hold his bladder for ten minutes?

"On the far end of the lobby, past the water feature, and to your left." She points to the little alcove.

"Thanks." He says the word, but he still doesn't move or take his eyes off of her.

I don't like it. And I don't like him.

"You're welcome."

"I'm Stephen Lund." He holds out his hand.

What the hell? This must be Douglas's son and golden boy, and he's decided to flirt with Nia? He'd better not be looking for an opening to ask her out. If he is, I'll shut the son of a bitch down and throw him out.

Maybe Stephen is the kind of guy who's capable of telling Nia he loves her.

I push the thought aside.

Slowly, she fits her hand into his. "Nia Wright. Do you need coffee?"

"I'm fine. Thank you."

She looks as baffled by their odd interaction as I am.

I turn to regard Douglas Lund, expecting impatience. Instead, he's watching the pair of them carefully. He must be an excellent poker player because I have absolutely no idea what he's thinking.

Whatever's going on makes my gut clench. I smell danger. Logically, I can't imagine how Lund Junior could hurt Nia in my lobby, but my instinct warns me to get him far from her.

"Nia, would you find Sebastian and tell him to join us?"

"Of course. Do you need me there to take notes?"

Normally, I would say yes. "No. We'll be fine. This won't take long."

The relief on her face is only obvious to me because I know her expressions well. "I'll make sure your eight o'clock is waiting when you're ready."

Then Nia is gone. Protectively, I watch her go. I want both Lunds to know she's off-limits.

"She seems efficient. You work well together," Douglas observes. "How long has she reported to you?"

"Three years. Do you want to talk about my assistant or present me an offer?"

"Present an offer, of course." Stephen walks up, suddenly all smiles, as if he wasn't just barking up Nia's skirt. If he senses my anger, he doesn't let it show. "My dad has been looking for a good assistant since his last one got married and moved away a few months ago. If you're at all amenable to us luring Nia away—"

"I'm not."

Stephen laughs. "Sorry, Dad. It was worth a try."

Douglas gives me a bland smile, and the two exchange a look. I don't believe them for a minute. Given how intently both stared at her, I don't think they were interested in her efficiency.

Silently, I fume as I lead the Lunds to my office. We've barely made our way inside when Sebastian enters and shuts the door. After some greetings and handshakes, Douglas doesn't let even a moment pass before he pulls a tablet from his briefcase.

"You have six minutes left." I don't care if I come off like a rude son of a bitch. They weren't invited. Their manners suck, and their behavior is even more suspect.

Lund clears his throat, and I see him shoving down his temper. "I've gone back to our investors. We've crunched more numbers, and we're able to present you an offer that includes all the protections you wanted for your employees, plus another ten million in cash."

This is exactly the deal I've been waiting for. Triumph spikes. I maintain my cool facade. I can't let my thrill show. But inside? I've won and I know it. The offer is above market value. The amount of cash they're throwing at me is almost obscene. As a bonus, my employees will be taken care of, too. As presented, I have no reason not to take it.

Sitting back in my chair, I study the two men. "What's the catch?"

"No catch," Douglas assures. "But there are a couple of changes from previous offers. We've restructured this deal so we can offer you more cash. For that reason, we're rescinding the clause that brings you on as COO for two years. You're expensive."

Since I never wanted to stay on as chief operating officer of my own company after I sold it, I'm not bothered. I've already been tossing around ideas for other parts of the tech sector to tackle. On the other hand, I'm talking to a group of investors, not computer engineers. If I don't run Stratus, who will?

I frown. "All the other terms are the same?"

"Minor differences. You can't work for a direct competitor for five years."

That stipulation doesn't bother me. Even if I sold out, I wouldn't work for someone in my own industry. I'd rather have a challenge that's totally new. "Fine."

"In exchange for the employee protections you requested, you'll have a two-year moratorium on hiring any of Stratus's employees, should you organize another start-up. Additionally, in exchange for these protections, we're going to ask all existing employees to sign employment contracts for that two-year period."

I pause. It's understandable they wouldn't want me to steal away the innovators and important contributors if they're going to assume the reins of the company. Ditto with employees wanting to leave. But their phrasing bugs me.

"I'd agree to that, provided the language specifies we're only talking about essential personnel."

"Define essential," Douglas insists.

"I'm taking Nia with me." As I say the words, I glare at Stephen. I can't be any clearer than that.

He's already shaking his head. "I'm afraid that clause applies to everyone. If Ms. Wright wants to resign and find another position with a different employer before the deal takes effect, of course we'll wish her well. But we hope to have the opportunity to encourage every employee familiar with the business to stay."

I understand Junior's logic, but the offer I was certain I would accept two minutes ago is now something my gut tells me to reject.

Turn down over a billion dollars for a woman you don't love who might never marry you?

Before I can formulate a reply, Bas jumps in. "Are the timeframes for acquisition and transition the same as previously proposed?"

"Absolutely. The payout structure is the same as well," Douglas assures. "I suggest you think long and hard about this offer, Mr. Cook. No one else will give you this sort of money."

They're probably right. And given how quickly technology changes, who knows how long before my data storage system, though revolutionary now, will become obsolete. That's something they must be aware of.

Until this moment, I never questioned why they wanted to buy Stratus. They aren't the first, but they are definitely the most cash-rich and persistent. I also want to know why their interest suddenly extends to Nia.

Whatever the reason, I want answers.

"Out of curiosity, what do you plan to do with Stratus? Leverage its capabilities to persuade another tech start-up to begin some other line of business with you? Sell the technology to a bigger player?"

"Neither. We'd like to grow it, maybe eventually merge it with some other technology we're developing in-house." Douglas shrugs. "See where that might go."

I don't believe his nonchalance for a moment. He's got a grand plan. Why else would he keep throwing cash at me like I'm a whore and he hasn't gotten laid in a decade?

I send Bas a glance. I see he's confounded, too.

"Email me the offer documents. I'll consider them and get back to you with an answer."

"We need signed agreements by December twenty-ninth or the offer expires."

Whatever they want, they want it bad. I need to do some investigating and figure out what.

"Duly noted." I glance at my watch and stand. "Now we're done, gentlemen. I've given you an extra four minutes and kept my first appointment waiting."

Both Lunds take the hint and rise to their feet. The elder looks annoyed as he picks up his briefcase.

That makes me smile. He assumed I would jump at his offer. No doubt, he did some research and heard I'm known for being calm and rational, that I always act in my financial best interest. So right now, he's confused as hell and irritated because he's wondering where he miscalculated.

Honestly, I'm doing the same. I should take it, persuade Nia to come with me—marry me—and walk into the proverbial sunset with her.

But what if she says no?

Then I lose her, both professionally and personally. And the Lunds know it.

Why are they trying to separate me from Nia?

It bugs the shit out of me that I have no clue. But I intend to find out. Douglas Lund has been a pushy asshole throughout this whole process. I plan to think this through thoroughly and make him wait until the very last minute. If he sweats about it… Oh, well.

I'm not usually vindictive, but they've rubbed me the wrong way, especially today. My impatience to show them out grows when Nia knocks and cracks the door, then sends me a questioning glance. Stephen's stare is all over her again. I grit my teeth.

I want him gone. In fact, I want both men out of my sight. Now.

As I nod at Nia, I approach and block the younger Lund's view of her with my body, then turn to face him and his father. "I'll let you know when I have an answer."

CHAPTER SEVEN

Friday, November 17

FRIDAY NIGHT CAN'T come soon enough. The week seems to drag on interminably. The one bright spot is that the Lunds have gone away and left me the hell alone for the last two days.

Bas, who says he's planning to quit before this deal goes through, seems relieved, too. We're investigating possible reasons Colossus wants to acquire Stratus Solutions—and Nia—so badly, especially without a COO. They're an investment corporation. They don't manufacture or service tech. This acquisition seemed logical when they intended to keep me around to run things and reap the rewards. Now that they want to operate everything themselves, it makes far less sense. Sure, the staff could assist them, but even collectively they can't run the company.

"We're doing all we can. Are you going to stop brooding?"

I turn to face Bas. He's been asking me this for days. The short answer is no. Not only do the Lunds bug me, I have this nagging worry that my blunt honesty isn't what Nia wanted on our last date. I shouldn't be surprised; what woman wants a husband who doesn't love her? But I doubt I'm capable of opening myself up again. It would be wrong and unfair to lie about that. Besides, there are plenty of logical reasons for her to say yes.

"Are you going to leave it alone?"

"Dude, I'm your best friend. If you need to talk to someone—"

"I don't."

Bas sighs. "Something is up. You and Nia have both been acting weird lately. Since I was raised by a single mom and I've got four pain-in-my-butt sisters, I speak female. You don't. I can help."

He wants me to be happy, and I don't want to be an ass, but… "I have to figure this out for myself."

"Listen, buddy. I think Nia is good for you, and I'd rather not see you screw this up. I overheard you say on the phone earlier that you two are going out tonight. Let me help. What are your plans?"

Since he means well, I can't be mad. "She's planning tonight, so I have no clue. I admit I'm anxious because I had no idea she enjoys performing in a burlesque show in her spare time. So who knows what she'll come up with for us to do?"

Bas laughs. "And you hate not being in control."

Almost as much as I hate him ribbing me about it. "Bite me."

"Do you know what you two are going to talk about?"

"I need an agenda on a date?"

He rolls his eyes. "No, but if you want to move your relationship forward and you're looking for a way to tell her that—"

"Nia knows exactly how interested I am. The ball is in her court." And it's going to be a long six weeks without knowing whether she'll be moving to Maui with me as my wife. Because even if I sell out, I'm moving. I can start a business on the island. There's nothing keeping me in Seattle.

But no matter what, I'm not letting Nia go to the Lunds.

"Okay. Well, if she gets back to you and you need to talk, I'm here."

"Thanks." Right now, there's simply nothing to say.

"Have fun tonight." Bas gives me a jaunty wave, then he's gone.

Since Nia left the office an hour ago and it's nearly six, I pack up and head to my place. She's supposed to meet me there at six thirty.

As soon as I hit the door, I pick up the few odds and ends lying around. My running shoes go in the closet. Yesterday's water glass goes in the dishwasher. I fluff up the comforter on my bed, which has clean sheets as of yesterday, thank you very much.

By the time I change my clothes, check my hair, and find a bottle of wine in case I can talk her into staying here for the evening, the bell rings.

"Hi." Somehow, I manage to breathe the word as she stands in my doorway.

I must look somewhere between bowled over and stupefied because she grins. "You like my dress?"

"Like isn't the right word."

She's wantable. Edible. Fuckable. I swallow, but I can't tear my gaze away from the thin straps grazing her shoulders, leading to a tight white, corset-style dress that dips low and hugs her plump breasts. My mouth is already watering as I take the visual tour lower and trace the nip of her waist, the womanly swell of her hips, and the lace trim that flirts with her thighs. Her white wedges show off her insanely gorgeous legs and a flash of turquoise toe polish.

"Are you going to invite me in?"

"Are we going to stay in so I can talk you out of that dress?"

She laughs and shakes her head. "No. We've got plans."

"I said that out loud?"

"You did."

"I…um, only meant to think it. Oops."

Nia smiles. "I see you took my wardrobe suggestions to heart. White shirt, black pants, black loafers. Perfect. Let's go."

When she takes my hand, I drag my feet. "Where are we going?"

"That's not how this works. You surprised me on Tuesday night. Now it's my turn." She tugs again.

I still resist. "Are we doing anything that's going to embarrass me in public?"

Why else would she have me dress so specifically if she didn't want me to show off somehow?

"You'll *be* in public. Embarrassment is relative since some people find most human contact uncomfortable."

She means me. And she's poking.

I scowl. "You're not answering my question."

"Just keeping a little mystery. Let's go or we're going to be late."

When I help her into my car and slide behind the wheel, I slant a stare her way. "Where to?"

Nia smiles as she fiddles with the radio. "You're not the only one with tricks up their sleeve. I'll give you directions. Head north on I-5 for now."

As she searches for a station, something slightly familiar hits my eardrums. She stops there with a little smile. "My grandmother used to love the Beach Boys. I remember listening with her when I was really little."

Then she falls silent, lost in her memories. I focus on the old tune. I don't remember the sleigh bells, and it seems funny on a non-Christmas carol? But okay…

That quirkiness aside, the opening lines resonate with me. I may not love Nia, but she should never doubt my sincerity. I will do whatever it takes to make her sure of us, of the fact I'll make her happy. Then the male vocalist croons with a plaintive tone something I should probably be asking myself when it comes to my lovely assistant-turned-girlfriend. Because really, God only knows what I'd be without her. Lost at work and home. Lost professionally and personally.

I can't let her go.

Twenty minutes of her meticulous navigation and a few more classic tunes later, we arrive. I'm not exactly sure why we're at an older strip mall in an unfamiliar but established neighborhood. The second I help her out of the car, she takes my hand in hers and drags me to an Italian place tucked away in the corner.

Once we're inside, it's obviously a casual, family-owned place. Nia catches sight of an older man, who suddenly beams. "Bella!"

"Hi, Lorenzo. I couldn't let another week go by without seeing my favorite chef."

The man is fifty-five if he's a day, and she still manages to make him blush as he comes forward and wraps her in a big bear hug. "Bah. It's not me you love; it's my pizza."

"Can't I love you both?"

He laughs and wags a finger at her. "Mateo is still single. I give you all the pizza if you marry him."

"Sorry. I can't do it, not even for that."

Lorenzo tosses his hands in the air. "I'll beat sense into him, make the man-whore settle down."

Suddenly, a broad woman with salt-and-pepper hair and a no-nonsense expression bustles into the room. "Don't you think I've tried? That son of ours..." She shakes her head and asks before giving Nia a hug. "Oh, bambina. Good to see you."

"Hi, Guilia. Good to see you, too. This is my...new boyfriend, Evan."

She frowns. "Same name as your boss?"

"Same man as my boss," she admits wryly.

"Evan Cook," I hold out my hand, fascinated by her closeness with the Italian couple.

"Nice to meet you. Be good to our girl or I'll find a way to marry her off to my son."

They treat it like a running joke, but I think they're at least half-serious. "Not if I marry her first. I've already asked, by the way."

I'm staking my claim, and I want everyone to know it.

Nia turns to me, stare pointed. Apparently, she didn't want me to mention that. I shrug.

"Have you now?" Guilia asks, then regards Nia. "Where is the ring?"

I pause. Valid question. Perhaps a ring wouldn't change Nia's answer, but it would prove I'm serious. After all, the notion of putting a ring on a woman's finger led me to proposing in the first place.

"I haven't said yes," Nia points out.

"Yet," I add. I may have overlooked something that, in retrospect, seems obvious, but I'm hardly done trying to convince her. "I'm not giving up."

"Okay, I like this one," the older woman says. "If I must give up the idea of you reforming Mateo, I can do that if this man loves you."

Her smile is jovial, but beside me Nia stiffens.

That L-word. Again. Why has everyone attached such illogical and often fleeting emotion to an arrangement that can be both practical and necessary? A home, safety, and financial security in exchange for sexual ease, domestic help, and companionship; the arrangement is enduring and timeless. Of course, Nia supports herself, but I can give her far more. And I'm convinced that she alone can give me everything I need.

"It's only our second date," she says into the awkward silence, then winks. "But I'm hopeful."

The older couple smiles and shows us to our table. We've barely opened a bottle of Chianti and enjoyed a few ravioli appetizers that melt in my mouth when Lorenzo delivers us a big, veggie-laden pie.

As much as I believe in clean eating, I have a weakness for pizza. After one bite, I'm hooked.

"This is fantastic. If the pizza is free, maybe you should marry Mateo and keep me on the side," I joke.

"Ha. You only say that because you can't cook. And because you haven't met Mateo."

Suddenly, something occurs to me. "Did you date him?"

"For about three months."

I don't like the way she gets quiet. "And?"

"Like Lorenzo said, he's a man-whore. The whole time he was dating me, he was sleeping with someone else."

And her. She doesn't say so, but it's implied.

"He hurt you?"

"Not really," she assures. "He pissed me off. Not caring as much as I should that he was boffing a co-worker was my clue that I needed to end things."

"How long ago was that?" I want her to tell me it was a long time ago. I want her to tell me it was way before we met.

"Two years ago. Remember when I told you I was spending a lot of time with friends on a houseboat in the bay that summer? I lived with Mateo in July, August, and part of September. So I spent a lot of time with Lorenzo and Guilia." She shrugs. "Everything ended when my mom got sick and passed away. Mateo wasn't there for me, but his parents were. I don't know how I would have made it through that time without them.

They're like family to me."

I have mixed feelings about that. When she sees them, I'll bet she sometimes runs into her ex-lover. That hardly thrills me. But I also know how much family and the bonds of closeness matter to her. Since she has none, it's understandable that she found people she adores to act as her surrogates. It's endearing, too. But it also proves that Nia is smart since she didn't marry Mateo simply to have one.

Isn't that what you did?

I shove the voice in my head aside. It doesn't understand. Becca and I were different. We were not only survivors and like minds, but well-matched. Kindred spirits, even. We'd been together long enough to know one other and understand what our marriage would be. Becca appreciated our quiet. Maybe we weren't as passionate as some couples, but she had been through a lot. Besides, there's more to life than sex.

Though I admit it's feeling a lot more important now that I'm with Nia.

I scowl at that observation.

"I'm not interested in him anymore, so wipe that frown off your face. I only brought you here tonight because of the amazing pizza."

As much as some stubborn part of me wants to argue with that, I can't. "It's delicious."

"And because it's really close to where we're heading next. I hope you're in the mood to dance."

Dance? I'm picturing a bar with loud music and strangers pressing against one another, getting more desperate as the night goes on. The good news is, people are usually having fun and getting drunk, so they shouldn't notice me. "I've never danced."

"Never?"

I don't know why she looks so shocked. "A lot of people have never danced."

She raises her brows. "I don't know any. Surely you danced at least once at your wedding reception."

"Rebecca and I were married at the county courthouse. After I paid for the marriage license and the costume-jewelry wedding rings, I had forty-three dollars to my name. Neither of us had family or friends attending. So no reception."

Nia looks stunned. "Diana didn't come?"

"She never liked Becca." And that always bothered me.

"Why?"

"According to Diana, I'm a 'strong personality,' and she thought I needed someone equally strong to balance me. Becca was fragile. As she matured and felt more secure, she grew a better sense of self. But Diana is the sort of person who makes up her mind once and there's no changing it."

Nia pauses. "Okay, so you didn't dance at your wedding. What about school events? The prom?"

I shake my head. "I spent most of my time with computers, and Becca's foster father would never have let her go to anything like that."

"Well, since you've missed out on all the fun of the dance floor, I'm going to help you make up for lost time."

"I'm going to be horrible at this."

She laughs. "First, we don't know that for sure. Second, everyone has to start somewhere."

"What about you? How did you start dancing?"

"My mom worked a lot. One of her friends owned a dance studio and watched me after school so I wouldn't be alone. I was six when I decided I didn't want to watch anymore." She shrugs. "I spent years dancing, lots of it competitively in high school. I've got ribbons and trophies galore if you want to see sometime."

"When did you find burlesque?" I'm displeased that she seeks attention from strangers by taking most of her clothes off on stage, but I still want to understand.

"My first year of college. I had a TA who danced on the side. She broke her ankle skiing and asked if I could fill in until she healed." Nia shrugs. "I've been hooked since. I know you think it's the same as stripping, but burlesque is an art form. It's a tease. No one is shoving bills in my thong. No one touches me. And no one gets to ask me for a lap dance. I have all the power to shake my thing, give the audience a wink, and go home alone."

"Do you get hit on at the club?" I don't know why that possibility hasn't occurred to me sooner. Heck, I don't even know why I bothered to ask now. "Of course you do."

"It happens. Most guys accept a gracious but firm no. For the ones who are a little more persistent, Kyle is usually around and willing to play boyfriend. It's not perfect, but it works."

Not for me, it doesn't. And it seems as if everywhere I turn, I'm confronted by Nia's exes.

"How many lovers have you had?" The question is out before I can stop it.

She tenses. "More than you. Is that a problem? It doesn't make me a slut."

"No. It doesn't. I-I didn't mean to imply—"

"Then what did you mean?"

This is my insecurity showing. This is me wondering if I can make her happy emotionally...and sexually. I lack her experience. It's not as if I can blame her for what she did before we got together. And I don't regret my years with Becca. After all, our choices have led us here.

Sex with Nia blew my mind, but I'm wondering if I can really do the same for her. The passion we shared in her dressing room was unexpected and urgent, like a sudden tornado that swept us both up. But if we deliberately planned to spend the night together, took our time and shared our pleasure slowly? I don't know if I could turn her inside out and persuade her to surrender herself to me. Once with Nia was enough to tell me that she's vastly different in bed than Becca. I'm wondering if I'm actually prepared for a woman like her.

"That I don't want to disappoint you."

She softens. "I don't think you can." I must still look unconvinced, because she sighs and takes my hand. "Look at it this way: I've had a little experience with a lot of guys. None of it lasted. None of it wowed me.

None of it was with anyone I loved. You have a lot of experience with one woman. You know what it's like to really connect, keep it fresh, and make something last. I don't think one kind of experience is better than the other. And I don't think any of that really matters. I'm not thinking about Kyle or Mateo when I'm with you. And I hope you're not thinking about Becca when you're with me."

"No." In truth, Nia seems to have settled somewhere inside me and taken over half my brain functions…and most of my cock.

"Then let's just be us. No labels, no judgment. No worries. If it's meant to be, we'll figure it out. If it's not, then we'll hope that we've each learned something from the experience and made one another feel good while it lasted."

I suspect she's right, but I prefer something more. "I'm looking to get married."

"And I'm only looking to get married for the right reasons."

Love. That's what she means. This conversation frustrates me because a poetic, idealized emotion is completely unnecessary. I'm even more annoyed that I have four more candidates I could interview for the position of wife, and yet I'm only interested in Nia. This is clearly a defect in my thought process. Maybe I should chalk it up to the sex drive not being logical. Whatever the reason, I'm not willing to give up trying to convince her that we could be happy together without silly Prince-Charming fantasies.

Instead of railing, I need to be rational and show her all the unmistakable, cogent reasons she should marry me, starting with family. She wants one? I have one. They'll love her. And she will absolutely adore them.

"I get it. And I appreciate the honesty," I say finally. "But I intend to marry you."

"Evan—"

"Before you protest, tell me what you're doing for Thanksgiving."

She frowns at the change of subject. "Well, I'm thinking about doing a 5K. I'll DVR the parade so I have something to do besides miss my mom. I'll probably eat Chinese takeout from down the street. You?"

I smile and go in for the kill. "I'm going to Maui. Come with me. If there's any chance we're going to spend our lives together, then I want to introduce you to my siblings and their spouses. Plus, you can get a feel for the island and make sure it's someplace you could actually see yourself living."

Nia hesitates, likely weighing the pros and cons. "Actually, that's a decent idea. It makes sense to see the island before I decide whether to move. And I'd like to meet your siblings."

I've got her. "I'm leaving Monday morning. I was planning to stay for twelve days."

"I don't have that much vacation time saved."

"I know the boss." I wink. "I'm pretty sure I can fix that for you."

"All right, then. That sounds really nice." She squeezes my hand. "I'm glad you're not spending your first holiday without Becca alone in your apartment."

"Me, too." I already knew I couldn't, but having Nia with me will give me so much more to be thankful for.

"I'll need to find a hotel and a flight. My credit card is going to hate me, but—"

"No, it's not. I'm flying charter. I think I can find you an extra seat on the plane, maybe the one next to me. And don't worry about hotel. We'll be staying with my sister and her husband."

Her eyes pop out. "You mean *the* Noah Weston?"

"Yes. You know football?"

"Um, yeah. Growing up in the south, you live and breathe it. Lots of the guys in high school idolized him. Are you sure he and Harlow won't mind?"

"They'll enjoy it. And we won't be in the way. They have a huge place with eight bedrooms. Right on the ocean. With a great pool. The weather will be fantastic." I grin her way. "Are you convinced yet?"

"Yes." She gives me a self-deprecating laugh. "Geez, I sound easy."

"Easy?" I shake my head. "No, I just said all the right things."

"Okay, we'll go with that conclusion."

Guilia boxes up the leftover pizza and waves off my credit card. They say goodbye to Nia with a big hug and a promise to get together soon.

When we reach the car, I unlock it and hold her door open. "Where am I going?"

Nia takes the box from my hand, tosses it in the front seat, then swings her hip into the door. It shuts with a click. "Right there."

She points across the parking lot at the side unit. The front is a huge floor-to-ceiling plate-glass window. Above is a tired sign lit in flashing red that reads DANCING DELIGHTS STUDIO. It's not a bar. It's not a club. It's… I don't know what it is.

"Explain," I demand.

"What?" She leads me across the asphalt. "I said we were going dancing."

"I assumed that meant someplace crowded and loud, where I could blend in and no one would care how I looked or that I've never danced. This…"

"Is a place where they teach people to ballroom dance."

"Fuck me." I close my eyes.

She giggles. "You'll be fine."

"Well, if I die of embarrassment, I know who to blame."

That makes her laugh harder. "You won't. I promise. Besides, we're both beginners. I've never done this, either."

"So…are we learning to waltz or foxtrot?" When Nia presses her lips together and shakes her head, I know immediately she's withholding something. "What? Tell me."

She sighs. "We're going to rumba."

I frown. "I know what a rhomboid is. I know what a rhombus is. I even know how to define a rumpus. But rumba doesn't compute."

"That's why we're here. To learn. And no, it's not a muscle, a shape you used in geometry, or a commotion."

"I'm going to suck at this. No telling Bas—or anyone. I'm swearing you to silence."

"Don't you want to know what the rumba is?"

"Only because I have to face it."

Nia takes my hand and leads me toward the studio's red door. "The dance of love."

No holding back a groan as we make our way inside. Four other couples are waiting, all of various ages and backgrounds with two things in common: the women look excited…while the men are looking for the exit.

We pause a few feet inside the door. The guys are sizing one another up, probably wondering who will be the worst at this. The answer is surely me, and the fact I'm still willing to do this for Nia says something, probably that I'm either brave or stupid.

"Good evening, everyone," says a man with brown hair, arms bulging out of his black tank. He's got tight pants and a Russian accent. "I am Pasha. And tonight, Lacie is my partner. We will teach you basics of my favorite Latin dance, rumba. It is dance of love. Before we begin, we will demonstrate so you feel movement's mood and pace. Watch."

The willowy blonde at his side presses a remote, and Latin music fills the air. It's slow and sultry and makes me think of humid breezes, warm evenings, and sex. Okay, this isn't bad…so far.

Then the pair starts moving, hips swinging in synch, as they move closer, circling one another. The footwork is intricate. Her arms create fluid lines and flourishes all around her body as she sways and shifts, seeming to lure him in. He stands tall, shoulders squared, seducing her with the flow of his movements and his eyes. He shifts his weight, undulating, posturing, and preening.

"Men's hips don't move like that." I whisper against Nia's ear.

She represses a laugh and gestures to Pasha. "Obviously, they do. Now, hush and pay attention."

By the end of their demonstration, I'm convinced I will never learn to do this dance half so well, especially in the three hours we'll be here. What I do think, however, is I'll get to watch Nia's lush, lithe body move in the sexiest ways. That, I can appreciate.

We spend some time learning basic movements—a box step, a slow-quick-quick-slow rhythm to our footwork, and something called a crossover. And let's be honest, I suck every bit as much as I thought. I'm a shit show with two left feet. But Nia is incredible. Watching her sway and flow while I rub up against her in the name of dance is a damn good time.

At the end of the three hours, we put everything we've learned together into a forty-second demonstration, and I'm more mesmerized by the way she lures me closer with a come-hither sweep of her fingers and her supple, seductive moves than counting my own steps.

God, everything about her draws me in. I don't know how or why I've overlooked her for months now. I only know I'm determined to have her tonight.

And for the rest of our lives.

At the end of the class, we're given a pat on the back and encouraged to come back for a six-week course of lessons beginning in January. I smile blandly. And I'm the first guy to pull his girl out the door and into the car.

When I toss the pizza box into the back and slide into the driver's seat beside her, she's frowning. "Evan, you practically ran a ten-yard dash out of that place. What's wrong—"

"I have to kiss you," I say in a rush before I fill my fingers with the loose curls at her crown, lower my head, and capture her lips.

As she gasps in surprise, I thrust deep. Our suddenly rough breaths fill the car. I'm cursing the console between us as our kiss turns endless. I devour her with a hunger I can't fight, and I'm vaguely aware of the momentary bright flash of headlights, signaling that the other couples have left the lot. Somewhere in my head, I know I need to release Nia, drive back to my place, then pray like hell I can persuade her to let me peel off her second-skin of a dress and take her to bed.

In the back of my mind, I'm still aware that I haven't nailed a few hundred women, like my brothers did before they married. I'm worried that puts me at a disadvantage when it comes to pleasing Nia, but I want her too badly to let that stop me from trying.

Suddenly, her hand drops to my thigh. I counter, gliding my palm up from her waist until I'm cupping her breast through the thin white fabric.

I brush the hard tip with my thumb, enjoying her throaty little moans and wishing like hell I had her naked.

When I reach inside the dress and lift her flesh from the confines of her bodice, she grips my forearm to stay me. "Evan, this is a parking lot."

She means it's a public place where people might be able to see us. I understand…but her panting little voice is subverting my brain.

"My windows are tinted."

"But—" she protests…until I glide my lips up her neck and my fingers tease her bare nipple. "Oh…"

I moan in return. She has the most gorgeous scent behind her ear, thick and swirling, like amber. She's musky, earthy…but with a hint of something sweet. It drives me wild. *She* drives me wild. For almost two weeks, I've questioned what happened in her dressing room. I've never been impulsive or felt so compelled to touch a woman. I never believed in an unstoppable need for sex, certainly never thought it could overtake my logic and overwhelm my better sense. Something about Nia has me questioning my preconceived notions. I'm revved up every moment I'm with her. And when I get close…

"You're like honey on my tongue." I lick my way up her throat, loving her whimpers as her nails curl into my thigh and she arches her breast into my hand. "So sweet. So addictive."

"Evan." Her head falls back, and she bares her neck in surrender. "Why do you make me feel this way?"

"I could ask you the same thing." I nip at her ear, then dip lower to nibble at her neck.

"You know we can't do this here."

No, I don't know that. As previously stated, my windows are tinted. But a glance around the interior of my car tells me I need to rethink this spatially. If we go much further, my six-foot-three frame won't fit anywhere that allows me to get inside her.

Unacceptable.

Gritting my teeth, I pull away, tug my phone from my pocket, and ask it, "What's the fastest way home?"

"Getting directions."

By the time the device pulls up a map, I've already revved the car out of the lot and zoomed toward the highway.

Traffic is light just before midnight. I'm racing down the road, my zipper crushed against my aching cock as I remember the way Nia dances and smells and kisses.

"What are you thinking?" she asks, her voice low in the charged silence.

"That you get to me in a way I've never felt." I swallow. "That when I touch you, I lose my head and my ability to see reason."

"Lust will do that." She sounds even quieter.

My first thought is to protest. I know simple lust. When I was married to Becca, I met beautiful women. Sometimes they even propositioned me, especially after I got rich. I never acted on the feeling. But the urgency flaring through my veins now isn't like that. It's…more. It's something I don't have a name for.

I don't speak for the rest of the drive. When we reach my place, I park in the garage and cut the engine. Nia reaches for the handle of the passenger door.

"Wait."

"Evan, it's late. And I have a late night tomorrow, too."

Because she'll be performing. With her ex. I grit my teeth. I know I should let her go; she's asked me to. I need to think about everything she said tonight. About everything I've realized.

It's the last thing I want.

"All right," I manage to say. "I had a good time tonight. Thanks for taking me to meet Lorenzo and Guilia, and for introducing me to the people you consider family."

"Since we're going to Hawaii, you'll be doing the same for me."

I am. And on some level, I realize that introducing her to my new family is more than a tactic to win her over. I want them to approve of her. And I want her to like them. I want to blend her into this new family of mine because what I feel for Nia is more than friendship. It's definitely more than lust, too. It doesn't have a name, but whatever it is, no matter how unsettling, I want more.

CHAPTER EIGHT

Plane over the Pacific Ocean
Monday, November 20

I'M SO RELIEVED when Monday evening rolls around and I finally have Nia all to myself—at least for the duration of this flight. I'm normally not a fan of being thirty-something thousand feet in the air for hours at a time. My logical mind understands how avionics function, but I still have trouble rationalizing the safety of something inherently dangerous like flying.

Beside me, Nia sips a glass of water and taps away on her laptop. She's been quiet since we took off. Maybe it has something to do with the way our last date ended. And my behavior Saturday night at the BBB Revue. I might have stayed less than two feet from Nia every moment I could. I might also have snarled whenever Kyle tried to talk to her. And I might have told him to back the fuck off when he walked into her dressing room uninvited after their performance.

Not my finest moment.

Why do I turn caveman every time a man looks at her? I can't understand it. I've never behaved this way in my life.

Guys often looked at Becca. She was a beautiful willow of a woman with long dark hair and bright eyes who always appeared as if she needed saving. Beings with Y chromosomes everywhere responded to that, and it never bothered me. But men don't look at Nia as if they want to save her. She's too obviously capable to need their help. They look at her as if they're desperate to fuck her. I'm not okay with that. Not at all.

"You're supposed to be on vacation," I remind her.

She slants a scowl my way. "Says the guy who spent the last hour reading the October financials."

"I told Bas I'd do it over the weekend. I didn't get to it." When she questions me with a raised brow, my gut clenches. "Because, I admit, I was wound up about Kyle."

"Clearly."

"You're mad."

"I'm not thrilled," she admits. "Look, if I wanted to be with Kyle, I would be. The fact I haven't let him touch me in nearly two years, despite the fact I see him at least twice a week, should tell you something about my non-feelings for him."

I understand her point, but it has no effect on my perspective. "He has feelings for you."

Which are too much like my own.

Nia shrugs. "That's his issue, and we've talked about it. He's hung up because I broke things off, and he's not used to hearing no. I already know that if I took him back, he'd lose interest in a month or less. We played that game once before, and I'm not doing it again. I did the rebound thing with him after I broke up with Mateo. I was sad about my mom's passing and the breakup…and I wanted comfort. But it was a disaster. There's nothing Kyle could say or do to win me back again, and you need to let it go. Besides, if you're determined to marry me for purely practical reasons, why does any of this matter to you?"

I have no answer and no basis to refute her. I sit back, blink, process as she resumes tapping out her email. Why does it bother me?

"I don't know. I just… I've never been through this."

She pauses. "No one ever hit on Becca?"

"That's not what I mean. Men hit on her all the time. It just never bothered me." Probably because I knew Becca had never had sex with any of those men who pursued her. But Nia has already assured me that she's not thinking about her exes when we're together; I'm the one who keeps bringing them up. She's right; I need to let it go.

"There's no reason for it to bother you now. I've been cheated on enough to know that it sucks. In my mind, going behind your lover's back to get some on the side before breaking it off is shitty. If we actually get married someday, I'll be with you, totally committed to you. That's the way I function. If there ever comes a day I decide I want someone else, I'll tell you to your face before anything happens. I expect the same of you."

I've never had a problem with commitment. "Of course. You have my word. And I'll try to keep my"—jealousy?—"issues with other men to a minimum."

"Thanks."

Nia doesn't say much for the rest of the flight, and I'm pensive. I try to lose myself in the listings of beautiful island properties Maxon and Griff have sent in advance. I'd like to get a living situation nailed down while I'm here. It's practical to be prepared to hit the ground running in January. And it gives me something to focus on now besides all the ways Nia unsettles me.

But price per square footage and number of bedrooms don't hold my interest for long. I pick one that seems more than livable and would probably be my best investment. Then my gaze strays to Nia.

Finally, she closes the lid on her laptop with a sigh. "What's wrong now?"

The fact that she realizes I'm struggling with disquiet, despite the fact I didn't say a word, says how well she knows me. "I'm not sure."

"Well, you're not bored. I know your bored face. This isn't it."

"No." I'm never bored around her. But there's something going on inside me that I don't comprehend. Maybe she knows me better than I know myself. "What do you think is bothering me?"

With a sudden shrug, she looks away. "You'll have to figure it out for yourself."

I've tried. Bas offered to help, but it didn't seem necessary at the time. All I know is the longer I'm with Nia—but not *with* her—the deeper I get into this funk.

Finally, the flight lands at the private airstrip. We make our way down the airstairs, greeted by the sunny skies and weather that's nearly thirty degrees warmer than Seattle. When the sun hits Nia, she pauses to close her eyes, tilt her head back, and soak in the warmth.

"I could get used to this," she murmurs.

If I have my way, she will. "It's definitely not so bad."

She nods, and at the bottom of the stairs, I can't resist touching her, so I take her hand.

Nia glances at our tangled fingers, and I can't tell whether she's amused or annoyed. Personally, I'm the latter. I didn't see the point of public displays of affections with Becca. We knew we were together. Why announce it to the world? With Nia, it's different. I want everyone to know—most especially her—that she belongs to me. I'd write it off as that insidious jealousy creeping in again, except there's no man here trying to snag her attention. Just the two of us and my need to be close to her.

It's a relief when she doesn't pull away, simply follows me into the red open-air building, glancing over her shoulder to take in the view of the ocean beyond the runway.

"Evan!" a man shouts.

I immediately identify that voice as Maxon's. To my right, I see him and Griff both rise to their feet, impeccably dressed in dark suits and crisp shirts. They approach, giving Nia—and our joined hands—a discreet once-over.

"Hi. I didn't expect you two here."

"We thought we'd be the welcoming committee," Maxon drawls as he gives me a bro hug.

Griff snorts as we bump shoulders. "Because we wanted to discuss the listings we sent you, and the wives have decreed there will be no shop talk tonight. But they didn't say anything about chatting in the car..."

I laugh. I'm not at all surprised they're eager to keep their wives happy. Not only do my older half brothers both seem devoted but, according to my sister, they're afraid to cross the women they married as pregnancy and hormones have progressed.

"We can do that. Guys, this is Nia. My…" How do I explain her? They already know from my previous visits here that she's my assistant, but by holding her hand I've made it clear she's more.

I should have decided before we landed what I intended to tell my family about our relationship. In truth, I wasn't sure they would care. I deeply suspect I miscalculated.

I seem to be doing that a lot lately.

"It's complicated," she says with a smile, saving me the awkward explanation.

Griff gives her a sanguine shrug. "Relationships are always complicated. Getting Britta to the altar was no breeze."

"That's because you were a stupid fuck-up. Hi. Maxon Reed." He thrusts his hand toward Nia. "Nice to meet you."

"Same." She shakes with my oldest brother, trying not to laugh. "I'm Nia Wright."

"Don't listen to the douchebag," Griff says as he takes her hand. "He's no smarter. I'm Griffin Reed, by the way."

Nia smiles at him.

"Oh, I'm so much smarter!" Maxon protests.

"Want me to ask Keeley?"

"You leave my wife out of this."

"You two can arm-wrestle for the douchebag title later," I say. "I need to arrange for the rental so I can get over to Noah and Harlow's place."

"We'll take you, and you don't need a rental. All of Noah's cars have arrived from the mainland since you were here last." Maxon laughs. "He has more cars than he has places to park them. Trust me, you won't be without wheels."

We grab the luggage and all pile into Maxon's SUV, jumping quickly into house-hunting talk.

"Everything you sent me looks great," I begin. "I think I know which is the best investment, but I'd like your local insight. I'm also going to hang on to my Seattle condo for a while, see how much I need to travel back and have a base there."

"Smart. And it will only appreciate," Griff points out.

"Absolutely." Maxon nods. "So, based on the listings we sent you, are you leaning more toward a house or a condo?"

"I see the upsides to both." Then I pause. If Nia marries me, I won't be the only one living in this place. I should ask her thoughts. Becca never cared, but Nia has an opinion about everything. "What do you think, honey?"

When the endearment rolls off my tongue, she turns a slow, questioning glance at me. Then her eyes widen. Yes, she remembers the last time I said that word to her. I was running my tongue up her neck and telling her that's what she tasted like. I very much want to have my tongue someplace else on her body right now to see how much sweeter she can be.

"Um…both sound great."

"But if you had to choose?" I prompt.

She shrugs. "What suits your needs? If you don't want a yard or the maintenance of a house, a condo is probably the way to go. You like yours now, right?"

I didn't consider the likability of the unit, only the practicality and suitability for my purposes. I know Nia views living quarters from a totally different perspective. "What do you like? You didn't go the apartment route. What was your rationale?"

"I'm afraid it's nothing terribly logical. I can't stand cookie-cutter stuff. I don't care much where I live as long as it has character. I'll take odd and quirky over predictable any day."

Given the little bit I saw of her cottage, I believe that. I reach into my computer bag and pull out the listings my brothers sent earlier. "What do you think of these? I've looked but…"

I'm aware of Maxon watching us in the rearview mirror as I hand the folder to Nia. She opens it and flips to the first description and its accompanying pictures.

"This seems nice," I prompt her. "A good investment."

She tries to smile but it's more like a grimace. "Twenty-nine million dollars?"

"I have the money, and price per square foot is actually an exceptional deal for that corner of Maui."

"Maybe, but what are you going to do with nine thousand square feet? And an acre? The maintenance alone…"

That's a reasonable point. "So, too big. Got it."

"Besides that, look at this place. It's…"

"Sleek?"

"Island modern?" Maxon suggests from the driver's seat.

"It looks kind of like a cruise ship. A new one, granted. A nice one…but who lives there?"

Griff laughs, then turns to Maxon. "Told you."

"Well, since Evan's place is on the contemporary side, I thought this might be his vibe," Maxon defends.

"I bought that for the investment. It came decorated." I was never there enough to change it, and Becca never said she wanted anything different.

"What about this one?" Griff points to one in the stack. "It's only fifty-five hundred square feet. And you'd be pretty close to me and Britta."

Nia flips through it halfheartedly. "It's still twenty million. Sorry. It's not my money, but I think that's silly. Plus…it looks a little Golden-Girls-go-on-vacation."

"What does that mean?" Her reference is lost on me.

"*The Golden Girls*? TV show about four older women who share a house in Miami? Betty White?" I must still look blank because she sighs. "The decor is little on the eighties side."

I frown. "The age or the decade?"

"Both."

Now that she mentions it, I see what she means. "And that's not the sort of character you want?"

"For me, no. But if you like it, then go for it."

If Nia is going to live there with me and character matters, then I want her to be happy. I can be comfortable almost anywhere. "What about this?"

She bobs her head a few times. "I can't fault anything about it. The price tag and size are coming down a little. It just…doesn't do much for me. The ocean views are insane, I admit. But it's…meh."

"What's your favorite style?" Griff asks.

When I look up, he's not watching Nia for her reply. He's staring at me, his expression dissecting. He's already figured out I'll let her choose the house. His raised brow also says he thinks that's very interesting…

"Oh!" Nia stops on a page suddenly, her eyes going wide.

"Yeah, when I looked at that, I wasn't sure what to make of it. It looks…"

"Totally charming." A smile lights up her face.

Really? "I was going to say mountain cabin meets tropical cabana."

She nods enthusiastically. "The rustic wooden beams framing the family room add so much visual interest. But then the carved balusters and iron spindles make it look more refined. The wainscoting around the room ties it all together. Nothing is predictable. The kitchen is transitional with an almost cottage vibe, but it's definitely big enough. And that Sub-Zero refrigerator!"

Griff warms to the subject. "Four patios, three facing the ocean. An outdoor shower, a library, a home office, a pool…"

"And a fireplace in the master," she breathes.

"Which you'll never use in Maui." Maxon chuffs. "Trust me, you'll look at it longingly a lot and turn on the ceiling fans."

"The fans sound practical," I mutter, wondering why anyone would build a fireplace in a home where the temperature rarely falls below seventy degrees.

The smile disappears from Nia's face. "You're right. Never mind."

Providing well for her is one of the things I can do. So is indulging her. If she wants a fireplace, I don't understand…but if that will help persuade her to marry me, she'll have a damn fireplace.

While she's looking out the window to her left, I catch Griff's stare and point to the listing in my hand. He nods and thankfully fills the rest of the drive by catching us up on some possible locations they've found for my offices.

Finally, we reach Noah and Harlow's massive place. Noah comes out to greet me, carrying a huge pair of tongs and wearing an apron that reads I TURN GRILLS ON. He gives me a brief, brotherly hug. "Good to see you, Evan."

"You, too. Thanks for letting me stay with you for the holiday."

"We're family, man."

I smile. After spending a lot of years without one, having the boisterous Reed clan is a blessing. "I hope you don't mind one more to the party. Noah, this is Nia. And she's a fan of yours."

"Then she's definitely welcome." He puts out his hand. "Hi."

"Oh, my god. Hi. If my mom was still alive, she'd be freaking right now with me. She was a fan, too."

"Thanks. Sorry for your loss."

"I appreciate that."

When she falls a little quiet, I wrap my arm around her, caress her shoulder. It's my silent way of telling her I'm here for her. I wasn't there much when her mother died. I gave her whatever time off she needed. I didn't attend the funeral; Becca didn't think it would be appropriate or welcome. I didn't see a reason to disagree. I assumed she had other friends and family to help her along. I didn't realize until now how alone she must have felt, and I regret that.

"Gorgeous place," Nia murmurs. "Thanks for letting me crash your holiday."

Noah takes in my possessive stance and smiles. "Not at all. We're glad you came."

Behind him, Harlow emerges in a red strapless dress, her dark hair a silky cloud of curls around her slender shoulders as she walks toward me without her normal easy gait.

I blink. "Wow, you look so pregnant."

Nia elbows me. "You did *not* just say that."

My sister laughs as she approaches me for a hug. "I am so pregnant. Blame the big guy."

"I don't mind being guilty." Noah presses a kiss to her cheek, then turns toward the patio. "I've got to get back to the grill before I burn dinner."

When he's gone, Harlow sizes Nia up with a glance and an approving smile. "Welcome. When the guys break away for 'man talk' after dinner, I'll ply you full of wine, pump you for information about this one"—she points at me—"and totally ask about your eye shadow technique. Whatever you did looks great."

Nia's smile widens, and I can tell she already likes my sister. "Deal, but I'll be asking you questions about your guy, too. How did you even meet?"

"Griff and Maxon had me housesitting this place before Noah moved in. I had no idea who he was when he showed up, but I told him I wanted sex." Harlow winks. "He let me stay."

While Nia apparently finds that funny, I groan. "I didn't need to hear that."

"Yeah, we didn't, either." Maxon grimaces.

Griff nods, and they both disappear into the house, rolling our luggage. I take my computer bag and follow as Keeley and Britta bustle forward. Actually, waddle might be a better word. They look even more pregnant than Harlow, but I refrain from mentioning that since it's apparently not tactful.

"Hey, cutie," Keeley says playfully as she moves in for a hug. "Happy to be out of Seattle's cold and rain?"

"I have to admit it's nice for a change." I turn to my side. "Ladies, this is Nia Wright."

"Your assistant?" Britta looks surprised as she hugs me, too.

"And…my girlfriend. I asked her to come with me for the holiday."

"We're glad you could make it. I'm Britta, Griff's wife." She smiles.

Keeley squeals as I finish off the introductions. "So the playlist I made for your first date was with Nia?"

"It was," I admit as I head into the cool, shaded house.

"I really liked the songs," Nia says. "Thanks for thinking of us."

Keeley beams and rubs her distended belly. "I have to do something now that the doctor wants me off my feet most of the time. I'm certainly not teaching any more yoga classes or singing karaoke unless I'm lying down."

"Is it a boy or girl?" Nia asks.

"I want it to be a surprise. My mom and Britta's mom know. They're arranging all the stuff for the nursery and they're going to decorate everything while we're recovering at the hospital." Keeley bites her lip. "I'm getting nervous. Less than two months to go now."

"You're going to be fine," Britta assures.

"Evan says you two are due at almost the same time," Nia mentions.

"It will be a race to see which of us gives birth first."

"I'm hoping it will be you," Keeley squeaks. "I've never done this birth thing. You're the pro…"

"Once doesn't make me a pro. It was just enough for me to know there are parts to the process I'd rather forget." Britta grins.

Nia smiles, too. "Do you know the sex of your baby?"

"We're having another boy. I was hoping we'd give our son, Jamie, a sister, but no."

"Next time…" Griff slides by his wife, pressing a kiss on her shoulder and a caress to her hip.

"I don't know about more babies, mister," she calls after him as he grabs a beer from the fridge and loosens his tie.

He pops the cap off the bottle and flashes her a smile that explains why he was able to seduce so many women before he married her.

Keeley giggles. "Maxon and I are talking about more. Well, Maxon is. I told him I have to see how this one goes. I really like sleep. I don't know how I'm going to function without it."

Everyone laughs.

Noah sticks his head in from the patio and informs everyone that dinner is almost ready. The women finish setting the table, and Nia does her best to help, though I'm sure she's tired from traveling.

Minutes later, we're sitting down to steaks and grilled vegetables, fresh pineapple, island breezes, and a lot of laughter. I just met these people a few months ago. Barged into their lives, really. It was awkward at first, and now…it's as if I belong. As if I've always belonged.

I think relocating to Maui is the right move. I intend to convince Nia to come with me as my wife.

We share a boisterous dinner to the soundtrack of one of Keeley's chill playlists in the background. I only recognize one Dido tune. Something about the best day of my life. Yeah, this is beginning to rank up there. There's beer for the guys, and true to her word, Harlow opens a bottle of red, despite the fact my girl is the only one who can drink it. There's laughs, gentle teasing, a lot of talk of the future, and a good time. I can picture the eight of us here over the years, growing closer as a family. I like the vision, except…they'll all have children, and I'm not ready or willing to endure the possibility of loss again. I've mourned Becca, but for the last few weeks in particular, I've felt the gnawing grief of wishing I was holding my son or daughter now…while knowing I never will.

It's a conundrum I'm unsure how to fix.

When the meal is over, everyone stands. By unspoken agreement, the guys start clearing the table and doing the dishes. The ladies pick up the rest of the vino and escort Nia outside, already deep in conversation.

"What's that about?" I ask the other men.

"Girl talk," Griff says cryptically with a saccharine smile.

In other words, they're going to grill her. Because they think she's not good enough for me? Because they suspect she pursued me for the wrong reasons? The notion makes me angry. "Nia is a great assistant, friend, and human being. She's not after my money. I'm the one who started this. She—"

"Hey, you don't have to justify her to us," Noah assures. "She seems great, and this is the happiest we've seen you."

"Exactly," Maxon puts in.

I let out a breath and frown. "Then why are your wives all circling her like they're vultures and she's prey?"

"They want answers," Griff supplies. "And all the juicy details. How was your first date?"

Maxon nods in agreement. "Your first kiss?"

"Your first..." Noah doesn't finish his question, just grins.

"She shouldn't have to explain us to anyone." I head off to rescue her.

My oldest brother stops me. "My wife will ply gently. You know Keeley. She'll joke and set Nia at ease, make her laugh. And if Nia doesn't feel like saying anything, she doesn't have to. I'm sure she has no trouble saying no. But they just want to know if she's content and invested...or if she could use a little help understanding how to speak Reed."

"God knows I needed help," Noah puts in.

"And they want to know if they should start planning a wedding," Griff adds.

I huff. "I hope they find out and pass the answer on to me."

The three of them exchange glances. "You don't know?"

"Everything is new. And we're still getting to know each other as something other than boss and assistant."

"But she's still working for you?" Griff asks.

"Yeah." For now. I don't want to think about what happens if she decides otherwise—or the Lunds manage to snatch her away.

"Is she making the move here, too?"

"Maybe. She's still deciding."

Noah rolls his eyes. "Dude, if you're moving here in six weeks and want her to come along, you have to help her make up her mind fast. The relationship might be new, but you two seem pretty serious."

Like their wives are doing to Nia, they're prying. It's embarrassing. On the other hand, they've all gotten married in the last year. And they all had to hustle like hell to get their wives to say "I do." It's possible they know something about women and relationships I don't.

"It is. I've asked her to marry me. I don't have any idea if she'll say yes. She's cautious and hard to read...and I'm used to Becca, who went along with whatever I thought was best. Nia is totally different."

"Does she love you?" Griff asks, his voice low and serious.

"I don't know, and it's not relevant. I'm not looking for romance, just a wife."

The three of them exchange a longer glance. Clearly, they think I'm insane. Whatever.

"And she knows how you feel about that?" Maxon prods me.

"Totally. I was honest. I'd never want to be anything less with her."

Maxon and Griff just groan.

"Well..." Noah scratches at his five o'clock shadow. "That's one way of doing it."

I frown. "What other way is there?"

The trio look at one another again before Noah speaks up. "The underhanded, not-going-to-take-no-for-an-answer way. Want pointers?"

"No. I want her to see the value of the arrangement and enter into it with her eyes wide open. I don't want to deceive or lie to her."

"That's not what we mean."

"Think of it as you giving her what she wants...so you can get what you want," Maxon clarifies.

"I don't understand."

"Put a positive spin on things," Griff adds. "Persuade her. Show her how good it can be using whatever you've got in your arsenal. Help her see you and your relationship from a different perspective."

Noah nods. "If you do this right, you're guaranteed to walk away with a wife."

I hesitate. When they put it like that, I can't do any worse with their advice than I've been doing on my own. Because the truth is, if I can't say or do the right things in the next six weeks, Nia will walk away. And how much will I kick myself for not trying harder? They've obviously mastered this romance shit I'm so clueless about.

"All right. I'll try. Tell me everything."

CHAPTER NINE

Wednesday, November 22

TWO DAYS LATER, Nia seems really comfortable with my family. I've studied the copious notes I took on everything my brothers and my sister's husband suggested. They're smart and they're slick. If they're right, the way I've gone about persuading Nia to marry me is all wrong.

So today, she's going to see a whole new Evan.

"Where are you taking me?" she asks from the passenger's seat of the black Mercedes convertible I borrowed from Noah.

I've never seen the point of a vehicle like this—until now. It's deeply impractical...but damn fun to drive. The weather in Hawaii is good enough to justify having such a car, so I might buy one, especially since Nia squealed in delight when I told her we'd be riding in this sweet two-seater today.

"Why would I tell you when it's supposed to be a surprise? It's my turn to plan the date, remember?"

Beside me, she huffs. Her little pout makes me laugh. As the wind whips around us and I head toward the north side of the island, I soothe her by taking her hand and brushing my thumb across her soft skin.

Since we're finally alone for the day, it's time to put my plan in motion. The advice I got rolls through my head.

Make her feel like she's the most beautiful woman in the world.

That won't be a problem. Nia *is* the most beautiful woman I know.

Make her feel like you can't wait to touch her.

Totally easy. I'm desperate to get my hands on her. I haven't in weeks. My damn well-meaning sister put Nia in her own room, so for the last two nights I've lain awake, alone and hard, wondering what Nia is doing on the other side of the wall and if she's thinking of me.

Make her feel like you can't wait to slide a ring on her finger.

Again, this shouldn't be difficult. The more time passes, the more I'm convinced this marriage makes sense. The more I'm certain she's the right choice. And the more I'm determined to see the stamp of my possession on her.

Make her come every single time you get her into bed.

I want to. I'm ready to try. I worry this sounds easier than it is, though. I lack her experience. I knew what buttons to push with Becca, but Nia is a completely different woman. Sure, the sex between us seemed scorching, but what if we're not as earth-shattering together as I remember? Anxiety and pent-up need gnaw at me, but if drowning a woman in pleasure is as effective as all three guys swore and our chemistry is everything I recall, then sex is a tool I should utilize now.

Make her feel like she's got you—body, heart, and soul.

Body, absolutely. I'll happily devote that to her. The rest of this notion is problematic, however. I don't think I can love again. Nia is certainly worthy, but once you love someone, logically you no longer have your heart to give to someone else. So…if I loved Becca, how could I possibly fall in love with Nia? It doesn't compute. But I will be a responsible, faithful, and dependable husband. No one will be more important to me. Can't that be enough?

"All right," Nia says finally. "I accept that it's your turn and you're probably not going to tell me what you've planned for us."

"I'm not."

"Meanie." Her pout deepens. "At least tell me where you went yesterday? You were gone for hours."

Does she want to know because she missed me? "Didn't you enjoy your time by the pool with the ladies?"

"I did. We had a lot of fun. They're great to hang out with and easy to talk to. And very curious about you."

"Well, Griff, Maxon, and I worked, scouting potential office spaces on the island, just in case." Which is true, but that's not all we accomplished.

"Any location you liked?"

"A few. Still narrowing it down. If the Stratus deal falls apart and I end up moving the company to the island, I'll pick somewhere close to the new house."

She cocks her head. "Why would it fall apart when you finally have the deal you want?"

"I never trust anything until the ink is dry."

"But you're planning to say yes?"

"Why would I say no? Granted, I don't like the fact they're trying to lock down all the employees for two years, and Lund has made it clear he's done negotiating. But—"

"*All* the employees? Does that apply to me, too?"

"Everyone, unless they leave Stratus before I sell." I try not to grit my teeth. "I intend to take you with me, Nia."

She looks wide-eyed. "When are you going to tell everyone so they can start deciding what they want to do?"

It's a fair question. I don't have an answer. "As soon as I read through the latest offer they sent, scan the details, and see if they've truly met all my terms so I can actually close the deal. You still think selling is a billion-dollar mistake?"

"I think they'll run your business into the ground in under twelve months because they don't have the knowledge or the passion you do. How would you feel if Stratus was no more?"

I can't imagine Douglas Lund would be dumb enough to spend that much money on a company only to kill it off. But hypothetically, it's possible. Weirder things have happened. "It would suck."

Years of hard work...gone. Logically, it shouldn't matter. I will have made an astronomical profit and gotten out at Stratus's peak—every entrepreneur's dream. But I admit, I don't much like that notion.

"It would, and I think you can build the company into something even bigger. But whatever you decide, at least you have a lot of amazing places to choose from once you relocate here."

"I do. They showed me a few areas yesterday so I could get a feel for the island." I peer over at Nia. "Can you see yourself living here?"

"I'm not sure. It's really different from Seattle."

"It is, but maybe we were both stuck in a rut there, and this move will be a good thing."

"Maybe. It's hard to say after only thirty-six hours. But your family is wonderful. I'm glad you all connected. Moving here will definitely be good for you."

"I want it to be good for us." I squeeze her hand. "Have you given more thought to marrying me?"

She nibbles pensively on her lip. "Every day. But nothing has changed, Evan. I can't marry you for purely practical reasons."

Because she wants love. I hold in a sigh. I have to take the guys' advice and prove I can make her deliriously happy, even if those three words will never cross my lips.

"You wouldn't be. There are a lot of wonderful reasons, too. But let's enjoy our time together today and worry about the future later."

As I suspected, my suggestion stuns her. "You, putting something off? Isn't that impractical?"

I grin wryly. "You wanted to date and get to know each other better, so this is me being wild and crazy…for you."

"Who are you and what have you done with Evan?"

"I have an unpredictable side," I insist. "You'll see."

I'm going to persuade you to say yes to being my wife.

Nia is still eyeing me like she's wondering what I'm up to. "Why?"

When I roll to a stop at a light, I reach across the car, wrap my palm around her nape, and drag her lips under mine. As soon as our mouths meet, we're connected by more than our kiss. I groan. It feels like forever since I've been this close to her.

She opens beneath me instantly, and I'm grateful as hell she's receptive after I've bungled everything up to this point. But she's right there with me, lips sliding open with a little pant of need, pressing in as if she can't get enough of me, either. Something about the way she tastes obliterates rational thought and rouses the primal animal in me.

Her tongue dances with mine. I grab her, lunge, thrust again, needing more. She throws herself against me, fingers clutching at me as she whimpers and falls deeper into the kiss.

Then suddenly she's pulling away.

"Nia..." I grip her nape tighter. "I don't want to stop."

"The light."

I look up. It's green, and I suddenly remember: traffic, civilization, the critical plans I have today. If I do this right, I'll be able to kiss her any day, any time, any way—forever.

Swallowing back a curse, I press on the accelerator and mingle with traffic.

Less than five silent minutes later, we arrive. As I park, I see her looking around. In typical Nia fashion, she understands immediately.

"We're taking a helicopter ride?"

"What better way to see the island than from above?"

I had to talk myself into this. Statistically, helicopters are one of the least safe forms of transportation, and I understand all too well the significance of weather, wind, and the reliability of the vehicle's maintenance and performance. Luckily, this is a nearly perfect day in Hawaii, and the pilot is someone Maxon and Griff know well. He's been flying for thirty years, and they swear there's no one better.

If showing Nia that I can be romantic will help sway her to say "I do," then I'm willing to take a few calculated risks.

We enter the no-nonsense office. Gary greets me, a smile lifting his graying beard as he shakes my hand. He's wearing a loud Hawaiian shirt and a tan that makes his blue eyes look almost electric.

"Welcome. You're one of Maxon and Griff's brothers, huh? They said you're moving here."

"I am. They seem really happy on the island, so why not?"

"I don't know if Maui is ready for another Reed." He chuckles.

I don't bother to explain that my last name is Cook and I'm the illegitimate offspring. It's too complicated. Besides, I came from the Reed line, and based on everything my siblings' spouses have said, there are some traits inherent in all of Barclay's children. Stubbornness ranks high on the list. So does a complicated love life.

"I'll try to keep the impact of my presence here to a dull roar," I promise.

Gary gives me a thumbs-up, then gets us suited up with safety gear, gives us preflight instructions, then takes us outside by his chopper. Nia is unusually quiet.

I glance her way as I take her hand. "You okay?"

"Nervous. I've never done this."

"It'll be a first for us both, then. But Maxon and Griff swear this will be amazing."

A tentative smile breaks across her face. "I've always wanted to ride in a helicopter, but I was too chicken."

I drop a kiss on her forehead, resisting the urge to go in for more. "So we'll tackle this together."

After Gary does his prefight check, we load up. Moments later, accompanied by the sound of whirring blades, we take off. Nia grips my hand, her nails digging into my knuckles. The airport gives way to surrounding civilization, then to lush fields of sugar cane and tempestuous blue water bashing against sand and rocks.

Gary gets his tour underway quickly. "The windward side of the island is a lush rainforest that gets about three hundred inches of rain annually. The leeward side is more like a desert. Its annual rainfall is less than twelve inches. There are even places on that side of the island with growing cacti and roaming scorpions."

We float around the shore, oohing and aahing over all the stunning sights of lush mountains, sheared cliffs, and sweeping waterfalls. We see a reef teeming with green sea turtles and blue, blue water. It's truly paradise.

"I've never been anywhere so beautiful," Nia breathes.

"Me, either." I squeeze her hand. "Even though I've been here twice before, I didn't appreciate it as much as I should have until now."

"Isn't it peaceful up here?" Gary asks into his mic, which links directly to our headphones. At our nods, he goes on. "Over there, that crescent-shaped island is a great place to snorkel. Lots of tropical fish. Heading back this way, we're going to take a climb above that ten-thousand-foot mountain."

Nia grips me as we glide into a cloud bank at the crest of a peak and seem to disappear into nowhere. I hope to hell Gary knows where he's going. I'm all for having my heart race today, but not in fear. But he's a pro, steering us through the cloud bank until we crest on the other side to another gorgeous view of the ocean.

For nearly two hours, he takes us around the island. After showing us the east coast, we move south, then fly back around to the west, over Wailea. When we hover above Lahaina, he identifies some points of interest before we're back out over the ocean, skirting the coast of Lanai before making our way up to Molokai. I'm shocked to find out that about half that island is completely off the grid.

Nia seems every bit as enthralled as I am until Gary finally turns back to Maui and puts the chopper down in the middle of a field near the coast.

She turns to me in confusion. "What are we doing here?"

"Enjoying ourselves for the afternoon. C'mon."

Gary helps us out, then takes off with a friendly wave.

She's still gaping when I snag her hand and lead her up a small hill, toward a sprawling white house shimmering in the tropical sun. I'm lucky my brothers seem to know everyone on the island and don't have any problem calling in favors. Of course, the fact I'm willing to spend money, especially if it advances the cause of Nia saying yes, helps a lot, too.

When we reach the house, the ocean views dazzle me all over again. The doors and windows are open to take advantage of the trade winds. There's seemingly no one around for miles.

"What are we doing here?"

"First, we're eating lunch."

When I urge her to follow me, she does slowly, gaping. "I don't understand."

"This is our private paradise for the day. You, me, an oasis for two, and no one to disturb us for hours." As we walk around the side of house, I ease her against the wall and face her, pressing my body against hers. "I enjoy being with my family, but I want time alone with you. So I planned today for us. No one to interfere. No other responsibilities or expectations. We can relax and talk and do whatever we want."

A little smile creeps across her lips as she stares at me as if she's trying to figure me out. "You're up to something."

I wink at her. "A lot of me is up to something."

Nia rolls her eyes and laughs. "You didn't have to do all this, you know."

"I wanted to." I cup her face in my hands and delve into her eyes. "You should know how important you are to me. I'll always do everything I can to make you feel special. And if your exes have been too stupid to do that, I'm here to prove I'm smarter, more determined, and ready to make you happy."

Her eyes tear up as she blinks at me. "What are you saying, Evan?"

I press a kiss to her lips and have to tear myself away before I get swept up in Nia again. "I'm saying you're the best thing that's happened to me in years. Maybe I should regret shoving my way into your dressing room and your life, but I don't want to be without you—now or ever. I'm hoping like hell you feel the same."

A silvery teardrop falls past her lashes and onto her dusky, satiny cheek. As I brush it away with my thumb, I feel my hand shake. The naked need on her face stuns me. For the first time, I'm convinced she feels something for me…

"Nia? You okay, honey?"

"I gave in to the pull between us that night because I couldn't help myself. But I've been wondering ever since if it was just sex and convenience for you, whether you saw me as an easy way to curb your grief and loneliness. And I…"

When more tears come, I caress her face and thumb her lower lip. "No. None of that."

I hate like hell that I ever made her feel insecure. Plenty of her exes have given her too many reasons to guard her heart. Even if she never loved them, their disregard for her feelings must have hurt. Until Maxon, Griff, and Noah verbally slapped me with some reality, I don't think I came across as any less selfish or focused on my own needs.

"Then I don't understand," she murmurs.

"I shouldn't be surprised. Communication in the office only works between us because you read my mind more often than not. Maybe I expected you to somehow understand how I saw our future together. But what we have isn't a meeting or a memo. I have to show you what I have in mind, so that's what I'm trying to do. My goal is for you to be wearing the brightest, happiest smile of your life when you say 'I do.'"

She sniffles as another tear falls. "When did you get romantic?"

"When I realized I was being an ass." I brush her tears away with my fingertips, then kiss their wet paths before I lead her toward the backyard again. "I'm sorry."

"Apology accepted." We emerge from the shady side yard and into the bright sun bathing the deck. She glances around the huge private space with a gasp, the sound nearly swallowed by gentle winds, swaying palms, and distant waves. Then she fixes her gaze on the tropical pool mere steps away. "Wow, if this is how you're going to say you're sorry, this place is worth a little suffering."

Her teasing makes me laugh—and gives me hope. "You keep me guessing. I like that, you know."

"Really?" She gives her lip a pensive nibble. "I've always had the feeling Becca was more predictable."

"She was."

"And you liked that about her. I've been thinking that's what you want."

How did I not know—or at least guess—she felt this way? Probably because I knew it was incorrect and, therefore, groundless. But Nia had no way of knowing. It's not her job to guess; it's my job to tell her. I can't thank Maxon, Griff, and Noah enough for that gem of wisdom.

"You know, when I decided to start looking for a wife, I probably did want that because I wanted order to the chaos in my life. But as time has gone on..." I shake my head. "No, as I spent more time with you, I realized I didn't need what I had before. The day I told you to place the wife-wanted ad, you asked if I that was how I intended to replace Becca. I told you no one could. It's true, and I can't bring her back. But I can honestly say after being with you that I don't need any semblance of my old life anymore. I need to move on and embrace the future. And I can't see doing that with anyone but you."

To my surprise—and delight—Nia comes closer. "If you don't stop, you're going to make me all mushy and melty."

I laugh. "I want you mushy and melty."

"Not until after the food. You promised me lunch."

Though I'm not excited about letting her go, I release her and lead her to the table. There's a feast, a bottle of champagne, and two flutes waiting for us.

We eat chicken, fruit, salad, and coconut pudding. Every bite is delicious, and the champagne takes the edge off my nerves. Instrumental mood music plays softly in the background as we talk about how incredible the helicopter tour was and how much the thought of living on this island already excites us. Our future stretches out in front of me. I can almost reach it. I'm getting closer... If I can just keep saying and doing the right things, maybe today will end exactly the way I planned it.

"Want to swim?" I ask as we stand and stretch, lazy from the food, booze, and sun.

"I didn't bring a suit."

"So?" I give her a sly smile.

Nia searches the deserted patio, her dark eyes dancing. "Are you proposing we skinny-dip?"

"I'm proposing marriage. But I'm suggesting skinny-dipping for now.

Interested?"

"In broad daylight? At a stranger's house?"

"Yes."

"You *are* full of surprises today."

I grin. "Is that a yes?"

"Why not?"

I expect her to find her way to the nearby cabana to take off her clothes. I envision her emerging in a tightly wrapped towel and finding the most shadowed corner of the backyard before she works up the courage to drop the length of terry cloth and jump in the water. But that's what Becca would have done—if she'd agreed to skinny-dip at all. Not Nia. She kicks her shoes off and under the table, pulls her T-shirt over her head, then shimmies out of her shorts. Suddenly, she's wearing nothing but a lacy underwire bra in a shimmering cinnamon shade and a pair of matching boy shorts that do a wonderfully inadequate job of covering everything I want my hands and mouth on.

I groan as I reach for the hem of my shirt, wondering how fast I can get everything off and feel her naked against me.

"You're moving slow," she taunts as she fiddles with one of her bra straps, flicking it down her shoulder, then the other, so the soft cups cling to her breasts.

"You're tormenting me."

Nia smiles, then drops her gaze to my stiff cock. "It's working."

Can't refute that. "Take off the rest. I want you naked."

At my command, her nostrils flare. Her breathing quickens. She licks her lips as she reaches behind her for the hook.

As I rip my shirt over my head and toss it across a chair, she turns away and manages to unfasten her bra. It slides from her body, baring her back to the shining sun. I'm fascinated by her skin, by its lush pigment, by the hues, shadows, and luster of it.

I can't stand not touching her for another minute.

Sidling up behind her, I hook my thumbs in her barely there underwear and kiss my way from her shoulder to her neck. "Hurry."

When I slide her panties over her hips, she shimmies. Her sweet backside sways and moves against me. I skim my hands back up her thighs, planting one on her hip and circling the other around her waist. I'm a tall man with big hands. When I lay my palm flat, I'm hyperaware of the fact that my pinky stretches so, so close to her pussy. Her heat rises up to my fingers.

She draws in a ragged breath. "Evan?"

"Want me to touch you?" I drift a little lower, my fingertip resting a fraction of an inch from her cleft.

"Yes."

She sounds breathy, aroused. I'm tall enough to peer over her shoulder and see that I'm right. Her chest rises and falls. Her taut, dark nipples shine in the sun. I want her now. My hands and mouth all over her. My cock deep inside her. In my head, I know I can't rush this; she's too important. On the other hand, I'm more than eager to dazzle her with orgasms...if I can.

I lower my hand, closing the distance between my touch and her nerve-laden clit. I don't even try to keep my hungry mouth off her skin. Instead, I drag my lips up her neck and toward her ear. Nia rewards me with a moan and a roll of her hips against my erection.

Pressing against her luscious backside, I skim my fingers down to find her slick folds. She gasps. Shit, she's soft as silk. I smell her arousal blending with the perfume of flowers in the air. Everything about this moment heightens my senses. I know I'm in the right place with the right woman at the right time.

As I run my fingers into her furrow and gather her moisture, I nip at the sensitive spot below her lobe. "I've missed you, honey. I've missed the taste of your kiss and the way you call my name when you're near climax. I've missed breathing you in when I'm inside you. I miss feeling close to you. I've missed feeling like you're mine."

She melts back into me, head braced against my shoulder, eyes closed. "I've missed you, too, Evan. More than you know."

Longing bleeds from her breathy admission. She's under my spell. I'll do whatever it takes to keep her there.

With a moan, I strum my fingers over her hardening bud. "Want to show me how much?"

Her breath catches. She gives a frantic nod as her body tightens around my touch. Power floods my veins. I'm holding her pleasure in my hand—literally. It thrills me. Becca had so many danger points and no-go zones in bed. Nia seems wide open and ready to do whatever pleases us both. The notion is dizzying.

I lift my free hand to her breast and thumb her nipple relentlessly. I hope she's sensitive here because I suddenly find myself fascinated. Her weight fills my palm. She tenses and whimpers as I pinch and stroke, envelop and twist the tip.

"Evan..." She reaches back to grip my thigh.

"Feel good?"

"Yeah," she breathes.

"Spread your legs. I want to touch you deeper."

Nia doesn't hesitate. I'm gratified when she slides her feet farther apart on the deck. I don't waste a second before plunging my fingers inside her. She's slick and tight and like something out of my fantasies. No wonder being inside her once somehow rewired my sex drive to respond to her completely.

As she sucks in a breath, I drag my fingers across her clit again, brushing, teasing, tormenting. Her nails dig into my thigh. I see her nipples tighten even more, the tips gleaming in the afternoon sun.

I don't let up. I don't stop for any moan, whimper, or plea. If orgasms will help her see how good we'll be together, she's going to have them. The fact I love giving them to her is a bonus.

Suddenly, her entire body seizes up. She's holding her breath, shuddering and tense against me. Her clit swells and hardens. Her pussy isn't merely slick anymore. She's wet. She's juicy.

She's mine.

"Come, honey. Right on my hand. Let me feel you. Let me hear you. Give it all to me."

Seconds later, climax comes fast and breaks hard. She keens out and convulses, chest buckling, hips rolling, lips parted with a scream of ecstasy. Pleasure suspends her for long moments, and I drink every moment in, teeming with triumph. Eagerness to be inside her—and to have the right to fill her every night—surges in a hot spill through my blood.

With a rhythmic sweep of my fingers, I ride out her climax all the way to her gasping, frenzied end. Nia has barely had time to go limp in my arms before I turn her to face me and grab her body against mine. As she wraps her legs around my waist, I drop my head and seize her mouth, plunging hot, fast, and deep—the way I intend to do with my body soon.

She clings, moaning into my mouth. As I cross the patio, she's completely attuned to me, every whimper and shudder given to me totally and freely. This heady willingness is unlike anything I've ever felt. I'm greedy for more.

When I reach the table, I swipe one arm across its cool, flat surface, tumbling empty cups onto their sides and moving dishes out of my damn way. Then I lay Nia across the cleared surface and stare. At her darkened eyes and skin. At her stiff nipples still begging for attention. At her swollen, saturated pussy.

Yes. To all of that, hell yes.

I pull up a chair and sit between her splayed legs, then grip her lush hips and drag her to the edge. "Come for me again."

Nia barely has time to take a breath before I'm on her once more, digging my tongue between her pouting folds and licking my way up her center, finally fucking tasting her.

Oh, god. If I thought I enjoyed stroking her to orgasm, I can already tell I'm going to love tonguing her to one way, way more.

Her taste isn't like anything I've ever had in my mouth. In some ways, she reminds me of wine—rich, complex, and intoxicating. But she's more. Mysterious, remarkable.

Mine.

I open my mouth wide, as if I can inhale every succulent part of her at once. I'm fucking greedy.

Cupping her thighs in my hands, I spread her wider and settle my tongue over her clit. I lap. She wriggles. I suckle. She jolts. I go deeper, demand more. Her reactions are instant, absolute, and perfect.

The man in me wants to witness every moment of her surrender. This time, I won't be satisfied by having her in a dark corner while she's half-covered by whatever she's wearing because I'm too frantic to be inside her. No, I want the golden sunlight around us as I catalog every dip, swell, valley, nook, and cranny of her body.

Easing away from her sweet sex, I thumb her clit and stare. Her sleek, dark thighs are slender and smooth. Her flat belly leads to a pair of breasts tipped with swelling nipples I can't wait to get my mouth on. She's tossed her head back to give me the perfect view of her arched throat, her graceful arms tossed above her head in abandon. Even her feet are dainty with high arches and bright toenails. The best part, however, is definitely in front of me.

Her pussy is spread open like a treat. She looks nothing like Becca, but that's especially true here. My wife was pale, pink, and shrouded in curls. Nia's sex is devoid of anything that shields her from me. Here, she's saturated with a darker hue than the rest of her skin. Because she's aroused? That idea sends my need for her higher.

I'm fascinated as I spread her open and take another long lick at her center. Beyond her folds, she's a deep, bold pink—almost red. The contrast is mesmerizing. I want to be right there, sliding my cock into that bright, snug clasp.

As soon as she comes again.

I redouble my effort to ramp her up so I can feel her shatter on my tongue. Under my lips, her whole body turns rigid. As I flick her clit, her breaths turn raspy. She keens, her back arching as she grips my hair and pulls me in closer.

It doesn't take long before she's thrashing, lifting to me, and encouraging me to give more.

"Evan… Evan, damn. So good. You make me feel… Yes!"

I love that she's vocal about her pleasure. I especially love that she lets me arouse her however I want.

Nia is close now. I can see her, smell her, taste the change in her flavor. I dive deeper, thrust two fingers into her empty, clutching opening, and feel her bud surge hard with blood and need against my tongue.

She's so ready.

Her fists grab at my hair as she rocks against my mouth, her breath turning to a heavy exhalation, then a squeal, followed by a throaty growl of satisfaction that lasts for long, electric moments. She holds nothing back, and this climax is twice as long and strong as the first. She jolts and shudders as her nails scratch at my scalp and she drags in more air so she can let out another howling cry. I can actually feel her pulsing. Knowing I can unravel her—and that she won't hide her reactions from me—is like nothing I've ever experienced.

Finally, she sighs and goes limp under my hands. "Oh, my gosh. I can't move."

I give her a satisfied smirk as I fish into my pocket for a condom. I planned ahead this time, and I'm beyond ready to lose myself inside her. She watches me with heavy-lidded eyes as I tear open the foil packet. Before I can roll it down my aching length, she takes it from my hand.

"Want help?" She doesn't wait for my reply, just sits up and fits the tip over the head.

It's the first time she's truly touched me, and damn if her fingers working the latex down my length isn't already undoing me.

"Nia..."

She smiles at my distress and continues on, slowly destroying my composure with each brush of her hand. By the time I'm sheathed, my chest is rising and falling, lungs audibly working. My entire body is tense. I'm losing my mind.

Somewhere, I find the sanity to lift her from the table. I ignore her squeal of surprise as I settle her onto my lap, her legs straddling me. Then I press against her opening and work her down every one of my desperate inches. By the time I'm balls deep, she's wide-eyed and shuddering.

"Evan..." My name is a gasp on her lips as her nails dig into my shoulders.

"I've dreamed of being inside you again. This feels amazing."

She gives me a silent, frantic nod before she plants her knees on either side of my hips and begins a torturous rhythm. I brace my hands on her waist and groan at the instant friction.

Clearly, I wasn't imagining how good we are together. At all. It's every bit as amazing as I remember—and more. Holy hell… I can't thrust into her fast enough. I can't surge into her deep enough. I can't suck her sweet nipples hard enough. Being with her is paradise and purgatory. Agony and ecstasy. It's wrenching and animal and shattering. And I want more.

Taking her ass in my hands, I rise to my feet and lift her. Automatically, she wraps her arms and legs around me. Our eyes meet. She looks breathless and stunned.

"What are you doing?"

"Taking you to bed."

"What?" She's clearly dazed.

Her question morphs into a whimper when I begin to trek across the patio—and gravity propels her farther onto my cock with every step. Her nails dig into my shoulders. Her eyes plead as she writhes and moans. As she wordlessly begs me for more.

I can't spare the brainpower to respond. I'd far rather put my energy into seizing her mouth than speaking anyway.

Once I fuse my lips to hers, I have to fight not to come undone. The house is only a dozen steps away, but as torqued up as I feel, it might as well be a thousand. I hope I fucking last until I can get her on her back.

I'm sweating as I step across the threshold. The cool shade and swirling air from the ceiling fans brush my damp skin. My head is swimming. I don't know how I'm holding it together. As my lips crush hers, my tongue dominates our kiss. I try to focus on her pleasure, as my hazy memory guides me into the master bedroom.

The instant we reach the cool space, I topple her onto the crisp white bed and follow her down, shoving myself even deeper into her body.

We groan together. The sensations are like a supernova—hot, unstable, never meant to last.

I set a pace that's rapid and harsh. It feels as amazing as the first time, but I'm fucking her with the desperation of a man worried that this time with her will be my last. I grip her hips, nip at her shoulder, and plunge my way into her with enough force to send her sliding up the slick sheets.

"Evan..."

Yes, I feel her tense. I'm right there with her, bucking and stroking toward the titanic explosion I know is almost on us.

"I'm here. Open your eyes. Look around." I have to hold myself together long enough for her to do that.

Her lashes flutter up so slowly, it's as if her body is using all its resources simply to breathe and process the pleasure. Finally, she blinks a few times and the room must come into focus because she gasps. "The fireplace!"

"And the house. They can be ours," I assure her between gritted teeth and hard strokes. "Just. Say. Yes."

Nia doesn't answer, simply drags in another breath and stares at me, stunned. Damn, I can't not kiss her. She's the song stuck in my head. She's the fever igniting in my blood. I can't not be inside her in every way possible.

I take her mouth under mine one more time, and the pace of my thrusts ramps up. She's clamping down like her orgasm is right there, and I can't slow down. For good measure, I grind against her on the downward stroke and drag my crest against all the spots that make her clutch me and mewl.

And that does it. Her thighs and her body begin to quiver. Her breaths get faster. Her moans sound throatier. "Evan..."

"Say yes."

"Evan..." She's wailing now. It's prolonged, low, and loud as her fingers bite into me. She looks at me like there's something she wants to say.

"Give it to me." *One word.* I can't voice the rest of my demand because ecstasy notches up and nearly pulls me under.

"Evan, I-I…" She blinks, parts her lips, and seems to lose herself in my stare for timeless seconds. "I love you!"

Then she falls into climax.

Her words trip across my brain. I'm stunned. I'm shocked. That admission should not turn me on more. But it fucking thrills and unhinges me. It undoes me.

As far as I'm concerned, that's a yes.

The orgasm I'd been holding at bay breaks my restraint. My body takes over. My blood surges. A growl tears from my throat. I erupt and give myself over to Nia. If I thought our first time was amazing, the second is beyond all comprehension. I'm never letting her go. She *will* be my wife.

My spine melts more with each thrust. I meld into her, become one with her, as we share the shuddering ecstasy.

I'm light-headed and panting when I've sated the desire. Slowly, my breath returns. Reason reasserts itself. And I remember my plan.

With a grimace, I withdraw from the hot clasp of her body. I don't want to, but it's essential.

"Evan?" She sits up, her face tightening. "Say something."

I've never seen her expression so hesitant, her eyes so vulnerable. Because I didn't tell her I love her. But I have more than words to bestow on her. The house. The sex. And the thing I should have given her weeks ago.

"Nia, honey… Everything is fine. In fact, everything is great." I reach into the nightstand beside her, pull out a box, then kneel at her feet. "Because you are everything I want and I can't imagine living the rest of my life without you. I want to make you smile. I want to make you happier than you've ever imagined. I want to devote myself to you. Every day." Then I open the box to reveal the massive engagement ring I bought last weekend. When her eyes flare in shock and she covers her gaping mouth, I smile. "Nia Wright, marry me?"

CHAPTER TEN

"OH, MY GOD," Nia gasps.

Why does she look shocked—and not in a good way? "Aren't you happy? I thought you were saying yes."

"No."

She's serious.

"What? You said you loved me." Gaping, I close the ring box and stagger to my feet. "Why are you saying no?"

"What I mean is, I'm not answering your proposal right now. I'm…processing."

I still don't understand. "Processing what? The fact I gave you a ring? I'm just showing you I'm completely serious about getting married."

"I appreciate that you arranged this grand romantic proposal, but I still don't know how you feel?"

"Excited about our lives together." I dodge the L-word because I'm focused on giving her everything I can, not what I can't. "I intended to get married for practical reasons—until I touched you. Until I looked right in front of me and realized you're exactly who I need. Who I want. You've dated a lot of guys who didn't treat you the way they should have. I'll be different. I'll be devoted. I'll be faithful. I'll show you every day that you're the best thing in my life. Say yes. Make me the happiest man."

She bites her lip. "I want to. I think you mean all that. Just like I think you believe it's enough."

Is Nia really going to refuse me?

"It is. There's no logical reason for you not to be my wife."

"Except that you don't love me." Nia swallows. "And I don't know that you intend to. Will you let yourself fall for me? Ever?"

I push the ring box into her hands. "Does this look like I won't adore you? Like I won't pamper you and shower you with affection?"

Nia barely glances at the five carats of cushion-cut solitaire before she sets the ring on the mattress beside her. "Evan, that's not the same as love."

Maybe not, but why isn't that close enough? I grit my teeth and try to hang on to my composure. "Don't say no."

She pauses such a long time, and I find myself holding my breath. If she refuses me, I'm not sure what else I can do to persuade her.

Finally, she presses her lips together. "I don't want to. But I told you how I feel. Being with you has made me feel things... The way you touched me just now, I would have sworn you felt the same way."

The fact I'm not professing my undying love hurts her. I'm surprised by how much knowing that hurts me in turn. "Nia, there's no one else for me. I will give you every part of myself—my attention, my protection, my dedication, my fortune, my commitment."

"But not your heart."

How do I reassure her without giving her the words simply because she wants to hear them? "I don't know what to say. I've never felt about any woman the way I feel about you, not even Becca. It's like...I'm connected to you in a way I can't explain. And I don't want to live the rest of my life without you by my side. I don't know what you call that. I don't know the words for it. But I know that's what's happening with me."

When I take her hand, she meets my stare with tear-filled eyes. "You confuse me."

"I'm confused, too. You're really not accepting my proposal?"

She cups my cheek. "Everything in my head tells me to say no and walk away, let you move to Maui alone. But I can't."

Hope burns hot and instant. "So...you're saying yes?"

Nia shakes her head. "The first time you asked me to marry you, you said I could give you my answer before you relocate here. I need the next six weeks to decide."

"We can't just keep dating." It's not working. I'm spending time with her, but we're not close enough. It's not intimate enough. We're working together but leading separate personal lives. That hardly gives me the opportunity to convince her I can make her deliriously content even if I never speak that trio of cliché words. "It's not enough."

She blows out a breath. "Let me think."

I disappear into the bathroom, fighting the completely irrational urge to punch a wall. Why is she clinging to some unnecessary, antiquated notion of hearts and flowers? Why doesn't her logical mind tell her that I'd be so good to her?

Because she leads with her heart. Always has.

Fuck.

After I dispose of the condom and take a minute to bank my frustration, I emerge to see her, legs gathered against her chest, chin on her knees, slowly rocking. She's distraught. Guilt assails me. I should back down, but that seems too much like giving up—something I'm not prepared to do.

"Are you…breaking up with me?"

Nia lifts her head and regards me, brows furrowed. "No. I won't deny there's something strong between us. You say you've never felt this way about anyone. I haven't, either. Ever."

"Then let's get married. We'll figure everything out together."

Before I even finish speaking, she's already shaking her head. "That's not what marriage is for. I only want to get married once."

"I wanted that, too. But guess what?" I snap. Instantly, I wish I could take the words back. It's not Nia's fault that Becca is gone. "I'm sorry. I shouldn't have said that."

"Her death hurt you, and I understand you never thought you'd find yourself single and searching again. You're entitled to be confused. Angry even. Maybe I should be the one backing off so you have more time to grieve and decide—"

"I don't need time. I know what I want." I grab her arms. "I want you."

"But not because you love me." She wriggles free. "I'm not a consolation prize."

"Damn it. Do you not understand?"

She shakes her head. "I'm trying to see this from your point of view. You don't want to be alone or with someone you don't like. And you don't want to be with someone you have lousy sex with. I'm available, we're friends, and when we're together, it's all blazing skies and fireworks. Check, check, check. But I'm more than items on your list. I'm a woman." She claps an emphatic hand to her chest. "Maybe you don't relate, but I have feelings and dreams. And never once did I imagine myself saying, 'Even though you don't love me, I'll marry you for your companionship and your checkbook, baby.' That's not who I am."

I sigh. She's right. "How can we compromise?"

Nia falls silent. I feel my blood pressure rise. I'm not angry at her, just at the situation I don't know how to solve. Why doesn't simple logic make this better?

Nia rises from the bed and disappears onto the patio. I zip up my shorts and follow her out to the streaming late afternoon sun. She's wriggling into her clothes with shoulders slumped, as if she feels defeated.

God, I can't stand that. I hate that I've made her feel that way.

As she slides into her sandals, I approach her from behind and cup her shoulders. "Nia? Honey…"

But I don't know what to say. I have no answer except that I know she's the woman I'm supposed to spend the rest of my life with. I'm also convinced that, despite being in love with me, Nia is perfectly capable of living without me.

"Right now, I don't see how we work this out," she admits.

"We need more time together." Maybe an afternoon isn't enough for her to see how sincere I am. "Not at work. Time for just the two of us to focus on nothing but each other."

Slowly, she nods, nibbling on her lip. That's her I've-got-an-idea face. She's still working it out; I can tell. But something is forming.

"What if we lived together for the next six weeks?" She turns her focus on me. "See what develops between us?"

I don't love the idea…but I don't hate it, either. It's better than the two of us heading back to the mainland to live in our respective pads, only to see each other in the office or on occasional dates. A few weeks ago, I would have celebrated home-cooked meals and a cleaner apartment. But just being next to Nia is way more important than any of that. Getting to kiss her good morning…and worship her body all night. It gives me time to truly sweep her off her feet so she can't say no.

"That makes sense. You want to be sure before you say yes, and this will help."

"And you don't?"

"I'm already sure. But if you need more time—"

"I do. And I honestly think you do, too. I know you want to move on, but I think you need to ask yourself where your heart lies. If you can tell me how you feel about me in six weeks and you still want to marry me, maybe I'll say yes."

What she means is, if I can spew out a confession of love.

Fuck. This kind of emotional tripe goes against my grain. She knows that. Does she expect that I'll suddenly become impractical and sentimental and fall madly in love? Even as invested as I was in my marriage to Becca, I wasn't that guy.

On the other hand, my only options are to convince her we should be married or for me to spend all my foreseeable days alone.

"I'll make sure that maybe is a yes. When we get back, you can move your things into my penthouse—"

"No."

I raise a brow at her. "Why not? I have a bigger place. It's closer to the office. I have an amazing view."

"All of that is true, but your wife's ghost is everywhere, and I won't be living with her, too."

I pause. Maybe there's some truth to that. I think of Becca less these days. I don't imagine I'm seeing her out of the corner of my eye as often. But so much of her presence still lingers there. Every morning when I get dressed for work, I pass her clothes. I've never packed them away. I open the home office we shared and her meticulously organized papers still take up half the desk drawers because I've never bothered to cull through them. The few personal pictures in the apartment are those she hung. The handful of knickknacks and throw pillows I possess, she bought.

I might hate to leave the comfort of my bed, my shower, and my quiet. But I wouldn't want to live in any space in which Nia has cohabitated with another man. Every time I got inside her, I would wonder if she remembered having sex with him in the same bed.

"Have you lived in your place with an ex-boyfriend?"

Her face softens. "No."

"Had one spend the night there?"

Her expression closes up. "I've had a sex life; we've established that."

"So that's a yes?" I clench my jaw and look for alternatives. "Then we need to find someplace else."

"To live for six weeks? That makes no sense." She sighs. "Look, before you, I hadn't had sex in nearly six months. I haven't had anyone stay over at my place in almost a year."

I don't intend to get stubborn, but I can't seem to help it. "But if you've fucked someone else on that mattress, it's a no for me."

She scowls at me. "Actually, we fucked on the couch, then we fucked on the bed. What is your problem?"

I bristle. "I don't want to imagine anyone else touching you. And I don't want you thinking about it, either."

"I'm here with *you*."

"Then humor me. Let me replace the couch and the mattress."

"You're serious?"

I slant her an expression that tells her my mind is absolutely set. "When am I not?"

Suddenly, she laughs. "If I told you we had sex on the kitchen counters, would you replace those, too?"

"Yes. Did you?"

"No. I just really despise them."

Despite the tension, I laugh, too. "If it will make you happy, I'll replace them anyway."

"No. The place is only a rental, but a girl can dream." Then she blinks and looks around, seeming to remember where we are. "Did you already...buy this place?"

"I leased it for the day."

"Just because I said I liked it?" She still sounds shocked.

"Yes. I wanted you to spend some time here to see if you liked it well enough to want to live here. With me." *As my wife.*

"Evan, this may not work out. *We* may not work out. And I may not be moving to the island at all."

"I'm going to think positive. Maxon and Griff have been negotiating with the listing agent. They've nearly brokered a deal everyone can live with. All you have to do is say you like it."

Her mouth gapes open. "This is millions of dollars. You have to like it, too."

"It has a bedroom, bathroom, kitchen, and couch, along with a great place for a flat screen and my gaming console. My needs are met."

She rolls her eyes. "That's such a man thing to say. You really don't care about style or decor or..."

"No. I care about making you happy."

A heavy sigh passes her lips. "If we can't agree on our future, why do you keep saying such nice things?"

She sounds conflicted, and I feel almost guilty. Almost...but not quite. It's my job not to take no for an answer. I have to convince Nia that those three words she thinks she can't do without aren't vital. It's my job to treat her like a princess and show her she needs me far more.

"I'm only ever honest with you." I scratch my chin with a deprecating grin. "Sometimes to my own detriment."

"I know." She sounds sad about that. "And I appreciate that you don't lie to me about your feelings."

"I never will, Nia. I promise."

She gives me a melancholy nod. She believes me…but it's still not enough.

Clearly, I need to focus on more of the good things I can give her. "Let's tour the house. Maybe after that we can, um…tour the bedroom again?"

"Sure."

I escort her inside and recite all the things the listing agent told me yesterday when we walked the house. She oohs over the kitchen and aahs over the rustic ceiling beams that caught her eye to start with. She loves the place. She loves the view. She loves our walk around the surrounding area. But despite the fact she loves everything I've shown her—and me—it's not enough to persuade her to say yes. Even after the hours we spend together, sharing one passion-filled orgasm after another, gorging on ecstasy until I'm not sure I'll be able to use my legs again, Nia doesn't seem any closer to saying yes.

As we leave late that night and head back to Harlow and Noah's, I'm wondering if I've miscalculated or misstepped along the way. I'm out of ideas. As Nia disappears into her solitary bedroom and asks for some time alone, I hold in a curse. What the hell is it going to take to make her change her mind?

Thursday, November 23

THE NEXT DAY, Nia and I sit down at the table with my siblings and their spouses for a big Thanksgiving. Around me, there's laughter, teasing, real happiness. But beside me, Nia is subdued, her smile stilted as she speaks, but only when spoken to. I'm preoccupied and, I admit, taciturn. She didn't refuse my proposal…but she didn't accept. Nothing—not a beautiful diamond, a gorgeous house in paradise, nor my pledge of undying fidelity—could distract her from insisting that I declare my till-death-do-us-part love. What void does she think my promise of an emotion that's neither tangible nor valuable will fill in her? Is she looking for adoration? Belonging? Security?

About halfway through the meal, I'm still in thought when Noah's younger brother, Trace, barrels through the front door, schlepping a huge tote on one shoulder covered in stars and rocket ships. In his other hand, he grips a baby carrier.

"Hi, gang. Sorry I'm late. Someone didn't want to wake up from his nap." He turns the carrier toward the crowd gathered at the table to reveal his infant son.

"Oh, he looks so precious," Harlow arches out of her chair and onto her feet, busting across the floor to lift the boy into her arms.

"He is." Trace looks absolutely enthralled by his newborn son. "Good eater. Good sleeper. This single-parent thing isn't so bad so far."

I know this story, mostly because Harlow has been keeping me up to date over the months. Trace met a woman named Mercedes at Noah's final Super Bowl victory party, just before he announced his retirement from football. Mercedes assumed Trace was Noah. It's an easy mistake since they look a lot alike. When she found out she was pregnant, she publicly named Noah as her baby's father. The accusation nearly tore Harlow and Noah apart. Finally, Trace realized he had fathered the boy that drunken night. When Mercedes caught wind of the fact her baby daddy was no meal ticket, she signed over her parental rights hours after giving birth to Ranger. Since then, Trace has been getting the hang of caring for an infant, apparently with a lot of help from Britta, who also cared for her infant son solo a few years before she and Griff reconciled and married.

The baby fusses a little, then quiets, seeming to stare up at Harlow with solemn eyes already turning dark. He looks exactly like his father, all the way down to the thick black hair and square chin.

If Becca were still here, our son or daughter would be this age.

I swallow, stare. My appetite disappears. My mood blackens.

Beside me, Nia rises to stand beside my sister, suddenly wearing a bright-eyed smile. "Oh… What a cutie. You're going to be a heartbreaker. Aren't you, big boy?" Then she looks up at Trace. "Sorry. We haven't met. I'm Nia."

"I have terrible manners." Harlow laughs at herself. "Trace, this is Evan's girlfriend." She turns to Nia. "This is Noah's brother."

"Good to meet you." Trace divests himself of all the baby accouterments. "And you're right about Ranger. He's already a heartbreaker. He and Daddy get along pretty well, but the minute a woman shows up, he smiles and flirts shamelessly. I could probably take tips from him."

"You know when babies are only a couple of weeks old the smiling is probably the relief of passing gas," Britta drawls.

Trace looks totally blindsided by that comment. The table erupts with laughter.

"Really?" Griff turns to his wife. "You're serious?"

She grins his way as she rubs her distended belly. "Just wait. Parenting a three-year-old is full of challenges, as you'll be reminded the minute Jamie wakes from his nap. But newborns? A whole different game…"

Suddenly, Griff looks nervous.

"Can I hold him?" Nia asks Trace.

"Sure. Just don't be surprised if he flirts with—or farts on—you, too."

With a laugh, she lifts the boy into her arms.

She coos at Ranger and strokes his cheek. I see warmth in her eyes. Her yearning. Her heart. My gut churns. Yes, Nia told me she wouldn't be content to remain childless. Some women are, and I'd hoped… But the way mine is immediately enthralled by the baby tells me she really will want at least one of her own—sooner rather than later.

Gulping, I stare. Today I'm supposed to give thanks for everything in my life. But what the hell do I have? Money and success, sure. Intelligence? I'm told I do. But my wife is gone, my son or daughter died before he or she had any chance at life, and now I can't convince the one woman I want to fill the emptiness to marry me. Looking at Nia with Ranger, I'm beginning to wonder if I could even make her happy.

"Wow, he's heavier than I thought," Nia remarks. "How much does he weigh?"

"Isn't he a chunker?" Trace laughs. "We saw the doctor yesterday, and he's already twelve pounds, two ounces. He's at the top of the height and weight chart, and he won't even be three weeks old until Saturday."

I do some mental math. Shock decimates me. "He was born November fourth?"

The question slips out before I can stop it.

Trace turns to me. "Hey, Evan. How you doing, man?"

When he sticks his hand in my direction, I stand and shake it. But I'm desperate for the answer to my question. I don't even know why. It shouldn't bother me that his son was born the day mine should have been. It's coincidence. Ranger isn't the child who was growing in Becca's womb. His birth won't bring my baby back.

But the something buckling my chest and smashing my composure isn't hearing logic.

"I'm good," I finally choke out. "You?"

"Better than expected. Yeah, November fourth. I took him home from the hospital the next day, and we've been baching it ever since. Haven't we, Ranger?" Trace glides a gentle finger over his son's cheek.

As the boy gurgles, the love on Trace's face is so obvious and naked. I frown, trying to understand my reaction. I'm both envious of his son yet determined not to have one of my own? I can't remember ever being this contradictory. I see things one way. It is or it isn't. It's light or dark. It's black or white. It's up or down. Nothing lies in the middle, and I never find myself of two minds about anything.

Except…I'm conflicted about having a child.

Keeley rises from her chair and elbows her husband, who gets to his feet, too. Soon, Trace has a place at the table, a cold beer, and a plate of food. He sits to eat while everyone passes his son around, bouncing him in their arms while making nonsensical sounds and comical faces for the infant's entertainment.

I push away my plate, any semblance of appetite gone. Before I can make an excuse and leave the scene, Griff turns to me, bundle of boy in hand. "You want to hold him?"

A big "no" sits on my tongue, ready to snap out like the crack of a whip. But everyone is staring at me, most wearing expressions of pity. They know that, if not for that rainstorm and the slick streets that April day in Seattle, I would have been a father by now. And they've all pegged me as concealing emotional wreckage I don't comprehend. If I refuse to hold Ranger, it will confirm their suspicions.

That bothers me. I'm not sure why. But it's a feeling, so it isn't real. I try to shake the annoying emotion away. But all the usual methods of focusing—mentally solving complex math problems, reciting the periodic table, or writing JavaScript in my head—aren't working.

The silence in the room seems oppressive. I'm aware of every eye on me, especially Nia's. I look at my brother holding the baby out to me, then the boy's little face. I swallow. I sweat.

I can't do it.

Scraping my chair against the floor, I stand. "No, thank you. Excuse me."

It's unreasonable and foolish to flee the table. Ranger is a human being, as is everyone else in the room, just a smaller version. What harm could come from holding him?

I don't know. I simply know the thought of doing it is more than I can manage. I haven't been blindsided by this kind of crushing tumult in months. Why is it back now, pressing down on my chest?

Once I've trekked out of the dining room and onto the patio, I drag in the scent of sunshine-filled salt, listen to the crashing waves, and head toward the beckoning ocean, desperately seeking my personal homeostasis.

What the hell happened just now? I really don't know.

"Evan?" Nia wraps soft fingers around my shoulder.

I stiffen, wishing she wasn't touching me while I feel so weak. Her gentle caress dissolves my composure even faster. This turmoil makes no sense, and the last thing I want to do is face her or try to explain why my mood is so foul. Why I didn't want to hold the baby.

"Go finish your dinner," I say finally, keeping my back to her. "I'm fine."

"You're not. And I'm not leaving you to grieve alone."

"I'm not grieving." *Am I*?

She sighs. "You don't like to admit to having feelings, I know. They don't make sense to you, but—"

"The only feeling I'm having is regret that a different decision on my part might have meant Becca and my child would be here with me."

"You don't know that. If you'd gone with them, you might have died, too."

I pause for long minutes. I don't want to talk about this. But I know Nia. She won't drop the subject simply because I want her to. My better bet is to reassure her that nothing is wrong. I'd much rather have her apply her mental energy toward deciding she should marry me.

"I've had similar thoughts. Maybe you're right. Obviously, we'll never know."

"We won't. I know you miss them, and I'm sorry for your loss. I'm also sorry I can't be the woman you want to celebrate Thanksgiving with, but I'll do whatever I can to cheer you up."

I cast her a frown over my shoulder. "You *are* the woman I want to be with."

As soon as the words are out, I realize I've admitted—both to Nia and myself—that I would rather be sharing today with her than my late wife. It shocks me. So does the realization that I meant what I said.

I whip my stare back out to the foaming blue waves. Nia may not be able to see my face, but I can't hide the truth. As time has marched on, Becca has faded from my memory. I can't recall her scent anymore. I can no longer recollect the exact blue of her eyes. Weeks ago, I heard a woman in the office with a laugh much like hers…then second-guessed myself. Had Becca sounded like that at all?

"Evan, I want to be here with you, too. I want to be here *for* you." Nia squeezes my shoulder, her voice so soft I barely feel it slicing me open. "I know you're hurting."

"I'm just in an odd mood. Join the others. I'll be inside soon."

I hope more than expect that she'll release me and return to the house with my family. Becca would have. Funny how I remember the way her mind worked more than the woman herself. But Nia… I already know she'll make a completely different choice.

"It's time we cut through the crap and have some straight conversation." She tries to turn me to face her.

I shrug off her touch, refusing to budge.

"Leave it," I tell her. Hell, I'm warning her. If she treads here, as agitated as my churning gut and boiling blood seem, I don't know what I'll do.

"No. Becca may have let you brood. Maybe her apathy didn't bother you. Maybe you were even grateful. I'm sorry she's gone, and I'm glad you want to be here with me. But there's no way I'm leaving you alone now. And there's no way I will believe for one minute that you aren't hurting." When I still don't reply, Nia huffs and marches around my unmoving form to plant herself in front of me. "You lost almost everything that meant something to you in a single afternoon. Grieving doesn't make you weak. You cared for Becca. You wanted your baby. Of course your first holiday without them is going to be difficult. Of course seeing a child born on the very day yours should have been is a shock."

How did she anticipate everything that would impact me when I didn't see those blows coming until they'd sucker-punched me?

I lick my suddenly dry lips and force myself to look at her. "It's illogical."

"It's normal," she argues. Her passion is persuasive, compelling, especially when she gives me a little shake. "There isn't a single person here tonight who doesn't feel your ache and doesn't wish they could make it better for you. It's okay if you weren't ready to hold the baby. No one blames you."

For some reason, her speech stirs up my anger. "They all stared, waiting, wondering, obviously thinking I'm a train wreck. I don't want their pity. I don't need yours, either."

"I don't pity you," she murmurs. "I love you. That means I'm concerned about you. I'm in your corner. I'm willing to listen whenever you want to talk. I'm here for *you*."

As I blow out a breath, I try again to tamp down my anger. I can't be mad at Nia when she's only trying to help. In fact, I should be grateful she even cares about this wretched mood of mine. But her words illuminate parts of my past I wish I could keep dark.

If Becca loved me too, why wasn't she ever willing to hear me when I was troubled? I excused her disinterest in my frustration during Stratus's early days as her lack of understanding about my business. Since she and I rarely fought about our personal life, I assumed she either walked away or acquiesced before disagreements got truly heated because she loathed conflict. Looking back, I wonder why she never fought for herself. For me. For us.

Did she ever really care at all? Or was I merely the protective barrier between her and the rest of the world?

"Evan?"

Nia is still waiting. She's done nothing but try to help. Whatever is plaguing my mood isn't something I can take out on her.

"It was a shock," I admit in something just above a whisper since I can't seem to find the rest of my voice. "I wasn't ready to hear that Ranger had been born the same day my son or daughter should have been."

"I know. But if things work out between us, we can have children."

"I don't want them."

"You say that now. The pain of your loss is still too fresh, so you're not ready to take a chance yet—"

"I doubt I'll ever be ready. It's not worth the risk."

"That's your grief talking."

Normally, I would have refuted her, told her that was my logic asserting itself. This time, I pause. Examine. I frown. Is she right?

"Maybe. But I don't think I'll change my mind, Nia."

And I worry about where that leaves us...and our future.

CHAPTER ELEVEN

Seattle, Washington
Saturday, November 25

BY MUTUAL AGREEMENT, we decided on Friday morning to head back to Seattle, rather than staying in Maui for another nine days. My siblings and their spouses were sorry to see us cut our visit short, but no one pressed us to stay, as if they understood that Nia and I need the time to figure out our next steps.

We arrived home to rain that hasn't let up since we landed. As we settle into the car, not many words pass between us. Nia isn't silent out of anger. Neither am I. It feels more like we simply don't know what to say.

As I near her house, I try to shake my lingering, puzzling disquiet. "What are we doing?"

"I assume you're taking me home."

"And then what? What's going on with us?" So much is unsettled. December is days away, and at its end I don't know whether she'll be working with me, living with me, marrying me—or completely out of my life.

Nia takes in a deep breath. "We continue as planned. You gather some things and move into my place when you're ready. We go back to work as scheduled. We spend the next five weeks together and figure out where we go from here…or if we call it quits. At some point, I guess you'll sign the papers to sell Stratus to Lund." She shrugs. "That's it."

That's not much of a plan. There's so much open-ended. My practical side rails, but I can't think of a better suggestion.

Will I be able to make Nia happy if I won't give her the love and children she craves? And if that's the case, should I be doing my damndest to marry her?

Maybe not...but I can't bring myself to let her go, either. Even considering it hurts like hell. Imagining life without her feels like a piece of myself is missing, like I'd become an emotional amputee.

I drop her off at her cottage with a promise to see her soon, then leave her with a kiss on her cheek. She doesn't press for more or even ask when I plan to show up at her door, suitcase in hand. I'm not terribly surprised. Nia knows me well. She must know I need the time alone to examine what I'm doing with my future and why. Hell, she probably knows that better than I do.

When I let myself into my apartment with a weary sigh, it feels immediately dark and still, heavy. Opening blinds and flinging back drapes to the stormy night does nothing to lift the oppressive air around me.

As I stand in the middle of my stark gray living room and stare out over the rainy bay, I feel alone. I can't remember ever feeling this isolated or gloomy. Not when the social worker dropped me off with my first foster family, who barely took notice of me. Not when I locked Diana's door behind me the morning of my eighteenth birthday with a duffel full of my things and one hundred twelve dollars to my name. Not even when I returned here after Becca's funeral and it finally hit me that she was really never coming back.

My sense of solitude now is gloomier. It's bone-deep. I don't know why this nagging misery followed me home from Maui, but staring out my twelve-foot wall of windows and onto the churning bay below magnifies it, along with my every concern, by reminding me precisely how alone I am.

"What are you doing here? I didn't expect you home for another week."

I whirl around to find Bas standing at the end of the hall, wearing a T-shirt and boxers. His hair looks mussed, and he's wearing a scowl.

"What are *you* doing here?" I glance at my watch. "And why do you look like you've already gone to bed when it's only eight o'clock?"

Bas scowls. "Last night, my toilet started leaking about midnight. I was bailing water until the plumber finally showed up a little after eight, so I'm freaking tired. I needed a place to crash while my place airs out, and you weren't supposed to be home for another week. I didn't think you'd mind. Why aren't you in Maui?"

Long fucking story. But is putting my best friend off even an option? "It's complicated."

Bas yawns and pads into my living room, tossing himself across the sofa. "Well, I managed a couple of hours of sleep, so I'm all yours. Start talking."

"I'd rather not. Go back to bed." I prop my suitcase against the wall and set down my briefcase with a sigh.

"Well, I'd rather not see you sulk because something's wrong that caused you to cut your vacation with your new family and your new girlfriend short. And...based on your expression, the family isn't the problem."

"No."

He rears back. "Are you and Nia still together?"

I sit at the end of the sofa and sigh tiredly. "I seriously don't want to talk about it."

My best friend is silent for a long minute. He bobs his head like he agrees and respects my privacy. But this is Bas we're talking about. He doesn't give two shits about privacy or boundaries or personal space.

"You must have seriously fucked up if you're on the outs with a woman who's totally in love with you."

That sends my gaze whipping over to him. "How did you know her feelings?"

But obviously he did, way before I did.

He rolls his eyes. "I'd ask if you're kidding but I know better. Dude, she offered to organize your life. She slept with you when she had a million reasons not to. She agreed to go with you over a major holiday to meet your family. She looks at you like she's head over heels. And you didn't figure that out?"

"I can figure out how to keep personal data stored safely, protected from hackers wielding every code and virus known to man, yet completely internet accessible." I shake my head. "I can't figure out how the woman's mind operates."

Bas braces his elbows on his knees. "She wants to get married and you don't?"

"The opposite, actually. I would marry her today. She only wants to get married if I can tell her I love her."

"Hmm. And you don't?"

"I loved Becca."

"Who's now gone," he says as if that's obvious.

"A heart isn't something you give twice. Once you've given it away, it's gone."

Bas laughs. "Why the hell would you believe that?"

"Because it's true," I bite out at his ridicule. "I don't expect you to understand. You probably think you're in love all the time and—"

"I don't. Lust? Yes," he concedes. "I was in love once. It didn't work out. She was married and I respected that. I had a good man cry about the fact she'd never be mine, then I told myself to move on. I've fucked around a lot to distract myself, I admit. But eventually, I'll fall in love again. I'll never love that woman less, but I'm ready to find someone new to fill my heart."

This is the first I'm hearing of Bas believing he was attached. "Who were you in love with?"

"Does it matter? It didn't work out. But the pain of losing her isn't stopping me from looking. If the right woman comes along at the right time, I'll happily give her my heart. I'm on the downhill slide to thirty, man. I'd like to hope that's going to be soon. But even if it takes until I'm eighty to fall in love again, I'll wait. It's worth it."

"Why? It can bring a lot of pain."

"It can also bring a fuck-ton of happiness. Look at it this way: If you didn't have people in your life, what would you have?"

I frown. "My business. My…hobbies."

Then I fall silent because I can't think of anything else.

"You'd have shit. You'd have meetings and balance sheets, taxes, paperwork, and strategic plans. In between all that…what hobbies? You'd have meals and errands, maybe a favorite TV show or two, a few meaningless lays when you could manage to pry yourself away from the office and scrape together a little charm at a local bar or do some random swiping right. You wouldn't even have painting since I'll bet you stopped doing that months ago. Am I wrong?"

I don't say a word because I'm stunned by how right he is.

"It would be empty as shit," he goes on. "Believe me, I know."

Something bleak in his eyes tells me he's not lying.

"What are you saying?"

"You want the short version?"

"Yes." Sitting in the semi-dark with my best friend in his underwear and talking about hearts and love just isn't very manly.

"Give love a try again. It's right in front of you. Don't piss it away."

"Like I already said, I can't give my heart twice. So why aren't friendship, commitment, and fidelity enough for Nia?"

Bas sighs. "I should have known the short version wouldn't convince you since you need logic for every fucking conclusion, even an emotional one."

"That's not a bad thing."

"In business, no. But that won't work with emotions. It's as if you're determined to treat love like a science experiment. You seem to have some hypothesis about love being a singular event. You get involved with Nia and stir the beaker a little, then start recording her reactions, studying the data and making comparisons so you can draw conclusions. Dude, no. She's a different woman than Becca. Nothing is going to be the same. Hell, *you're* not the same."

I want to refute him. And I can't. On some level, I've assumed that, because my relationship with Nia isn't like the one I shared with Becca it can't be love. But I didn't take into account the variables, like the fact that my control samples are totally different.

Sitting back, I regard him with a solemn stare.

"And the kicker is..." He shakes his head as if he's reluctant. "Never mind."

"No. I'm listening." Because I suspect he's on to something.

"You'll just get pissed off. So, let's talk about something else. I've been doing some digging into Lund, trying to figure out why he has such a hard-on to buy Stratus, but I've hit a brick wall, so—"

"We'll get back to that. But first I want to know what you won't tell me."

"No, you don't."

"Jesus." I want to throttle him. "I do or I wouldn't be asking you."

He pauses. "I guess you'd only be asking me if you're actually listening. All right. Here's the truth: You didn't love Becca."

Gritting my teeth in fury, I jump to my feet. "That's bullshit."

"No, it's not. I watched you two for years. She was your friendly helpmate. You were her savior. She respected you. You relied on her. But that's it. And that's not love."

"You don't know the first fucking thing—"

"How often did you and Becca have sex?"

"That's a low blow. You know she had a lot of personal demons to overcome and—"

"How often?"

I rake a hand through my hair. "Maybe every couple of weeks. It always took her time to...deal with it."

"Uh-huh. And did you want it more? Feel desperate when you couldn't have her?"

"Sex isn't the only measure of love." I don't know why I'm so defensive.

"It's a fucking big one. Compare that to the way you want Nia. Think about how much you crave her when you can't have her."

His logic punches me in the gut. I can't breathe. For a moment, I'm stunned and disoriented.

"If not love, what do you think I felt for Becca?"

"Responsibility and guilt. I'm not saying you didn't like her. She took care of your life. Hell, she was able to put up with you. And you were faithful to her for months after she died. There was nothing wrong with that. It's commendable. You weren't unhappy with her. But look me in the face and tell me that being with Nia isn't somehow brighter, more intense. Like the difference between flipping on a light and sticking your finger in a socket. Like staring at the sun and being willing to go blind for the privilege because you can't not look at her."

No, he's right. His words seem to have unraveled the tourniquet around my perception. Suddenly, I see my marriage from a completely different perspective.

I've missed what Becca did for me. I've missed the space she filled beside me. Have I actually once missed her yoga pants hanging from the shower door? Or the way she used a whole bag of oranges to squeeze her juice every Sunday? Have I even missed the way she'd curl up to me after having a nightmare about her foster father? If I'm being brutally honest, no. I haven't kept her possessions because I'm loath to let my last vestiges of her go. I've kept them because I haven't wanted to admit I'm alone and I haven't wanted to expend the energy to make that even more obvious.

"So you think I still have my heart to give…and that I should give it to Nia?"

Bas shakes his head. "I think you *had* your heart to give until a few weeks ago, but it's Nia's now. But you should stop trying to put labels on what you two have and just go with it."

"Go with it?" I raise a brow at him. "You've met me, haven't you? You know I'm not good at that."

He laughs. "Yeah, you suck. But here's the thing: If you keep fucking around with this, trying to name it and figure out how it fits in your practical view of the world, she's going to slip through your fingers. Then I think you'll grieve the loss of a woman for the first time because she won't come back. Then, you're right, there might not be any recovering.

And you really will spend the rest of your fucking life alone."

AS I MARCH up Nia's walkway, the icy rain pours, sluicing down my face and seeping into my clothes. I really don't care. I hit the button of the fob of my sedan, drag the suitcase I didn't even bother to unpack, and start pounding on her front door.

"Nia! I need to talk to you."

The whole drive over, I considered what Sebastian said, pondered the probability that he's right. Am I in love with Nia and I've been too blind to see it? I need more time with her to know for sure, but the concept no longer feels impossible.

Mostly because I'm beginning to suspect he's also right about the fact I didn't love Becca.

That fills me with guilt. Shame. I'm an asshole for that, right? My wife devoted her life to me, and I didn't give her even half of myself. As least I know now why I would rather have been with Nia than Becca on Thanksgiving Day. I also know why my sex drive has been in hyper mode since I first touched the assistant I should have left at a professional distance. And I definitely know why I challenge Nia and her feelings, rather than simply placating her. They matter. She matters.

How the fuck did I not see any of this?

Suddenly, she opens the door. She's wearing a berry-colored pajama top and a coordinating pair of floral pants that are far more practical than sexy, but at the sight of her, instant need fires through my blood.

Nia gasps at me. "Oh, my god. Come in. It's got to be freezing out there, and you're soaking wet."

I step inside and shut the door. "I had to see you."

"I'm just making a cup of Bangkok tea. Do you want some?"

I don't even know what that is, but I don't care. "No. I want you."

She studies me, and something shifts on her face. "Let me get you a towel and—"

When she turns away, I grab her arm and haul her back against me. I'm drenching her clothes and dripping on her floor. I'm invading her space. It's impulsive and impractical. Probably unreasonable, too.

And I can't stop.

I cup my hand around her nape and drag her face under mine. Her gaze skitters. Her lips part. Our stares meet. Then I crush her lips with my own, instantly opening her to me and claiming her with a thrust of my tongue.

For an instant, she's shocked stiff. Then her fingers crawl up my biceps. Her arms curl around my neck. She loses herself in the kiss.

My blood goes up in flames.

As I kick off my ruined loafers, I attack the big white buttons down the front of her pajamas. I'm thanking god they seem to melt under my hands, especially when she attacks the fly of my jeans and moans.

I tear my mouth away, panting. The sofa, where I already know she's taken another man into her body, taunts me. I also refuse to take her on her bed for the same reason. "Where can I fuck you?"

She blinks at me as if she's trying to understand my question. As I wait impatiently for her answer, I spread the lapels of her flannel top wide.

She's not wearing a bra.

"Too late," I growl. "Let's go."

Suddenly, I know the perfect spot.

Wrapping my hands around Nia, I fill my palms with her ass and lift her against my body, seizing her mouth as I cross the room and deposit her on the counter next to the kitchen sink.

"Take off your pants," I demand as I reach behind my head and pull my wet shirt off and dump it in the sink. I barely notice when it lands with a splat. "Now."

Then I'm lifting her breast and bending to take her nipple in my mouth. Beneath me, she wriggles, shifting her weight from one side to the other until she's finally shoving her pants past her knees and kicking them away.

As soon as I push the top off Nia's shoulders, she's naked. She's got my fly open and her hands around my cock. We're both breathing hard as she presses kisses across my chest. I close my eyes and groan. I want to get inside her. I want to feel her close around me. The urge is so strong. It's not like anything I've ever felt.

Bas's words float through my head. Being with Nia really is like sticking my finger in a light socket—in a good way. She lights me up, makes me feel alive.

"I didn't think you'd be back so soon," she murmurs. "After the way we left things, I worried you wouldn't show up for days."

I shake my head, fighting to find words as she gives my length another heated stroke. "Need you too much."

"Condom?" she asks.

Fuck. "In my suitcase."

"Mine are on the other side of the house. Can you wait?"

I know the practical, responsible answer. But… "No."

Surprisingly, her lips curl up in a smile. Then she gives my chest a little shove and hops off the counter, onto her feet.

Instant denial flares through me as I grab her wrist. "Don't go."

If she leaves me, even for thirty seconds, I won't make it. It sounds ridiculously melodramatic, but my breath is heaving, my heart thudding. It's as if my whole body is a live wire. More electrical pulses are frying my brain and melting my defenses. I need Nia to take the surge and ground me before I overload.

"I'm not going anywhere," she promises as she brushes a kiss across my mouth.

Then she drops to her knees.

I barely have time to gape and process the new charge to my revving heart before Nia's tongue flicks around the head of my cock, then she slips my crest between her lips.

The hot velvet of her mouth has me groaning in an instant. I stiffen and try to process all the pleasure she's giving me. Before I can, her lips purse tighter around me and she sucks me deeper. It's a scalding, silken paradise.

Then I feel my tip at the back of her throat and her tongue cradling my shaft. She hums, digging her nails into my ass. When did she shove my pants around my ankles? I don't know. I don't care. All I know is that, as she glides her pretty, pouty mouth up my length, my only imperative is to nudge her back down until she takes all of me.

I slip my hands in her hair, grabbing tight fistfuls at the crown, and push. She doesn't panic or protest or cry. Not Nia. She complies with a hearty moan and engulfs even more of my cock in her mouth, then swallows slowly when I bottom out.

"Jesus..." I mutter, feeling conscious control slip away in a matter of seconds.

Around me, she whimpers, the sound becoming a crescendo as I start ruthlessly fucking the back of her throat.

The sensations are a revelation, like the videos of those color-blind people wearing specialized glasses for the first time that allow them to truly see. Feeling Nia take every wild pump of my hips as my dick shuttles past her lips, over her tongue, and deeper than I imagined is completely blowing my mind...and unraveling my body. I both love and hate that she knows exactly what to do to dismantle my composure and drive me to climax.

Her firm hand wraps around the base of my shaft, sliding up and down with her mouth. Her tongue wraps all around me. The gentle nip of teeth slides over my sensitive crest before she takes me deep enough to feel her swallow again.

"Fuck," I mutter.

"Oh, we will. Eventually," she taunts before she cups my balls and licks the underside of my shaft before taking me impossibly deeper.

I grip the edge of the sink, my body pulsing with energy. My toes grip the tile floor. I'm trying like hell to stay upright. My knees feel like melted butter. The higher my pleasure climbs, the more my head spins. When her cheeks hollow out, blood pounds through my veins. My heartbeat hammers like I'm a drummer on speed. My skin feels too tight. I'm going up in flames, burning to death. And I don't give two shits. As long as Nia doesn't stop…

Her breathing turns harsh. I can feel her willing my ecstasy as she digs her nails deeper into me with one hand and gently tugs on my testicles with the other. As those sensations rack up, she nips at me again, then sucks me deep and performs some maneuver where I swear I feel the head of my cock slip past her throat and…

Holy hell. I'm done for. I can't stop bellowing for breath, can't stop the electricity from boiling my blood, liquefying my veins, lighting up every nerve ending in my body. I tense. My balls feel tight and heavy. I swell. I turn atomic.

I'm going to come.

"Nia…" I manage to grind out as I fist her hair and fuck her mouth hard.

She can't answer with words, but she moans. Encouraging. Inviting.

"If you don't want me like this, in your mouth…" I grit my teeth and try to find the strength to pull away.

Nia sucks me deeper, holds me tighter. Her mewls sound like a protest.

I grip the sink tighter. This orgasm is coming hard and fast. It's going to be like crashing into a concrete wall at warp speed. It's going to mean certain death—and I don't think twice. I let it happen.

"Jesus. Motherfucking… Oh, my… Yeah. Nia… Honey! I'm—"

Climax rips away the rest of my nonsensical babble. In its place is the most astonishing, spine-bending explosion, a nuclear mushroom cloud that's somehow a good thing. It's peeling the skin from my flesh, tearing the muscle from my bone. It's utterly dissolving me. And it feels so good I'd give my entire fortune to do it again.

Slowly, consciousness returns. Nia laps at my softening cock and hums in what sounds like satisfaction. My ragged breathing and the pelting of raindrops on the roof fill the rest of the space.

Struggling to assimilate, I tug on her silky hair and stare down at her. She relinquishes my cock from her mouth with a soft pop, then blinks up at me with fluttering lashes and a temptress's smile.

Two thoughts hit me at once. First, she has every right to feel supremely satisfied with what she's done. Second, I don't want to know how many times she had to perform that act on other guys to do it so perfectly.

Like everything else with Nia, she infuriates me. She enthralls me. She conflicts me.

"Evan?"

Still struggling to find words, I help her to her feet and search her face. "Nia."

She presses her lips together. "Has any woman ever done that to you?"

Slowly, I shake my head.

"Seriously?"

Nia is probably thinking it's crazy that a grown-ass man has never had a blow job. I'm thinking how brain-bending it is that, in less than five minutes, she redefined pleasure. I still can't wrap my head around it.

"Seriously."

She regards me with solemn eyes. "Becca *never*…?"

I squeeze my eyes shut and shake my head. "Becca… Remember I said her foster father abused her? Yeah. Sexually. He especially liked to force her to give him head. So when we got married, she tried, but she couldn't bring herself to…"

"Without having flashbacks. Got it. What else couldn't she do?"

The list is long, and in the face of Nia's obvious experience, I'm almost embarrassed to admit all the sexual acts and positions I've never performed.

"I need to know," she says softly. "If we're going to live together for the next few weeks and really give us a try, then—"

"She…" I swallow nervously. "She preferred to be on top."

"Where she was in control?"

"Yes."

"And you let her."

"Yes."

"Even though it went against your grain?"

"How did you know?"

Nia sighs. "Evan, you like to control everything, all the way down to the kind of pencils we buy in the office. Why would sex be any different for you?"

I open my mouth to refute her, but can I? Should I? Unlike Becca, she's not crying or blaming me for being insensitive to her past. She's simply trying to understand me. "You're right; it's not."

My whispered admission seems loud in the room.

She cups my face. "You have nothing to be ashamed of. Nothing."

"I'm overbearing. Demanding." At least according to Becca.

"No, you're not." She seems to laugh at my contention. "You obviously restrained yourself to accommodate her. But at some point, she had to concede that you aren't her rapist."

"Sex…was something she did for me."

"Not for her own pleasure. I see." Nia frowns. "Missionary?"

"Every once in a blue moon, usually only when I couldn't climax with her on top."

"Could she climax?"

"Eventually. It took a lot of effort. I learned patience, figured out her body, and discovered a lot of shortcuts and tricks."

"No wonder you always seem so focused on making me come and you can do it so fast," she murmurs. "What else? Did she like it when you went down on her?"

"Yeah. That was a guaranteed orgasm. Jesus, why am I spitting all this out? What I really want to know is how many blow jobs you've given to be that good at it."

"I don't know and it doesn't matter. I don't have any sexual baggage that's going to stop us from being happy in bed. But I think you have a whole lot of unexplored territory. Why couldn't Becca stand missionary sex?"

"Because that bastard fucking climbed on top of her, pinned her down, and took her virginity against her will. I don't want to talk about her hang-ups. I want to talk about you."

"And I'd rather talk about us," she says calmly. "Tell me your fantasies."

I blink at her. I'm standing in the middle of her kitchen, hair still wet, shivering, with my pants around my ankles. And she wants to know what I think about when I jack off?

"Nia..." I shake my head. "The sex seems to be pretty fucking awesome without this conversation."

She raises a brow at me. "Just because Becca never wanted to talk about sex doesn't mean I don't. I do. I *really* do. Don't filter. Don't worry that whatever you're thinking is something she wouldn't have approved of. I'm willing to try anything once. If I don't like it, I'll tell you. But I want to devote the next week to letting you try whatever your heart—and cock—desires and hopefully put a huge smile on your face." She leans in and places her lips against my ear. "Tell me."

I shudder. "I'll never get tired of being on top of you."

"I'll never get tired of you being there. But I know there's more. I'll bet there's way more."

She's not wrong, and I should be freaked out that she sees me so deeply. Instead, I'm relieved. "I want to fuck you from behind."

She smiles. "Hmm. And?"

If I'm really going to let my mind go there, I have a lot more to say. "I want to fuck you in the office."

Her smile turns naughty. Her teeth nip my ear just before she whispers, "That's one of my favorite fantasies, too. You bending me over your desk and muttering filthy words to me while you smother my mouth with your hand to keep me from screaming out in pleasure."

I just had an orgasm less than five minutes ago, but her words stiffen my cock. "Yeah, that. Totally that."

"Keep going."

"I want to fuck you against a wall. I want to finger your pussy in public, under a table, where you can't do anything but take the pleasure I give you and figure out how to stifle your cries when I make you come."

Nia shivers. "Hell, yes. What else?"

Do I dare go on? The rest of my fantasies are filthier, things Becca would never have consented to, no matter how slowly I took them, no matter how much therapy she had. Nia is clearly more open and irritatingly more experienced, but that doesn't mean she's willing to go to these dark places with me.

"Evan, you're thinking, not talking. Lay it on me. Every bit."

I huff in a breath. She's serious. My brain races, but I keep coming to the same conclusion: I'm either going to freak her out or light her up.

"All right." I drag in a bracing breath. *Here goes nothing*… "Anal?"

"Yeah." She sounds breathless.

I'm both thrilled and piqued. "You've already tried that?"

Nia is silent for a long minute as she regards me with a little furrow between her brows. "I'm a girl who likes to be touched. I don't have a lot of hang-ups about sex. In my mind, any expression of affection and pleasure between two consenting adults is good. I like to fully enjoy whomever I'm with, doing things I want and trying things he likes, too. So yes."

She's not saying anything wrong. Logically, I know that's the way sex should be—without fears and limits and artificial boundaries. I've simply never had that. I'm jealous of her experience, both that it's been so easy and that she's had more than me. But I'm the man with her now. She'll give me her sexual curiosity and passion if I stop fixating on who she's fucked before. She wants me. I need to embrace that and let the other shit go.

"Bondage?"

Her breath catches. "I'd like to try."

I let out a breath. Finally, something we can explore together. I'm stupidly relieved that we'll be on a level playing field for something.

"When?"

She shrugs. "Whenever. Tonight, why don't we have tea and talk some more and—"

"I want inside you."

A big smile curls up her lips, and I can't stop staring at the full, pouty bow and remembering it wrapped around me. "When you look at me like that, there's no way I can say no."

Kicking my pants away, I stalk naked to my suitcase, conscious of her gaze on me as she follows. I hear her footsteps behind as I crouch to retrieve the box of prophylactics. Then I toss it on the coffee table and grab a fuzzy white blanket off the back of the couch. Ignoring the wrinkle of confusion between her brows, I spread it out on the living room floor.

"What's that for?" she asks.

But her voice sounds suggestive, challenging. She knows exactly what I want. "On the blanket. Hands and knees."

Nia looks between the furry throw and my face. She must see the resolution there because she draws in a shaky breath, for the first time looking nervous. "What do you have in mind?"

"Did I forget to mention that I've fantasized about spanking you?"

CHAPTER TWELVE

MY WORDS RING through the room. Long moments of silence pass.

Nia bites her lip with a little shiver. "You didn't mention that."

"Now I am. Will you let me?"

She doesn't answer with words, simply walks to the middle of the blanket and drops to her knees in a graceful slide. Next, she falls on her hands and arches her back, lifting to me.

I almost lose my fucking mind. That ass. It's right in front of me—juicy, taut, round. And between her legs, I see her pouting pussy, wet and plump and dark with need.

I fall to my knees behind her. Keeping my hands off her flesh is too much to ask. As if they have a mind of their own, my palms glide over the small of her back, down her butt in a caress that should tell her exactly how much I covet her, then dip between her thighs. Yes, she's as drenched as she looks.

Bending to her, I whisper in her ear, "Do you like being spanked?"

"M-Maybe."

That tells me nothing. I need more information to proceed, and my patience is thinning. My hands are shaking. My cock stands up, stretching desperately as if I haven't had an orgasm in months, rather than minutes.

"Explain," I demand.

"I've only done this twice. Once, it was..." She shakes her head. "Wrong mood, I guess. Too playful, maybe? I giggled the whole time."

"I'm not feeling playful."

Nia turns her gaze over her shoulder at me. "I know."

"The second time?"

"It hurt. A lot. He was angry."

I glower, my hand tightening protectively on her flesh. "No man should ever hit you in anger."

"That's why it's the last time he ever touched me."

Gnashing my teeth, I resist the urge to ask who and when and where to find this prick. I want to beat the shit out of him. I want to make sure he understands that he should never have touched Nia at all, much less in any way that hurt or scared her.

"Evan..." Her gentle voice sounds like she's talking me off a ledge. "It's okay."

"It's not."

"I'm fine."

"He doesn't deserve to breathe."

That makes her smile. "He was an insecure, immature asshole, and that's why we're done now. Let it go."

I'd rather not, but I understand her point. This is about us.

I drag in a steadying breath and trail my gaze over her exposed backside again. I want that. I want her. But I want to give her pleasure, too.

"Tell me exactly how this makes you feel."

"What?"

I lift my hand. Adrenaline surges through my system, but I restrain myself. The last thing I want to do is frighten her or give her any reason to think we're incompatible and she needs to show me the door.

My swat lands on her right cheek, a dull thud meant to test her reaction more than assuage the hunger roaring inside me, which I don't fully understand.

"Nia?"

She tilts her head to look at me again. "Are you testing to see if I'm awake? Because I am and that wasn't a spanking."

"Do you want it harder?"

"What do *you* want?"

I swallow, gather my thoughts. She's been open-minded and receptive so far. If she doesn't like something, she'll let me know.

"To spank you harder. To make you claw, gasp, and beg."

"What's stopping you?"

Fuck, this woman has a way of peering inside my head and knowing exactly how to put me on edge. I like it. No, I love it and I want more.

"Absolutely nothing."

Except the fact I don't really know how this is done. But is there a science to it? Spanking classes I should take? I swallow a scoff. I don't need to logic this through. I just need to do it.

Rearing back, I lift my hand to her again. I swoop down with a *whoosh* and strike her left cheek. Satisfaction winds through me at the sound of the crack of my palm to her skin. At the way her breath catches and her body braces. At the visual of my big, pale hands against her soft, dark flesh. Everything about it turns me on. Everything about *her* turns me on.

"One," she counts, her voice almost a breathy sob.

I don't ask if she likes it. Her body language and the hitch in that one syllable tell me she does.

"We'll go to ten," I tell her.

I hope that will be enough to satisfy the straining, stretching dark side rooting around in my body and filling my brain with more sensual images than I can process.

"Yes, Sir."

That shouldn't turn me on half as much as it does, but yeah... The impatience to slowly, sensually spank her to incoherent arousal before I fuck her into panting, screaming sobs claws at my restraint.

"Damn it, Nia..." I curse her even as I land another blow to her right cheek, this one higher and harder than the first.

Her body bucks. "Two."

After that, I get into a rhythm. Left and low. Right and high. In the center. On her thigh.

"Six."

She's panting now, and something inside me I don't understand is eating this up. I cup her pussy and find she's even wetter than before. At my touch, she tosses her head, wriggles her hips…

"Evan?"

She wants me to forget seven through ten and simply get inside her.

I fist her hair and lean over her as I force her to look at me, shaking my head in answer. "No. I made you a promise. Unless something hurts too much to carry on?"

But I already know she's not in pain, and I can't deny that I'm enjoying this even more than I imagined.

I remember reading once that the body's biggest sex organ is the brain. I'm finally understanding what that means.

"It does," she protests.

"Where?"

"My clit."

"I'll make it all better…eventually." I laugh, mimicking her earlier words.

She mewls in protest, but when I nudge her thighs wider apart, she doesn't do anything except rush to comply. Blows eight and nine fall in the center of each cheek. The last strike I can't resist. I swing low, far gentler than before, and swat her swollen sex.

That makes Nia gasp, then let out a low, aroused moan.

"What number was that?" I prompt.

Why am I enjoying this so much? I'm not sure. We both know the answer to my question, but I *need* to hear her say it. Because, for the first time in my life, I'm able to have more than a cursory say-so about the sex I have? Because I'm finally able to act out the fantasies in my head? I'm sure there's a rationale here, but puzzling through it now is the last thing I want to do.

"Ten," she keens out. "Evan, please…"

I linger, my fingers tracing her slick folds, breezing over her hard clit. "Did you enjoy that?"

Again, I know the answer. I like making her admit the truth. I enjoy feeling arousal at more than a physical level, beyond skin and bone and cock. Our exchange now? It's as if we've entered something forbidden together. As if my brain being engaged is ramping up the rest of my responses.

"Yes. God, yes."

Her panting confession tells me it's the same for her.

Maybe a stronger man would toy with her, make her wait more. But she already sounds desperate. No denying I'm more aroused than I've ever been, and it's all I can do to make my shaking hands rip into the condom. It still feels foreign to roll it down my length, but I do it hastily, then position my knees between her spread calves and grip her hips.

"Good. I did, too. Ready?"

Nia doesn't answer with words, simply arches her back, lifts her ass even higher, and wiggles impatiently.

I'll never turn down that invitation.

Fitting my cock against her opening, I slide into her slick sex. And I groan long and low, filling the room with the sound of my need. She's scalding and tight, and the fact she's fulfilling another one of my fantasies notches me up even more.

Urgency drives me. I set a hard pace, shuttling in and out so fast it's a blur. Nia throws her head back, digs her fingers into the blanket, wailing for more. She tightens—a good sign. But I'm already dangerously close to orgasm. After sharing something I've wanted for a decade with the woman I want more than any other? It's a recipe to lose control.

"Reach down," she manages to pant out. "Rub my clit."

Happily. I want to do whatever she needs to climax. If my brain was functioning, I would have figured out that manual stimulation would get her there faster. Not that I want to rush this, but I'm like a freight train without brakes. There's no slowing this down.

The second I get my fingers right where she needs them, Nia lets out a needy, high-pitched cry and jolts in orgasm. Around me, I feel her contract, squeeze, milk me. It's all over, then. After a handful of harsh, jerking thrusts, I'm shuddering and bellowing and shouting out a rough growl of ecstasy.

It seems like hours before my breath turns normal, before the sheen of sweat covering my body begins to cool, before I can even move.

Finally, I press a kiss to her shoulder, then gently withdraw and lay another kiss at the base of her spine. "You okay?"

She turns to face me with a loopy smile and nuzzles my neck. "Better than okay. I feel..." She stretches happily, even wiggling her toes. "Fantastic."

Smiling from ear to ear, I head to the kitchen and dispose of the condom. When I return, I take in her nudity as she fluffs her hair and sighs with satisfaction.

"How are your cuddling skills?" she asks.

We've had sex multiple times, but I realize we've never lingered. I haven't really touched her afterward.

"Probably terrible." I wince.

"Too impatient?"

"No experience. Becca didn't like to be touched after sex." Honestly, she didn't like to be touched much at all.

"Oh, I'm the opposite. This will be new. Shall we go to bed and give it a try?"

Where she's been with other men. "No. Let's do it here."

"You're serious about avoiding my mattress?" She scans my face and rolls her eyes. "Of course you are. Okay..."

Nia wraps her arms around me and urges me down to the floor. We lie face-to-face, and she slings her thigh over me, caressing my face and kissing me softly. "I'm not going to stop telling you I love you."

Her words don't shock me as much as they did the first time. I don't hate them; I simply don't comprehend what I feel.

"I don't think I want you to," I admit softly, kissing the tip of her nose.

Being so close to her, so intimate, without the burning heat of passion, is novel. It's...nice.

I pull her closer. "I'm not going to stop asking you to marry me."

She smiles back at me. "I don't think I want you to."

"Then what do we do?" About our futures? About our impasse?

"Evan, let it lie for now. We don't need the answers tonight. We just need to be with one another. We'll figure it out."

Despite the fact I hate leaving tasks unfinished, I don't know what else to do. My usual silent calm is a humming swing-sway of energy. It's as if someone barged into my brain, took the orderly boxes I've stacked all my thoughts and notions into, then upended them, forcing the lids open and spilling the contents everywhere. In the resulting chaos, I don't know what to think. Feelings are unavoidable. I can't seem to process them. They pelt me with pinpricks from every direction.

Is this love? Is what I'm feeling for Nia that I didn't feel for Becca finally, truly the real thing? I don't know. But as I pull her closer and she lays her head against my chest, I'm happy. No, I'm ecstatic. So instead of trying to apply different forms of logic to my thoughts to reach a reasonable conclusion, I'm going to take Bas's advice and just go with it. Why not? So far, it feels really damn good.

Monday, November 27

MONDAY COMES, AND I find myself falling into familiar routines. I'm not used to vacation. In the years since I started Stratus, I can't think of any real time off I've taken. Hell, I barely left the office for seven hours when Becca died—the afternoon of the wreck and the morning of the funeral. Despite everyone encouraging me to take more time to grieve, I didn't see how hanging around my empty house would help me cope with losing my wife. Now that I'm with Nia, I'm determined to enjoy this time we have together...but she has to wake up first.

Damn, I'm envious of her ability to sleep.

After kissing her forehead, I rise up from our pallet on the floor with a groan. That's a backache I could have done without. Tonight we'll spend in a comfortable bed, damn it. I'm getting us a new mattress today.

After quickly brushing my teeth, I fish out last week's gym clothes from my suitcase, vowing to swing by my apartment and pick up more after my workout. Then I down half a cup of coffee and pick up a bottle of water. I make it to the gym by five thirty a.m.

I slacked off on workouts when I was in Maui, and I feel lethargic this morning. All the lazy satisfaction humming in my veins could be contributing, too. I push myself through a grueling hour and a half, then remove my earbuds and head out.

When I exit and make my way toward my car in the relatively empty lot, I spot a blonde dressed in an impeccable gray suit and a crisp white blouse standing beside it. She's looking at me expectantly, as if she's been waiting.

"Mr. Cook?"

"Yeah." I approach cautiously. "Who are you? Is there a problem?"

"I'd like to talk to you. My name is Bethany Banks…but I'm also a Reed."

Her words have the impact of a gut-punch. "You're Barclay's other daughter?"

"Yes."

So she's my missing half sister. Holy shit.

I know from talking to Maxon that our old man likes to boff his assistants. A lot. He seemed to take a particular perverse pleasure in impregnating them. My mother wasn't the first or the last. In fact, Bethany is a few years older than me, and up until now, none of the Reed children have ever spoken to her. No one knew where to find her. I can't help but wonder why she picked me and why she chose now to make contact.

"Wow. This is a surprise. I…um, it's good to meet you. Are you here because you want to know your siblings?"

"Just you. I have no interest in the others. They're ungrateful offspring who are apparently relishing their father's misery and downfall. I'm hoping you're different and that your opinion is more open since your contact with him has been limited."

"You know him well?" I frown.

"I grew up with him. I've worked for him my entire adult life. Look, I know the others have told you stories about what a terrible human being he supposedly is. The tall tales are greatly exaggerated. There's another side to the story I think you should hear. Is there someplace we can talk?"

There is and we could, but I still have questions. "How did you find me?"

She frowns as if the question is so simple it's almost beneath answering. "You're a creature of habit. Except for last week, you leave the gym no later than seven every morning. I merely waited, hoping to intercept you."

My mind is blown. "You've been following me?"

She hesitates. "I've suspected for a while we might need to have this conversation. Now, circumstances have arisen that make me realize I was right. Where can we go?"

For the most part, I don't want to talk to her. I don't know everything Barclay inflicted on my siblings, but I can't forget my personal experience with the bastard. He's dismissive, self-absorbed, and manipulating. I can't imagine what Bethany can say to change my opinion or why she's even bothering to try. On the other hand, I'm curious. If she's not interested in family dynamics, what does she want? I don't know, but at the very least, Maxon, Griff, and Harlow will want information about the sister they've never met.

"Not from Seattle?"

Bethany shakes her head. "I'm based in San Diego."

She traveled twelve hundred miles to see me? This exchange is getting weirder and weirder.

"Around the corner. There's a bagel and organic coffee place." I've never been, but it's close by. And I want answers. This place will work.

I give her directions and she meets me there three minutes later. I'm first to enter, and when she walks in, I'm not surprised that male heads turn. Now that I'm looking at her, she's got an exotic quality. She's slender, petite. But her presence seems much bigger than her stature. Her almond-shaped eyes are striking, especially since they're an unusual shade of gray. In fact, everything about her comes off as severe, yet there's something under that facade I can't put my finger on. It's a vulnerability. She's not as confident as she wants everyone to believe. Somewhere along the way she's suffered. I've experienced enough of the bad to know the hallmarks. Bethany has secrets—deep, dark ones. I'd bet everything on that.

Now I'm even more intrigued.

I wave her over, and she sits. A college-age waitress in a logo'd T-shirt appears. We both order black coffee and skip the carbs.

"You've got my attention," I say as soon as the girl is gone. "What do we need to discuss?"

"Barclay."

Not Father or Dad or any other term to express one's paternal unit.

I frown. "I'm listening."

"The rest of your siblings may have poisoned you against him, but I'm here to give you a different side of the story…and ask for your help."

Right to the point, and without any acknowledgement that we're, in fact, siblings, too. The old me would probably have accepted that approach without complaint. Heck, in some ways I'm still okay with it. But something niggles at me. If I'm supposed to be paying attention to my heart or whatever, I'm not going to let her bark questions at me and leave without trying to see if there could be any sibling bond between us. I also find myself wanting to know what the heck that chink in her armor of confidence is about.

"I have some questions first. You say you grew up with Barclay?"

She sighs. "Do you need me to prove that I am who I say I am?"

Actually, that hadn't occurred to me. She's got too many of the Reed characteristics not to be authentic—Maxon's stubborn chin, Griff's dissecting gaze, and Harlow's sharply feminine features, the green tinge to her unusual eyes we all have.

"No. I want to understand your perspective. You're right that I've heard nothing good about the man, and my one interaction with him didn't leave a positive impression."

She waves my words away. "He suspected you were already poisoned against him."

"Yet he still tried to persuade me to invest with him."

"Everyone should want to make money, regardless of the people you're making it with."

A very Barclay answer. On the other hand, I can't logically disagree. Whether I've earned money with people I like or hate, it spends the same. "Point taken. Tell me about growing up with Barclay."

"That's not important."

"Because you want me to invest money, too?"

"I wouldn't be opposed."

"What about all the people he's cheated out of their savings? It's three billion dollars. He's likely going to prison."

Bethany wrings her hands for a moment before she seemingly catches herself and stills. For whatever reason, she's nervous.

"Allegedly cheated. It's a giant misunderstanding. Which is actually why I need your help. You see, he invested the money for those people, like he promised. He can produce it all and clear up this mess quite easily. And he will." She shifts, crossing her legs and clasping her hands. "But Lund is a thorn in his side."

I rear back. "Douglas Lund?"

"The same one trying to buy Stratus, yes."

"That's an unconfirmed rumor." I frown.

After the waitress sets down our coffee with a quick murmur, Bethany leans across the table. "Cut the BS. We both know it's true. Lund wants his hands on Stratus. Have you figured out why yet?"

I've been trying to understand that for weeks, but so far...nothing. I'm loath to admit that. It would be giving Bethany the upper hand. The woman might be my half sister, but she's all Reed, which means she's part shark. If she thinks there's blood in the water, she'll treat me like chum and come at me, teeth bared.

"I have some guesses," I bluff.

"Let's say I believe you." But clearly she doesn't. "The truth is, Lund's number one goal is to bring Barclay down."

"Because?"

"Barclay has a wandering dick. The fact that we're both sitting here is a testament to that fact." She sighs. "Earlier this year, his latest perky, young assistant gave birth to a baby boy. When I realized he'd zeroed in on her, I told him to leave the girl alone or get a vasectomy. At least wear a condom. But obviously none of that happened. So Amanda gave birth. Did I mention that Lund is her last name and Douglas is her father? He's absolutely pissed that Barclay knocked up his baby girl, so he's on a personal vendetta to tear our father down. Right now, Lund can't do any further damage—beyond framing Barclay, of course—so he's going after one of the man's children."

What? I peer at her. Blink. That's so twisted it barely makes sense. "Lund framed him?"

"Like I said, the whole mess is a misunderstanding. Lund contorted all the evidence to make Barclay look guilty."

Is that possible? "Even if that's true, why come after me? It accomplishes nothing. My biological father barely knows I exist."

Besides, why would Lund have offered me an amount of money for Stratus that's more than fair if he's merely screwing Barclay through me?

"I don't think that matters to Douglas Lund. Barclay may not acknowledge the slight, but there's no way he won't take notice. They both know it. As soon as he can prove Lund is full of hot air, he'll be out of jail and the truth will be revealed."

"Why tell me all this?"

"I'm trying to be a decent human being and warn you."

"So you're doing this for me?" I say skeptically.

"And for Barclay," she admits. "You're crucial to not letting Lund win. You can't sell Stratus to him."

"Because he'll have revenge?"

"Exactly."

I sit back and cross my arms over my chest. "That's not a compelling reason for me to turn down a billion dollars."

When I toss out that figure, I see her repress a wince. "Think of your family."

"Maxon, Griff, and Harlow are my family." I take a sip of brew. "Tell me why you think I should save a man who screws his assistants and—"

"Are you really in any position to cast stones, given the fact you're screwing Nia? Isn't that her name?"

I almost come across the table. "Why the fuck are you poking in my personal life?"

"I'm merely doing my homework, and as far as I can see, Mr. Cook, the apple hasn't fallen far from the tree."

I barely bite back an ugly curse. "Nia is more than a warm body to me. And I certainly haven't gone out of my way to impregnate her."

Except I remember the night at the burlesque club. I didn't do anything to *not* impregnate her...

"Aww, are you in love?" She snorts. "Are you really naive enough to choose pussy over the man who gave you life?"

I narrow my eyes. "Don't manipulate me. If Barclay were in my shoes, he would sell, too. In fact, he'd have zero respect for me if I forfeited a fortune for anyone, much less someone I'd met once."

Bethany presses her lips together. "So you don't care if Lund is only using you to get to Barclay?"

"Not really. I still walk away with a billion dollars."

Her face softens. "You think our father doesn't care about you. He does. Admittedly, he's not a warm man. But are any of the Reeds?"

"Did he send you here to make this ridiculous pitch? To tell me not to take a profitable deal simply so he can save face?"

"No, so we can prevent you from having to watch Lund dismantle your business. That's exactly what he'll do, simply for spite. He'll happily tear it apart in front of your face to see you squirm. There won't be a damn thing you can do to stop him."

The possibility that he'll break Stratus apart occurred to me. In the past, I shoved the notion aside and refused to let it bother me. Now...I can't deny a twinge of something like denial and regret. Could I watch that asshole disassemble everything I've spent years building? I would hate every minute. I also can't stand that he's trying to take Nia from me, too. Unless I can convince her to quit before I sign the papers, she'll be out of my professional reach for two years. If she won't marry me and won't follow me to another endeavor, I may lose her altogether.

Too many possibilities scroll through my head. And this woman across the table might be my sister biologically, but she's not my friend. I don't think for one moment her ploy has anything to do with protecting me and my interests.

I need to do some digging, find some answers.

"I'll think about it. I have a month to make up my mind. How can I contact you?"

"Why would you? I don't have anything else to add."

"I might have questions."

"I've given you all the information I know."

With a shrug, I study her, trying to figure her out. She's got a more than passable poker face. Only her odd gestures give away her nerves. "Don't you want to know what I decide?"

She taps a finger on the table, then finally reaches into her purse and pulls out a business card and a pen. Quickly, she scribbles something on the back. "Here's my cell number. Call me once you've made your decision."

Then she tosses ten bucks on the table, rises, and leaves before I can say another word. I'm left staring after her, wondering what the hell kind of rabbit hole I just went down and what will happen next.

CHAPTER THIRTEEN

I'M NOT IN a great mood when I get back to Nia's house. I managed to pick up some clean clothes from my place without waking Bas. I need to call my siblings, let them know about Bethany and our meeting that felt a hell of a lot like a chess match. But it's still the middle of the night Hawaii time, so it will have to wait.

By the time I return to the cottage, it's almost nine. Nia is up. A slow R&B tune blares from a Bluetooth speaker in the kitchen. She's swaying to the sensual beat as she stirs something in a bowl.

Suddenly, I'm less interested in the things Bethany said to me and more focused on continuing the sexual exploration Nia and I started last night.

I approach her from behind and wrap my arms around her waist. She freezes for a second, then looks over her shoulder at me, closes her eyes, and smiles, hips still rocking.

"Morning," she purrs.

"Morning, honey." I try to move with her. "What are you making?"

"Pancakes. Want some?"

"I can think of other things I want far more." I slide one hand down from her waist, over her stomach, then brush my fingers across her pajamas until I'm cupping her pussy through the cotton.

"Hmm. I like that. But I have to eat something first. You wore me out last night."

A low laugh breaks from my chest. "Having trouble keeping up?"

She raises a dark brow. "Give me some breakfast, and we'll see who has trouble keeping up."

We stand close, swaying to the music for a wordless moment. I've never heard this song, but I like it. Sexy. Romantic. The female vocalist says she's head over heels in love. She tells her man to look no further, that everything he wants is right in front of him. I'm in total agreement as I press kisses down her neck and across her exposed shoulder, covered only by the spaghetti strap of her tank.

"I'm looking forward to it."

Nia rolls her hips, grinding back into me. I groan as the woman sings that her heart goes ba-dum, biddy-da-dum. I relate.

"I like this. I want to play it while I fuck you." I make my point by dragging my thumb over the top of her cleft, hovering over her clit.

Her breath catches. "Yeah…"

"What's the name of this song?"

"'Boo'd Up' by Ella Mai."

"You got more music like this?"

"Like what?"

"Sexy." When she nods, I smile as I nip at her lobe. "How long did you say those pancakes will take?"

"Ten minutes." Her voice strains as she gyrates back against me.

"The faster you're done, the sooner I can make you feel really good." To make sure she gets my point, I tease between her legs again until I hear her breath hitch, until I feel her body tense.

"Maybe we can skip pancakes, after all."

"Eager?" I taunt.

"You do this to me, Evan. Always have, since the first time you touched me."

"Same, honey." I grab her a little tighter. "I can't seem to get enough."

Nia turns in my arms. "Try not to, okay?"

There's something in her eyes… She's vulnerable, anxious. Does she really think I could get tired of her? Leave her? I don't know if this is love. Maybe. I never felt it with Becca so I'd know for sure. But I'm pretty certain of a few things…

"I never want what we've got to end. I'm always going to crave you. You're not like anything I've felt or imagined. Believe that."

She nods slowly, but I see on her face that she's wondering if that will be enough.

As I caress a stray dark wave away from her cheek, I know she wants reassurance. She wants to know if I love her.

I need to figure my shit out. Nia deserves that.

"Eat. I'm going to take a quick shower."

"You want some pancakes?"

"I'll make eggs," I hedge.

She cocks her head and gives me a little pout. "But I make amazing pancakes. I slip in a little vanilla and cinnamon. They're so light and fluffy and—"

"I have no doubt they're delicious." Even the sound of them makes my mouth water.

She sighs. "But they're not healthy enough, right?"

"You know me. I try to keep my diet high in protein, low in fat and carbs. It promotes a healthy weight and blood pressure, not to mention—"

"Of course it does. But it's a lot less fun and interesting. Let me make you one at least?"

"All right. One." I can't turn her down when giving in would make her happier. "But if you want me to keep these abs you seemed so fond of licking last night, you can't feed me empty calories."

As she laughs, I leave her with a kiss on the cheek and jog to the shower. When I return to the kitchen in clean clothes a few minutes later, she's already setting two full plates onto her little bistro table, one piled high with pancakes. The other contains nothing but eggs and oatmeal. "Good timing. It's ready."

"Where's the pancake you wheedled me into?"

A slow smile spreads across her face. "I got to thinking… Rather than putting it on your plate, I have a better idea for giving you a taste."

Immediately, I'm intrigued. "Yeah? Let me have it."

"In a minute. Once we start that…I'm not sure I'll get to finish my breakfast. You tend to make me lose my head."

I love that, despite my relative inexperience, I can rev and rattle her. "Okay. I'll wait, just not patiently."

As she butters her pancakes and pours the syrup, she sends me a flirty grin seemingly full of secrets. "So how was the gym?"

In the haze of promised pleasure, I forgot about Bethany. My smile falls. "Well, I met my mystery half sister. She accosted me in the parking lot, actually."

Nia takes her first bite and, in mid-chew, stops. "What?"

As I dig into my food, I explain the meeting, Bethany's behavior, and the reason she doesn't want me to sell Stratus.

"She doesn't want anything to do with the rest of your siblings?" Nia asks.

"Apparently not."

"But they're great people."

I nod. "The whole thing makes me more suspicious and less inclined to listen to her."

"Why would you, since she's clearly on Barclay's side?

"Good point. She said she grew up with him."

"That bothers you, doesn't it? Because he had nothing to do with you once you became an orphan."

I swallow more eggs, then sip coffee. "Something like that. I'm torn between being jealous and pitying her."

"And you don't know which to feel because you don't know the man well." At my nod, she frowns. "That's a lot to take in. What are you going to do?"

"Nothing she said changes the way I feel." Well, not really. I don't love the idea of anyone taking Stratus apart, especially as a fuck you. But is saving it for the sake of sentiment and pride worth a billion dollars? "If selling upsets Barclay, that's not my problem."

"It's not," she agrees. "You know…I've been giving that thought. I was against you selling Stratus at first, but maybe I was looking at it selfishly. I didn't want things changing that much. I'm comfortable with our office and its vibe. Working with you has always been great." She turns quiet for a moment. "But everything has changed anyway."

I can't refute that.

"And you're looking at this deal more logically. It's a lot of money. Why shouldn't you profit from your hard work? You're totally young enough to start over and do something else if you want. And if you don't... Well, I don't know. I can't picture you lying around drinking mai tais all day."

"No. I'd definitely find something to do. But whatever that might be, I want you to come with me. You will, right?"

She shrugs, looking somewhere between undecided and uncomfortable. My gut tightens.

"I think we'll have to figure out where we're at when you're ready to sign the papers. We've still got a month."

Gritting my teeth, I lean in. "You have to think about whether you're staying with me professionally? I know our personal lives are in limbo but..."

"How can I still be your assistant if you're my ex? Besides, you're moving to Maui. If we're not together anymore, Evan, I'll be staying here."

"Would you work for the Lunds, too?" That possibility leaves me feeling vaguely betrayed and a lot angry.

She shrugs. "It's a good job, and they'd need the help. But maybe we'll wind up together. Who knows?"

I set down my fork with a clatter. "We would know for sure if you'd just say yes to marrying me."

"You know it's not that simple." She reaches for my hand. "We've barely been together for three weeks. Most people even don't talk about marriage in less than three months."

I want to argue with that, but I can't. She needs more time before she's ready to commit. Hell, maybe I do, too. Maybe I'll figure out by then what love is and whether I'm truly in it.

Forcing myself to relax, I push away my empty plate. "In the meantime, are you going to eat the rest of those pancakes?"

She glances down at the last few bites on her plate, then up at me with an unsteady grin as she stands. "No. You are."

Then she clears my plate and our empty coffee cups onto a nearby counter. Next, she strips off her shirt and drapes herself across the table. I flash hot as she sets the plate on her bare abdomen, drags her finger through the syrup, then smears it over her taut nipples.

Stunned, I stare. Yeah… I just ate a whole meal, but suddenly I'm starving.

Plucking a scrap of pancake off her plate, I shove the bite in my mouth and moan. "It's good, but it needs a little something…"

All but tossing the plate in a nearby chair, I lunge over Nia and take her breast in my mouth, drinking in the sticky-sweet syrup and her skin with a long, low moan.

It's a long hour later before we come up for air. We're both sated—at least for now. But Nia's sensuality, her sense of sexual play, and her ability to make me feel not only like a man but like the best she's ever had keep me ravenous. But I'm beginning to wonder if, like Sebastian suggested, there's more between us. Some emotion. Something binding. Something lasting.

Right now, I can't imagine ever letting her go.

Is Bas right? Am I in love for the first time in my life? Have I fallen for Nia?

Tuesday, November 28

AFTER ANOTHER NIGHT with Nia, wrapped in her arms and her body, I wake up beside her on our new mattress, which I managed to have delivered same day. A new sofa, too.

Beside me, she lies curled on her side, facing the wall. Her dark hair looks glossy and lustrous strewn across her pale pillow. She's naked, and her bare shoulder peeks above the covers, tempting me. Even in the predawn light, I see the faint marks of a love bite I left on her neck last night. I was unabashed, unrestrained, and unapologetic as I took her during the night. Now, I'm happily sated and pretty damn cheerful.

Until I look at the date on my phone. The twenty-eighth—exactly seven months since Becca's death.

Reality hits me, but instead of her absence felling me like a battering ram, it stings more like the prick of a needle.

Logically, Becca not haunting my thoughts anymore is healthy. But the change stuns me. A month ago, I was grappling with a lingering black pall and struggling to process all the changes in my day-to-day existence. Today, it's as if I've been reborn and emerged on the other side a completely different man with a whole new outlook.

Guilt gnaws at me for that, biting and tenacious. It's worse because I can't deny how happy I am, maybe more than I've ever been.

Another sign I wasn't in love with Becca? Or merely that I've moved on and am totally infatuated with Nia?

I don't know.

But there's one issue—person—I can't seem to forget and haven't recovered from: The child I lost seven months ago today. The child I'll never get to hold. The child who will never know life.

Into my lamenting, my phone buzzes. I glance at the screen, wondering if it's one of my siblings checking in before they go to bed in Hawaii. They were glad to hear I'd found Bethany—or rather that she'd found me—but shocked to learn she was both loyal to Barclay and utterly disinterested in meeting them. I'm okay to write the woman off. She's a stranger—granted one who shares half my DNA—but it seems counterproductive to badger someone hostile into becoming a part of my life.

Instead, the message is from Sebastian. `If you're not at the gym yet, want company?`

I grin. Bas has a love-hate relationship with fitness. He likes sleeping in and drinking way more than I do, which isn't conducive to maintaining peak physical condition. But he doesn't look as if he's been skipping too many workouts. He was a college athlete, so it doesn't take much for him to keep muscle tone, lucky bastard. Because I didn't get in shape until my early twenties, I have to work a lot harder at it. That's okay, though. I've worked hard for everything I've got. Besides, having this time every morning helps me keep my head clear.

I drop a kiss on Nia's temple, then roll out of bed with a stretch. After brushing my teeth and drinking my customary half a cup of coffee, I meet my buddy at the gym by five thirty.

"You're up early," I comment as we head inside.

The place is barely awake, like most people at this hour. I prefer to start my day before the sun. I can get a lot accomplished. Nia would rather be a night owl. The later the hour grows, the more she seems to come alive. I'm not getting much sleep these days...and I'm not complaining. If she keeps making me feel this good, I'll be happy to sleep when I'm dead.

"I'm almost ready to move out of your digs. I got up early to do a little more cleanup at my place. Some of us aren't on vacation this week, you know," Bas drawls.

"No rush. I've moved in with Nia until I relocate to Maui. She and I, um...need to figure out where we're at and what's next for us."

"You mean you're still trying to decide whether you're in love with her?" He laughs and shakes his head. "Dumb ass. Guess I shouldn't be surprised. It took you a month just to choose the perfect shade of blue for Stratus's logo. Deciding what's in your heart is a much bigger decision. At this rate, you might be collecting Social Security before you figure it out."

Snorting, I head for the free weights. "Thanks for the vote of confidence. Do your thing. I'll do mine."

Ninety minutes later, I've made the weight circuit and logged forty-five minutes of intense cardio. I feel sweaty. Bas looks bedraggled. We leave, and I follow him to my penthouse to pick up more clothes. The weather is getting cooler. I need a coat.

After we take turns showering, I help him pack up, and we decide to grab breakfast so he can fill me in on what's been happening at the office in my absence. It's nearly noon when I finally duck into Nia's quaint cottage. In fact, I'm surprised I haven't heard from her yet today. Is she really still sleeping?

Once glance inside the place tells me she's not.

Nia paces the kitchen with a hand pressed to her rapidly rising-and-falling chest. She turns in my direction, and I see tears streaming down her stunned face.

Her expression hits me square in the chest like a semi. When she spots me, her eyes flare wide and guilty. Her anxiety thickens. My heart stops.

What the hell is going on?

"Nia?"

"Evan." She swallows. "Oh, my god. I…"

I cross the room and take her shoulders, delving into her darting stare. She wriggles out of my grasp.

"Tell me what's wrong."

Nia shakes her head, not in refusal but as if she's swimming through disbelief to find words. "You'll be angry. Upset."

Shit. Has she met someone else? Is she done with me? Those possibilities plop a two-ton weight on my chest. I need information ASAP. But first I have to calm her.

I drag a chair from the kitchen table across the floor and set her in it. I manage to resist the urge to grab her up in my arms again by gripping the back of her chair and looking directly into her eyes. "We'll figure it out together. Tell me why you're crying."

She blinks up at me, mouth contorting as more tears spill. They tear at my guts. This is beyond mere anxiety. She's in pain. I feel it. I've never experienced this transfer of emotion, and I'm unsure why I hurt before she's even said a word. I only know I need to help and comfort her.

"I-I had a doctor appointment at nine. I scheduled it months ago. It's my annual well woman…"

A sob interrupts her. The sound tightens every muscle and rips through my chest. "And they gave you bad news?"

I wrack my brain, trying to imagine what they might have told her. Cancer? Something worse? I can't even wrap my head around what that might be.

"I-I'm pregnant."

Those two words penetrate my brain, pelt my composure. I couldn't possibly have heard her correctly. But a mental replay of her trembling voice assures me I did.

Shit.

I don't have to guess who, when, where, or how it happened. I know all too well. Me. Twenty-four days ago. Her dressing room at the Bawdy Boudoir Burlesque Revue. On top of her, plowing away without thought, caution, or condom.

I release her chair, stand upright, and force myself to breathe. "You're sure?"

It's a stupid question, and some rational part of me recognizes it's a stall tactic to give my brain time to catch up to reality.

She sends me a shaky nod. "They asked the first day of my last period. I couldn't remember. I have an app that tracks… I realized I was a few days overdue. When they asked if I could be pregnant, I-I said yes. Ten minutes later, they confirmed… I came home to break the news." Then she sniffles and looks up at me with dark eyes desperate for something. Forgiveness? Reassurance? "I didn't know how."

At my sides, my hands curl into fists, like the ones seeming to choke the air from my lungs. Then a thought burns through my brain: She's not upset for herself; she's apprehensive about my reaction.

"How do you feel?" I ask.

"Shocked."

"We both are. Beyond that?"

"Worried."

I allay the only other concern she might have. "You'll be a great mother."

"I guess. I hope. I had a great role model." She frowns. "But that's not why I'm worried."

So I was right. "Forget about my reaction for a minute. How do *you* feel?"

"Um, it's a lot and it's unexpected. I'm not unhappy. I already know I'll love my son or daughter, no matter what." She grabs the front of my shirt. "Please tell me what you're thinking."

How do I admit that I have no idea? "Just this morning, I was thinking about the child I lost seven months ago, the one who would be an infant now."

Is this baby Nia and I conceived a second chance? Is this Fate's way of replacing what I lost? I don't really believe in such things, but this seems somehow too serendipitous to be totally random.

"And?" Her voice shakes.

"And...that's as far as I've processed."

"We're going to be parents, and I don't know what we should do next." Suddenly, she can't look at me. "If your marriage proposal is off the table, I get it. This is more than you bargained for, right? My own father didn't want me, either. Since you and I got together, I've had trouble believing the hot, rich white guy would really stay with a girl like me, so—"

"Wait a minute." Her words jar me. Infuriate me. I don't bother with the back of her chair this time, just clutch her shoulders and kneel in front of her so we're eye-to-eye. "I never said anything about retracting my marriage proposal. And I never thought any of those things you're thinking."

"But it makes sense."

"To who? Don't compare me to your deadbeat father. And don't think for one second that I care what color either one of us is. You're beautiful, smart, and sexy. I've been wondering what you're doing with a tech geek like me," I swear. "I would never abandon you or our child. Hell, you know I want to marry you. I bought you a ring you're still not wearing. I was willing to give you the house you wanted. I'm living with you. I'm sleeping beside you. I'm doing my best to heap pleasure on you. I don't know what else..."

She could want. But yes, I do. And an instant later, she takes the words right out of my mouth.

"You don't love me." Her words are almost a whimper, accompanied by tears.

Everything about her reply stabs me in the chest. I'm not sure what to say.

"I have no idea what I feel." In the midst of some of the most shocking news of my life, I can't help but laugh. "In case it's escaped your notice, I'm terrible with emotion. There's something between us that's unlike anything I've ever experienced. I've got no clue what that means. But if you really need to hear three words to say 'I do,' I don't know where that leaves us."

She dissolves into tears and wraps her arms around herself. "I never meant for this to happen."

"You can't blame yourself. *I* barged in. *I* demanded. *I* didn't glove up. I didn't think. It's my fault. I'll help you deal with the consequences."

That only makes her sob harder. "You didn't want children. All you wanted was relief. And now…everything is a mess. I need to go."

"What? Go where? This is your house." I shake my head. "No."

When Nia sniffles again and I sense another tear-storm brewing, I glance around for a box of tissues. Nothing. *Goddamn it.*

"Stay right there."

I hustle out of the room and haul down to the bathroom. It seems so odd to be terribly concerned about something as mundane as a tissue when the world as I know it is collapsing in on me.

A baby.

Fuck, I'm not ready to confront being a father again. I'm not ready to handle the fear of losing my child.

But what choice do I have?

Now that Nia isn't in right front of me, her dark eyes haunting me with questions I can't answer, I grab the cardboard box off the vanity and drag in a steadying breath. Vaguely, I'm aware of my fingers crushing the flimsy container, but I can't stop. Or care.

A baby.

Nothing logical or coherent is happening in my head right now. It's swimming in shock. I release the tissue box, grasp the edge of the sink, tell myself to breathe.

It doesn't help.

When I lost Becca and the baby, I wasn't sure I'd ever want a wife or a child again. The necessity of getting married soon became apparent, however. I could barely function without organization, and my practicality persuaded me that finding another wife was the best solution. Fine. Then Nia came along. Not exactly as planned, but in many ways better than I dared to hope. Yet more hellish because I never wanted to feel again. And now?

A baby.

That news keeps flashing through my brain like a neon sign, but it hasn't really sunk in. I resist the urge to punch the framed mirror over the sink. I'm not a violent man, and I won't stoop to a childish, destructive compulsion. But it's tempting.

I need to return to Nia. I need to say something that will make it better. First, I need to figure out what that might be.

Yeah, I'm freaked out. But she's scared. She's worried she's going to end up like her mother—alone and single because the selfish prick she gave herself to left. But I know all too well what it's like to be without a father. I know how many years I spent resenting the hell out of Barclay Reed for leaving me to the dubious mercy of the foster care system because the son he'd inconveniently conceived with his secretary cramped his style or whatever.

That won't happen to my child.

I'm going to go back into the living room, hold Nia's hands, and find some way to convince that woman to be my wife. We're going to have this baby together. I will not lose my shit because she's pregnant. I will not walk away. I refuse to hurt her.

A baby.

I let out a shuddering breath, then somehow manage to compose myself, grab the box of tissues, and head back down the hall to comfort the woman I intend to marry.

But when I reach the living room again, Nia, her tears, and her purse are all gone.

CHAPTER FOURTEEN

THIRTEEN TEXTS AND half a dozen phone calls to Nia. All of them unanswered.

In the middle of that, I searched her social media and found the names of friends and past lovers. Methodically, I hunted down their phone numbers and called each one. I even gritted my teeth as I talked to Kyle.

No one has seen her tonight.

Afterward, I spent two hours driving to places I thought she might go. Lorenzo and Guilia haven't laid eyes on her. Ditto for Bas. The BBB Revue was locked up tight.

Still no sign of Nia.

It's damn near ten p.m. Anger and panic are carving up my composure. Where the fuck could she be? The waiting. The wondering. They remind me too much of that fucking April afternoon I never saw Becca again. That time, I hadn't known anything was wrong until the police arrived at my office. Her death disordered my world.

Losing Nia would destroy me.

Terrified, I grip the steering wheel with one hand and begin dialing police stations with the other, barking questions and damn near biting people's heads off.

If—no, when—I catch up with Nia, I'm putting a tracker on her car, her phone, and anywhere else I can think of. I can't believe she fucking walked out of the house and left me. Is she trying to say we're through?

No. It can't be over. I won't let it be, not unless she says that to my face. Even then, I intend to do everything in my power to persuade her to stay in my life. I'll beg her to marry me. Hell, I'll skywrite my proposal.

Will you tell her you love her?

Do I? I'm starting to have suspicions, but how am I supposed to know for sure? Even if I've totally fallen, would she believe me if I said the words now?

Just in case she went to my penthouse, I stop there. The minute I walk in the door, I know the unit is empty. Not only is no one inside, but it's devoid of emotion. It always has been. After spending time with Nia, I comprehend that.

I lived under this roof for three years. Becca and I rarely smiled or laughed here. We never argued here. We hardly had sex here, either. We didn't share passion. We didn't share hopes. We shared hours. We shared space. We shared money.

That wasn't a marriage.

Jesus, I didn't love her.

I'll have to call Bas later and tell him he was right. He'll enjoy that.

Suddenly, my phone buzzes in my pocket. Fresh hope and panic twist around in my gut as I pull the device free. Nia's name and text flash across my screen. Relief floods my veins.

`Sorry I ran out. I had to clear my head. I'll be home by midnight if you want to talk.`

In two hours? I poise my thumbs over the screen, ready to demand she come back now before I pound her with a horde of questions. *Where have you been? Where are you? How are you feeling? What are you thinking?* But she texted—rather than called—because she wants to avoid answering all that until she's ready. One thing I'm quickly learning about Nia? Rushing her, no matter how badly I want to, accomplishes nothing.

Finally, I tap back, `I'll be there. And we will talk.`

She doesn't respond, but I see she's read my message. For now, it will do.

That gives me time to get calm, figure out exactly what I'm going to say. First, I have to find some way—no fucking idea how—to quiet the doubts and demons in my head.

I turn a slow circle around my darkened living room, looking for distraction. I don't feel like TV. If I go to Nia's place now, I'll spend two hours climbing the walls. I don't want a drink. I'm not hungry for dinner.

I can think of only one solution.

With ground-eating strides, I make my way to my bedroom and drag out a half-finished canvas from under my bed. In less than ten minutes, I've stripped down to a pair of shorts, dragged everything I need into the kitchen, and prepared a palette.

As every light in the place blazes, I stare at the beginnings of a painting I barely remember starting months ago. It's mechanical, gears and spokes turning in circles, working together for a common purpose. The dominant colors are cool grays and blues with a hint of green and rust to depict shadow, wear, and age. It's competent, not representative of the way I'm feeling now. There's no sense of barely leashed wildness. Not one brush stroke is out of place. It's too meticulous and methodical.

I can't finish it.

After shoving the half-finished piece aside, I retrieve a fresh canvas and set it on my easel. I dip a brush in the paint and stare at the blank white space. What am I bringing to life with pigment? I've always been into technical and mechanical themes. Precision and order—that's how my brain usually works.

Not today. In fact, not since Nia.

Raising the brush, I let it hover over the canvas and close my eyes. The cacophony of shock, worry, and terror begins to quiet. I encourage the monotone hum working its way up through the background of my thoughts. And without looking, I flip the brush across the blank space once, twice, a few more times.

A minute later, I risk a peek. Yeah, I have no idea what I'm doing. Is this a landscape? A portrait? An abstract? So far, it's a disorganized blob...which is an accurate representation of my current thoughts.

With a disgusted sigh, I set the palette down, clear everything away, and toss my clothes on once more. I don't know why my steadying, go-to activity still isn't working. Since I actually put a brush to canvas, I managed more today than any time since Becca's death. But I miss sinking into the steadying strokes, letting my subconscious take over as my world rights itself once more.

None of that happened tonight. I'm still as confused as ever.

Cursing, I grab my keys and lock the penthouse behind me, ridiculously eager to be away from here. In fact, when I move to Maui, I might sell this place after all. It's not logical. It may cost me money in the long run since the value of this unit will only increase over time. But there's nothing here I want to revisit. There's no reason for me to return.

Wondering when I stopped being so practical, I head to Nia's. The house is still dark when I walk in.

Thankfully, she's only a few minutes behind me. When she finally steps through the front door, I'm desperate to hold her. Fuck, she looks tired. She's clearly been crying.

I tear across the room toward Nia. Her expression turns resolute as she raises a hand between us to stop me. "Don't. I have to say this without being clouded by your nearness."

Though the distance she's putting between us makes me anxious, I do my best to respect it. "I'm listening. But before you say anything, remember that I wanted to marry you before you found out you were pregnant. I still do. Don't think for one instant that me being your boss, the size of our bank accounts, or the different colors of our skin changes anything for me."

"I know you mean that. I'm sorry if I upset you. That was my insecurity talking. It wasn't fair to lump you in with my father." Nia slowly drops her hand to her side. "I've been driving around, thinking. I went by the house I grew up in. I visited my mother's grave. I even went to the office after hours. Finally, I came to some conclusions. A baby changes everything. We both grew up in homes that weren't picture-perfect. I don't want that for my child."

What is she saying? Why is my chest buckling, my throat tightening? "I don't, either."

"Some people may call my decision old-fashioned, but they don't have to live with it. I do. And I believe this baby will be better off with two parents."

"Ones who have the same last name and live in the same house." I want to be clear about my expectations.

She nods. "Yes. The practical choice is to get married."

Part of me rejoices. I've won; I've got her. But another part bleeds. I cheated my way into her future. Not intentionally. I hardly set out to get her pregnant in the hopes she'd marry me. Yet I hate the resignation on her face. She's not making this decision lightly—or happily. She wants love. She wants the romantic fairy tale. That's not what she's getting, and I don't know if I can ever give it to her. I respect her too much to lie now and hope it will be true later.

My one consolation? I'm prepared to make our engagement official.

From my pants, I pull out the box containing the engagement ring I bought before Thanksgiving. I lift the lid and extract the diamond from the cushion. Then I take her hand, surprised to find my fingers shaking. "This may not be the circumstance you wanted when you said yes, but I swear I'll do everything I can to make you happy and—"

"It's not about me and my heart anymore. Or even our feelings." She slides a palm over her still-flat stomach. "It's about the life we made together."

After being with Nia these past few weeks, I've felt the passion and connection Becca and I lacked. I won't have another gray, void marriage.

"It should be about us, as well."

"I can't think about that right now. I have a responsibility to this child. All my life, my mother put me first. She's not here anymore for me to thank, but I'm a better person for her love. I intend to give our baby the same kind of devotion."

It's admirable, commendable. I'm sure Nia will shower our child with all the love he or she could ever want. But I'm not thinking about a being that's the size of a seed right now. I'm thinking about the woman standing in front of me, cheeks stained with silver paths, whom I plan to speak vows to and spend my life with.

"Of course." I slide the ring on her finger, gratified when it fits perfectly.

The sparkle of the diamond is a striking contrast with her rich brown skin. Every man will see the stamp of my possession. I've never been the caveman sort, but Nia is nearly mine in every sense of the word. This isn't a joyous occasion for her, but I have to swallow down the urge to whoop and beat my chest.

Until she speaks.

"Can you do that?" Nia questions. "Less than a week ago, you said you didn't want children. You couldn't even hold Trace's son. I wrestled all day about whether it was selfish to marry you when you're not sure you ever want kids. I nearly decided that if my mother could raise a daughter alone, I could do the same with my baby—"

"No. That's *my* baby, too." I already lost one this year. I'm not losing another.

She anchors her hands on her hips. "How are you going to handle it?"

Honestly, I don't know. I don't feel any more ready to be a father than I was last Thursday. I'm terrified as hell of Nia being pregnant, of fathering another child who may never be born. But here we are, and bowing to fear will only hurt us all.

"I just will."

"All right." Finally, she looks down at the ring on her finger and swallows. "It's really beautiful. I'm sorry I didn't tell you that when you gave it to me the first time."

I squeeze her hand. "It looks perfect on you."

The smile she gives me doesn't convey happiness. "If we're going to get married, I'd like to do this quickly."

"Absolutely. Do you mind if we get married in Maui? Maxon and Keeley's place is perfect for weddings. The Reed clan is all the family I have, and I don't know if they can travel here—"

"The wives are all too pregnant to come to Seattle now. A wedding in Hawaii would be nice." She tries to muster enthusiasm. "I only have a few people to invite. Lorenzo and Guilia. Some girlfriends. My second cousin Annabelle. Remember me telling you about her? The one who lives in New Orleans with her three guys?"

Vaguely, but if she wants them at our wedding… "Sure. I'll call Britta. She's the organizer. All three of my siblings have put together quick weddings, so they're pros. Britta's mom caters. Keeley works really closely with a great florist and photographer. Harlow is clever. It'll come together."

She nods absently. "I'll figure out a dress."

Becca always wanted something elaborate, and at the time we married, the money simply wasn't there. I don't want Nia to regret anything else about her decision to marry me.

I grab her shoulders. "As far as I'm concerned, you're only getting married once, and that's to me. So whatever dress will make you happy, I want you to have it."

"I don't need anything extravagant."

"But what do you *want*? Whatever that is, I'll give it to you."

Normally, I'd grit my teeth about the impractical pomp of weddings and stew about how illogical it is to spend thousands of dollars to speak a few words in front of some people simply so we can become man and wife. But until the baby, Nia wasn't even sure she wanted to marry me. I've forever changed her life with one rash decision made in a haze of possessive anger and lust. How can I not give her the small consolation of the wedding of her dreams?

"You don't have to do that, Evan. I don't mind keeping it small and simple."

Suddenly, I mind. "Our ceremony should be memorable, not expedient."

She sighs. I don't know whether she's conceding my point or simply too tired to argue. "You'll be having a prenuptial agreement drawn up, I suppose?"

It's illogical but I instantly resent her suggestion, like she's already concerned about our divorce before we're even married. Still, my practical side kicks in. "Yes, but let's not worry about it now. Shouldn't we..." Break open a bottle of champagne and toast? No, we can't do that since she's pregnant. "Celebrate somehow? We're engaged."

Nia looks at me for a long moment. "I don't feel like celebrating, Evan. I feel like going to bed. I'm tired."

It's been a day full of shock and exhaustion—for both of us. A few earlier searches on my phone informed me that her hormones are probably raging, and it's not uncommon for her to feel exhausted. But knowing that doesn't help. We're planning to spend our lives together, yet I've never felt further apart from her.

When she makes her way down the hall, I follow, gripping her arm to stop her when we reach the bedroom. "You're unhappy, and it's...hurting me."

She turns with a little furrow between her brows. "I didn't plan this. You didn't, either. I thought I knew where my life was going. But..." She pauses. "I'm happy about the baby. I've always wanted kids. I'm just sad because I wanted them with someone who would love me for the rest of my life."

Her words stab me in the chest.

"Please understand. I'm not saying that to make you feel guilty," she carries on. "You can't help how you feel any more than I can. I know you're not ready to fall in love again and—"

"I never loved Becca. I realized that today."

Nia rears back, searches my face, then cups my cheek. "And you're confused?"

"Incredibly. But I know that for sure."

She looks stunned. "What are you saying?"

I'm not sure she believes me. Why should she when it took me years to realize something that's been staring me in the face? "You've changed me somehow. Made me look at everything differently."

"Or you've just gotten used to something new." She shrugs. "I'm not even sure it matters."

Then she eases free from my grip and heads for the shower, peeling her clothes off along the way. It's not seductive. It's automatic, as if I'm not even here. As if I'm not important at all.

That fucking hurts. Nia never doesn't want to talk. She's never not wanted to be with me.

Tonight, I might as well be invisible.

I sit back on the bed and watch her close the door between us. Everything inside me tells me to storm in there, strip down and climb in the shower with her, then grab her tight and kiss her until she melts against me. Until she curls herself around me.

I don't. It goes against everything inside me to sit idle, but I do.

When she emerges ten minutes later, she's wearing a cotton nightgown in a soft pink shade, trimmed in lace. Her face is clean, but her eyes are swollen. She's been crying again. Her ring finger is bare.

Fury swells. Not at her. At myself. She's bitterly disappointed, and I don't know to ease her. I fucking hate how impotent that makes me feel. If I could to go back in time and undo that night—No. I still wouldn't. I didn't expect any of this. Sure, I'd hoped I would be getting married, but to someone who roused only easy companionship, not a woman who makes me want her until I can't breathe. I certainly never imagined I'd be expecting a child again.

But I wouldn't change anything. I only want to move forward.

Nia climbs into bed and turns off the light, then rolls away from me. I ease down beside her. I may not know exactly what to do, but I know she needs my comfort.

When I wrap an arm around her, she stiffens. I don't relent, just press a kiss to her shoulder and wait. Slowly, she relaxes, her breathing evening out as she falls asleep in my arms.

I lie awake for hours, feeling her warmth against me, wondering how and when I'll figure out a way to make her happy for the rest of our lives.

Maui, Hawaii
Saturday, December 9

ELEVEN DAYS LATER, the day of our wedding dawns. It should be one of the happiest days of our lives. Instead, I've never seen Nia more withdrawn, as if she's preparing to walk to the hangman's noose, not the altar. Every time I look at her face, I see second thoughts and regrets. I can't stand it. And I can't marry her like this. She might have said yes, but I know damn well she answered me under duress.

It's stupid-early when I knock on Maxon and Keeley's door. It takes a good two minutes before my oldest brother opens with a yawn. "What's up? You're about eight hours early for the wedding, bro."

"I need to see Nia."

The gravity in my voice halts his stretch. "You okay? I didn't want to say anything, but you guys haven't seemed the same since you arrived."

How do I answer that? "I don't know what to think."

"Want to talk?"

"About how I feel?" I toss my hands in the air. "I can't answer that. Is shitty an emotion?"

Maxon grabs me by the arm and leads me into the kitchen. "You've got Reed genes, so yeah. I feel you. Coffee?"

"Please."

He prepares the single-cup brewer, then glances at me over his shoulder. "You have cold feet? Worried you two won't last?"

"No." With everything between us tense and uncertain, I probably should be. She's been closed off since she learned about the baby. I haven't wanted to push her. But my gut still tells me this is the right move. "She wants a father for our child. I..."

My brother stares at me as coffee drips and I grapple for words. I could explain that I'm loyal and I keep my promises but what's happening between us is more than that.

"I want to be with her." That's the best way I know how to put it.

Handing me a cup of steaming brew, Maxon nods and opens his mouth to speak.

It's interrupted by another knock at the door.

"Grab that. Will you?"

Wondering who the hell else could be here at the ass crack of dawn, I yank the door open again, stunned to find Bas and Griff. "What are you doing here?"

When I step back, they enter.

Griff slaps me on the back. "Thought I'd come by. Britta was having contractions earlier. For a while, I suspected we'd be having a baby and a wedding today. But it was false labor. It stopped about two hours ago. I came over because Noah called me and said he saw you leave his place at oh-dark-thirty. I picked up Sebastian along the way."

I nod. "I just, um…"

"Needs his head screwed on straight," Maxon supplies. "Before you knocked, Evan was explaining that he doesn't know how he feels about Nia. He's both male and a Reed, so naturally he has his head up his ass."

"Can't say I'm surprised. Welcome to the family," Griff drawls, then regards me with a slap on the shoulder. "It took three years and almost losing Britta for me to tell her I love her."

"I was faster with Keeley, but it was…messy." Maxon winces.

"How did you know?"

"My feelings?" Griff asks, then shrugs. "Process of elimination. Do you feel miserable without Nia?"

"Yes."

"Does it get under your skin and make you panic a little when she's angry or not speaking to you?"

The last week and a half has been anxiety-ridden and gut churning. "Yes."

"Does it bug the shit out of you when another guy so much as glances at her?"

"A lot." Even thinking about her exes and all the ways they've touched her makes me want to punch them all.

"Do you want her more than any woman you've ever known?"

From the first moment I saw her as something more than my assistant. "Yes."

"Have you ever felt this way before?"

I shake my head. "I didn't know I could."

Bas tsks at me as Maxon hands him coffee. "Dude, you're in love." He looks at my brothers. "I've been telling him this for a while."

He was right about the fact I didn't love Becca. Maybe he's right about this, too.

Maxon points at Sebastian. "See? I rest my case. You, my brother, just need to believe. You need to take that leap of faith."

"What he said," Griff puts in.

They make it sound so easy…

"What's going on, guys?" Keeley steps into the room, wrapped in a silky, pale robe, belted around the swelling of her belly. "Did you decide you wanted a bachelor party after all, Evan? I have to say, six a.m. is a pretty interesting time…"

Nia will look that pregnant come summer. I did some calculating. Our baby will be born late in July. We have our first appointment with a new obstetrician while we're on the island. We haven't talked about the fact that we're moving here, but as far as I'm concerned, it's a done deal.

"We're just convincing Evan that he's head over heels for his bride-to-be," Maxon quips.

Keeley frowns and blinks. "Of course. I mean, something has been troubling you both since you got here, and I guess neither of you were expecting to have a baby so soon. But I've known since you two came for Thanksgiving that you're mad for each other."

Head reeling, I set my coffee down and leave the men behind. Maxon's wife knew, too? Before I even suspected?

I take Keeley aside. "How's Nia?"

She stayed here the night before the wedding since everyone insists it's bad luck for the groom to see the bride before the ceremony. I think that's a foolish, antiquated notion, but Nia agreed with the superstition, so I acquiesced. I haven't seen her in almost twelve hours. She looked particularly pensive last night. I've been awake for hours, worrying she'll wake up this morning and tell me she's changed her mind.

"She seemed happy that everything is ready. Britta's mom finished the food last night. The florist will be here at eleven to drop off all the bouquets and arrangements. Lono will be here a little after one, a good hour before he performs the ceremony. The photographer will show up about the same time. The seamstress finished the alterations for Nia's dress and we picked it up. Thankfully, she found one off the rack that fit her almost perfectly. Otherwise—"

"That's not what I asked. How is *she*?"

Keeley takes a long time answering. "Nervous."

"Hesitant."

Maxon's wife pauses even longer before she nods. "But she loves you."

Right. The problem is, she thinks I don't love her. I may not know what love is, but I know what it isn't. I know that, since being with her, I've become full of nonsensical notions and something else I can't explain: feelings. Even though they have no basis in logic, I can no longer deny them. They exist.

In the background, my brothers and Bas rib each other about something. I focus on my racing thoughts and pounding heart. "I need to see her."

For a moment, Keeley looks as if she's going to object, then she presses her lips together and gives me a decisive nod. "Follow me."

As she leads me through the kitchen, pausing to accept a soft kiss from her husband, I follow.

"Evan?" Bas asks.

"Where you going?" Griff calls out.

Maxon follows up. "What are you doing?"

I raise my hand and wave them off. "I think…I'm leaping."

Behind me, they celebrate and immediately start arguing about who was right first. I don't care. I'm focused on Nia as I trail Keeley behind their bed and breakfast, toward the private *ohana* they've recently renovated into a suite.

We creep through the humid predawn and dewy grass until we reach the beachy blue door.

Keeley knocks. "Nia?"

A minute later, my bride opens with a sleepy yawn. Her face closes up the instant she sees me. "Evan?"

"I need to talk to you."

Something I don't like skitters across her face. "Come in."

"You two going to be okay?" Keeley asks, seemingly reluctant to leave us.

Nia doesn't answer. She's worried. That I'm here to call it off? Or that she wants to end it and doesn't know how to tell me?

"We'll be fine," I assure my brother's wife as I nudge her aside and head straight for Nia.

"Call me if you need—"

"Thanks," I assure Keeley. "I appreciate it. I've got it from here."

Well, I'm trying to. My palms are sweating. My throat begins to clamp tight. I catch sight of Nia's wedding dress hanging from the bathroom door. I can't see details since the room is shadowy and the white confection is shrouded by its protective plastic bag. But I'm not here for a sneak peek. I'm here purely to work out everything between me and Nia.

I shut the door and turn to her.

Her heart seems to stop. "What's wrong?"

Shit. Where do I start? What do I say? "I…"

The sight of a manila folder on her nightstand catches my attention. The prenuptial agreement.

"Did you sign that?" I ask.

If she divorces me in the first ten years of our marriage, all the assets and possessions I brought into the union belong to me. She'll walk away with nothing but child support. If I end the union at any time, she's entitled to half of everything. The agreement is practical. My attorney insisted on it.

Right now, I'm finding it distasteful and divisive.

Nia swallows, bristling. "I said I would and I did. Look, if you're having second thoughts—"

"Not about marrying you, no. About everything you're thinking? Yes. We need to clear up a few things. First, that document isn't... That's not how I feel."

As I storm across the room and pluck the paper from its folder, she gapes at me. A quick scan assures me she's signed and dated it, as promised.

"Does this bother you?"

Nia doesn't answer right away. "I know it shouldn't."

"But it does."

"You're entitled to protect yourself financially. In fact, you should."

"If you think that, why does having a prenuptial upset you?"

She fidgets in the shadowy room. "In my head, if we're building a future and spending the rest of our lives together, talking about the division of assets before we've spoken our vows feels like we've already given up."

Exactly. "I'm never going to divorce you. And I don't believe we're making a mistake."

Before she can say another word, I grasp the prenuptial paperwork in my hands and rip it in two.

"What are you doing?" She gapes at me.

I prowl toward her. Nia backs up a step. I come closer. She frowns and retreats again. I lunge for her. Her back hits the wall. I cage her in with a smile.

"Trying to make you happy. We're going to have a marriage, not a business partnership. I want to be with you. And I trust you, the way I hope you trust me. The only piece of paper we need between us is the one legally declaring us man and wife."

Nia blinks. "You're willing to give up your financial protection simply to make a point?"

I gesture to the scraps of legal document. "I already did. For you."

"Why? You went to a lot of trouble to—"

"Have my attorney draw up the papers quickly? Yes. Now I wish I hadn't bothered." I swallow. "Nia, you probably know how I feel better than I do."

"I don't."

"You have no guess?"

She looks away, biting her lip. "I don't want to be wrong."

There's no way she is.

"Do you still love me?"

Her eyes close. "I don't see how I'll ever stop."

Her admission makes something in my chest flip over. My heart. That crazy, cursed, uncontrollable organ slowly rousing like a sleeping giant. It's frantically thundering between my ears, far louder than my common sense. It's taking over my brain.

"I'm slow to understand how something non-logical works. You know that. I never meant to hurt you or ruin your life or—"

"You didn't." Nia looks almost confused by my statement. "I've been worried I ruined yours."

I cup her face. "Honey, no. You've *made* my life. Nothing would be right without you. Know why?" I shake my head because I can't wait for her to either guess or demur. "Because I think—no, I know—I love you, too."

Her breathing stops. Tears fill her eyes. Her fingers try in vain to grip the wall behind her. "You don't have to tell me what you think I want to hear. I'm going to marry you regardless."

"No." I grab her shoulders. "I'm telling you what I'm finally comprehending. What I probably should have figured out a long time ago but was too emotionally numb and disconnected to understand. I. Love. You. If you need me to say it again—"

Tears spill down her cheeks. A sob hitches her chest. "Don't."

I'm so confused. "Don't tell you how I feel?"

"D-don't lie."

Her voice sounds small and broken. My heart contracts and thuds again. I actually feel her pain as if it was my own. It's disconcerting and awful and amazing all at once.

"Never," I vow. "I'm just sorry it took me so long to realize what I should have known weeks ago. I think I fell for you the first time I touched you. I just didn't know."

She sniffles and finally opens her eyes. Hope, sharp and bright, illuminates her dark eyes. "You're not just saying that?"

Before she's even finished, I'm shaking my head. "You know I'm not a liar, just like you know I'm not good at sparing anyone's feelings. I finally understand what's in my heart. But if you still don't believe me, I'll be happy to repeat it until you do. Preferably while I'm inside you."

Finally, she laughs through her tears. "I love you so much."

Gently, I swipe my thumbs across her cheeks to dry them. "I know. And I feel like the worst ass imaginable for putting you through weeks of worrying and wondering and uncertainty."

"It's okay. I know you've been struggling. I just thought… When I opened the door, I was worried you were coming to tell me you weren't ready for a baby, so you couldn't marry me."

I'm still not entirely sure I'm ready for the fatherhood thing. But Nia and our child are a package deal, and I have months to figure it out.

I lean in, kiss her forehead and the tip of her nose before sliding down to brush the softest buss over her lips. "What do you say we start over? Today marks the beginning of our lives together, and I can't think of a better way to celebrate than by getting married to the woman who's changed my life, my heart, and my future."

"That might be the sweetest thing you've ever said to me." Softly, she nods. "Yes. A thousand times yes. See you at the altar at two."

"Are you kicking me out?" I frown.

"I am. I have a wedding to get ready for."

"Damn, I thought I was taking you to bed so I could show you how much I love you."

Now Nia is downright giggling, and it makes my heart feel so light. "Save it for our wedding night, mister."

A big smile breaks across my face. I feel triumphant, like the time I built a life-size Mars Exploration Rover for the hell of it and made it roam the nearby park. The project was frustrating and took a shitload of time and brainpower. But once I managed, success felt really damn rewarding.

"Oh, I have so many plans for you, my soon-to-be Mrs. Cook."

She winks. "I'm counting on it."

CHAPTER FIFTEEN

TWO O'CLOCK FINALLY rolls around. It's a balmy, breezy day. Blindingly sunny. Cheerful. Hopeful.

Wearing a dark gray tuxedo, I stand in front of a tall, rectangular trellis on Keeley and Maxon's lawn, framing a stretch of Hawaiian beach mere feet beyond. It's wrapped in flowing white drapes and trimmed with what seems like hundreds of white tropical flowers. In fact, everything around me is white—the bows around the chairs, the ribbons, the runner down the middle of the aisle. It's all pristine and beautiful. Classic.

Keeley, Britta, and Harlow have done a fantastic job tossing these nuptials together in under two weeks. It's a far cry from my wedding to Becca. This is a true celebration of the union between me and the first woman to truly hold my heart.

I'm past caring if that sounds illogical. It's undeniable. Sebastian advised me to just go with it. I am. He's my best man. We've been friends for nearly a decade and apparently he gives damn good advice. I wouldn't be here today without him.

As if he knows what I'm thinking, Bas claps me on the back. "You look happy."

I nod. "Maybe for the first time ever. I never thought I'd say this, but thank you for taking me to the burlesque club to show me a nearly naked Nia."

"You're welcome." Bas winks. "I had a suspicion you'd like the view."

"I did. But after that, I couldn't not see her as a woman. I needed that." Just like I needed Nia, her open arms, and her big heart.

He laughs. "Did you ever..."

The ending strains of a song floats through the salt-heavy air, just above the distant sounds of the crashing surf. A woman on a pre-recorded track is waxing vocally through the speakers about her special man and wanting a couple of forevers with him. I hope Nia feels that way about me. I hope we spend the next fifty years together, raising our children and building a good life. I refuse to think something terrible could happen to take her or the baby from me. Not today, not when I'm just beginning to really live.

Maxon, Griff, and Noah finish escorting the last of our guests to their chairs, then take their own seats. My side of the aisle is more crowded than Nia's. Even so, I couldn't miss her cousin Annabelle—a lovely African-American woman flanked by three hovering lawyers. Hard to believe she's committed to them all. It's an unconventional relationship, but it works for them. Eric and Kellan seem like decent guys, but I really connected with Tate. If they lived closer, I'll bet he and I would be great friends.

On one side of the altar, Keeley's bright red hair glints in the sun as her bohemian blue dress flows around her ankles. She smiles at me, microphone in hand. Britta and Harlow both stand at the back in the open doorway of the picturesque bed-and-breakfast, waiting for their musical cue.

Finally the song ends. Harlow lifts her arm and holds up her thumb. Nia is ready. This is it, the moment I've been wanting all day. Hell, for weeks.

She's really going to marry me.

The opening notes to another song begins. A piano taps out slow, almost thoughtful groups of notes. Then Keeley chimes in with a slow ballad about having her lover's heart forever. More instruments join in. A drum. A violin. The musicians must be behind the drape. It's still a simple arrangement. It's also sweeping and romantic.

As Nia comes toward me on Lorenzo's arm, the song echoes the sentiment in my heart. I am truly in love, truly head-over-heels. I need her. I may be tying myself to her today, but her devotion, quite simply, has set me free.

She draws closer—and steals my breath dressed in a simple sheath dress. Sheer straps cling to her shoulders and mirror the lace that covers her from the tops of her breasts to the bottoms of her ankles. A band of white flowers flows along the top of her head. A long stretch of tulle falls from it, all the way to the floor.

And she's smiling at me. The expression is open, genuine, and full of joy. She's ecstatic to be marrying me. My heart feels so light, as if it's so filled with helium it might float out of my chest.

As Keeley finishes singing, Nia reaches my side, white bouquet in hand. Lorenzo hands her off to me with a smile as bright as any proud father's and gives me a clap on the back. "Take care of her."

"I will," I vow.

To my left, I hear Guilia quietly sniffling. On my right, my foster mother, Diana, does the same. My siblings and their spouses are all smiling. And my wife-to-be looks at me like she can't wait to say "I do."

Lono starts the ceremony, his loud Hawaiian shirt billowing in the breeze. Nia's hands shake when he tells me to take them in mine. We speak our vows, looking into one another's eyes. Her voice trembles. My heart thuds.

The last few years flash through my memories. The day I interviewed her, she entered my tiny office wearing a confident tilt of her head and a purple suit, demonstrating an organized style that blew me away. I remember the first time Becca was too overwhelmed by a corporate event I needed her to organize so I could woo a client. Nia stepped in at the last minute to play hostess, decked in a red dress that stole the show and had my potential customer panting. I definitely can't forget the night she came to my place to make me gumbo and I first saw her not just as a female but as a beautiful woman I desire.

Finally, Lono says to kiss my bride. No one needs to tell me twice.

With a smile, I bend and cup Nia's face. "You're mine now, wife."

"Kiss me, husband."

Her words are faint but unmistakable above the Hawaiian breeze. And I take them to heart, sealing our vows with the first meeting of our mouths, signaling the beginning of our lives together.

God, we haven't made love since Nia discovered she was pregnant. She was withdrawn after the news. Then there wasn't time. All the wedding preparations seemed endless. My two weeks of vacation from the office turned into three. I missed a December second meeting with Lund, I think. I don't know right now. I don't care, either. He can wait until December twenty-ninth. I'll call him if I have questions.

The only things that matters to me—the only things that will truly matter for the rest of my life—are this woman I'm kissing passionately and the child she's carrying.

"Come up for air," Bas advises softly in my ear with a chuckle.

I ignore him. Instead, I press my lips to Nia's again and again. Then… Fuck it, I'm going in for tongue. I've missed her like hell. I love her like mad. I want her to know. Screw what everyone else thinks.

"Oh, my gosh… Get a room!" Harlow calls from the audience.

Everyone laughs, even Nia. Reluctantly, I end the kiss and step back.

"Now that I'm not worried we'll be witnessing the consummation of this marriage at the altar, I pronounce you man and wife," Lono jokes. "Mr. and Mrs. Evan Cook, everyone!"

Our guests all chuckle. Nia looks as if she can't decide whether to be excited or embarrassed. I have no such problem making up my mind. I'm proud as hell as I raise our joined hands and run back down the aisle while everyone tosses white petals our way.

We have a few precious moments alone inside the cool, shaded tent set up on the far side of the lawn. I don't waste a single second. I simply grab Nia in my arms and pull her against me, covering her mouth with mine until I hear people approaching.

Reluctantly, I end with one last peck, then back away. "I've missed you."

Her face softens. "I've missed you, too. Your visit this morning meant everything to me. You love me."

"I do."

The most radiant smile lights her up. I dare any man to show me a more beautiful bride. He'd fail, I'm sure of it.

"I love you, too. And we're going to have a great wedding night."

"Damn right we are."

She's laughing as our collective friends and family all approach. Congratulations begin. Lorenzo and Guilia reach us first, the big man full of hugs and boisterous laughter. Guilia dabs at tears and embraces Nia as lovingly as she would her very own daughter.

Diana grabs me in an uncharacteristic bear hug. "I'm so happy for you."

She surprised me by flying in late last night. I haven't seen her since Becca's funeral and I didn't expect her to come from her artistic pilgrimage through Asia to see me get married a second time. "It means a lot to me that you came."

"I had to see this woman for myself. But Nia is perfect for you. We talked for a few minutes last night." Diana smiles genuinely. "She's got enough ambition and spark to both keep up with and challenge you."

Becca didn't, according to my foster mother. She's right, but now isn't the time to talk about the past. "I think Nia is perfect, too."

Others join in. Music begins. Drinks flow. Food and cake follow. Dancing commences. I even learned how for Nia. Well, kind of. I'm sure I look like a dolt, but I don't care. It's a celebration in every sense of the word.

As evening wanes, Nia talks animatedly with Keeley, Britta, Harlow, and Annabelle a few feet away, so Eric, Kellan, and Tate sidle up to me, looking toward their woman, as if they never let her too far out of their sight.

"Thanks for coming all the way from New Orleans, especially on short notice. I know having family here makes Nia happy."

"Our pleasure," Eric says. "We're glad we could see Nia tie the knot."

Kellan nods. "In truth, the Hawaiian getaway made our Belle happy, too."

"Exactly," Tate agrees. "We always look for ways to tell her that we love her. But the best way is with our penises."

I nearly spit out my drink. Eric snickers.

Kellan groans. "Dude..."

"What? We always show Belle we love her with our penises. And this vacation we're hoping to say it with our sperm, as well. We're trying to conceive a baby."

I barely manage to swallow my scotch without coughing it down. "Well...good luck with that."

"Seriously, Tate..." Kellan looks ready to clobber his buddy. "They didn't need to know that."

"I don't see the problem." Tate gestures my way. "I'm pretty sure Evan is going to show Nia how much he loves her with his penis tonight. Maybe even his sperm."

The people around Tate may see him as embarrassing or socially awkward, but he's candid, factual, and logical.

"Absolutely," I assure him with a laugh.

Within minutes, Tate and I find ourselves in a heated debate of Edison versus Tesla, who was better and why. While Eric and Kellan seem to glaze over, I'm defending the fact that AC current was in every way superior to DC and that Edison was kind of a vindictive asshole to Tesla. Then Nia strolls up and threads her arm through mine.

At the same time, I see Annabelle sandwich herself between Eric and Kellan, then reach a hand out to cup Tate's shoulder and soothe him. "Hi, baby."

"Just a minute, Belle. I'm telling junior over here all the reasons he's wrong."

Before I can say a word, Annabelle leans in. "So, you don't want to go to our room and..."

She whispers the rest of her suggestion in his ear.

Tate's eyes widen. When she eases away, Tate actually flushes. A whole different kind of electricity pings off him.

"Yes, I do. And yes, we should. Night, all." He wraps his arm around Annabelle and makes to haul her away.

"Let's do the same," I tell my wife.

Grinning, Annabelle calls over her shoulder to Nia, "I think you and I went shopping at the same husband store."

We all laugh.

Eric and Kellan follow them out. The crowd is winding down. Most of my family has already left, as the wives don't seem to have as much energy now that they're nearing the end of their pregnancies.

I bring Nia against me. "Let's take this celebration private. What do you say?"

She sends me a sly smile. "Are you going to show me how much you love me with your penis?"

After twelve long, aching nights without her? Now that she's finally my wife?

I scoop Nia up into my arms, lift her against my chest, and plant a hard kiss on her lips. "Oh, yeah. All night."

"WHERE ARE WE going?" Nia asks a few minutes later as I speed down a two-lane road in one of Noah's high-performance sports cars.

I've got one suitcase, two bottles of sparkling cider, and a whole slew of dirty thoughts on board.

"You'll see."

She sends me a curious glance. "What are you up to?"

"At least eight inches."

That makes her giggle. "I meant, what do you have up your sleeve?"

"You should know by now that what I have is down my pants." I wink. "Want to see?"

She rolls her eyes at my bad joke. "If I peek while you're driving, we'll probably have to pull over on the side of the road. Then we'll never make it to wherever we're going."

I glance at Nia. She was a beautiful bride, but now she's my incredibly alluring wife. I want her all to myself.

"Sadly, you're right. I'm afraid if you even breathe on me too much right now, I'll be all over you."

"Gosh, that sounds terrible," she teases.

"Positively awful, right?"

"The worst." She drops her hand on my thigh.

"Nia…"

"It's so"—she drags her palm up my leg until her fingers trail over my balls, then she cups my shaft—"*hard* to figure out how I'm going to endure your attention. I'll have to think *long*…" She moans as she strokes my length through my tuxedo pants, which are suddenly way too constricting.

"About what?" I choke out.

"How to put up with you tonight. I have ideas…"

"I do, too."

"Tell me."

Clamping my fingers around her wrist, I drag her hand away from my cock. I need to take control of this situation or we won't make it to our romantic destination before I fall on her and fuck her like a madman. "Lift your dress, take off your panties, and show me your pussy."

Nia gapes at me. The air seems to dissipate from the car. She freezes, except for her harsh breathing, and stares at me.

"Now," I insist softly. "I want to see you, wife."

She closes her eyes. "Your command shouldn't turn me on that much."

But it does, and I'm a lucky son of a bitch. I feel even luckier when she pulls up her dress to the tops of her thighs and reaches under the lace sheath. With a shift and a wriggle, she comes up clutching a tiny taupe-colored thong.

I hold out my hand. "Give it to me."

"W-what are you going to do?"

"Keep it."

She lets out a shuddering breath and sets the scrap of hot silk in my hand.

I shove it in my coat pocket and cast her an impatient stare. "Thank you. But I can't see your pussy yet."

"What if someone pulls up beside us?"

"Who? There's no one on this road, and if another driver comes close, it's my problem. I'll handle it. Show me your pussy, Nia. Now."

"You're awfully demanding."

"It's your fault. I was never this way before you."

That makes her smile. The expression is hesitant and nervous. And aroused. It's so beautifully female.

Then she raises her dress around her hips. I wish like hell I had more light in the car, but I know her bare ass rests against the seat. I see her pressing her slender thighs together. I laugh. As if that's going to soothe her ache… I already know it won't because even in the shadowy interior, I see her sex shimmering with wetness.

"Touch yourself for me."

If I do it, we definitely won't make it out of this car. And fucking my wife here, even if I could figure out how logistically, would be decidedly unromantic, especially for our first time as man and wife. She deserves better.

"You mean like this?" Nia spreads her thighs just enough to tease me and begins to rub her clit.

The sight of her fingers on her pussy has me gripping the wheel tighter. "Exactly like that."

"Hmm. How much longer until we reach wherever?" She licks her lips. "Enough time for me to make myself come?"

As much as I'd like the show, no.

I grab her wrist again. "Your first orgasm as my wife is mine, Nia. You can get yourself wet and hot and ready, but you're going to give me that first scream while I'm on top of you, inside you, kissing you, and making sure you know you belong to me."

Vaguely, I'm aware that I sound decidedly unevolved. Being with Nia isn't strictly about sex…but I enjoy every moment I spend in bed with her. I'm not against her making autonomous decisions about her pleasure, generally speaking. But not tonight. From now until the sun comes up, she—and all her orgasms—are mine.

Nia shivers. "All right."

Slowly, I release her wrist. Her fingers delve between her folds again. It only takes a second before her back is arching, her hips lifting.

"What are you thinking about?" I demand.

"You."

"What am I doing?"

"Making love to me. Slowly. Carefully. Touching me everywhere. Wringing pleasure from me. Telling me you love me."

I can picture that, too. "That's what you want tonight?"

Her head falls back against the seat and she closes her eyes. "Please."

"Why? Because that's 'wedding night' sex?"

She shakes her head. "Because no one has ever done that."

Really? She's had playful sex, intense sex, spontaneous sex, even slightly kinky sex. But she's never had thoughtful, lingering, meaningful sex, the kind where someone revered her body, stoked her heart, and consumed her soul at once?

Come to think of it, neither have I.

"Then we'll share this first together."

The smile Nia gives me leaves me basking in anticipation and reeling with need.

Two torturous minutes later, I pull into the driveway and stop the car. Thank god we made it.

She blinks in the darkness and lifts her hand from between her legs slowly, looking disoriented by her lingering haze of self-pleasure. "We've been here."

I nod, waiting for her to catch on. "We have."

As she takes it all in, I exit the car and run to open her door.

"Have you guessed yet?" I almost hold my breath, hoping she's happy with my surprise.

"Is this the house where you proposed to me?" she asks as she steps out.

"It is."

"The house I picked out from the stack of listings? The one with the fireplace?"

A smile splits my face. "It is. And it's ours."

She gasps, a smile spreading across her face. "Seriously?"

"I accepted their counter offer the day after you agreed to marry me. I signed the paperwork at eleven this morning. I thought it would be fitting to spend our first night as a married couple here, so we can start building memories."

Her smile almost blinds me. "That's perfect. You got me a fireplace! I always wanted one as a kid."

And she never had one. I'm so fucking glad I can be the man to give it to her. "Now, it's all yours."

Nia squeals. There's no other way to put it. She throws her arms around my neck, jumps up and down excitedly, and peppers my face with kisses. "You did this for me?"

"We needed a place to live."

"But you picked the one I chose, even though it wasn't the best investment of all the properties you saw."

"I did."

"You chose the non-logical place simply to make me happy. I know how major that is for you, Evan. Thank you. I love it!" She brushes a kiss across my lips. "I love you."

Her response is everything I'd hoped. "You're welcome. You can refurnish anything you want, however you want. We'll be living here permanently in just over three weeks, then you can redecorate and—"

"I'll have plenty of time to set up the perfect nursery."

My smile turns down. Her words jolt me with anxiousness. Fear. Will she purchase a bunch of items meant to welcome and care for a new baby that I'll again have to cancel and return because fate stole my wife and child from me?

I can't think that. I can't be that unfortunate twice. Nia will be fine. She'll have a baby—our baby—and we'll raise him or her together. I refuse to accept any other possible future.

She squeals again, grabs my hand, and tries to drag me toward the door. "Let's go inside."

"One minute."

I grab all the stuff out of the trunk and lug it up to the front porch. Harlow, bless her, set up everything to turn our master bedroom into the perfect honeymoon suite. I didn't give her much in the way of instruction, just asked her to make it romantic and conducive to hours of pleasure. She gave me a wink and assured me she'd take care of it.

Beside me, Nia opens the door in excitement. Before she can step over the threshold, I ease the bags I'm carrying down on the porch step and reach for my bride.

"You don't get to walk inside. Tradition."

I'm more than delighted to pick her up, fold her against my chest, and carry her over the threshold. She slides an arm around my neck and cuddles closer. Instead of looking around her new house, she sees only me. The love shining from her eyes nearly blinds me.

"I want to kiss you right now."

Her smile widens. "I want you to do more than kiss me."

"My pleasure, Mrs. Cook."

Without wasting a second, I hustle her toward the bedroom. In the doorway, I almost stop short because I don't recognize the place. Harlow has managed to shroud the huge mahogany tester bed in gauzy white drapes. New white bedcovers and pillows in watery shades of blue add to the romantic feel. Candles provide a soft glow all around. A second glance tells me they're all battery operated, but the effect is still idyllic. Sultry scents of vanilla, jasmine, and sea salt blend in the air. The overhead fan sways lazily, but the fireplace is cracking and jumping merrily for my wife. Outside the open double doors, I see the low lights surrounding the patio and the pool, then the shift of the ocean beyond, visible under the moonlight.

I'm going to share all of this—and the rest of my life—with Nia.

I set her on her feet. "Wait here."

She nods slowly, taking the place in. "Wow."

Grinning stupidly, I jog back to retrieve the rest of our things, then haul them into the bedroom. Shoving the suitcase to one side—I'm hoping we won't need clothes until we fly back to Seattle on Monday night—I grip the sparkling cider by its neck, find the two plastic glasses, and open the bottle.

The cork pops free, and I manage to contain the overspill into a glass just before I pour us each a few sips. I hand her one and hold it up.

She joins suit. "What are we toasting? Us?"

I nod. "You know I'm not good with words or sentiments. And today, I've got so many things running through my head." Not to mention clogging my throat. "Now that we're married and starting our lives together, it all seems so big. No, sharp. That's not exactly it, either. More like soft but important. I can't put it into words…"

"Poignant? Emotional?"

Those are words that have barely been in my vocabulary before now. I was aware of their meaning in an academic way before Nia. "Yes. That's what I mean. We've had an…interesting road to get here."

"By interesting, do you mean the fact you failed to notice I'm female for years?"

"Yes," I admit sheepishly, then frown. "Wait. Are you saying you noticed me as a man before that night at the BBB Revue?"

Nia rolls her eyes. "Evan, of course. I was professional, not blind. I would have never acted on my attraction, especially while you were married to Becca. But…I always wondered what you'd be like if you turned all that considerable focus and attention to detail on me." Then she smiles. "Besides, I'm a sucker for green eyes."

That makes me laugh. "Well, I'm a sucker for this one beautiful woman who turned my life upside down." Then I sober and cup her cheek. "I can't imagine ever being this happy without you. Here's hoping we have fifty amazing years together."

She clinks her glass with mine. "I'm greedy; I want more."

I could point out that if I live another fifty years, it would extend me beyond the average life expectancy of the American male and that we can't know whether I have any heretofore unknown medical conditions or an unfortunate incident might cut my life short. But her point is sentimental, not logical.

"I want more, too," I assure her. "But right now, I want you out of that dress."

As I turn her away from me, I shuck my tuxedo jacket. Next, I lower her zipper. It's a quiet, suggestive hiss in the room.

"It's beautiful here," she says, trembling. "Thank you. I can't think of a more perfect place to spend our wedding night."

The dress folds away from her body, leaving the smooth expanse of her back to gleam by the candlelight. As I ease it down her hips, I spread kisses across her shoulders and up her neck. "I can't wait to take advantage of this romantic atmosphere—and you."

"Evan…" she murmurs as I nip at her lobe.

"Yes, wife?"

I circle my hand around her middle and lay my palm over her flat-for-now abdomen. Tonight, I'm not thinking about the baby or what might happen. I'm focused on this moment, on her.

I shift up to cradle her breast, reveling when her head falls back to my chest with a little moan.

"Be with me. Stay with me. Love me."

Her words fill me with something I can't describe. Rightness. Not the sort of certainty that comes from being correct when I've solved a complex equation or a complicated business dilemma. It's not straightforward. It's not tangible. It…just is. This rightness comes from somewhere deeper than my brain. It's louder than my logic. It's pure bliss. It's a certainty stemming straight from my heart that I am where I'm meant to be with the woman who completes me.

Until now, that's another notion that always confused me. Each person is an individual unto themselves, so how could they need another person to complete them? Maybe it's finally feeling genuine love that's helped me to understand. But as sure as I'm standing here now, I know my world will never be the same again if I don't have Nia by my side.

"My pleasure."

I'm not even conscious of what we do next. Our clothes seem to melt away as we embrace. We stand closer with every touch. Suddenly, we're in the middle of our king-size bed, and Nia is under me as I kiss her, looking for new places on her body to both conquer and worship. Those seemingly contradictory urges should strike me as odd, but feeling them simultaneously tonight seems somehow normal.

With my lips, I feel my way over her neck, across her breasts, down her stomach. With my tongue, I adore her hips, her thighs, her pussy. When she cries out and reaches for me, I have to be closer. I have to be with her. I have to be inside her.

As I ease into the snug heat of Nia's body, I fit my mouth over hers and possess her in every way I know how. She opens her arms, her legs, her heart to me. I sink deep—body and soul. It's more than a meeting of mere flesh and passion. Slowly, we move together. Until now I've never tried sex with this kind of unhurried reverence. I never needed my joining with a woman to be more than two bodies seeking mutual satisfaction.

Tonight, with Nia, everything is different. We're making love.

As I stroke deep and steady into her, I bend to wrap my lips around her nipple, drag my way up her neck, then whisper in her ear, "I'll never get enough of you."

"As long as you love me, too, neither will I."

Our pleasure rises, bright and inexorable. It's as if the restraint we're exercising to make it last makes the blaze between us burn hotter. Our feelings power the desire we share into something more mesmerizing than the mere rubbing together of bodies. I would never have believed how much emotions could heighten ecstasy if I wasn't experiencing these stunning sensations for myself.

As we reach a gasping, cataclysmic, mutual end, I feel satiated, content, and far more wrapped up in another human being than I thought myself capable of feeling. This is my *wife*, to have and to hold from this day forward. I may have been married before, but for the first time, I actually know what that means. I'm going to love, honor, and cherish Nia for the rest of my days.

I tuck her damp body against me and wrap my arms around her. She closes her eyes with a sigh of satisfaction, making me smile all over again. If this is marital bliss, sign me up for more.

CHAPTER SIXTEEN

Seattle, Washington
Sunday, December 17

AFTER A FEW idyllic days at our new place in Maui, we squeezed in a quick visit with the new obstetrician before heading back to Seattle. The next time we step foot on the island, we'll be new residents.

Unfortunately, that means I have a lot of packing up of my penthouse to do in the next week, especially since I've decided to sell the place after all. Engaging a good Realtor to list it eight days before Christmas might be less than simple, but I'm determined to get rid of the old baggage and start fresh with Nia.

I've just finished sorting out Becca's half of the closet—finally. I'm giving away all of her clothes and shoes to a local women's shelter that needs the donations, according to Nia. Becca's jewelry I've consigned with a reputable jeweler. Now that everything is in boxes and I'm staring at the empty racks beside my neatly arranged dress shirts and suits, I feel lighter, as if I've lifted a huge weight off my chest.

While I drag the last of the boxes to the foyer, someone knocks on my door.

"You there, bro? Or you busy boinking your bride?"

Bas. I've hardly seen him since I returned from Maui. We've both been busy as hell, preparing year-end reports, dealing with a new malware designed to take down our security, a particularly insistent hacker, and our respective upcoming moves. I'm glad he stopped in now.

I open the door to find him lounging against the frame. "Hey, man. What are you doing?"

He takes in the boxes I've stacked against the wall. "Same as you, culling through crap and trying to decide what to take and what to ditch. I've lived in my little place for five years. I didn't realize how much shit I've collected."

"For real. I've barely managed to get through Becca's closet and it's taken me all morning."

He turns quieter. "Was it hard?"

"No." I thought memories, guilt—something—would nag me, but…nothing.

"So you're putting her behind you once and for all?"

"It's time." Actually beyond, but I don't say what we both know.

Bas nods, his golden hair gleaming in the sun pouring through the windows. "Good for you. Where's Nia?"

"Organizing and purging at her place. She's also got to sell her furniture since she can't bring it with us and her landlord doesn't want it."

Besides, I didn't want her to have to toil here with me as I finish closing the chapter of my life with another woman. I needed to say my final goodbye to Becca alone.

"Gotcha. So…how's married life?"

I can't wipe the stupid smile off my face. "Great."

"You reconciled to the fact you two are having a baby?"

That's the one dark spot in my bright pool of joy. "Still working on that."

Shock and denial still slap me every time I think about it. I don't know when or how I'm going to embrace pending fatherhood again. Even the thought terrifies me.

"You'll get there. I'm just glad you're finally happy. I had a feeling about you and Nia. But your announcement shocked the hell out of everyone at the office."

"That it did."

The whispers about us started just before Thanksgiving, but most everyone thought it was a lurid, unsubstantiated rumor—until we came back from Maui married. By mutual agreement, we decided not to say anything publicly about our relationship before we tied the knot. We didn't want the gossip, and it was none of anyone's business anyway.

"The employees may not even be your employees for much longer. You still waiting to agree to Lund's deal until the very last moment?"

I give him a head bob that's neither yes or no. "That was the plan. But now…I don't know. The sale is worth a billion dollars, and I stand to make a huge profit. Then I can do anything else I want with my life. I get all of that. The thing is, when I think about it, I realize I'm already doing what I want with my life. I love Stratus."

"What are you saying?"

"Maybe I don't sell."

Bas raises a brow at me. "Seriously?"

I shrug. I've been reluctant to mention this to my best friend, but since he works for me and is one of my chief officers, he needs to know. "So if you were already out job hunting—"

"Hell, no. For selfish reasons, I hoped you'd keep Stratus. I wasn't going to start looking for another job until I had to. But I'm definitely not working for Lund. He seems like an asshole and that son of his…"

"The douche who couldn't take his eyes off my wife? Yeah, that's the other thing. I really don't want to give Lund or his junior anything they want. It's spiteful, but they both rubbed me wrong."

"What about your biological father? Refusing to sell helps him, at least according to your whacked-out half sister."

I'm not worried about Bethany or Barclay. "That can't be helped. There's no perfect solution. But the more I think about the situation, it would be hard to turn over the business I've built from the ground up. This year, we have twenty percent market penetration. Next year, we're projected to top twenty-eight. We could be as high as thirty-four percent in the next three years. I know you've done the math on this; it's your job. That's a lot of return, especially since we've already done the majority of the capital investment. And when I think about keeping what's mine versus letting an asshole potentially tear it apart... Well, I've already got a lot of money and a solid revenue stream. I don't need his billion dollars."

That makes Bas smile bigger than I've seen in months. He claps me on the back. "Look at you, thinking with something other than your logic."

He's right; I am thinking with my heart. "Why not? It seems to be working for me these days."

"Damn straight. What does Nia think?"

"I asked her this morning. She seems more focused on our future and the baby than business."

"So...she wants you to go through with the deal?"

I shrug. "She never came out and said that. But I think so. She told me once that she didn't want things to change around the office for us. They already have. Even if I wanted to, I can't undo any of that. So I'm not sure what to do."

"And you've got twelve days to make up your mind?"

"Pretty much. Hey, want a beer? Maybe we can talk this out while I declutter my home office."

"Sure. I'd love to watch you organize your crap while I take a break from jacking with mine."

Laughing, I fetch us each a pale ale and toss one his way. "So you're not going to help?"

"Think of me as moral support." He twists off the cap as we make our way down the hall. "After all, what are friends for?"

"Strangling?"

We both chuckle as I settle behind the big desk, into the leather chair I've barely used in months. All of this can be sold off or donated since there's a great home office with perfectly adequate furniture in the Maui house.

Sipping on my beer, I pull open the drawers on the left, where Becca kept her things. "You mostly packed up?"

"Getting there. Are you spending Christmas in Maui?"

With everything else going on, I'd forgotten about the holidays. Bas sometimes joins me since most of his family lives on the East Coast.

"Yeah. We're going to spend the twenty-third at a party with some of her friends. Lorenzo and Guilia are hosting it. You're welcome to join us."

"Actually, I'm flying to my mom's house this year, but thanks anyway. So…you finally get to meet Nia's ex?"

I grit my teeth, then remind myself that I ended up with the woman, not Mateo. "Probably. I'm hoping that if I ignore him, the prick will leave us alone."

Yeah, it's probably wishful thinking, but I can't beat up my hosts' son for something he did to my wife before I married her. Though that doesn't stop me from wanting to.

I try to distract myself by sorting through the few papers Becca kept in the desk. Some are invoices for her membership to a yoga studio. Shredder. Reading suggestions from a book club she joined a few years back. Trash. Receipts for the repair to the kitchen sink we needed a few weeks before her death. Keep for next owner. Then I find a file folder with business cards stapled on the inside flap. A hairdresser. A few potential nannies. A painter. I also find fabric swatches and a carpet sample. All can be tossed. Drawer one empty.

"You okay?" Bas asks.

I look up. His expression is tense. Almost…pained. "Fine. Are you?"

"It doesn't bother you to see her handwriting one more time? To toss away things she collected and valued?"

His question strikes me as odd. "I don't need them."

Blowing out a breath, he eases back, staring at a note Becca jotted on the file folder about paint samples and a lead on someone who could create a great mural in the nursery. "Yeah. I guess…I'm just sentimental by nature. It's still so shocking that she's gone."

"It felt that way to me for a while, but I've finally admitted that I didn't love her. I've been able to let go of her and my guilt."

He nods. "And you found someone else to help you with that."

Why is Becca's absence impacting Sebastian now? I must be misunderstanding. Surely he isn't intimating that he needs to find another woman to forget my wife.

Frowning, I turn the exchange over in my head and open the next drawer. Becca's birth certificate and our marriage license. I set those aside for legal purposes, just in case. More file folders, some with magazines containing articles about romantic dream vacations flagged. I scowl. Becca wasn't idealistic or starry-eyed. She rarely liked to leave home at all. Odd… I set those aside.

Under that I find a few notebooks. The top three are empty. I'm not surprised. Becca stocked up because she was forever writing notes and keeping lists. Given her OCD, she needed absolute order to function. I understood and often encouraged her. Now that I've experienced Nia's laid-back, more natural organizational style, with a bit of spontaneity thrown in, I prefer it.

The fourth notebook, the one on the bottom, is filled. I scan the first few pages. It's a journal of sorts. I had no idea she kept one.

On the first page, she wrote about being listless and confused. That entry is dated nearly a two years ago. On another, she mentioned resisting what she knew was wrong. I frown. What does that mean?

"What is it?" Bas asks.

"I'm not even sure. Hang on…"

I flip further into her entries, read a tad more closely. As time passed, she admitted to being unable to not notice "him," especially since she saw him so often. That spring, she was thinking about him, wondering what he was doing, if he was happy or seeing anyone. By summer, she was fantasizing about him. She wanted him sexually.

I read that again, completely stunned. Becca, who could rarely stand intimacy, wrote that she twisted in her lonely bed with desire for him. She clearly doesn't mean me.

Who is this guy?

By that fall, she confided to her journal that she was in passionate, undying love with him. She didn't know how she'd ever fall out. And he had no idea how she felt.

My thoughts race as I try to discern who this mystery man could possibly be. All thoughts lead back to one person.

With numb fingers, I set the notebook down. "Sebastian, were you in love with Becca?"

He stiffens. "Why?"

I notice he didn't answer the question.

"So, that's a yes." I rake my hand through my hair. "Holy shit."

Suddenly, it's hard to breathe. Shock does that to me. It mimics a stupor, as if the capabilities of my body are gobbled up by my brain when I have to process something blindsiding.

How did I never see what was right in front of me?

My best friend of nearly a decade holds up his hands as he backs away. "I never touched her. I never told her how I felt. I never gave her any indication… I respected you too much. But I couldn't help how I felt." He frowns. "H-how did you guess?"

"The pieces all came together just now. Once, you said you loved a married woman. And Becca's journal…" I blow out a hard breath, wondering whether the truth will be a curse or a comfort to him. "I think she loved you, too."

Sebastian pales, looking stunned and heartbroken. "She said that?"

I nod absently. "She didn't mention you by name, but looking at her words now, it seems obvious."

Maybe I should be angry or feel betrayed. Most people would, right? But shock still has me reeling, and I don't see fury charging in to replace it once I'm over the surprise. Instead, the whole situation seems tragic.

If I'd known… If Becca had given me any indication she wanted someone else… I'm not sure what I would have done. I like to think I would have let her go. Why didn't she ever speak up? If she was so in love with Sebastian, why did she come to me just after the holidays last year and tell me how much she wanted a baby?

"I wasn't the only one who felt that way? Oh, god…" He sounds devastated as he falls against the wall like he needs the support to remain upright.

In retrospect, he sounded this devastated the day of Becca's funeral. I thought his grief was for me. But it was for himself. For the loss of what he believed was unrequited love.

"Man, you have to believe me," Bas implores. "I would have never let anything happen between us. Ever."

My chest feels tight, my palms sweaty, as I reach for the journal again. I scan page after page, until I come to the answer. "Did you start dating Ashley last winter to distract yourself from Becca?"

He swallows. "Yes. I tried. I tried so hard… I jumped in with her—no safety net. I laid on the PDA so thick last New Year's Eve at your party. I don't know if I wanted to prove to myself or to Becca that I wasn't ridiculously in love with her."

He did. I remember thinking something was off with them. "Becca told me she wanted a baby two days later."

Bas groans miserably, and I suspect a baby was my first wife's way of distracting herself from her heartache over Sebastian.

"When I heard she was pregnant, I pasted on a smile and pretended to be happy for you two. But I was dying inside. I wanted that to be me. To be my baby. Goddamn it." He pounds a fist against the wall and grits his teeth against tears.

I feel for him. He loved Becca in a way I never did. I blithely spent every day of my life without any clue how much they wanted one another. I'm shocked, yes. But given how much I love Nia and how much I loathe knowing about all her other sexual partners… I can only imagine how deep Sebastian's pain was to discover the woman he loved was pregnant by his best friend, who didn't love her at all.

"I'm sorry."

"*You're* sorry? I'm the asshole who couldn't keep my heart in line." He sighs. "But it's such a guilty relief that you finally know."

Oddly, I understand his anguish. After all, I didn't set out to fall for Nia. It just happened. The way I'm assuming it happened for them.

"What did you love about Becca?"

He pauses. "Everything."

"She was very quiet."

"Which made finding a way to coax her to talk interesting."

"She was OCD."

A momentary smile breaks up his grief. "She was particular. She wanted things neat and organized. The way her brain worked fascinated me. I loved watching her make tea. A spoonful and a half of sugar. No more, no less. She brought that exacting concentration to everything she did."

Not with me, but I don't dwell on that. "She wasn't a sexual creature."

Bas drops his gaze to the floor and fresh guilt flashes across his face. "I think you're wrong. I don't know for sure. But…she blushed at anything I said to her. Last fall, I remember telling her that I was hanging my coat in the hall closet, and she turned all rosy. So I talked to her about nothing, told her jokes, simply to see her react. I sometimes I thought the way she looked at me meant something, but then she'd clear her throat, tsk at me, and walk away. She never betrayed you, either."

Logic tells me they pined, and it doesn't matter that they never consummated their feelings. It's still a betrayal. But I simply can't muster anger, only regret. "I must have been too self-absorbed. I never saw how either of you felt."

I hate that.

With a heavy sigh, I turn to the next page of Becca's journal, dated January twentieth. Stapled to the page is a business card for a divorce attorney I've never heard of. My heart stops.

"What?" Bas asks. "You turned pale as shit."

"She thought about leaving me for you."

"What? I never encouraged—"

I hold up a hand and start reading. "'The most terrible, wonderful thing happened today. A man approached me as I left the yoga studio. I worried at first. This stranger was waiting for me. Apparently, he and his son want to buy Stratus. My stubborn husband won't agree to their terms, so they hatched a plan to force his hand. They need my help…'"

"Lund?" Bas sounds as alarmed as I feel. "How did Becca think that snake-oil salesman was going to force you to do anything? And why would she go along with it?"

I scan on. The passage is long, but it doesn't take more than a few seconds to get the gist of her entry.

This is a betrayal I can't forgive her for. Never. Ever.

"She was going to divorce me. Washington is a community property state. I would have been forced to sell Stratus to buy Becca out. The Lunds were waiting, money in hand. And they promised her fifteen percent of the sale price, in cash. Once the deal closed, she'd have the money to be free and finally be happy. She was going to ask you to run away with her."

"Oh, jesus." He looks stricken, as if I punched him. "I had no idea. I swear."

"I know." Becca's journal entries make that clear. But I don't ask whether he would have left with her if she'd gone through with the plan. I probably don't want the answer. Hell, he probably doesn't want to envision what he would have done. "The Lunds referred her to the attorney, apparently." I flip the page, stunned to find my hand shaking. "She met this shyster the following Monday." I flip another page. "By Wednesday, she decided to go through with it and they were drawing up papers to serve me. They had it all set up for Monday, the thirtieth."

Bas closes his eyes. "But she discovered she was pregnant over the weekend. I'll never forget that Saturday afternoon you called me to tell me. You were so thrilled. I tried to be happy for you. But I knew that was the nail in our coffin."

I scan a few more pages. "She knew it, too. She dropped all proceedings the day she intended to serve me. And, in her words, she spiraled into depression."

She wrote no more journal entries after that.

"I knew something was wrong." Bas sounds tortured.

Really? I didn't suspect a thing. Did I pay so little attention to my own wife that I never realized the extent of her heartache?

Yep. I feel blind, stupid, double-crossed, and utterly bowled over.

I'm also angry as hell. Yes, at Becca for clamming up and plotting to blindside me, rather than finding the courage to tell me how she felt. But I'm seething in fury at the Lunds for scheming and interfering and having no compunction at all about ripping my life apart for their financial gain.

"I didn't know how to help her," Bas goes on miserably. "I didn't know what was wrong. And I couldn't step over the line..."

"Thank you for..." *Not resenting me when I stood between you and happiness. Being my friend. Staying true, even when it cost you.*

He hangs his head. "Please don't hate me."

"I can't. You did everything you could in a shitty situation."

Bas's head pops up. As if on autopilot, I stand and round the desk. I'm aware suddenly that in all the years I've known Bas, I've never hugged him. In the past, I wasn't a fan of these male expressions of friendly affection. But over the last seven and a half months, everything has become different. I lost my wife, met my siblings, fell in love... My head has changed. My heart has changed.

I back up my words by bringing Sebastian against me and giving him a hearty man-slap on the back. He does the same. I feel him swallow. I sense the sob he holds in. I hurt for him, knowing he'll never have the lover he pined for.

He backs away, managing to hold himself together. "Thanks...brother."

"Brother." I nod. "I hope you fall in love again and that she's everything you ever wanted or needed. I hope she makes you sublimely happy for the rest of your lives."

"Thanks. I hope that happens, too. I'm so fucking tired of being alone."

"I know. Now, if you don't mind me leaving this brofest, I'm going to kick the Lunds' asses."

CHAPTER SEVENTEEN

As I'm driving to Nia's cottage, I seethe. Douglas Lund didn't think twice about tearing apart my life with Becca. I'll be damned if he gets the chance to try again with Nia.

I dial my wife. I need to tell her I'm heading over. She needs to know the Lunds are scum.

No answer. I scowl and dial again. Nothing. That's unlike her. I try not to let it, but worry bares its teeth and gnaws at my gut.

Please, God, don't let anything happen to her…

Maybe she simply has her head in a moving box. Or better yet, in the shower. Yeah, I'd like her all naked and wet and available for me to pleasure as soon as I tell her what's up.

In the nine days we've been married, it's crazy how much my need for her has grown. We spent last night locked in each other's arms, drowning in kiss after kiss, touch after touch. I want her again. I want her more than ever. I'll want her always.

But she doesn't just fire my blood. I admire her, respect her. Weirdly, she also soothes and comforts me just by being near.

There's no doubt about it; I'm hopelessly, irrevocably in love with Nia.

Learning the extent of Becca's duplicity only helps me realize how much deeper and more substantial my relationship with Nia is. I'm in a far better place with the right woman.

And Sebastian… I feel sorry as hell for him.

As I cruise down the main drag outside of Nia's neighborhood, her little blue compact in the corner of the parking lot of a cafe catches my eye. What is she doing here? It's two in the afternoon. Maybe she got hungry. But if she's there, why didn't she take her phone inside? Is she grabbing a quick takeout order?

Frowning, I pull into the lot and park near the door. I can't see past the restaurant's tinted windows for a glance inside, but now that I think about it, she's mentioned this place once or twice. According to her, they make a mean peach pie, and my wife definitely likes her sweets.

With a little smile, I head for the door. I'll surprise her, maybe even order something and eat with her as I fill her in on the day's events. She might have some insight. Not that I'm not handling the situation. I think I'm actually doing a decent job. The old me would have been pissed enough with Bas to burn bridges. Logic would have dictated that by coveting my wife, he was betraying me. The old me didn't understand love. This me? I get it.

But my heart isn't all mush. Nia may try to talk me out of squashing the Lunds. I'm disinclined to hear reason. I'm definitely not selling them a fucking thing. They want Stratus? They'll have to pry it out of my cold, dead hands.

I don't give a shit that my decision will cost me a billion dollars. I'm going to do everything humanly possible to grow my business into a mega empire. I'm going to become untouchable. Nia will be at my side, helping me. So will Sebastian. Together, we'll ensure that neither Douglas nor his shitbag son can lay a hand on the company we've worked so hard to build. We can grow Stratus so big I'll be Jeff Bezos rich. Then the Lunds can go fuck themselves.

In my pocket, my phone rings. I pull it out, half expecting Nia's name to pop up on my display. I'm hoping she'll tell me she's at this cafe and ask me to join her.

Instead, the caller ID indicates it's Bethany.

What the hell? I didn't think we'd talk until I decided Stratus's future—if even then.

I almost don't answer, but Nia still seems to be inside, and I can say a few words right now to make my ice queen of a biological half sister go away. Giving her what she wants is distasteful, but her wishes align with mine for the moment, so this shit is unavoidable.

"I'm not selling to Lund," I say without any preamble or greeting. "You're getting your wish. Congratulations."

I expect to hear her gloating, even a chilly laugh. Instead, she sobs.

"E-everyone was right. *You* were right."

Bethany sounds desolate and nearly incomprehensible. What's going on? She rubbed me wrong when we first met…but now I can't help responding to the pain in her voice.

"About what?"

"Barclay. He…" She stops to cry in noisy, heart-rending gasps. "He lied to me. Almost nothing he told me was the truth."

This doesn't surprise me nearly as much as it does her, and I don't know why she called me, of all people. But weirdly, I feel for her. "What happened?"

"The FBI started questioning me about what I knew. When Barclay told me all the pending charges against him were a misunderstanding, I had no reason not to believe him. I told the police everything I knew. Or thought I knew. They started showing me evidence to prove Barclay had been lying to me—and everyone else—all along. He stole from those people. All of them. Their life's savings in some instances. Without remorse. I was…shocked. And I knew I had to find answers for myself."

She breaks down again, her jerky, stuttering breaths almost painful to hear.

"What did you do?" I prompt gently.

Compassion isn't something I've exercised much in the past. But it's softening my attitude now whether I want it to or not. Her world has fallen apart. I know that feeling.

It takes a long moment, but she manages to gather herself. "Just before he got arrested, he installed a safe in my condo. He said it was because he needed to hide things from Linda because his divorce from that bitch was getting ugly. I had no doubt he was right, so I never snooped. Until today." She lets out a shuddering breath. "I hope you're sitting down."

I'm not but whatever she has to say has likely rocked her world far more than it's going to upend mine. "Go ahead."

"Over the years, Barclay stole money from a lot of people, including the Lunds."

Taking money from the man *and* impregnating his daughter? Wow, my biological father is a real peach…

"They want to buy Stratus because they want access to Barclay's secret account on your storage cloud network," she goes on. "He didn't register it under his name or email address. If he had, the feds would have already found it. I discovered the login information in his safe and accessed it. Swiss bank account numbers. Records of client funds he exchanged for precious metals and stashed in safe deposit boxes offshore… He's got money in every form, everywhere, hidden from everyone—his wife, the IRS, the investors he swindled. If I hadn't seen all the proof for myself, I still wouldn't believe it. I just can't… Oh, my god. He let me spit out one falsehood after another to clients. To the FBI. If the feds hadn't believed me, I could have gone to prison. How could my own father betray me like this?"

She's totally disillusioned. She's imploding and trying not to crumble.

"I'm sorry."

"That I was wrong?" she spits.

"That he hurt you. I grew up knowing he was an asshole. You only realized that today."

I'm still not sure why she chose me to call, except that I have the ability to look into Barclay's records, maybe help give the people who lost their money a chance to see some of it back.

"I'll lock down his files for you."

"Thank you. I'll text you his login ID, along with the name of the FBI agent on the case."

She's asking me to turn her father in. Maybe she can't bring herself to do it...or even say it. Maybe she's still reeling too much. Whatever the reason, I respect her terrible, brave choice.

"I'll take it from there," I assure her. "Bethany, you're doing the right thing."

"I needed to hear that. I've devoted my entire life to that man, and some part of me still can't believe I'm turning on him. But I'm not. He betrayed me. I just need to make everything right." She drags in a shuddering breath. "There's more you need to hear."

Seriously? "I'm listening."

"Barclay kept what he called a 'blackmail book.' Every dirty, hidden fact he knew about anyone and everyone he wrote down, along with details about where he heard the information and how he verified it." She hesitates, and I hear the nerves in her voice. "He made lists of the people he could hurt most with it."

Tension twists my stomach. "What do you know that I should?"

"Were you aware that Barclay and Lund were friends?"

"No."

"They were, for years...until Barclay got Amanda Lund pregnant and Douglas realized his pal had stolen almost two hundred million dollars from him."

The information shocks me...yet it doesn't. Barclay and Douglas seem like birds of a feather. Why wouldn't the high-rolling scumbags be buddies?

"So Lund was going to buy Stratus, get Barclay's financial information, recoup his losses, and make a killing for himself by taking the rest of the stolen money?"

"That's my guess. If you had to spend a billion dollars to get almost three billion in return, wouldn't you do it?"

"If I wasn't breaking the law and hurting people, absolutely. Fuck..." The Lunds were willing to procure and destroy my business for revenge and greed. I wish I could say I'm having trouble believing it. But I'm not.

"I'm not done yet, Evan. I'm sorry."

Holy shit, what else could there be? "Go on."

"Barclay knew some of the skeletons in Douglas's closet. Lots of them, actually. For instance, he was there years ago when Lund was carrying on a torrid affair with his maid. Barclay didn't tell Douglas's wife at the time, even when the maid got pregnant. Douglas paid the maid off and provided financial support for the child. But thinking she might be helpful someday if Lund ever proved…difficult, Barclay kept track of Douglas's illegitimate daughter. His bi-racial daughter. You must know who I mean."

I freeze. Bethany can't be right.

"You're saying Nia…"

"Is Lund's daughter, yes. Small world, isn't it? I'm emailing you a picture of Nia's original birth certificate right now."

I open my email, find Bethany's missive, and launch the attachment. Everything she said stabs me with the truth. Unless this is one hell of a forgery—and why would my half sister bother?—Douglas Lund really is Nia's biological father.

Holy shit.

Here comes that debilitating grip on my lungs. I can't quite stand upright.

I swallow and lean against the side of the cafe. "How…"

Shock has even rendered me unable to speak.

"How did I get my hands on this? Lund was dumb enough to give it to Barclay for safekeeping shortly after Nia was born, maybe so his wife wouldn't find it. I don't know. Of course, within a month Lund had paid Nia's mother to petition the courts to have his name removed from the birth certificate. That's why Nia's copy says the father is 'unknown' instead."

"Why didn't Barclay threaten Lund with blackmail if he had all this information?"

"I'll bet he did. But all these years later and after his wife's passing, I don't think Lund cared anymore. He just wanted his money back."

So all this information remained in the safe. *Jesus.* This explains why the Lunds were so damn interested in Nia last month when they barged into my office to give me their final offer. Maybe that's why they insisted on keeping my staff—Nia especially—on board if they bought Stratus out from under me.

"That, and revenge. Lund wanted that, too. I suspect he's the one who tipped off the FBI. He's the reason Barclay is awaiting trial now."

"You're probably right." And even though Douglas Lund is on my shit list, I have to give him credit for doing something right.

"Do you think Nia has any idea Lund is her biological father?" Bethany asks.

"According to my wife, her mother took the secret of his identity to her grave."

And how devastated will she be to learn that the man who contributed half of her DNA has been paying more attention to acquiring my company than to mending fences with his daughter?

"Are you sure? In one of my last conversations with Barclay, he said Lund would never have made multiple attempts to buy a company from such a resistant seller without some inside help. You know, like an ace in the hole."

I don't mention that the bastard tried to use Becca against me first—and would have succeeded if fate hadn't intervened. On the other hand, Bethany may be right. And Lund continued with the lucrative offers well after Becca's death.

Does that asshole really have someone helping him from the inside?

"What are you suggesting?"

"I would congratulate you on your recent marriage…except I think you may have married the enemy. You know, it's funny. Given our childhoods, we had a million reasons never to trust people. But look at us being optimistic, wanting to believe and giving others our faith. You'd think we would have learned better."

"Listen to me," I snap. "Nia barely knows Lund. She wouldn't help him stab me in the back."

"You keep thinking that. I did, despite the number of people who told me Barclay is a thief, a liar, and a son of a bitch. I loved him. I never thought he would betray me like that…" She lets loose a bitter laugh. "Look in front of you, Evan. You have a new wife whose father intends to take your company from you. Tell me, has she encouraged you to sell?"

Not at first. And not that it matters. Nia wants what's best for me. She's been by my side for years. She loves me. I'm not letting Bethany's subversive questions crawl in my head. "Thanks for the information. I have my marriage under control."

"You think you can't be betrayed by the people who should be in your corner?"

No, I know I can. Becca proved that. But Bethany is simply drowning in her own bitterness now. She doesn't know Nia like I do.

"Is there anything else you need to tell me?" I really hope not. I've had enough bombshells for one day.

"That's it." She backs down. "I hope for your sake everything with Nia is all you hope and want it to be. Disillusionment is a bitch."

With that, three beeps sound in my ear, telling me she ended the call.

Sighing, I pocket the phone. Her suggestions about Nia's loyalty piss me off, but she's in a bad place. Maybe, after time passes, I'll reach out to her again. Maybe she'll want to meet the rest of our siblings and she'll see that we've all suffered at Barclay's hands but still managed to come out happy. I think she'll need some hope.

Right now, I need to see my wife. I have to decide if I should tell her. No, when. She deserves the truth about her biological father. I can't keep that information from her. I don't know how she'll take it. I don't know how much it will matter to her. But that's for her to decide. All I can do is hold her and be supportive.

Dragging in a steadying breath, I shove the door to the cafe open and glance around. The place is largely empty. There's a busboy cleaning up the last of the lunch rush. I see a hostess wiping down menus. A waiter hustles across the room with a carafe of coffee to an elderly couple a few feet away, holding hands. My day is shit, but their affection still makes me smile.

Until I catch sight of Nia in the far corner. And I realize she's not alone.

NIA STANDS WITH Stephen Lund, that male-model wannabe, next to a table piled with discarded dishes and half-empty iced tea glasses. Apparently, they just finished a cozy lunch.

Motherfucking son of a bitch. What is he doing in town? What is he doing with Nia?

Then he reaches for her. My wife is letting the jackass hug her? Yes. She's standing on her tiptoes, arms around him, totally returning the gesture. Like he's a friend. No, like he's her brother—and she knows it. Lund junior gives her a brotherly pat between the shoulder blades and murmurs something in her ear.

What the hell is going on?

Dread weighs heavily inside me. Suspicion races through my veins.

I sidle closer and hide behind a column in the middle of the room. This feels wrong. Vaguely, I'm aware that if I trust Nia, I should simply approach her and ask for an explanation. On the other hand, nothing about this meeting looks good—or right. Since when is she friendly with Stephen Lund? Last time they met, she seemed almost eager to get away from him.

At least that's what she wanted me to think.

I shove down my distrust. I don't know for certain what they're talking about. Maybe it has nothing to do with me or Stratus. Maybe today's bombshells and Bethany's voice in my head are messing with me. Maybe Nia isn't plotting to stab me in the back at all.

"We can make this work," Lund says.

"I hope you're right." She sounds nervous but upbeat.

He gives her hand a reassuring squeeze. "I am. I've given this a lot of thought. It's for the best. For everyone."

"I'm not sure Evan will see it that way."

"But this is for *you*, for *your* future. Don't forget that."

She nods. It's hesitant at first, then the gesture builds steam. "You're right. I can't have everything I want if I don't do this."

"Exactly." He gives her a peck on the cheek. "Call me if you need anything. I'll be more than happy to talk you off the ledge, like a good big brother should."

"Thanks. That means a lot to me."

They say their goodbyes and leave via the door on the far side of the room, never seeing me. I watch them go, dumbfounded.

Denial fights with common sense. I don't know precisely what that exchange was about. It could be anything, and I shouldn't jump to conclusions. But it's fucking hard not to. My new wife is meeting with Lund Junior in the middle of our negotiations. And they just happen to be siblings. Who knew? They look pretty damn close, too. She's thinking about her future and she's prepared to act, even if I won't like it. Logically, there are only so many things that could mean.

The most obvious is that they're plotting to sell me out.

Clenching my fists at my sides, I storm toward the door, ducking under a waiter carrying a food-laden tray, and crash outside. Nia and her car are already gone.

Fuck.

Throwing myself into my sedan, I slam the door and burn rubber out of the parking lot. I'm going to find her and demand she tell me I'm wrong.

My righteous anger simmers just under a rolling boil. I try to tamp it down, tell myself to ask questions before I hurl accusations. But if she's up to what I suspect she is? How fucking dare she stab me in the back. I opened up for her. I trusted her. I defended her. I gave my heart to her.

As I reach Nia's cottage, I see her car parked in its usual spot. Good. We need to have this out. I'd rather do it in private.

In my pocket, my phone buzzes. I pull it free as I step from the car and glance at the screen. Nia sent me a text. What ironic timing…

`Can you come home? There's something we need to talk about.`

Pocketing my phone again, I charge up toward her house. Yeah, hers. It's not our temporary digs anymore. We don't have any home together, not if she's going to even consider betraying me.

I could forgive Becca for her treachery because I didn't give her what she needed. I took her for granted. I gave her a name and a house—and nothing more. Sure, her plot was twisted, cold, and shitty. But on some level, I understand.

With Nia, I'm confused as fuck. What have I not given that woman? She has my name and my love. Hell, she has my fucking soul. Know what I don't have? A prenuptial. Yep. She talked me out of it at the last minute, made it seem as if tearing it up was a grand romantic gesture on my part to prove how much I loved her so we could be truly happy on our wedding day.

And I was such an idiot. I totally fell for it.

Has she been laughing these last nine days, since I took her hand, promised to love, honor, and cherish her, then said "I do?"

God, none of this makes sense. Nia has never been a liar. If anything, she's always been wincingly straightforward with me. Why would she start all this subterfuge and lying now? And how long has she known she was Lund Junior's sister? Maybe the answer to my previous question matches the answer to my last. I don't know anymore. I'm so confused. And I'm afraid I won't like the truth. There's a gaping hole in my chest. I'm twisted up by the terrible, wrenching hope that all my suspicions are wrong. But my head is telling me I can't be.

When I reach the door, I shove it open to see Nia standing at the kitchen table. Her moving boxes are stacked neatly against one wall. She looks tired but excited. And decidedly nervous.

"That was fast. I just texted you thirty seconds ago. How did you—"

"It didn't take me long to drive here from that cafe where you fucking met Lund Junior for lunch. And I guess some conspiratorial plotting?"

She freezes. "You saw us?"

"Oh, I heard you, too."

At that, Nia cocks her head. "What do you think you heard?"

She's going to give me attitude? Is she fucking serious?

"Are you going to deny that asshole is your half brother?"

She gasps. "How did you find out?"

"I have my ways, honey," I snarl out. "And I heard all about your big plans for the future. It's 'best' for everyone. Well, except me. I've got to hand it to you. You didn't directly target my business, where I'm smart and guarded. Nope. You slithered toward me where you know I'm stupid. You preyed on my emotions."

"Slithered? Preyed?" She anchors her hands on her hips and glares at me, suddenly pissed-off female. "What the hell do you think I'm plotting?"

"To sell Stratus out from under me. This is same song, different verse for the Lunds. Did you know they convinced Becca to divorce me so I'd be forced to sell them the company, too?" When shock crosses Nia's face, I give her a mocking nod. "Yep. I found that out today. She wanted the money to run away with Sebastian. Because she was in love with him. I also found that out today. But you..." I point an accusing finger at her. "I guess you decided to help your long-lost family screw me over and make a buck in the process. So they'd accept you? Never mind that none of them have been here for you your entire life. And never mind that I fucking loved you. Nope. I guess you were all about winning their favor so you wouldn't be a sad little girl with no daddy anymore. And if you got to fuck me in more ways than one, even better."

Her mouth gapes open. "Seriously? You think I'm guilty of all that? Are you listening to yourself?"

"I notice you're not refuting anything I'm saying, Nia. I don't hear a shred of logic."

"Logic? Remember, *you* came after me. You proposed to me. You insisted on marrying me." She sighs in frustration. "I chose to be your wife. I'm carrying your baby. How could you think I'd plot to take Stratus from you?"

"Um, you were having lunch with him behind my back."

"That's not what happened. He said he wanted to talk to me and swore it wasn't about the buyout. I didn't see any reason not to listen. I thought maybe I might even get some inside information to help you."

Convenient. "Or get the same deal the Lunds were willing to cut Becca. One hundred fifty million dollars—plus half of all my assets from the divorce, of course. I can't fault you for being greedy or needy or whatever. I fault myself for being too emotional to see it. Fuck that. Never again."

There doesn't seem to be anything left to say. Looking at her hurts. I know every angle of her face. I know each curve of her body intimately. I thought I knew her heart equally well, and to be proven so viciously wrong is stabbing me in the chest and wrecking my soul.

I spin around and march for the door.

"If you leave this house without talking it out, we're done," she warns. "That will tell me you don't love me and you're not ready to be married."

She's threatening me...but not refuting me. Oh, she asked me some rhetorical questions designed to make me think twice, but she didn't really defend her decision. Because she fucking can't.

My throat closes up. My chest buckles. Why did she have to break me like this?

"Oh, honey, we were done the minute you made a deal with the devil. I can't stop you from cutting off my balls and forcing me to sell Stratus in order to give you half its value in the divorce. I wasn't smart enough to protect myself. But you'll have to live with the fact I'll never forgive you."

As I slam my way out the door, she follows and yanks it open, calling after me. "You'll have to live with being completely wrong. You want the truth? Here you go: I have loved you since the moment I came to work for you. I said yes to you that night at the burlesque club because there was no way I could say no after pining for three years. I have *never* betrayed you. I never would. Stephen told me a freaking hour ago that I'm his sister. He sought me out against his father's wishes. What you overheard was the two of us planning to let everyone know that we intend to recognize each other as family. That's what I thought you wouldn't be happy about. But now that I know what you really think of me, Evan? Go. And don't let the door hit you on the way out."

Nia gives said door a decisive slam and locks herself inside the cottage.

I blink, stare, replay her speech in my head. The heat begins to bleed from my anger. Is it possible she's telling me the truth, that Lund Junior approached her a mere hour ago? That they weren't talking about betraying me? Is there any chance I misunderstood everything and was wrong about everything? Most especially about her?

CHAPTER EIGHTEEN

Maui, Hawaii
Sunday, December 24

FUCK, I SHOULD have stayed in Seattle. I could have sulked in the cold. It would have better matched my mood. Instead, I came to paradise for the holidays, where I married and first made love to Nia as my wife.

For some reason, my misery is more acute since it's sunny and seventy-two degrees. Or is that my imagination and I'd be despondent regardless of where I am? Yeah, that's the more likely scenario.

I'm not functioning well without Nia—and not because I can't cook or clean or do my own laundry. I've learned to be a lot more self-sufficient because of her. But since we split, sleeping is a no-go. Concentration is even more laughable. Socializing is an absolute fail. And screw holiday cheer. I arrived in Maui yesterday, and I've barely mustered the energy to talk to Harlow and Noah. I'm staying with them because they have a ton of bedrooms in their palatial love nest, and I can't sleep in the house I bought for Nia and me to spend our lives together. Nor can I bring myself to sell it. I'm not ready to let go of the memories. The minute I landed on the island, I went there, sat on the bed, and just…remembered.

She's never coming back. I deeply suspect that. I've had a week to come to the conclusion that I irrevocably fucked up the best thing that ever happened to me.

An hour after I left Nia's cottage that confusing, awful day, she texted to say my stuff was on her front porch. Twenty minutes later, I had two emails in my inbox. The first was a resignation letter, effective immediately. The second stated that she rescinded any and all claim to Stratus in the event of our divorce.

I spent the rest of the day mulling over everything, sorting through the facts to find a logical conclusion. But my common sense no longer functions properly when it comes to Nia. I'm not sure it ever did. Her conversation with Stephen Lund seemed to prove her obvious guilt, so I acted accordingly.

But as soon as she slammed the door between us for the final time, instinct kicked in. I started second-guessing everything.

Would Nia, the woman who's been my invaluable right hand for years, betray me? Or try to separate me from Stratus for her own gain? Would she really cheat me? Would she bother to release me from my financial obligations if she was simply plotting to climb over me to brighten her future?

No.

She's smarter than that. She's also more honest.

Within hours, I was convinced of that fact, but I slept on it. The following morning, I resolved to call her to talk everything through face-to-face. Sure, I didn't want to spend another wretched night like the previous one—in the condo I shared with Becca, feeling utterly lost and crushed. But it was more. I needed to be near Nia again. Only she can make me whole.

But when I rang, I discovered she'd disconnected her number.

She didn't appear for work. In fact, her desk had already been emptied, and her badge lay next to my computer, along with a list of appointments, passwords, and files.

When I stopped by her cottage, prepared to beg her, she refused to answer the door.

I've tried to make contact with her every day since our breakup. No response. My Facebook messages go unanswered and unread, as do my emails.

She's spending time with Lund Junior, according to her social media.

They even publicly recognized one another as siblings and posed together for pictures in the park. In the photos, I see her smiling, but she doesn't look happy.

I'm falling apart.

Why won't she talk to me?

Because I was a douche who accused her of terrible shit. Because I didn't listen to my heart.

"You okay?"

I turn to find Harlow lingering uncertainly in the doorway of their home office. I've been holed up here all morning, trying to focus on work...but there's not a lot coming my way right now. It's Christmas Eve, and I'm wasting my time. No, I'm hiding out.

"Sure. How are you?" I see her hand on her belly. "Is the baby active this morning?"

"He's getting restless. It's nothing new." She shrugs. "Want to talk about it?"

No sense in pretending I don't know what she's talking about. "Not really."

It won't change anything.

"Well, that's too bad. I hate to be the buzzkill at your pity party—okay, no, I don't—but you need to figure this out. You and Nia are married."

Yes, but for how much longer?

"More than that, you belong together. You two are having a baby," she goes on. "You have a million reasons to work things out with her."

"I don't know where to start. She's not speaking to me."

"Whatever you did must have been messed up because that woman is in love with you."

I close my eyes, but there's no escaping the pain. "It was. And it was entirely my fault."

Harlow sighs. "All of Barclay Reed's children have an unfortunate genetic predisposition to mistrust and stupidity when it comes to relationships. Maxon took Keeley for granted and almost lost her. Griff threw Britta away once and nearly failed to believe in her the second time. And me? Noah is a saint for putting up with all my hot-and-cold mood swings and my skittishness in committing. My brothers and I have learned to admit when we're wrong. For the record, it sucks, but the skill is admittedly helpful because we have to use it a lot. Tell Nia you're sorry. She'll listen."

"I accused her of marrying me to swindle me. So probably not. Besides, I've tried."

Harlow winces. "Wow, that's a fucked-up low, even for a Reed. I don't know whether to bow to you or just shake my damn head. What a dumb ass."

"I deserve to be called worse."

"Um…yeah, but I won't heap on you when you're obviously miserable. So you need to find a way to reach her, beyond the usual lame flowers and pitiful groveling."

"Yes, but what's going to persuade her to forgive me? I've wracked my brain. I've got nothing."

"One thing I've learned—that all us Reed kids have—is that actions speak louder than words. If you accused her of something seriously awful, you need to show her that you know better now. You need to prove that you believe her."

"How do I do that?"

Harlow shrugs. "If I were in her shoes, I'd want something meaningful. And sacrificial. I'm not saying you should offer her your balls on an altar of apology literally…but figuratively? Absolutely."

I would be willing to do that, but there's that sliver of worry inside me that keeps asking if I truly know how to be that vulnerable with anyone. "Can't she just believe me when I say I'm sorry? Understand that I'm miserable as fuck and would do anything to have her back?"

"How will any of that convince her you understand the gravity of your BS and that you won't dive into another steaming mass in the future?"

Point taken. If Nia had accused me of dirty, underhanded shit, especially without listening to me, I would be disinclined to hear some feeble-ass apology. Words are easy. People say them every day. They schmooze. They charm. They lie.

A gesture that would not only tell Nia I know I was wrong but that I trust her in every way is what I need. Maybe then she'll listen. Maybe not. But if I craft the right apology and give it to her with my whole heart, at least I'll know I did everything I could to win her back.

"Think it over. It's not a decision you can rush. Oh… Wait here." Harlow runs down the stairs, then huffs and puffs her way back up before handing me a thumb drive. "Here are some musical inspirations from Keeley. It may sound corny, but she seems to know exactly the right songs to help someone move forward. Give them a listen. Maybe they'll inspire you."

This is probably a collection of schmaltzy love songs I would normally never listen to, but I don't have anything better to do or anything to lose by trying another tactic.

"Thanks," I say to Harlow. "I'm going to hang here and check this out."

She pauses and nods. "I'm here if you want to talk more. No pressure or anything, but what you do next may determine your whole future."

I'm well aware of that. "Sure. No pressure at all."

"Just ask yourself what's the most convincing, least dumb ass move. Then do that."

Speaking of least dumbass moves… "Before you go, you should know that I probably ended Barclay's days as a free man."

She raises a dark brow at me. "Do tell. I don't relish anyone's misfortune, but after all the shit he's pulled, he deserves to go down."

Since I've already explained my contact with Bethany to my siblings, I don't have to preface this much. "I found Barclay's information on Stratus's platform and turned it over to the FBI. It's the direct link they've been needing between him and the missing money. The feds won't be able to seize all of it, given where he stashed the funds. But some. I hope it will help his victims."

And it will screw Douglas Lund out of taking it all for himself. So win-win.

"Good for you. Did you tell Bethany?"

I nod. "I called her earlier this morning."

"How's she doing?"

The only answer I can give Harlow is a shrug. "About as well as can be expected when you find yourself suddenly and completely alone."

Something I know about too well.

"And it's the holidays." My sister holds out her hand to me. "Give me your phone."

I reach into my pocket and pull the device free. "Okay, but you can't call Nia for me. I don't know her new number anyway."

She scowls at me. "I wasn't going to. That's between you two. But Bethany needs someone now, and this gathering of ol' Barclay's children could sure use more estrogen. Between you, Maxon, and Griff, the testosterone cloud is choking. I know she said she wasn't interested in meeting any of us…but it's the holidays. I'm willing to be the bigger person and offer her a hand when she needs it."

"I think she'll appreciate it. If not today, then eventually."

I unlock my phone and hand it to Harlow. She puts the call on speaker. Bethany answers on the second ring.

"Hi, Evan. Thanks again for sending all the evidence to the feds. It needed to be done."

"Actually, it's Harlow, your younger sister. I conned Evan out of his phone. I want to talk to you."

"About what?" Suddenly, Bethany sounds guarded.

"Look, I don't want to rip you a new one or anything. You fell for Daddy's bullshit. Don't feel bad. You're not the first." Harlow pauses. "Who are you spending the holidays with?"

"N-no one. I don't… You know Barclay's views on relationships."

"Oh, I do. I've never met a more cynical, unromantic sociopath."

"Right. I was pretty much a workaholic anyway, so I don't have any other connections."

Sympathy crosses Harlow's face. "Come to Maui. Today."

"What? I can't barge—"

"You're not barging. I'm inviting you. Say yes. You can join the small but distinguished club of Reed offspring Barclay has royally screwed. We'll swap stories and sing songs. It'll be fun."

"You're serious?"

"She is, Bethany. I only met this clan six months ago, but they've been awesome and welcoming. Trust me, they get what you're going through."

"Come," Harlow says again. "Seriously. Don't spend the holidays alone."

"Um...how will I get there? Christmas is tomorrow, and I don't have a plane ticket. I don't have a job to pay for one, either. And the feds have frozen my accounts until my part in this mess Barclay created is sorted out."

"I'll handle it," I tell her. "Start packing your bags, and I'll send you the details in a few hours."

She falls very quiet, and I only know she's still on the line because I hear her breathing and what sounds like a sniffle she's trying to suppress. "Thank you. Really, I appreciate everything."

"You're welcome," I say gently. "See you soon."

We hang up, and Harlow smiles. "This will be a good thing. I'm going to go tell Noah to expect one more for dinner. You go figure out how to get your wife back soon, huh?"

As she leaves me with a kiss on the cheek, Diana texts me from Tokyo to wish me a Merry Christmas. I don't have the heart—or the balls—to tell her that the marriage she attended mere days ago is already in shambles. Instead, I text back my holiday well wishes, promise we'll get together when she returns to the States again, and stare into my bottle of water.

I shake off my maudlin thoughts and make calls until I find a charter flight for Bethany. It's going to cost me a pretty penny to get her to Maui by tonight, but she needs to meet people who will truly be family to her—if she lets them.

But now that task is off my to-do list, and I have to figure out how to fix my own damn life.

With a sigh, I slide on my noise-canceling headphones and pop in the thumb drive Keeley made for me.

I'm not surprised the intro to the first song isn't familiar. I search around and discover Maxon's wife included a list of songs on the portable storage device, so I launch it.

"Goodbye" by Natalie Imbruglia is up first. Never heard of her. Nice voice. The tune itself is slow and sad, and the female vocalist manages to convey melancholy desolation perfectly. It resonates on every level because I'm feeling it, too. When she sings that every day is the same and she feels them all merge, I completely get it. It's only been a week without Nia, and I'm in this never-ending malaise I can't shake. Oh, and the singer's lilting high note when she croons that people are telling her she'll be fine and it will all get better? Heartbreaking bullshit. She knows it—just like I do.

This song makes me certain I'll be feeling this way for the rest of my life if I can't figure out a way to tell Nia how sorry I am.

Next up, another ballad, accompanied by a simple piano-drum duo. It's stripped down, and when the opening line is about the car being parked and the bags being packed, I know this is going to hurt. By the time Sara Bareilles starts singing that her lover is all she has and all she needs, the one she's pining for is the very air she would kill to breathe, I'm choking up. That's exactly how I feel about Nia.

Fuck, this song is an ax to the heart.

Suddenly, something wet drips on the desk. I look down. I see another drop. Then I realize the wetness is coming from me.

I'm crying.

I haven't done that since I was five, when my mother died. Odd that I just realized I never mourned for Becca like this. I was lost, yes. But I didn't feel this aching, empty hole in my existence because she was gone. I totally feel it for Nia. Every morning, every night. Every moment. Yes, it hurts to be here. And I hope I'll breathe again.

But I can only do that with my wife.

The next song cues up immediately after the last one. Another female starts singing after a short musical interlude, almost whining the observation that they fell out of love, but they can fall back in. What can I do or change to make that happen? Good question. I'd like to know.

Here comes another onslaught of tears. They aren't manly. They aren't logical. And yet I can't stop them.

Crap, I want to blame Keeley. She likes chick ballads, which are admittedly effective in dissecting a shitty situation. But I'm also feeling a bit like I'm having my heart ripped out through my ass. It's not remotely comfortable.

"Fall Back In" by Plumb rolls on. Yes, everything used to come so easily for Nia and me. I could have found her in the dark. I could have found her blindfolded, wearing earmuffs, with my hands tied behind my back. When I was with her, I had this feeling of ease and peace and rightness. That's all gone.

Really, what the fuck was I thinking when I opened my mouth and accused her of trying to hurt me? That I'd hurt her back? I don't even know anymore.

There's definitely something between us, like the song suggests, and if I throw it away, I'll regret it like hell. I already do.

I close my eyes. How do I make this maudlin shit stop?

When the song ends, a rock tune blessedly hits my ears next. A guitar accompanies a man's gravelly voice saying he was blown away. Daughtry. I recognize this song, though I haven't heard it in years. Yeah, it did all seem to make sense—at the time. Becca's betrayal. Bethany's bombshell. Then Nia's seeming stab in the back. It simply didn't make sense in the end. He implores his lover that they should start over, swears they're wasting too much time. Amen to all of that.

Weirdly, this anthem is giving me hope.

The last song on the list is from Lifehouse. I listen, letting the lyrics sink in, nodding along to the mellow tune before the chorus smacks me across the face. I will do whatever it takes to turn this relationship around. I have no doubt what's at stake, just like I know I utterly let her down. I did worse than that, but I still relate to these words. The singer begs that if she'll just give him a chance, he'll do everything he can to keep them together. He makes another plea that's brilliant: that they to hold on to each other above everything else. That they start over.

I want that, too. So badly. And suddenly, all of these songs blend together in my head and form a message. Ideas have been swirling as tears have been falling. Now, I wipe my face clean and stand. I know what I have to do to win Nia back.

With a grim smile, I pick up my phone and proceed to gamble my entire future on one apology.

CHAPTER NINETEEN

Seattle, Washington
Thursday, December 28

TODAY IS THE day—my last chance with Nia.

I arrived in Seattle late last night to a voicemail from my Realtor. She has an offer for my penthouse—asking price, all cash. They want to take possession in two weeks. One quick phone call later, and the deal was done. After that, I crashed for a few hours, until sleep deserted me. It's as if everything inside me woke up to the fact that lying in bed is an unproductive waste of my time right now. Sure, I have a condo to pack up.

More importantly, I have a wife to win back.

Still, getting up sucks. After traveling across three time zones twice in less than five days, I'm jet-lagged. The sun won't be up for hours, but if I do everything right today, I might have the rest of my life to sleep next to Nia.

And if I fuck up, I'm doomed.

Shoving the thought away, I brush my teeth and get busy. I have to give her the apology she deserves and show her how much I love her. It's my only hope.

In the hush, I assemble my setup in the kitchen. Tarp, easel, paints, and the canvas with the blob I tried to paint…was that exactly a month ago?

Yes. I have thirty days of mostly wonderful memories. But my situation has changed so much. Now, everything hurts, especially when it hits me that if I can't figure out how to win Nia back, we'll never make another memory together again.

No. Fuck no. I made mistakes—colossal ones. I'm learning from them. But *we* aren't a mistake.

Our story can't end this way, not when I'm still so in love with the woman who helped me create it.

When I try to lift my brush to canvas, the silence proves too soft to drown the thoughts in my head. The doubts rush in to overwhelm me. I need distraction. I need noise. Keeley seems to have the right idea. Music.

I grab my phone and scroll through my song selections. I don't download many songs for myself, but I have for technically challenged Diana over the years. They're mostly oldies I listened to in the car with her as a teenager. One song jumps out at me.

It's perfect.

Putting the tune on repeat, I let the admittedly cheesy seventies intro roll between my ears and through my brain. "If" is an epically romantic ode from a man who shares an imperfect love with an unforgettable woman. His voice is—there's no other way to put it—desperately yearning. He asks why, if a picture paints a thousand words, can't he paint her.

Interesting point.

I'm going to paint Nia as I see her. As I see us.

The us we should be.

Inspiration rushes me. I grab my brush and let it find its path over the canvas. I still don't know how I'll depict what's in my head, just like I don't know what Nia and I will be someday. Loving spouses or bitter exes? We'll always be soul mates, I know that.

I never put much stock in that concept before; it never made logical sense. The idea of having a single person as one's destiny sounded preposterous on multiple levels. The logistics of that alone don't add up. After all, what are the odds of finding that singularly perfect person on a planet of nearly eight billion people? But now I suspect that fate puts everyone on the right path to the right people at the right time to help us grow. To teach us to be better people. It's up to every individual to embrace and value their soul mate.

I didn't do enough of that, and I've got to now or I'm going to wind up a miserable fucking bastard.

As the song goes on, I can't disagree when the guy sings that if a man could be in two places at one time, he'd be with her. I'd be with Nia right now if she'd let me. And every day thereafter.

For the rest of our forevers.

It's hours before my painting takes shape. Once I realize what this image needs to be, I can't swipe my brush across the canvas fast enough. The good part? I'm centered. I see so clearly what I need to do and say. I may not win Nia back, but if I convey everything pouring from my soul, at least I'll know I gave us my all.

And I'll have empty decades in front of me to correct my fatal flaw: relying too much on logic and not listening enough to my heart.

When I'm finally done, my shoulder aches. I'm so tired my head feels stuffed with cotton. My eyes are gritty. But as I stand back and survey my work, a grin breaks across my face. I'm back—alert and present—but I'm changed, thanks to Nia. I'm reborn. I'm better for having loved her.

No matter what happens next, I'll always be thankful to her for that.

I leave the canvas to climb back into bed for a couple of hours. When I wake at noon, I start dialing people, calling in favors, and even begging strangers until everything is in place.

Finally, evening unfurls when the delivery truck I hired pulls up in front of Nia's cottage. I'm relieved to see her car here and the lights on.

"You got everything, man?" the driver asks as I lift the unwieldy rectangular bundle I brought for her, wrapped in plain brown paper.

"Yep. Thanks for letting me hitch a ride with you...what was your name again?"

"Garth. It's no problem."

"Here's the five hundred bucks I promised you." I withdraw the cash from my pocket. "I hope you don't lose your job over this."

"Nah. It's the end of my shift, and it wasn't even half a mile off my route. If anyone asks, I'll say I took a wrong turn." He glances down at the cash. "But, um…you could keep that if you'd look at my résumé."

"Your résumé?"

"I know who you are, Mr. Cook. And I don't want to drive a delivery truck for the rest of my life. I'm a coder. Self-taught, but I'm damn good. And I used to break into systems for fun, just to see if I could. So I can think like a hacker. I've written some pretty complicated viruses, too. Not that I ever unleashed them on anyone."

He reminds me of myself a half dozen years ago. Normally, I don't look at anyone without significant work experience, but my gut tells me I'd be passing up someone valuable.

"Take the money and email me your résumé, Garth. I'll take a look as soon as I can." With a grin, he hands me a pencil, and I jot my personal email address on the back of the envelope.

As I press the bundle of cash into his hands, his eyes widen. "Wow. Thanks! And hey, I hope this girl lets you in. You seem really into her. When I first heard your plan—before I knew who you were—I was thinking you're a crazy bastard to be so hung up on one chick…"

"She's worth it."

Garth, who's barely legal to drink, doesn't get it yet.

"Sure. Good luck," he says with a wave as I hop off the truck. "I'll be in touch. You sure you don't want me to come back and take you to your car?"

"I parked two blocks down the road, but thanks."

As I nod at him, I position the package in front of my face and head up Nia's walk. If she's looking out the window, she'll see nothing but a giant delivery. I never imagined I'd be making a plea to my wife not to leave me forever while wearing a brown uniform. But if that's what it takes, I'll do it.

My heart jerks and hammers as I ring her bell. It kicks up another notch when she opens the door between us. I can't see her, but I sense her, smell her. It's like coming home. Like my heart is awakening from a dark slumber. I have to exercise all my restraint not to grab her in my arms.

"Oh, my gosh," she exclaims. "Is this for me?"

"Yes. I've got more, too." I muffle my voice.

"Okay. It's kinda big. You want to set it in the foyer?"

"Sure."

By mutual agreement, now that I'm inside Nia's cottage, I hear Garth drive off in a screech of tires.

"Um, is your partner driving away without you?"

I drag in a breath and lower the package, setting it on end at my feet and revealing my face.

With hungry eyes, I take in every detail. Nia is barefaced and already in her pajamas for the night. She looks a little tired, but still so beautiful I can't find words. My knees almost buckle. I'm filled with sharp, bittersweet agony.

"No, honey. I'm right where I'm supposed to be."

She gapes at me, looking utterly stunned. "Evan... What are you doing here?"

"Apologizing to you. Fighting for us."

The words are barely out before her face closes up. She opens her mouth. Nothing good is going to come out of it.

I have to cut her off before she says something we can't take back.

"Please don't kick me out before I admit I was a complete asshole who can't give you a good reason why I accused you of ugly things. I'd just like to try to explain as best I can."

Nia bites her lip and stares. She says nothing for excruciating moments while she gauges my sincerity. Finally, she sighs. "Fifteen minutes. I'm supposed to fly out early in the morning."

That stops my heart cold. "Where are you going?"

She hesitates, then shakes her head. "Evan, why would I stay here? I don't have a job, and my rental is too expensive with no income. And to be honest, the memories are...too much. I'm from Georgia originally, so I thought maybe I'd fly home and see if—"

"Douglas Lund isn't hiring you or helping you or..." He's her fucking father, after all. And now that the truth is out, why wouldn't he?

"No. Stephen is happy to recognize me as his sister. Douglas..." She shrugs. "We've talked. We'll see what happens. He's spent twenty-five years denying I exist. I don't know that he's eager to shout to the rooftops that he did his maid or has an ethnic daughter or whatever."

"Then he's a douchebag. But I was, too. I should never have spit all those awful accusations at you. My only defense is that I'd found out mere minutes prior that Becca was brewing plans to divorce me and force me to sell Stratus so she could be with Sebastian."

"You said that. Was he in on it, too?"

"He had no idea," I assure her. "But it was a shock to know that, even after I'd genuinely tried with Becca, she was willing to stab me in the back and sell me out for a chance at a life with someone else. I didn't love her, and she didn't love me, either."

"I get it. You were in a bad headspace when you followed me home. But—"

"That's not all. I was literally standing in front of the cafe when Bethany called me. She'd figured out earlier that day that Douglas Lund was your father. She put the suggestion in my head that you'd married me to screw me out of Stratus. I didn't really believe her. After all, she doesn't know you. And Barclay Reed had just destroyed her every illusion, so she was brittle. But then...I overheard you and Stephen talking about making your plan work and it being best for everyone but me. He argued it was for your future, and you agreed that you couldn't have everything you wanted if you didn't go through with it. Instantly, my thoughts went to dark places."

"You thought I was willing to sell you out to be accepted by the Lunds." She frowns. "That I'd rather have them over the family you and I were building together?"

The tone of her voice says that's ridiculous.

I wince. "He's your father, and I thought you would—"

"Throw you under the bus for a man who walked away from me before I was even born?"

Sighing, I shake my head. "I knew shortly after our fight that I'd been dumb. But I didn't quite realize until now just how stupid. For the record, I couldn't imagine what else you and Stephen were talking about."

"Douglas," she answers. "Stephen has known about his dad's illegitimate daughter for years, and when we literally ran into each other in Stratus's lobby, he wanted to get to know his sister. When you and I came back from Maui after the wedding, he reached out to offer his congratulations and said he needed to see me. I was wary until he explained. After some talk, we decided we want to be family. So we hatched a plan to approach our father together and see if he would accept me." She shrugs. "But no. He only said he wanted to keep me on staff because it seemed to yank your chain. That day we fought, I imagined you wouldn't like the plan Stephen and I had concocted because of the negotiations. And because you never liked Douglas."

"I like him even less now," I grumble. "Funny how we're both in the same place—wealthy, powerful men as fathers, neither of whom wanted to recognize us. I don't need Barclay, and you don't need Douglas."

"I don't." She nods. "If he comes around, fine. I'll listen. If he doesn't, I have a brother in Stephen. He's been really great."

"Thanks for explaining." Even though anxiety is grinding up my guts, I take her hands. "If having him in your life brings you happiness or peace, then I'm glad. You deserve...everything. I didn't give you that, so I need to rectify the situation. I've given this a lot of thought, Nia. I had a miserable Christmas without you."

She presses her lips together. Her expression says she had a craptastic holiday without me, too. But she doesn't admit it aloud.

"The thing I trashed most the day I walked away from you was trust. The thing I took most from you was your voice. So I'm here to give those back to you. I know you would never have sold me out and now I need to prove that to you."

Nia folds her hands together. "Are you sure? The accusations you hurled at me—"

"Were terrible and unfair. And I know this world doesn't often give second chances. So if you don't feel like extending me one, I understand. But I have to ask."

"You can't just say and do those awful things, then sprinkle a few words of apology around like pixie dust, and poof. All the goodness and trust come back." She shakes her head. "I don't work like that."

"I know. Harlow pointed out that words are easy. You deserve more. So…will you lift your arms, palms up for me?"

Quietly, she does, and it kills me to see she's not wearing her wedding ring. "What are you doing?"

I lay three envelopes in her grip. "I'm putting everything in your hands, for you to decide. First, I've given you divorce papers. Technically, I know I'm supposed to hire someone to serve you, but I couldn't do that without talking to you, apologizing, and explaining. Splitting for good isn't what I want; I need you to know that. Just like I want you to know that I love you. You're smart and sassy and sexy. You're loyal and funny and wonderful. And you showed me who I am. But if you want to be free of me, I've granted you the means. In that document, you have full custody of our son or daughter, but I'm here if he or she ever wants to know me. I'm also giving you half of my assets, with the exception of Stratus."

Her eyes tear up. "Evan—"

"Let me finish. In the second envelope is a document that transfers one hundred percent ownership of Stratus to you. I've already signed it. Once you do the same and have it notarized, the entire company is yours—to keep or sell as you see fit."

Nia's jaw drops. "It's worth a billion dollars."

I nod.

"You've spent your adult life building it."

I nod again.

"You can't give it away. That's not logical."

"It's not." I want to touch her so badly I can barely breathe. "But I don't care. Nothing means anything to me without you."

Tears well in her eyes, then fall down her cheeks. "Evan…"

Jesus, I'm going to lose it, too. My eyes sting, my throat constricts. I suck it up. I need to keep myself together—for her.

"The third envelope is a plane ticket from Seattle to Maui. If you can forgive me and you want to try again, I'll be there. It leaves on Sunday. If I see you get off the plane, I'll know you still love me, too. And that you want to ring in the New Year and our new future together. If not"—I swallow—"then I'll probably never see you again. In either case, this is for you." I thrust the package forward. "You asked me the evening you came to the penthouse to help me clean if the canvases under my bed were Becca's." I shake my head. "They were mine. I hadn't been able to paint since her death. You not only made me function again, you taught me to feel. I want you to know how I see us, how I see our forever. In my head, this is the way we'll always be."

"Oh, my god." She reaches for my offering, tears now streaming crystal paths down her face.

I work up the courage to wrap my fingers around hers. "Wait to open it until after I'm gone. Please. Then look at everything I've left you. I hope to see you on New Year's Eve because you're my everything. But if I don't..." I lean in and kiss her softly one last time, our lips clinging, our breaths mingling. It kills me to pull away, knowing I may never be this close to her again. "Then I understand. And I'll always love you."

CHAPTER TWENTY

Nia

I BLINK AT the door Evan closed between us, then stare at the envelopes in my hand.

What has he done? I can't breathe. My heart hurts. I tremble.

But I have to know what he's saying to me.

Swallowing, I dig into the envelope on top. It's the plane ticket he mentioned. I set it on the hall table beside me, then reach for the next set of documents. The papers giving me total ownership and control of Stratus. I scan them.

Oh, god.

This is surreal. This is crazy.

"Evan…why?"

But I know why. He's showing me he trusts me. In the strongest way possible, he's telling me he doesn't believe I'll sell him out to my biological father. And he's doing it without uttering a word.

I can't sign this. I can't take this man's work from him. He's birthed it, lived and breathed it for years. As much as I would love for my own father to recognize me someday, I would never buy his affections by selling Evan's blood, sweat, and tears, then pocketing the cash. Nor would I want Douglas's affection if Stratus is the price.

If I have to choose between loyalty to the man who helped give me life or the man I pledged my future to, there's really no choice.

I miss Evan so much. Christmas was awful. I spent the morning with

Lorenzo and Guilia. Mateo offered me "comfort" as he dropped his hand to my thigh. I elbowed him in the stomach and flipped him the bird. Stephen picked me up for the evening. We shared pictures and swapped childhood stories. When I refused his offer of wine, he figured out I'm pregnant. Then he asked me what had gone wrong between Evan and me. Sad and lonely and heartbroken, I cried in his arms and explained. As he held me, he promised that Evan wouldn't give up. He swore that Evan loves me.

My brother was right. I knew it even then…but is love enough? What good is it without trust? If Evan can't believe I would always be his helpmate and his champion—that I would always choose him—how could we stay together?

I never expected him to prove how much he loves me by tossing aside every shred of his logic and sacrificing his future simply to say he's sorry. He's making me rethink my decision to end this and go.

I don't want to open the last envelope, the one I know holds divorce papers. I stare at it like a snake, terrified it will bite me. The heartache of even holding these documents sears my veins like venom, wrecking me.

With a gasp, I toss the closed envelope on the hall table. I'm not opening it. I don't want to read what's inside. I don't even want to touch the documents.

Now that the opportunity to be free is in front of me, I don't want a divorce.

Where does that leave me?

Evan hurt me with his wild, awful accusations; I can't deny that. But to never see him again, never hold him, never share the joy of our baby or our tomorrows with him?

My breath shudders as I close my eyes. I'm not ready to face that possibility. I resigned from my job and changed my number in anger. I cleaned out my desk and refused to answer my door because I wasn't ready to forgive him. I stayed away over the holidays because I knew that if I looked at him once… Well, I love him too much to hold out.

And now every shred of my anger is gone. A seven-hundred-pound sorrow sits in its place, crushing my chest.

I'm putting everything in your hands, for you to decide.

But what decision should I make?

Things aren't perfect between us…but I don't want perfect. I want our push-pull. I want our silly debates about head versus heart. I want to teach him to vacuum. I want him to show me quantum physics. I want to curl up on the couch and watch him grapple to comprehend some of my favorite goofy films. I want to grow old with him.

The tears that began spilling during his heartfelt apology become a wrenching sob. I hold the wall for support, but still feel as if I'll crumble if he doesn't hold me.

I first fell in love with Evan James Cook when he glanced at me across his cheap rented desk, my résumé in his hand, and proceeded not to ask boring questions about my work experience or where I saw myself in five years. Instead, he tested my grit by asking about a time I wanted something so badly that I was unstoppable in pursuing it. Then he inquired about my sense of curiosity, wanting to know the last thing that made me geek out. He inquired about teamwork, ownership, and organizational impact. He wasn't just looking for a cute assistant; he wanted someone with a brain. And he had such an interesting one of his own.

Oh, I dated off and on over the years I worked for him, tried to fall in love with someone who wasn't already married.

I was utterly, wholly, ridiculously unsuccessful.

I'm still in love with Evan James Cook.

You can have him.

The voice in my head is coming straight from my heart. It's impulsive. But I need to be rational, think of my future. Can I be with this man? He might always struggle with trust and emotion. He'll be better at solving Mensa puzzles than sharing his feelings. He will never be an easy man to live with. But I love him so much and he's come so far to not just tell me but *show* me that he loves me.

How can I not choose life with him?

My head spins as I lean against the wall and resist the urge to call him back until I've thought this through.

As I rest my forehead against the cool drywall and try not to cry, my knee bumps something. My startled gasp is loud in the silence until I realize it's the package Evan brought with him. The painting he made.

Of us.

I have to see.

My heartbeat slams against my chest quick and hard as I tear into the paper and rip it away with one hand. With the other, I turn on the quirky chandelier in my foyer. When the space is illuminated, I find myself looking at the back of the canvas.

Breath held, I turn it around.

Against a soft gray background, a man and a woman sit facing each other, hands clasped as they look into one another's eyes, legs twined. They have no color, no age, no identifying characteristics except the devotion in their eyes. They're soul mates. They're equals.

Together, their shapes form a perfect heart.

The sight destroys my composure—and my resistance. Suddenly, I can't stand. I fall to my knees and stare at the couple.

That could be us—Evan and me—for the rest of our lives.

All I have to do is tell him I want, trust, and love him.

My tomorrows, if I choose a life without him, loom before me. I could go to Georgia, get a new job, start over, hope I meet someone who will be half the man Evan is, and probably be miserable for all my days. Or…

Pressing my hand to my shaking chest, I swallow down a sob, collect all the papers he gave me, and lurch for my door. I don't care that my feet are bare, that I'm wearing pajamas, that any one of my neighbors could see me make a fool of myself.

The only thing that matters is reaching Evan.

My body trembles, heart thundering as I run down the walkway and stare up the street. In the distance, I see his familiar form, broad shoulders slumped as he slowly walks away. He reaches his car and hits the fob. With a listless tug, he opens the door, then pauses, bracing his arm against the doorframe. He lays his forehead on it and hesitates, as if he can't bring himself to get in the car and drive away.

My heart leaps.

"Evan!" I run after him, screaming with every ounce of my energy, praying to God I'm not too late. "Evan!"

He jerks, head snapping up before he zips his stare in my direction. Cautiously, he takes a half dozen steps around the car, climbs onto the sidewalk, then starts an uncertain jog in my direction. "Nia?"

The closer I get the more my lungs burn, my eyes sting, and my heart feels as if it will explode. But I refuse to give up. I'll never give up on this man.

"Evan..." My voice catches, wails.

He must hear my pleading, because suddenly, he runs toward me. "Nia!"

The closer we get the harder my tears fall. I can't reach him fast enough. I can't live without him another moment. I can't be whole if he's not my friend, my partner, and my husband.

Finally, we're almost within touching distance. I launch straight at him. He opens his arms. We crash together. He lifts me, and I wrap myself around him. Our mouths meet for a long, wet, tear-filled kiss.

Instead of tearing me down, as the last eleven days apart have done, this embrace puts me back together, healing the pain, washing away the anger, blame, and despair. Now there's just Evan. And I never want to let go.

When he eases his mouth free, he searches my face under the halo of the nearby streetlight. "Honey?"

I wriggle out of his arms and stand, swallowing down my nerves as I flip through all the documents I'm still clutching. I come across the agreement giving me ownership of Stratus. And I rip it in two. Then in two again. I repeat the process until I throw the confetti in his face.

"What was that?"

"You're not giving your company to me. I don't want Stratus. I certainly don't want to sell it out from under you. And you're not selling it to

Douglas Lund. You *are* Stratus. The company has no heart without you. It belongs to you."

Evan shakes his head. "You've been its heart for a long time. I've just been its brain."

Weeping, I shake my head. "Don't be an idiot. You've made it everything it is today. It will never function right without you. Neither will I." With that, I take the envelope of divorce papers, holding one end in each hand, and give them it a mighty tug until I hear the most satisfying rip. "So you're not divorcing me, either. Ever."

He freezes. "You still want me?"

"I've always wanted you. I can't not want you. I wanted you when I shouldn't have. I loved you when it was impossible. I can't unlove you. I'm not going to try again."

His hand shakes as he raises it to my cheek. "I love you so much, Nia Cook."

I manage a lopsided smile as I press the plane ticket to my chest. "I'm keeping the plane ticket to Maui."

A wry grin spreads across his face. "Good. I have the seat next to you. I figured if you got on that plane, there was at least a shred of hope and I could spend the next six hours convincing you to take me back."

I have to laugh at his crazy, sneaky, kinda brilliant ploy. "You don't have to convince me of anything. I want to be with you, always."

He swallows nervously. "You forgive me?"

I nod. "That shit is behind us."

He lets loose a relieved sigh and pulls me close. "Thank god."

"C'mon. You had to know I would take you back..."

"I didn't. I hoped."

Tsking, I shoot him a skeptical glance. "You're too smart not to know better."

"I knew nothing about my heart until you." He lays his lips over mine as he settles his hands across my stomach. "The day we got married, you said you wanted more than fifty years with me. I want that, too. Just like I want more than this one child with you."

I melt all over him. "You're ready to be a father? You're not afraid anymore?"

"No, I'm still terrified. I don't know how to come back from the sudden loss of a baby. I'm taking that day by day. But whatever happens, we'll deal with it together. If I have you and your love, I have everything I need."

"You do."

A little grin spreads across his face. "This all started because I intended to put out a personal ad for a wife. If I could go back and rewrite the copy now, it would say, 'Stupid, left-brained entrepreneur seeks partner, lover, and soul mate. Ideal candidate is polished, intelligent, organized, educated, attractive—and under my nose, but I'm too blind to see it. Children and romance a must. Sense of humor a definite yes. Please relocate with me to Hawaii.'"

I giggle through my tears. "Well, if you're asking me now, the answer is yes. A million times, yes. And the first thing I want to do is hang your beautiful painting in our bedroom. Thank you for that. It touched me more than you know."

"It was my pleasure. I thought of you with every stroke of the brush and imagined…"

He trails off, looking too choked up to finish his sentence. "Evan?"

"I imagined touching you again."

"Don't imagine." I squeeze his hand. "Take me home and make love to me. Never let me go."

"Ever." He seals the vow with a kiss.

The End

Look for the next More Than Words novel, MORE THAN TEMPT YOU, coming from Shayla Black in early 2019!

Read on for more from the book that started it all…

Inspired by my 25th wedding anniversary trip, the More Than Words series is set mainly on the beautiful Hawaiian island of Maui. The More Than Words series comes from deep in my heart. I love creating real human connections and strong character-driven stories with romantic themes like redemption, second chance at love, and friends-turned-lovers.

MORE THAN WANT YOU

More Than Words, Book 1
By Shayla Black
NOW AVAILABLE!

A sexy and emotional contemporary romance series by Shayla Black...

I'm Maxon Reed—real estate mogul, shark, asshole. If a deal isn't high profile and big money, I pass. Now that I've found the property of a lifetime, I'm jumping. But one tenacious bastard stands between me and success—my brother. I'll need one hell of a devious ploy to distract cynical Griff. Then fate drops a luscious redhead in my lap who's just his type.

Sassy college senior Keeley Kent accepts my challenge to learn how to become Griff's perfect girlfriend. But somewhere between the makeover and the witty conversation, I'm having trouble resisting her. The quirky dreamer is everything I usually don't tolerate. But she's beyond charming. I more than want her; I'm desperate to own her. I'm not even sure how drastic I'm willing to get to make her mine—but I'm about to find out.

"THIS WILL BE our last song for the set. If you have requests, write them down and leave them in the jar." She points to the clear vessel at her feet. "We'll be back to play in thirty. If you have a dirty proposition, I'll entertain them at the bar in five." She says the words like she's kidding.

I, however, am totally serious.

Keeley starts her next song, a more recent pop tune, in a breathy, a capella murmur. "Can't keep my hands to myself."

She taps her thigh in a rhythm only she can hear until the band joins during the crescendo to the chorus. Keeley bounces her way through the lyrics with a flirty smile. It's both alluring and fun, a tease of a song.

Though I rarely smile, I find myself grinning along.

As she finishes, I glance around. There's more than one hungry dog with a bone in this damn bar.

I didn't get ahead in business or life by being polite or waiting my turn. She hasn't even wrapped her vocal cords around the last note but I'm on my feet and charging across the room.

I'm the first one to reach the corner of the bar closest to the stage. I prop my elbow on the slightly sticky wood to claim my territory, then glare back at the three other men who think they should end Keeley's supposed sex drought. They are not watering her garden, and my snarl makes that clear.

One sees my face, stops in his tracks, and immediately backs off. Smart man.

Number Two looks like a smarmy car salesman. He rakes Keeley up and down with his gaze like she's a slab of beef, but she's flirting my way as she tucks her mic on its stand. I smile back.

She's not really my type, but man, I'd love to hit that.

Out of the corner of my eye, I watch the approaching dirtbag finger his porn 'stouche. To stake my claim, I reach out to help Keeley off the stage. She looks pleasantly surprised by my gesture as she wraps her fingers around mine.

I can be a gentleman…when it suits me.

Fuck, she's warm and velvety, and her touch makes my cock jolt. Her second would-be one-night stand curses then slinks back to his seat.

That leaves me to fend off Number Three. He looks like a WWE reject—hulking and hit in the face too many times. If she prefers brawn over brains, I'll have to find another D-cup distraction for Griff.

That would truly suck. My gut tells me Keeley is perfect for the job.

Would it be really awful if I slept with her before I introduced her to my brother?

MORE THAN WORDS SERIES

DEVOTED TO PLEASURE

Devoted Lovers, Book 1

By Shayla Black

NOW AVAILABLE!

Bodyguard and former military man Cutter Bryant has always done his duty–no matter what the personal cost. Now he's taking one last high-octane, high-dollar assignment before settling down in a new role that means sacrificing his chance at love. But he never expects to share an irresistible chemistry with his beautiful new client.

Fame claimed Shealyn West suddenly and with a vengeance after starring in a steamy television drama, but it has come at the expense of her heart. Though she's pretending to date a co-star for her image, a past mistake has come back to haunt her. With a blackmailer watching her every move and the threat of career-ending exposure looming, Shealyn hires Cutter to shore up her security, never imagining their attraction will be too powerful to contain.

As Shealyn and Cutter navigate the scintillating line between business and pleasure, they unravel a web of secrets that threaten their relationship and their lives. When danger strikes, Cutter must decide whether to follow his heart for the first time, or risk losing Shealyn forever.

"CUTTER?"

She sounded unsure. Was she afraid of the dark? Of what had happened with her blackmailer earlier? Or what might happen between the two of them next?

He moved closer slowly, giving her plenty of time to back away. "I'm here."

Shealyn allayed his worries when, instead of retreating or flipping the light switch beside her, she reached for him, fingers curling around his arm like she was grabbing a lifeline.

Cutter edged into her personal space. She didn't put distance between them, just exhaled in relief and pressed herself against him.

Oh, god. She wanted something from him that didn't feel merely like comfort.

He was going to have to deal with the two dirtbags who were after Shealyn and convince her to let him hunt them down to see justice served. To do that, he would have to focus on something besides her sweet, addicting mouth.

But unless someone charged in, gun drawn, threats spewing, that wasn't happening now.

The thought that she was here, safe, and wanting his touch tore the leash from his restraint.

Cutter took her shoulders in hand and nudged her back against the wall. She went with a gasp. In one motion, he flattened himself against her, palms braced above her head, hips rocking against the soft pad of her pussy. He couldn't hold in the groan that tore from his chest.

"I shouldn't do this but . . . goddamn it. If you don't want this, stop me. A word will do it." Cutter tried to wait for her assent, but the sensual curve of her throat beckoned him. He bent, inhaled her, grew dizzy from her scent. It reminded him of the gardenias Mama used to grow in the spring. Blended with that scent was the thick aroma of her arousal, pungent and dizzying. "Say it now, sweetheart."

Shealyn ignored him, rocking against him, her head falling to the side as she offered him her neck—and any other part of her he wanted. "Why would I tell you to go when I want you closer?"

She wasn't going to stop him. And she wouldn't save him from himself. Drowning in her would be a singular pleasure that would be worth whatever the price—even his heart.

Cutter fastened his mouth to hers again and tugged on the bottom of her turtleneck, only breaking the kiss when the sweater came between them. The moment he yanked it over her head and tossed it to the floor, he captured her lips once more, growling at the heady feel of the warm, smooth skin of her back, bare under his palms.

Shealyn moved restlessly against him, fisting his T-shirt in her hands and giving it a tug. She raised the thin cotton over his abdomen and chest, but got stuck at his shoulders. Her moan pleaded with him. She wanted the shirt gone and she wanted it now.

Cutter took over, tearing his mouth from hers and shrugging off the holster. When it fell to the tile with a seemingly distant clang, he reached behind his neck and jerked the T-shirt from his body. Using one hand, he tossed it aside. The other slid down Shealyn's spine to cup her pretty, pert ass.

Jesus, she was like all his hottest fantasies, but better. Because she was real and, right now, she desired him.

When his second hand joined the first on her luscious backside, he bent and lifted her, parting her legs and sliding between them with a growl. She wrapped her legs around him, clutched his shoulders, and swayed against him as if she wanted nothing more than to be as close as two people could.

The attraction between them was chemical, animal—unlike anything he'd ever felt. He needed to get on top of her, be inside of her, root as deep into her as he could. The wall had been convenient for a mere kiss, but it was a damn hindrance now. He couldn't have Shealyn the way he craved her here.

"Hold on to me," he demanded as he clasped her tighter and trekked down the hall, across the expansive living room and the glitzy view, then strode into her bedroom.

The stars of L.A. beckoned beyond the French doors. He didn't give them a second glance, not when he had Shealyn West in his arms.

She pressed kisses to his jaw, his lips, his forehead. She nipped at his earlobe, her soft pant a shiver down his spine. "Cutter . . . I-I need you."

Yeah, he understood her perfectly, even though nothing between them made a damn lick of sense. But tonight had flipped some switch inside him. He could no longer pretend—to her or himself—that his feelings for her were strictly professional. No, he craved her alive and responding, clawing, wailing, begging, seemingly his . . . even if it wouldn't last.

"I'm here." He laid her across the bed and climbed over her, settling his hips between her legs. He wished they were naked. He wished he was inside of her, already one with her as he pressed his erection to her softness. "I'm not going anywhere unless you want me to."

She paused and blinked up at him as if she was trying to gauge how much he really meant that. Why would she doubt him? Or her own appeal, given how quickly she'd dismantled his self-control?

"I don't want you anywhere else." She skated her palms over his shoulders, even as she parted her thighs to take him deeper.

Her touch sent an electric reaction zipping through his veins. He curled his fingers around one of her shoulders in return, lowering her bra strap. When she didn't object, he tugged down the lacy cup and exposed her breast.

Holy hell. He had to have that taut pink flesh in his mouth now. He had to savor her, suck her like a sweet summer berry. He craved his lips against her skin.

Without another thought, he lowered his head and lapped her rigid peak with his tongue. She gasped, arched up, clasping him like she never wanted him to let go. He sucked harder.

He'd known she would be beautiful. He'd known she would feel like heaven. He had never expected her to respond so perfectly to him, with little catches of breath as she burrowed her fingers in his hair, urging him closer.

Under his body, Shealyn writhed, trying to shimmy out of her bra. She couldn't reach the clasp—and he couldn't bring himself to allow enough space between them for her to do the job—but she still managed to work the other strap down and peel the cup away.

Cutter seized the unclaimed space instantly. He broke the suction from the first peak and shifted to the other. Oh, hell yes. Soft and velvety, her breasts beckoned him the way the rest of her did—every part from her pouty lips to her sweetly sassy spirit. He loved that she wasn't all bones, hadn't subscribed to the Hollywood belief that a woman with hips should immediately begin starving to save her career.

He couldn't wait to see Shealyn naked, wrap his arms around her, sink into her. Take her. Make her his for the few golden hours it lasted.

With a move Cage had taught him in high school, Cutter slid a hand beneath her and pinched the clasp of her bra. The undergarment propped free, and he stripped it from her body.

A voice in the back of his head reminded him that getting inside her shouldn't be his top priority. But a primal fever burned him, urging him on. It wouldn't cool and it wouldn't bow to logic or civility. It didn't give a shit right now if he was professional. It could care less what else was going on in their lives. It wanted to claim Shealyn, mark her as his woman.

ABOUT SHAYLA BLACK

Shayla Black is the *New York Times* and *USA Today* bestselling author of more than sixty novels. For twenty years, she's written contemporary, erotic, paranormal, and historical romances via traditional, independent, foreign, and audio publishers. Her books have sold millions of copies and been published in a dozen languages.

Raised an only child, Shayla occupied herself with lots of daydreaming, much to the chagrin of her teachers. In college, she found her love for reading and realized that she could have a career publishing the stories spinning in her imagination. Though she graduated with a degree in Marketing/Advertising and embarked on a stint in corporate America to pay the bills, her heart has always been with her characters. She's thrilled that she's been living her dream as a full-time author for the past nine years.

Shayla currently lives in North Texas with her wonderfully supportive husband, her daughter, and two spoiled tabbies. In her "free" time, she enjoys reality TV, reading, and listening to an eclectic blend of music.

Connect with me online:
Website: shaylablack.com
VIP Reader Newsletter: shayla.link/nwsltr
Facebook Author Page: facebook.com/ShaylaBlackAuthor
Facebook Book Beauties Chat Group: shayla.link/FBChat
Instagram: instagram.com/ShaylaBlack
Twitter: twitter.com/Shayla_Black
Google +: shayla.link/googleplus
Amazon Author: shayla.link/AmazonFollow
BookBub: shayla.link/BookBub
Goodreads: shayla.link/goodreads
YouTube: shayla.link/youtube

If you enjoyed this book, please review it or recommend it to others so they can find it, too.

Keep in touch by engaging with me through one of the links above. Subscribe to my VIP Readers newsletter for exclusive excerpts and hang out in my Facebook Book Beauties group for live weekly video chats and other fun stuff. I love interacting with readers!

OTHER BOOKS BY SHAYLA BLACK

CONTEMPORARY ROMANCE

More Than Words

More Than Want You
More Than Need You
More Than Love You
More Than Crave You

Coming Soon:
More Than Tempt You (2019)

The Wicked Lovers (Complete Series)

Wicked Ties
Decadent
Delicious
Surrender to Me
Belong to Me
"Wicked to Love" (novella)
Mine to Hold
"Wicked All the Way" (novella)
Ours to Love
"Wicked All Night" (novella)
"Forever Wicked" (novella)
Theirs to Cherish
His to Take
"Pure Wicked" (novella)
Wicked for You
Falling in Deeper
"Dirty Wicked" (novella)
"A Very Wicked Christmas" (short)
Holding on Tighter

The Devoted Lovers

Devoted to Pleasure

"Devoted to Wicked" (novella)

Coming Soon:

Devoted to Love (July 2, 2019)

Sexy Capers

Bound And Determined

Strip Search

"Arresting Desire" (Hot In Handcuffs Anthology)

The Perfect Gentlemen (by Shayla Black and Lexi Blake)

Scandal Never Sleeps

Seduction in Session

Big Easy Temptation

Smoke and Sin

Coming Soon:

At the Pleasure of the President (Fall 2018)

Masters Of Ménage (by Shayla Black and Lexi Blake)

Their Virgin Captive

Their Virgin's Secret

Their Virgin Concubine

Their Virgin Princess

Their Virgin Hostage

Their Virgin Secretary

Their Virgin Mistress

Coming Soon:

Their Virgin Bride (TBD)

DOMS OF HER LIFE
(by Shayla Black, Jenna Jacob, and Isabella LaPearl)
Raine Falling Collection (Complete Series)

One Dom To Love
The Young And The Submissive
The Bold and The Dominant
The Edge of Dominance

Heavenly Rising Collection
The Choice

Coming Soon:
The Chase (2019)

THE MISADVENTURES SERIES

Misadventures of a Backup Bride

Coming Soon:
Misadventures with My Ex (December 25, 2018)

STANDALONE TITLES

Naughty Little Secret
Watch Me
Dangerous Boys And Their Toy
"Her Fantasy Men" (Four Play Anthology)
A Perfect Match
His Undeniable Secret (Sexy Short)

HISTORICAL ROMANCE (as Shelley Bradley)

The Lady And The Dragon
One Wicked Night
Strictly Seduction
Strictly Forbidden

BROTHERS IN ARMS MEDIEVAL TRILOGY

His Lady Bride (Book 1)
His Stolen Bride (Book 2)
His Rebel Bride (Book 3)

PARANORMAL ROMANCE

THE DOOMSDAY BRETHREN

Tempt Me With Darkness
"Fated" (e-novella)
Seduce Me In Shadow
Possess Me At Midnight
"Mated" – Haunted By Your Touch Anthology
Entice Me At Twilight
Embrace Me At Dawn

Join the

*Shayla*BLACK

Book Beauties

Facebook Group

http://shayla.link/FBChat

Join me for live, interactive video chats every #WineWednesday. Be there for breaking Shayla news, fun, positive community, giveaways, and more!

VIP Readers

NEWSLETTER

at ShaylaBlack.com

Be among the first to get your greedy hands on Shayla Black news, juicy excerpts, cool VIP giveaways–and more!

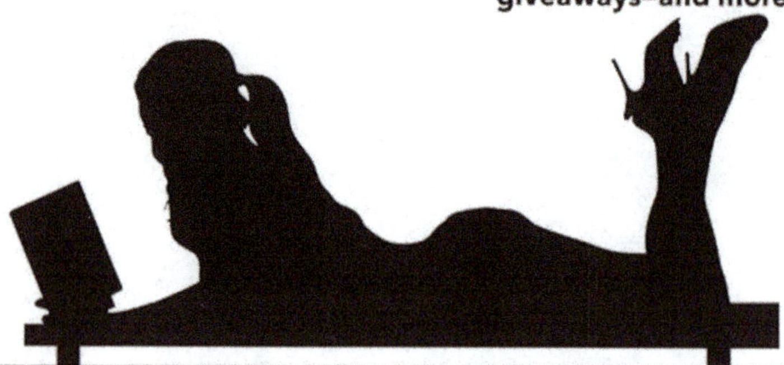

CPSIA information can be obtained
at www.ICGtesting.com
Printed in the USA
LVHW03s1846200918
590799LV00011B/954/P

9 781936 596508